SHOWTIME IN CLEVELAND

The Hanna Theatre

COPYRIGHTED

Lee and J.J. Shubert and Crosby Gaige

Lessees & Managers

Showtime

IN CLEVELAND

THE RISE OF A REGIONAL THEATER CENTER

John Vacha

THE KENT STATE UNIVERSITY PRESS

Kent, Ohio, and London

Frontis: A cover from an early Hanna Theatre program. *Collection of Author*

©2001 by The Kent State University Press, Kent, Ohio 44242
All rights reserved
Library of Congress Catalog Card Number 00-012106
ISBN 0-87338-697-3
Manufactured in the United States of America

07   06   05   04   03   02   01   5   4   3   2   1

Vacha, John.
    Showtime in Cleveland: the rise of a regional theater center/by John Vacha.
      p.   cm.
    Includes bibliographical references and index.
    ISBN 0-87338-697-3 (alk. paper)
      1. Theater—Ohio—Cleveland—History—20th century.   2. Theater—Ohio—
Cleveland—History—19th century.   3. Performing arts—Ohio—Cleveland—History—
20th century.   4. Performing arts—Ohio—Cleveland—History—19th century.   I. Title.
PN2277.C57 V33 2001
792'.09771'32—dc21   00-012106

British Library Cataloging-in-Publication data are available.

FOR *Ruta,* BEST OF THEATER COMPANIONS

Contents

Preface

I CAN'T REALLY SAY that I come from theatergoing folk. My mother did take us once to the Hanna Theatre—to see Blackstone the Magician. And a grandfather shepherded us all to Cain Park one summer's evening for the Czech national opera, Smetana's *The Bartered Bride*. Movies were a different story, and I was taken by my parents for Saturday matinees at all the downtown movie palaces during their heyday, before the advent of multiplex cinemas. That was about it until the obligatory high school field trips to the annual Shakespearean offerings of the Cleveland Play House.

When I was finally ready for theater, however, I soon discovered just how much Cleveland had to offer. There were touring Broadway shows at the Hanna, classics and contemporary drama at the Play House and Karamu, the golden age of American musicals at Musicarnival, and entertaining comedies both old and new on community stages. As public interests and tastes broadened, new groups appeared to serve them: Great Lakes Theatre, Dobama, Beck Center, and many more. Later, becoming involved in the field of local history, I naturally began collecting materials on the rich tradition of the stage in Cleveland. There was clearly enough to fill a book, yet there was none covering the subject in its entirety—hence, *Showtime in Cleveland*.

In organizing this history of theater in Cleveland, I have elected to focus on what is regarded as the "legitimate" theater of live, spoken drama. Less formal entertainments occasionally make the cut, especially in the earlier periods before the lines between the venues were strictly drawn. Musical theater, short of opera, is part of the story inasmuch as it shared the same stages, personnel, and audiences with its "straight," nonlyric counterparts. Movies, though, are brought in only occasionally, mainly for their impact on live theater. The narrative is aimed at the general reader or theater buff, which accounts for the virtual elimination of footnotes. As an aid to further study, the text is liberally sprinkled with dates, but the casual reader may feel free to ignore them; there won't be any quizzes.

Finally, there are a great many debts to acknowledge. In the remote past I owe much to the late William McCollom of Case Western Reserve University, who first "hooked" me on theater as literature. It was the late David Van Tassel and John Grabowski of *The Encyclopedia of Cleveland History* project who got me involved in the pursuit of local history.

More immediately, the literature department of the Cleveland Public Library, headed by Evelyn M. Ward, proved an invaluable resource for its collections of programs and original manuscripts. Theater people who generously gave of their time and experience for interviews include John L. Price Jr., Reuben and Dorothy Silver, Margaret Lynch, Jackie Demaline, Don Bianchi, and Ed Henry; I have also drawn upon earlier interviews with Milton Krantz and Ray Shepardson. Needless to say, no one but myself is responsible for any error of fact or judgment that may be found in this work.

I am especially grateful for the constant help, encouragement, and advice of my wife, Ruta, over a period far antedating the gestation of this book. For bringing my manuscript into conformity with the dictates of the computer age, I am indebted to my niece, Audrey Hopkins.

One

EARLY STAGES

i write to no how about the show bisnes in Cleeveland
—Artemus Ward in his first letter to
the *Cleveland Plain Dealer* in 1858

ARTEMUS WARD, OF COURSE, was a figment of the imagination of Charles F. Browne, the *Plain Dealer's* new city editor from Toledo. Browne introduced him as a semi-literate itinerant showman plying the circuit of Midwestern cities just emerging from the frontier stage: "i have a show consisting in part of a Californy Bare two snakes tame foxies &c also wax works my wax works is hard to beat, all say they is life and nateral curiosities among my wax works is Our Saveyer Gen taylor and Dockter Webster in the akt of killing Parkmen. now mr. Editor scratch off a few lines and tel me how is the show bisnis in your good city i shal have hanbils printed at your offis you scratch my back and i will scratch your back, also git up a grate blow in the paper about my show don't forgit the wax works."

With due allowance for comic exaggeration, many of Browne's readers probably could recall the days when what passed for "show bisnes" was not that far removed from Artemus Ward's playbill. Cleveland was barely sixty years old when Browne arrived on the scene, and the city's early growth had been glacial. The Cuyahoga River "Flats" are nationally renowned today as an entertainment district, but the earliest settlers tended to rush past their malarial miasma with hands over noses, heading for the healthier environs of Doan's Corners and Newburgh. In the two dozen years between its founding in 1796 and 1820, in fact, Cleaveland (as it was then spelled) had managed to attract little more than six hundred inhabitants.

Nevertheless, the population was enough to draw the city's first visit from professional actors, and a troupe under the management of William B. Blanchard made its appearance in March of 1820. As there was no theater in which to perform, they made do with the single-story, slab-sided structure known as Mowrey's Hall, appended to the rear of the city's principal hostelry, Mowrey's Tavern. Also known as Cleveland House, the inn occupied the southwest corner of Superior Avenue and Public Square, a location inherited by successively more imposing hotels and culminating in the present Renaissance Cleveland Hotel.

Since the original Mowrey's fronted Superior, the hall behind stretched out along the Public Square side of the structure. It was a plain room normally used for banquets and meetings. Blanchard and company, seven or eight strong, probably had to make their entrances on a makeshift platform for a stage. An audience said to have come from miles away paid fifty cents a head, children half-price, to view the initial offering of *The Purse; or, the Benevolent Tar.*

By candlelight, the first thing patrons saw would have been the villain, Theodore, alone in a room, chewing up whatever served as scenery with the following exposition: "Curs'd infatuation!—madness! To risque so vast a sum! and not my own too! gaming will mark my ruin. The baron's partiality must decrease when he discovers this embezzlement!—against his return must my accounts be truly stated.—what's to be done?—how to look him in the face I know not." It was a fair sample of what was to follow, dramatically, for the rest of the nineteenth century. Suffice it to say that by the end of the evening the villain was unmasked and the baron's rightful son restored to his inheritance, all of which was accomplished, to the accompaniment of an occasional song, by the returning sailor of the title.

Blanchard and his players, at least half of whom were members of his own family, stayed in town for at least three performances. As was the custom of the day, each bill consisted of a main *pièce de résistance* such as *The Purse* supplemented by a farce and other shorter entertainment.

Following performances of the heroic drama *Douglas* and a melodrama, *The Mountaineers,* the Blanchard troupe left Cleveland as they had come, aboard a sailing vessel named the *Tiger.*

Not only was that the first professional dramatic performance in Cleveland, but it may well have been the first one recorded in the entire Great Lakes region. Of course, the key word in that claim is "recorded," since Blanchard and company had to come from somewhere on the lakes. Still, one historian could find no earlier evidence of professional theater activity in Buffalo, Detroit, Columbus, or Indianapolis.

Even in Cleveland, though, there had been some amateur dramatic stirrings prior to Blanchard. For example, dramatic readings were performed in the school exhibition conducted under Mr. Stephen Peet in 1815. These included a pair of short morality skits, *The Conjuror* and *The Dissipated Oxford Student,* as well as a scene from *Julius Caesar.*

A group of amateur thespians organized themselves into the Theatre Royal Society in 1819. For a short period of time, they gave performances every Friday evening in a hall known as the Shakespeare Gallery, located on the northeast corner of Superior and what is now known as West 9th Street. Admission was a rather steep dollar a head, but the profits, if any, were supposed to be donated to the village. While no record of their repertoire has survived, at least one of their members surfaced many years later as a performer with a visiting professional company. Thomas Colahan, then, may be considered Cleveland's first actor.

The coming of theater to Cleveland was part of a general cultural awakening in the slowly germinating village. The first schoolhouse had been erected in 1817, and a two-story brick academy would follow five years later. A bookstore was opened in 1820 by Herschel Foote, who advertised tomes on theology, history, and travel. Most important, at least from the standpoint of theater, was the establishment in 1818 of the town's first newspaper.

Artemus Ward aptly described the symbiotic relationship that would develop between journalism and show business during the course of the nineteenth century: "you scratch my back & i will scratch your back." Theatrical enterprises relied on newspapers to publicize their appearances, while newspaper editors reaped the benefits not only of paid advertisements in their columns but also handbill and program orders for their job-printing offices. By the time of Blanchard's arrival, the *Cleaveland Gazette & Commercial Register* had been succeeded by the more permanent *Cleveland Herald.* In advertising the appearance of this troupe, the *Herald* was also leaving a record of its performance for posterity. It was involvement enough for the times; dramatic criticism would come later.

While Blanchard's visit had broken the dramatic ice, it hardly opened the floodgates for future performances. Five years would pass before the appearance of another, unnamed company was recorded, though that does not mean that Clevelanders lacked entertainment in the interim. Nearly forty years before the introduction of Artemus Ward, in 1819 a real wax museum had been exhibited. A demonstration of the "exhilarating effects of nitrous oxide gas" tickled the curious a few years later. In 1825 the *Herald* carried an advertisement for the exhibition of a "Large and Learned Elephant," among whose accomplishments was the ability to "draw a cork from a filled bottle, and drink the contents, and then present the empty bottle and cork to the keeper." No details were supplied as to the nature of the contents. The performing pachyderm was backed by a supporting cast consisting of an "Asiatic Lion" and other animals "Too tedious to mention." Other attractions arrived to test their drawing power. In 1827 it was an Egyptian mummy, which was followed a few years later by the Siamese twins Chang and Eng.

Against such varied competition, what would come to be called "legitimate" theater made sporadic progress. A company led by H. H. Fuller, following an engagement in Detroit, came to town the same year as the Egyptian mummy. This appearance was noteworthy for the introduction of Shakespeare to Cleveland, in the guise of *Catherine and Petrucchio,* David Garrick's adaptation of *The Taming of the Shrew.* The Bard of Avon would become a pillar of the nineteenth-century repertoire in Cleveland, even if generally in heavily edited versions.

Another notable attraction of Fuller's visit assumed the compact form of a low comedian named William S. Forrest. Barely five feet tall and seventeen years of age at the time, Forrest would become a familiar figure on Cleveland stages as he returned with other companies and even managed a season here himself. He became quite a famous comedian, acknowledged as such, unfortunately, even when forced to double in more serious parts.

A ten-year-old child prodigy named Louisa Lane was the chief attraction of a troupe that came to town in 1830. Fresh from a successful upriver tour from New Orleans to Cincinnati, Miss Lane opened a three-night stand with a "polite comedy" and the usual farce. Many seasons and a couple of marriages later, she would be revered as Mrs.

John Drew, matriarch of the legendary Barrymore clan. Lane and company performed in a temporary theater prepared in a building behind the *Herald* office.

Another troupe appeared at the Masonic Hall, while other acts such as "the American Fire King," a fire-eater, favored the Franklin House. The new brick courthouse built in 1828 on Public Square was also pressed into use as a theater, where the Gilbert and Trowbridge company in 1831 gave Clevelanders another helping of Shakespeare. Due to the realities of travel on the frontier, most dramatic visitations were confined to the summer months.

Travel conditions were not the only hazards faced by theatrical enterprises. A troupe headed by a couple named Mestayer broke up in Cleveland in 1832 for lack of funds, leaving its members on their own resources to return east. Those without money, including the Mestayers, resorted to the time-honored device of singing for their passage, presenting comic sketches and other acts in Seth Abbey's tavern. A tradition holds that the comedian Dan Marble made his show-business debut during these improvised performances. He would return some

In the days before Cleveland had a proper theater, visiting troupes made do in such venues as the second Cuyahoga County Courthouse in the southwest quadrant of Public Square. The Gilbert and Trowbridge company presented Shakespeare there in 1831. One of the buildings to the right likely is Mowrey's Hall, site of the city's first professional dramatic performance eleven years earlier. *Western Reserve Historical Society, Cleveland* half-dozen times in the popular stock characters of the shrewd Yankee, Jonathan, or Sam Patch.

Three events occurred in the early 1830s that accelerated the development of theater in Cleveland. The first was not theatrical in nature, but it filled the role of catalyst for the others. This was the completion in 1832 of the Ohio and Erie Canal.

Seven years of mostly manual labor and $4.3 million had gone into the 308-mile ditch, and the results more than justified the investment. Providing a water connection from Portsmouth on the Ohio River to Lake Erie at Cleveland, the canal propelled the latter from village to city status. Barely surpassing one thousand residents in 1830, Cleveland could count more than six thousand citizens ten years later, placing it among the nation's fifty largest cities.

Some of the increased prosperity brought by the canal was evident in the construction of Cleveland's first practical theater building. Named Italian Hall for some reason now lost in obscurity, it was located on the third floor of the Erie Building, one of the city's earliest brick structures. It stood at 19–23 Water Street (now West 9th) opposite the intersection of Center (now Frankfort) Street. Known today as the Warehouse District, the neighborhood was Cleveland's original theater district.

Though not designed exclusively for the drama, Italian Hall did feature an inclined seating arrangement for an audience of about five hundred. There was a stage framed by a proscenium arch but evidently scant arrangements backstage for actors. Thespis shared the premises with a variety of other activities, from exhibitions to public meetings.

After the canal and Italian Hall, the third theatrical milestone of the 1830s was the advent of the Dean and McKinney lake circuit. Edwin Dean had appeared in Cleveland with a manager named Charles Parson in 1833. He returned the following year with David D. McKinney as partner and set up a stock company in Italian Hall. Their plan called for touring the company along a triangular route on Lake Erie, from Buffalo to Cleveland to Detroit, with occasional trips to towns in the hinterlands.

Dean and McKinney's Cleveland seasons steadily expanded from three weeks to eight by 1837. They transformed theater from an occasional novelty to an expected amenity of town life. Arrangements were made to have both ferries on the Cuyahoga River in operation each night after the play to take patrons from Ohio City back to the west side.

Inevitably, the partners provided the city with a great many local premieres—nearly one a night in the 1835 season. Shakespeare was represented in the repertoire with *Othello, Macbeth, The Merchant of Venice,* and *Much Ado about Nothing.* Other classics included Otway's *Venice Preserved* and Schiller's *William Tell.* Farce was present with the performance of such titles as *The Honest Thieves, My Neighbor's Wife,* and *The Youth Who Never Saw a Woman.*

Faces both fresh and familiar appeared in the casts. Dan Marble played his comic Yankee in three seasons, while droll Billy Forrest returned for two. On the serious side, John R. Scott portrayed the title roles in *Macbeth* and *The Merchant of Venice.* Charles Eaton's performance as Richard III, in the opinion of the *Cleveland Herald,* was superior to that of the elder Booth. Cleveland was fortunate to have seen it, for Eaton died five years later at the age of thirty.

Perhaps the most renowned of those early visitors was the husband-and-wife team of Augustus A. Adams and Mary Duff. They opened the 1836 season in the lead roles of *Hamlet,* followed by *Richard III* and *Othello.* Adams's portrayal of the latter had been favorably compared to that of Edwin Forrest, but by the time Cleveland saw him again in 1848, Adams's career and life had been nearly ended by drinking.

As their seasons lengthened and prospered, Dean and McKinney began laying plans for their own theater in Cleveland. Italian Hall, though invested by the partners with new scenery, decorations, and a "splendid drop curtain," had become too cramped for their expanded operation. Organizing a commercial stock company, they began raising a projected $25,000 for a new 750-seat theater on Water Street. As described in Cleveland's first city directory in 1837, it would measure three hundred by seventy-five feet and "rank with the principal public buildings in western America."

But it was never built. The project became an early victim of the Panic of 1837, and so too, apparently, were the Dean and McKinney partnership and their lake circuit. In their brief local career, they had given Cleveland its first real taste of what theater could be. Fifteen years later, the *Cleveland Herald* still considered their productions to be superior to any that had followed.

For a time, other managers kept drama alive in Italian Hall. Under D. Marsh and Joseph Parker, respectively, the 1838 and 1839 seasons even expanded to a maximum of ten weeks or more. As the full effects of the depression reached Cleveland, however, the theatrical seasons began to taper off to five weeks, then a few days, and finally to nothing at all in 1843. It was the last year the theaters would remain completely dark in Cleveland.

There were elements in the community who would not have been loathe to see it go for good. Cleveland originally was settled heavily by New England Congregational and Presbyterian stock, which tended to view theater as one of the devil's snares. The Reverend Samuel C. Aiken dredged up a seventeenth-century attack on the English stage as the basis for an anti-theatrical sermon in his First Presbyterian Church (later known as the "Old Stone") in 1836. He was answered by the editor of the *Cleveland Advertiser,* who viewed the theater as a useful diversion from the drudgery of a ten-to-twelve-hour working day.

A letter from "Senex" to the editor of the *Cleveland Whig* enumerated several objections against the drama: for example, (1) presenting an unrealistic picture of life, (2) greatly inflaming the passions, (3) being enacted by persons of the lowest class, and (4) causing youths to stray through keeping late hours. "On the whole, Providence has always opposed the theatre," summarized Senex, "pious parents dread it for their children; the dying profligate has often cursed the day he ever entered it; and it may be said of the Thespian harlot, as of the false church. . . . 'He knoweth not that the dead are there, and her guests are in the depths of hell.'"

Opinion was divided among members of the Fourth Estate. As late as 1848, the *Daily True Democrat* advocated driving all theatrical nuisances from the city and converting the temple of the muses into a house of worship. The *Herald* and the *Cleveland Plain Dealer* took a more constructive stand, defending the theater as an institution while calling for better plays and actors. The city itself maintained a morally neutral stance. While making no attempt at censorship, it asserted its authority by enacting a licensing fee of $75 per troupe per year in 1836, increased to $150 by the longer season of 1853.

When theater made a comeback from the dark season of 1843, it did so in a genre unlikely to offend even the most pious—that of the temperance play. Three companies gave a total of twenty performances of antidrinking dramas in 1844. Recommending one called the *Drama of the Reformed Drunkard* to the editor of the *Herald,* a reader commented, "The whole performance was strikingly true to nature and highly creditable to the actors." The editor concurred, though "a little suspicious that it was done in the spirit."

Most of the temperance presentations were given in Apollo Hall, a space seating about four hundred located far down Superior in the Flats. As a demonstration of its morally elevated purpose, this hall resorted to the nineteenth-century fiction of being attached to a museum, the museum in this instance consisting of a total of nine items on exhibition. The most notable practitioner of this device, of course, was New York's P. T. Barnum, who would bring his own production of *The Drunkard* to Cleveland in 1853.

Another genre that made its Cleveland debut during this period was the minstrel show. Not long after its introduction in New York in 1843, a group calling itself the Cleveland Amateur Minstrels put on a local version of this entertainment. Visiting companies during the following decade included the Christy Minstrels, the Campbell Minstrels, and Sanford's Opera Troupe with T. D. Rice.

Legitimate drama also made its return. It was led by John S. Potter, who came in 1846 for a four-night stand and was encouraged by full houses to remain a week and a half. Returning yearly for longer stays, he even purchased a home and set about building his own theater in the city.

Situated down the street from Italian Hall, Potter's Water Street Theater was the first edifice in Cleveland to be intended primarily for theatrical productions. It was located on the east side of Water Street about a block north of St. Clair Avenue and just outside of the business district. The frame structure, built for an estimated cost of only $6,000, measured fifty-seven feet wide by seventy-five feet long.

Inside, the 1,500-seat house contained a large pit flanked near the stage by two tiers of boxes. The stage measured thirty-four feet in width by twenty-eight feet in depth. All was lit by chandeliers and solar lamps, but the apparent absence of a heating system made the theater habitable only during the summer.

Potter installed a stock company in his new theater, headed by his wife, Estelle, as leading lady. Foremost among the visiting stars was the returning A. A. Adams, who introduced Clevelanders to *Brutus,* by American playwright John Howard Payne. Another local Payne premiere, *Clari,* featuring Estelle Potter, had opening-night patrons humming "Home, Sweet Home" on their way out of the theater.

George Jamieson, a familiar face on the Southern theater circuits, made his Cleveland debut in 1849 and also decided to settle in the "Forest City." Former child star Louisa Lane, not yet Mrs. Drew but at this time Mrs. Mossup, appeared in eight local premieres during a return engagement. In one play she assumed a male role opposite Mrs. Potter, a common practice among female stars of the period.

At the end of its first summer season, Potter vacated the unheated Water Street Theater for a warmer venue. A few days later, on the night of September 14, 1849, Cleveland's first proper theater became the victim of the city's first theater fire. Fortunately, no one was killed in the flames, though a neighbor died of an apparent heart attack during the excitement. The uninsured building, together with much of the scenery, was a total loss. "There can be no regret that this nuisance is destroyed," chided the *Daily True Democrat*. The *Plain Dealer* speculated that "the same hand that has undoubtedly applied the torch many times before this summer, was not wanting last night."

Theater was sufficiently established in Cleveland by this time to overcome even disaster. Potter was ruined along with his theater, but other managers and halls were at hand. Potter himself, when not using his ill-fated Water Street Theater, had used Apollo Hall and Watson's Hall. The latter was an all-purpose structure built in the early 1840s on Superior near Seneca (West 3rd) Street. While it had a spacious auditorium with a thousand seats, its stage was an extremely shallow fifteen feet in depth. Nonetheless, it enjoyed a long and useful life under a succession of names, becoming Melodeon Hall, Brainard's Opera House, and finally the Globe Theater.

Another stage, making its appearance around 1848, was somewhat more answerable for theatrical purposes but handicapped by an inconvenient location. This was the Center Street Theater, built by Gennett Overrocker on a narrow byway north of Superior between Bank (West 6th) and Water Streets. Center Street would later become Frankfort Avenue, and the theater itself would be known first as the Cleveland Theater and later, infamously, as the Theatre Comique. It was poorly ventilated, making it uncomfortable during the summer theater season. However, it became the first Cleveland theater to use gas to illuminate both the stage and auditorium.

It was in the Center Street, or Cleveland, Theater that William Forrest returned to pick up the torch (unfortunate metaphor though it be) dropped by Potter. Though he soon proved to be a better comedian than manager, Forrest's brief administration if nothing else was distinguished for the Cleveland debut of Charlotte Cushman. Undoubtedly the brightest star to shine on the Cleveland stage up to that time, the tragedienne stopped off in 1851 during an American tour following several years in England. She played to packed houses in the city for five performances, including her two most celebrated portrayals, Lady Macbeth in *Macbeth* and Meg Merrilies in *Guy Mannerling*. The *Plain Dealer* considered the former to be "a standard for all future representations of the same character," one notable for "a careful avoidance of rant and vulgar stage effect."

Unfortunately, things went downhill from there for Forrest and his partner, William Hield. Personally, Forrest was enterprising enough, appearing in sixty-four productions in 1851 and eighty-nine the following season. His stock company was a different matter, earning criticism for failure to memorize lines or learn their characters' stage business. In an age when actors were still responsible for providing their own costumes, some of Forrest's company made their appearances in incongruous get-ups.

Such loose standards on stage seemed to invite similar disrespect from the audience. It was generally a young audience, representative of the growing community. A lingering aura of disrepute lingering around the theater also made it a predominantly male audience. Women and the "best society" tended to sequester themselves in the boxes, leaving the pit and the galleries to the laborers and the "b'hoys." Beginning in 1851, blacks were segregated in a section of the gallery.

Abetted by the presence of a bar on the second tier, the Center Street audiences grew increasingly disruptive. Speaking for untold generations of future theatergoers, actor J. R. Scott stepped out of character one evening to caustically suggest that "if persons would talk no louder than the actors, listeners might by chance hear." J. A. J. Neafie on another occasion rebuked the "rowdies in the pit and gallery" in more direct terms. "It is high time that the proprietors of the Theatre put a stop to the 'caterwauling' of the pit," commented the *Herald*. "The time for these displays in Cleveland has gone by. The people want a first class Theatre and they will patronize no other."

That sounded like an entrance cue, and Joseph Foster of Pittsburgh just then happened to appear on the scene. Foster, who had managed theaters in Philadelphia and Buffalo as well as the Iron City, turned out to be the best thing to happen for theater in Cleveland since the days of Dean and McKinney. Not the least of his contributions was the fact that he was the one who first brought the Ellslers to Cleveland.

Taking over the Cleveland Theater in 1853, Foster first set about to turn it into a first-class house. To make it more accessible, he installed a boardwalk along Center Street over the muddy approaches from Bank Street to the theater. Inside, he raised the floor of the pit for better sightlines, carpeted the floor, papered the walls, and covered the seats in the parquette. On stage, he added a few feet to the apron, giving the actors a better-lighted playing area. The wings on either side were partitioned into private boxes.

Having done over the theater, Foster gave it his own name and then undertook to elevate the behavior of the audience. He made sure that the theater was cleaned after every performance and provided sergeants-at-arms, an early version of ushers, to put down disturbances. Editorials in the Cleveland newspapers seconded Foster's efforts in this direction.

The most effective measure in improving audience behavior, however, was providing playgoers with an improved product. Foster came through with polished productions anchored by a solid resident stock company. It was headed by his son Charles Foster, who played 125 varied roles throughout the season as the juvenile leading man. George C. Boniface was the light comedian, while Felix Vincent filled in as low comedian. Then there were the Ellslers: John Adam Ellsler, who played old men, and his wife, Euphemia, or Effie Ellsler. "They are the life of the theater," wrote the *Herald* of the couple.

Foster also offered a varied repertoire, including his own adaptation of *The Three Musketeers,* renamed *The Three Guardsmen.* Irish characters, increasingly popular with theatergoers, were portrayed by William Florence and his wife, Malvina, as Ragged Pat and Judy O'Treat in *Ireland as It Is.* Opera was often mixed in with straight dramatic fare, as when Caroline Richings appeared in *The Daughter of the Regiment.*

The roster of visiting stars continued to expand. James E. Murdoch appeared, enabling Clevelanders to compare his Hamlet with that of A. A. Adams. Murdoch gave way to Charles E. Couldock, who offered his interpretations of *Richard III, Catherine and Petrucchio,* and Bulwer-Lytton's *Richelieu.* Couldock also introduced *The Willow Copse,* a recent play by Dion Boucicault, in which he portrayed a farmer driven insane by his daughter's debauchery. The Shakespearean canon expanded along with the visitors, as Julia Bennett Barrow performed as Rosalind in *As You Like It.*

Foster's Theater had to put on a good show, for it wasn't the only show in town. On the south side of Superior, opposite Bank Street, was an auditorium that had opened around 1850 as Kelley's Hall. With a seating capacity of more than one thousand, it had been booked by

Legendary showman Phineas Taylor Barnum brought his American Museum company to Cleveland in 1853 with its production of W. H. Smith's temperance play, *The Drunkard*. It also gave Barnum a chance to help out a kinsman, E. T. Nichols, who managed Cleveland's Atheneum Theater. *Western Reserve Historical Society*

P. T. Barnum for the Cleveland stop on the legendary American tour of Jenny Lind in 1851. The "Swedish Nightingale" sang there on November 7 to an overflow crowd of 1,125 that even climbed to the roof to see her through the domed skylight—and came close to breaking up the concert when their pressure shattered the glass.

Shortly afterward, a cousin of Barnum named E. T. Nichols moved into Kelley's and operated it as the Atheneum Theater. Barnum helped get his kinsman off to a resounding start by bringing in his American Museum company from New York. Among the players were Douglas Stewart, who would gain renown under the name of E. A. Sothern, and Emily Mestayer, whose parents had once been stranded in Cleveland.

The highlight of the company's visit was its celebrated rendition of *The Drunkard.* It was promoted by Barnum himself, who spoke at a local temperance meeting, and by the attendance of several ministers at one of the performances in the Atheneum.

Nichols had enlarged his theater's stage to a generous fifty-two-foot width by fifty-foot depth. He also increased its capacity to 1,500 seats and introduced ushers and reserved seating. Barnum's American Museum company was followed at the Atheneum by James Rodgers's National Dramatic Troupe from Cincinnati. This attraction proved less popular, but Nichols was ready with a blockbuster even bigger than Barnum.

On Monday evening, November 7, 1853, the Marsh Family began an open-ended engagement of *Uncle Tom's Cabin* at the Atheneum. Coming from a twelve-week stand in New York, it featured six-year-old "Little Mary Guerineau Marsh" as Little Eva. This was the popular George L. Aiken version, "embracing the entire work of Mrs. Harriet Beecher Stowe" in six acts, eight tableaux, and thirty scenes.

Uncle Tom's Cabin took Cleveland by storm. It was hailed as the "Great American Drama" by the *Daily Forest City Democrat,* a descendant of the *Daily True Democrat,* which had had no use at all for the theater. "The reason for this continued attraction is not idle curiosity, nor the brilliancy of the players, but the *subject,"* thundered the *Democrat,* now edited by a firebrand from central Ohio named Joseph Medill. "Thousands have left the Atheneum with a deeper hatred and loathing towards the Institution [of slavery] than they ever before experienced." They kept coming by the thousands until November 30, giving *Uncle Tom's Cabin* an unprecedented local run of twenty-two consecutive performances. Not the least of the play's accomplishments was its demonstration that the stage might do more than merely entertain. "The Marsh family are the best anti-slavery preachers that ever visited our State," concluded the *Democrat.*

For their 1854 season at the Atheneum, Nichols and his manager, J. G. Cartlitch, installed a resident stock company backed by the usual visiting stars. Charles Couldock and Julia Bennett Barrow, who had appeared with Foster's company, took their turns on the Atheneum stage. Margaret Mitchell emerged as a star playing boys' roles, and young male admirers appeared on the streets of Cleveland wearing "Maggie Mitchell scarfs."

By far the most sensational event of the 1854 season was the farewell appearance at the Atheneum of Anna Cora Mowatt, actress and author of *Fashion,* one of the most successful American plays of its time. Demand for tickets to an earlier appearance had been so great that they were sold at auction, with the surplus profits thus generated being donated to the Cleveland Orphan Asylum. She took her bows "with her arms literally filled with the bouquets" thrown by admirers from the boxes. A month later, her farewell appearance was so applauded by a full house that the captain of her steamer consented to delay his departure to allow an extra performance the following evening.

In answer to the heightened level of competition from the Atheneum, Joseph Foster moved in the summer of 1854 from his old quarters on Center Street to a splendid new theater. Built by a group of investors on the east side of Bank Street, the National Hall had opened on April 16, 1853, with a production of *The School for Scandal*. Moving his stock company into the new house, Foster promptly renamed it Foster's Varieties. In time, it would become famous as the Academy of Music.

Professional quality had improved steadily over the past few seasons, and the seasons themselves had gradually been expanded to half a year in length. With the opening of National Hall and Foster's Varieties, Cleveland now had one of the finest theatrical facilities in the country. Plainly, theater in Cleveland was ready to take the stage for a new and promising act.

UNCLE TOM'S CABIN: THE ORIGINAL MEGAHIT

The "bloodhounds" often were comparatively docile Great Danes, and the "ice floes" in the Ohio River generally were upturned soapboxes. That never seemed to bother nineteenth-century audiences, though, who made *Uncle Tom's Cabin* the most popular drama in the history of the American stage.

Cleveland was one of the first places it played, which was only fitting: the book upon which the drama was based, after all, had been copublished in 1851 by the Cleveland firm of Jewett, Proctor, and Worthington. The most popular dramatization, that by George Aiken, hit the boards in New York City in June 1853. A few months later it arrived in Cleveland, where it achieved the first extended run in the city's theatrical annals with twenty-two consecutive performances.

Over the next three decades, the play maintained its popularity in Cleveland with a total of nearly two hundred performances. Draper's

Mammoth Uncle Tom's Cabin Company justified its adjective by producing "300 darkies at work" on the stage. C. S. Smith's Boston Double Uncle Tom's Cabin Company delivered, as advertised, two Topsys, two donkeys, and six bloodhounds. Perhaps that was the production that provoked one reviewer to note, "The dogs gave an excellent performance, but received little support from the rest of the company."

Most of these companies, known as "Tommers," made a career out of touring Uncle Tom's Cabin. They were "a race of actors apart," according to Cleveland theater historian Harlowe R. Hoyt: "A 'Tommer' never played anything but a Tom show. A girl started as Little Eva. If it was a boy, they clapped a wig on him and nobody was the wiser. A feminine Little Eva graduated into Topsy. When the demands of the part became too exacting, she might become Eliza, or Mrs. St. Clair, or Aunt Ophelia, depending upon physique and countenance. Or if she was very bad, they made her play Cassy."*

If a company had to subsist on only a single play, it could not find a better vehicle than Uncle Tom's Cabin. The play offered both comedy in Topsy and tragedy in the fate of Uncle Tom. Those who preferred melodrama could thrill to Eliza crossing the river. As for villains, the very name of Simon Legree became synonymous with that stock character of the nineteenth-century stage.

Such dramatic assets kept Uncle Tom's Cabin before the footlights long after the Civil War had ended its political relevance. Unfortunately, the antislavery message of the original quickly became subordinated to stereotypical comic treatment of many of the play's Negro characters. That these invariably were portrayed by whites in blackface, often in the broad style of minstrelsy, didn't help matters. In an era of racial segregation, that aspect of casting was no hindrance to the play's popularity.

In Cleveland, Uncle Tom's Cabin often served as a pièce d'occasion. It closed the Globe Theater in 1880. It was Gus Hartz's first production at the Euclid Avenue Opera House and the last to ring down the curtain at that theater forty years later. James O'Neill played it in this city in the late nineteenth century, and Vaughan Glaser early in the twentieth. For years it was an annual attraction at the Cleveland Theatre on St. Clair Avenue.

The play made a final bow locally in 1934, when the Cleveland Play House scraped off the excrescences of nearly a hundred years and re-

*Harlowe R. Hoyt, Town Hall Tonight (Englewood Cliffs, N.J.: Prentice-Hall, 1955), 57–58.

A dramatic highlight in any production of *Uncle Tom's Cabin* was the scene of Eliza crossing to freedom over the ice on the Ohio River. It was enacted here by Virginia Dillon in the 1934 revival of the nineteenth-century melodrama at the Cleveland Play House. The only thing missing, according to *Plain Dealer* critic William McDermott, was the bloodhounds. *Photograph by Gordon Cowner; Cleveland Play House*

vived it as a period piece of American history. Even then, it was still performed by an all-white cast, with Esther Mullin as Eva and Dorothy Paxton in blackface as Topsy. Nonetheless, said William McDermott in the *Plain Dealer,* "you get a clear echo in this performance of the power it must once have had and which, to some degree, it still possesses." The critic's only objection was to the absence of bloodhounds, since "'Uncle Tom' without bloodhounds is 'Hamlet' without Hamlet."

With the post–World War II revolution in civil rights, *Uncle Tom's Cabin* went the way of the minstrel shows and Jim Crow legislation. That "Uncle Tom" became a pejorative in the movement, in fact, reflected more on the excesses of the various dramatic versions than on the Harriet Beecher Stowe novel that inspired them.

But a good story is hard to keep down. Stowe's characters still ply the boards to this day, even if in the guise of a fanciful Siamese version of *The Small House of Uncle Thomas.* As such, they may be seen in every revival of one of the most beloved of modern musicals, *The King and I.*

Two

THE ELLSLER ERA

EARLY IN 1855, CLEVELANDERS may have taken note of a small dark man cutting a dignified figure with little apparent effort, even against the final gusts of winter coming from the lakefront. If not exactly handsome, his face was nonetheless striking with its full flowing hairline, prominent cheekbones, and long straight nose. His large expressive eyes were his most arresting feature, twinkling with expectancy as he hurried back and forth along the streets of the Warehouse District. Those who were not strangers to the theater might have recognized him as John Ellsler, an actor who had attracted favorable notice with Joseph Foster's company a couple of seasons past.

For his part, Ellsler might have seen a city seemingly poised on the threshold of bigger things. Only the year before, Cleveland had annexed the smaller town of Ohio City on the west bank of the Cuyahoga River, boosting the city's population over twenty thousand. By 1860 that figure would be more than doubled. With the arrival of the railroads during the decade, the city was freed from the seasonal limitations of its lake and canal lifelines. From the Flats to Public Square, the Cleveland skyline was dominated by commercial structures of three to four stories, broken only by the spires of more than a dozen churches.

Cultural amenities duly followed in the wake of physical progress. A new high school was being built, though one of its students, John D.

Rockefeller, would drop out before its completion to begin his business career. Formation of the St. Cecilia Society had recently given the city its first permanent orchestra, while the Cleveland Mendelssohn Society provided an outlet for such vocal performances as Haydn's *The Creation*. Cleveland was preparing to host its first Saengerfest that year, in which German singing societies from across America would gather for a monster concert on Public Square. Stirrings were also being felt in the visual arts, with all of six professional artists listed in a directory of the period.

There were four theatrical facilities of varying suitability in town. Watson's Hall on Superior, briefly used for drama in the 1840s by John Potter, was now known as the Melodeon. It served the city as an all-purpose venue for lectures, panoramas, concerts, and minstrel shows. Louis Kossuth, the Hungarian freedom fighter, had spoken there in 1852. On Center Street, Foster's old Cleveland Theater would become the National Amphitheatre and harbor a circus before a further transformation into the Theatre Comique.

That left two first-class houses in Cleveland: the Atheneum and Foster's Varieties. The Atheneum was the old Kelley's Hall on Superior, refurbished, improved, and renamed by P. T. Barnum's cousin, E. T. Nichols. Foster's Varieties occupied the new National Hall on Bank Street, leased and renamed by Joseph Foster of Pittsburgh. Only two years old, it was unquestionably the city's premier theatrical house.

But Foster had failed after only a single season in the new facility. Some thought that mismanagement was at fault, but others were doubtful that the city could support more than one quality theater operation. This is the quandary that brought Ellsler to town. Determined to keep National Hall lit for the drama, its stockholders engaged Ellsler as manager on the recommendation of Dr. Charles Reese. A former Baltimorean, Reese had known the Ellslers from their appearances in Foster's companies both in Pittsburgh and Cleveland.

"Mr. E. is one of the best actors on the American Stage; and it is reasonable to anticipate a company of a high order of histrionic talent," claimed the *Cleveland Leader* in announcing Ellsler's engagement. As the new season approached, the *Leader* seemed to be thinking in terms of a theatrical new deal for the city: "The day has passed when the citizens of Cleveland will put up with a Theatrical Company, the highest attainments of whose members is to rant in the worst style of the worst actors in the Bowery, or to grin at the foot-lights and repeat the latest cant of the bar rooms. . . . Give us no more of such acting in Cleveland,

Theater became an integral part of Cleveland's cultural life with the arrival in 1855 of John Ellsler. For more than twenty years, Ellsler managed the city's first permanent resident stock company. That, plus his specialization in "old men" roles, earned him the cognomen "Uncle John." *Western Reserve Historical Society*

but give us something worthy of the city, of the age, and of the profession, and we will give you the assurance of a hearty cooperation and of a success commensurate with the talent and worth of the Company."

Thirty-three-year-old John Adam Ellsler had been bitten by the theatrical bug as a printer's devil in Baltimore, where one of his duties was to deliver posters and programs to the city's two theaters, and one of the fringe benefits was inclusion on the "dead head" list for free passes. His apprenticeship completed, he left the printing shop to become "a sort of general factotum" around the theater. Upon returning to his native Philadelphia, he became a full-fledged member of the acting company at Peale's Museum, sharing the boards with another young player named Joseph Jefferson.

As Ellsler once explained to a member of his company, he lacked the self-assertion to claim the starring roles. He may have been confirmed in this assessment by a glance in the mirror, which revealed a shade too much nose and not quite enough chin for an ideal leading man. Whatever the reason, Ellsler decided before the end of his first season to specialize in old men, "crying old men or broad farce-comedy old men," according to the demands of the script. Having opted for a subordinate role, he nevertheless put all the art at his command into it. Clara Morris recalled him as "one of the most versatile of actors," whose "greatest pleasure was in acting some 'bit' that he could elaborate into a valuable character." He could transform a twenty-line role such as the switchman in *Under the Gaslight* into a character "so cheery, so jolly, so kindly an old soul, everyone was sorry when he left the stage."

Ellsler acquired not only a lifelong profession in Philadelphia but also a wife, marrying the former Euphemia Murray, a daughter of an old theatrical family. Together with Jefferson and his wife, the Ellslers then managed stock companies for a couple of seasons in the southern states. Ellsler had complete autonomy in the "front" of the house—that is, the business end—while Jefferson supervised everything behind the curtain. A tradition later arose, though undocumented, that it was Ellsler, with his knowledge of German, who taught Jefferson the "Dutch" dialect for his signature role of Rip Van Winkle. Upon the dissolution of this partnership, the Ellslers played seasons in various localities from Baltimore to Pittsburgh. They were managing the Utica Museum in upstate New York when the call came from Cleveland.

With Foster out of the picture, Ellsler changed the name of his house from Foster's Varieties to the Cleveland Theatre. He had at his disposal a theater "equal, if not superior to any edifice of its character and capacity in America," according to the *Cleveland Leader*. Like most theaters of the time, it occupied the top floor of a three-story building, with offices and businesses below to provide a cushion against the roller-coaster economics of show business. The brick structure was located on Bank Street (now West 6th) opposite the Johnson Block in today's Warehouse District.

From 1853 to 1875, the Academy of Music was Cleveland's paramount theater. Located on Bank (now West 6th) Street between Superior and St. Clair Avenues, it enjoyed a national reputation as a "school of the drama" under the management of John Ellsler. Its theatrical career was ended by the 1890s, but the building itself survived into the 1960s. *Cleveland Press Collection, Cleveland State University Library*

The theater inside offered a large forty-foot stage with a depth of sixty-five feet. It was lit by 120 gas footlights in front of its plush red curtain. The auditorium reputedly could accommodate 2,000 people under its high central chandelier.* Gas had not reached this part of the house yet: hundreds of china candles in the chandelier were painstakingly lit each evening from the balcony by means of a long rod. In a bid for respectability, Ellsler announced that no drinks would be served on the premises.

*Later allusions suggested that the seating capacity was less than half this figure (see below, p. 44). One possible explanation for the discrepancy may have been a sacrifice of seats through various renovations undertaken to adapt what was originally an all-purpose hall into a legitimate theater.

The Cleveland Theater raised its curtain on April 2, 1855, two months before Nichols began his season in the Atheneum. It played to good houses until the opening of the other theater began cutting into its audience. According to Ellsler, the Atheneum sought to undercut him by not only reducing ticket prices but also by conducting lotteries for ticket buyers. Ellsler's response was a "grand Oriental Melo dramatic spectacle" entitled *Aladdin; or the Wonderful Lamp,* which began an open-ended run at the Cleveland on November 5. Among its advertised enticements were "beautiful, complicated and brilliant stage paraphernalia," a "costly and superb wardrobe," "spirited marches . . . with an increased Orchestra," and "wonderful machinery, transformations &c."

With Euphemia Ellsler in the title role, *Aladdin* ran for twenty-four performances, breaking the recent Cleveland record set by *Uncle Tom's Cabin.* Determined to give no quarter, Ellsler followed up with another spectacle, *The Naiad Queen,* which ran nearly as long. Nichols came to the Cleveland Theatre with a white flag, offering to close his doors in exchange for a financial settlement. Ellsler called his bluff, and the Atheneum closed anyway the following day.

Before he could launch his second season, however, Ellsler faced an even more formidable obstacle in the form of the Cleveland City Council. In January 1856 the councilmen enacted an ordinance that hiked the fees for a theatrical license to $10 a night, $200 a month, or $1,000 a year. The prohibitive intent of the measure was revealed in the remarks of one of its supporters. "The Theaters were of no benefit to our city," Councilman Stanley was paraphrased as saying. "There always congregate at the Theaters all classes; the young, the old, the prostitute and loafer. The tendency of such places was immoral."

According to the *Daily Clevelander,* Stanley's animus was really motivated by the recent conduct of E. T. Nichols, who had evidently run up a lot of bad debts among local merchants in order to support his "gambling operations," probably a reference to the Atheneum's lottery nights. Coming to the defense of Ellsler's Cleveland Theatre, the *Daily Clevelander* vouched for the reputations of the company members:

> We have known ladies in that Company, whose characters are as unimpeachable as those of any friends of Council members, who, after two rehearsals, (a day's work,) have appeared in the night's play, and in the scenes where they did not appear, have plied the needle on costumes for a new spectacle.

Gentlemen of the Council, you can be sure of having a Theater in Cleveland—people like it, and will sustain it. Will you have ELLSLER & REESE's, the best managed in the West—or will you *tax* it out, and have a *hole* in its stead? The Cleveland Theater has paid Cleveland people more money that it has received from them.

While the council pondered that conundrum, Ellsler and his partner, Dr. Reese, planned to test the ordinance by playing without a license. At length the council members reconsidered and passed a compromise measure setting a more realistic fee of $3 a night or $25 a month. "Some Conscientious Fathers opposed this, on account of the wickedness of theaters, but were willing to legalize this wickedness if it would pay $1,000 a year!" contemptuously observed the *Daily Clevelander.* When Ellsler opened the new season in April, his wife was ready with an "Opening Address" that began:

> Prejudice, the twin-brother of *Ignorance* has sought,
> To crush the work that centuries have wrought,
> To raise [raze] the temple where MELOPOMENE reigns,
> And shackle SHAKESPEARE with *golden* chains; . . .
> In vain in this enlightened age
> As in an elder day, to crush the Stage!

Ellsler carried on without further incident for two more seasons in the Cleveland Theatre. The culmination of this period was reached in 1857 with an appearance by the greatest American tragedian of the day, Edwin Forrest. When Ellsler wrote asking how long a stand he would play, Forrest replied, "If the weather is warm, ten nights; if cold, ten minutes." It must have been unseasonably warm in Cleveland that fall, for Forrest showed up the first week in December. He came on the heels of Charlotte Cushman, who had offered Clevelanders a second look at her specialties in *Guy Mannerling* and *Macbeth.*

If anything, Forrest's opening performance in *Virginius* on December 7 brought out an overly enthusiastic house. "[W]e are pained when we say that we witnessed some of the worst acting we ever beheld inside the walls of a theater," stated the *Cleveland Leader,* quickly explaining that it referred to neither Forrest nor his supporting cast but rather to their audience. According to the *Cleveland Herald,* the trouble started when a dog brought into one of the private boxes reacted to one of

John Ellsler's heroic declamations "in a most *dogged* manner," after which standards in general went to the dogs. The cracking of chestnuts and munching of peanuts were so loud that the *Leader* suggested that the management "impose a duty on all refreshments more noisy than popcorn." Both papers complained of bothersome distractions from promenaders in the lobby during the performance, and the *Leader* added the annoyance of young gallants explaining "Every scene, speech and action" to their ladies, "to enlighten the ignorance of the damsels and to show off their own erudition." To remedy this particular problem, the *Leader* anticipated Brecht by recommending "the exhibition of large labels at the commencement of every scene, explaining all about the forthcoming movements, in the manner of the ancient 'chorus.' "

Manners were evidently much improved for subsequent performances. The only complaint of the *Herald*'s writer a couple of days later was of a house so packed that, "our knowledge of the performance was obtained from furtive glances under the arms and between the heads of those in front of us." A popular demand arose to see Forrest in *Metamora,* a vehicle especially written in response to his call for plays on American themes. "I utterly despise the play," Forrest "growled" to Ellsler, "but for God's sake, as the people like it, put it on, and let's get it over." The public obviously was not as sated with it as was Forrest, the *Herald* reporting, "During Friday and Saturday evenings the town was 'Metamora' crazy."

Forrest took Ellsler along one morning on one of his habitual walks before breakfast. They hiked out on Euclid Avenue for a few miles and then headed north to return along the lakefront. Winter had finally caught up with Forrest, and he paused dramatically to look out over a gray and wind-whipped Lake Erie. With a rhetorical flourish, he asked Ellsler over the crashing breakers whether Cleveland harbored any infidels, "Because, if there are any infidels, let them come here, and look upon this magnificent element of creation, and then let them go home and pray."

For a man reluctant to spend more than ten minutes in a cold climate, Forrest should have exercised more prudence in the face of a Cleveland winter. Scheduled performances of *Damon and Pythias* and *Hamlet* had to be cancelled due to the actor's indisposition, disappointing a large number who had journeyed in from the country to see him play. A "Farewell Benefit" of *Hamlet* was added to the schedule, but that too fell victim to the state of Forrest's health. Ellsler gave up and closed the Cleveland Theatre for the season. Possibly, Forrest's impromptu impersonation of King Lear on the windswept bluff overlooking the lake had cost Clevelanders the opportunity to see his Hamlet.

Ellsler reopened the following April but was forced to close prematurely two months later. Like Dean and McKinney twenty years earlier, he had become the victim of another general economic downturn. A different manager gave the Cleveland a try in August and just as quickly folded. Ellsler took his wife and baby daughter Effie, born in the city, to try his luck in Detroit. From there they migrated to Cincinnati, where they were engaged in George Wood's company. With Wood, they came to Cleveland for a short engagement a year later but then returned again to the Queen City.

For three years, Cleveland endured a series of lackluster theater seasons under a revolving-door regimen of management. Ironically, this dramatic drought happened to occur just at the time that Cleveland acquired its first dramatic critic of distinct personality. Charles Farrar Browne came to the *Cleveland Plain Dealer* in the fall of 1857. Still in his early twenties, he was an ungainly looking beanpole topped by a large head of tousled hair, with a quizzical look in a pair of enormous eyes. As the paper's city editor, his principal responsibility was writing the daily "City Facts and Fancies" column on page three. That included the dramatic beat, such as it was.

Theater was practically nonexistent in 1859, the city's darkest drama season since the depression of the early 1840s. As a matter of fact, the entire "season" consisted of a two-week stand at the Cleveland Theatre by Wood's company from Cincinnati in April and a one-night stand organized by local actor George Jamieson on the Fourth of July. There were also dramatic readings at the Melodeon by Fanny Kemble, who included *The Merry Wives of Windsor* and *Measure for Measure* in her programs. "All the reports that have reached us of the remarkable powers of this lady were true," wrote Browne. "[W]e see, not the lady in plain black, sitting at a table and reading from a book, but bullying, bragging, intriguing, sack-drinking yet philosophiest [*sic*] and witty Sir John Falstaff."

Reviewing the staged productions that year, Browne seemed more critical of the plots than the productions. "The last act is certainly bloody enough," he said of Webster's *The Duchess of Malfi,* "and we almost wondered why the few remaining characters didn't suddenly discover they had been poisoned, wrap themselves up in a capacious star spangled banner and die simultaneously with frightful rattles in their throats." When it came to *Othello* and *Macbeth,* Browne indulged in outrageously detailed plot summaries translated into a sort of frontier idiom and enlivened with an occasional flash of wit, as when he observed apropos of Lady Macbeth, "This is not the only time when a woman has got her husband into trouble."

For the most part, Browne's retellings make for tedious reading today—and perhaps the readers of his own day felt similarly. Their only redeeming value may be the practice they provided Browne in honing his skills as a humorist. Rendered orally, they might have sounded a little like Andy Griffith's account of Bizet's *Carmen;* it's not surprising that Browne, in the persona of Artemus Ward, should have gone on to achieve his greatest fame as a performer on the lecture circuit.

Perhaps sobered by the passing of nearly an entire year with little theater to speak of, Browne took his critical duties more seriously the following season. When Harry S. Eytinge of Cincinnati announced plans for a Cleveland season, the *Sandusky Register* caustically observed that the Cleveland Theatre had been "established on a firm basis" a dozen times over the past couple of years, adding, "We pity Mr. Eytinge." "Reserve your sympathy, Mr. *Register,* for some of your own citizens, who need it badly enough," shot back Browne. "Sandusky and other people in the 'provinces' must come up and see the show."

Browne became an unabashed drama booster that season, noting with approval that Eytinge and company had attracted several "solid" citizens and their families to the dress circle. "Theatrically, Cleveland is the most eccentric place that we ever had the felicity of residing in," wrote Browne, wondering how opera in a foreign language and "boring lectures" could draw full houses, while "an admirable company of actors . . . are permitted to play to half-filled benches." When Peter and Caroline Richings were given a benefit performance, Browne exhorted: "Let every lover of pure drama go and take his wife. Let young men go and take their sisters. If they have no sisters of their own, let them take somebody else's sisters. We are told it don't make much difference."

Unfortunately, Browne did not stick around to see the outcome of his campaign. When the management of the *Plain Dealer* objected to sharing his output with other publications, he left for New York. *Artemus Ward: His Book,* from which Abraham Lincoln read excerpts to his cabinet, was compiled largely from recycled *Plain Dealer* pieces, including a mercifully edited version of his irreverent look at Shakespeare. Browne died quite prematurely of tuberculosis in England, his final thoughts returning to his days in Cleveland.

If Clevelanders realized what they had lost with the departure of Browne, they might have consoled themselves with the fact that they soon had John Ellsler back. "After wandering from one point to another," he recalled, "so much encouraged did we feel by the friendship extended to ourselves and family that we decided to give Cleveland a regular season and a home company." He brought his growing family back to the familiar stand on Bank Street, which in his absence had been renamed the Academy of Music. They opened with a production of *Uncle Tom's Cabin* featuring Ellsler in the title role, his wife as Eliza, and "Little Effie Ellsler as the Angelic Eva."

Ellsler's stock company established a seasonal routine in which they would open in Cleveland and then travel to Columbus in April to play the state capital during the legislative session. Returning to Cleveland, they closed the season on the Fourth of July. On several occasions, the company then took a summer tour through northeastern Ohio. On one of these, they played a full month in Akron and two weeks in Canton. They continued all the way to New Philadelphia, where they drew a theater party from the socialistic commune at Zoar.

There were the usual appearances by the visiting stars of the day. Most notable during the Civil War period, not entirely for theatrical reasons, was a pair of visits by a dark, devilishly handsome man with a wild glint in his black eyes. This was John Wilkes Booth, youngest son of the great Junius Brutus Booth, whom Ellsler had known from his Southern barnstorming days. Billed as J. Wilkes Booth, he arrived at the Academy of Music in November and December of 1863 for one of his last professional appearances on the stage. His eight performances included an appearance as Hamlet, opposite the Polonius and Ophelia of the Ellslers, and his first (and undoubtedly last) Iago in *Othello*.

Booth's specialty, though, was *Richard III*. "His combat with *Richmond* is unequalled," said the *Cleveland Leader* in anticipation, "and on his visit last season, the whole audience rose to their feet with excitement as the combat went on." According to Ellsler, "John Wilkes, as Richard, never knew when he was conquered, consequently he was never ready to die, until it was evident to him that his death was necessary to preserve Richmond's life . . . and the text of the tragedy." He described one performance in which a desperate Richmond had whispered, "For God's sake, John, die! Die! If you don't I shall."

There were two performances of *Richard III* in this stand. The *Herald* called Booth "undoubtedly the best *Richard* on the stage," and Ellsler considered him the "only" Richard after his father. While expressing some disappointment in Booth's choice of *The Stranger* for his benefit performance, the *Herald* concluded overall that he was "an actor of talent and great promise." His final performance in Cleveland was in Schiller's *The Robbers* on December 5, 1863. A couple of weeks after he left, Ellsler put on *Our American Cousin*.

Some sixteen months later the Academy company was in Columbus when news reached them of Abraham Lincoln's assassination. They couldn't believe the rumors associating Wilkes Booth with the act until Ellsler arrived, uncommonly pale, to confirm the reports. Euphemia Ellsler, who rarely cried, broke into tears for the actor her husband called "as manly a man as God ever made." A mass meeting had been called in Capital Square, but Ellsler prudently advised members of the company not to put in an appearance.

In the hysterical pursuit for Lincoln's killers, Ellsler himself came close to suspicion because of a business venture he had shared with Booth in the Pennsylvania oil fields. Only the previous summer, the two actors had met there to share a cabin and develop the property. Ellsler claimed he later received an offer of $80,000 for the property but could no longer get in touch with Booth. In the end he realized only $700, and even that was lost in a bank fire. It would not be the last fortune that slipped through his fingers.

A more fortunate engagement at the Academy had begun shortly after Ellsler's return to Cleveland. One of his actresses appeared at the theater one spring day with a twelve-year-old from her boarding house to fill a need for an extra ballet girl. Ellsler would remember seeing the girl still wearing a short pale blue dress with her hair done in long braids ending in ribbons. A brown straw hat completed the ensemble while an oversized umbrella constituted her sole accessory. He noted, "Her eyes were distinctly blue and were plainly big with fright."

Preoccupied at the moment with a business matter, Ellsler brushed the newcomer off with the flippant observation that he wanted women, not children. He turned to go but was arrested by the eyes of the silent girl: "I had noticed their blueness a moment before—now they were almost black, so swiftly had the pupils dilated. All the father in me shrank under the child's bitter disappointment; all the actor in me thrilled at the power of expression in the girl's face." He told her to come back in a day or two.

Her name was Clara Morrison, but Ellsler's stage manager carelessly recorded it as Morris, and it was as Clara Morris that the timorous

Clara Morris became the most famous "graduate" of John Ellsler's "school of the drama" at the Academy of Music. As America's leading "emotional actress," she often returned to Cleveland in such vehicles as Alixe, in which she is pictured here. *Cleveland Press Collection*

child ripened into the most famous product of the Academy of Music's "drama school."

Though born in Toronto, Clara Morris often listed Cleveland as her birthplace in an effort to be accepted as an American actress. She had an unnaturally peripatetic childhood due to her mother's efforts to escape the claims of a bigamous husband; they finally settled in Cleveland after learning of the father's death. According to Morris, her mother had once rejected with righteous indignation an offer from a popular actress to adopt Clara and educate her for a stage career. "It would be better for her to starve trying to lead a clean and honorable life, than to be exposed to such publicity and such awful temptations!" she recalled as her mother's response.

If so, continued privation must have worked a change of attitude toward the stage. Her mother found a job assisting the owner of a boarding house patronized by actors, giving them a more accurate notion of the morals of stage people. Clara became a member of the Academy's corps de ballet for $3 a week, evidently with mother's blessing. She soon caught Ellsler's eye with her pluck, stepping unrehearsed into a bit part when an older girl suffered an attack of stage fright. He invited her to return the following season as a full member of the company.

Morris later seemed to take a debunking attitude toward the Academy's reputation as a school of the drama. The only lesson she ever received there, she claimed, was one on how to apply her makeup, given by a fellow actress on her first night as a ballet girl. Whatever she learned since then had been "by observation, study, and direct inquiry—but never by instruction, either free or paid for." The sum total of Ellsler's advice had been to speak loud and distinctly.

Those who think of drama schools in terms of improvisation drills and method exercises certainly would not recognize the Academy as a school. In fact, there were no such drama schools in the nineteenth century. Young apprentices were expected to observe and learn from their elders, especially when that elder happened to be a famous visiting star who expected members of the local stock company to be in harmony with his or her interpretation of a role. When necessary, Ellsler also included "the courtesies that mark the well-bred man or woman" in the curriculum.

Such as it may have been, the Ellsler "method" worked well enough for Clara Morris. She was promoted to small roles and gained her first notice, the *Herald* observing, "Clara Morris played the small part allotted to her well." Paradoxically, each advance could bring a temporary monetary setback, as actors were still responsible for supplying their own costumes. Ellsler related how one actor who came to play Hamlet was nonplussed to see the company's Horatio show up at dress rehearsal in a costume identical to his own. "We will play *Hamlet*," he finally decreed, "but—without—Horatio!"

Morris did not seem to run into any problems with visiting stars. She played Gertrude opposite the Hamlet of Edwin Booth, and C. W. Couldock affectionately dubbed her his "crummie girl"—a Yorkshire term for someone round faced. She continued to collect ever more glowing notices. "Miss Clara Morris, who has been deservedly advanced in the company, was received with especial marks of favor, the applause continuing for some moments," reported the *Leader* at the beginning of her fifth season. It regarded the demonstration as "a flattering testimonial to that ladies' [*sic*] merits in her profession, and an assurance that Miss Morris cannot but feel gratefully sensible of."

In a way, that became part of the problem. No matter how much praise she garnered outside the company, Morris saw that Mrs. Ellsler continued to be given preference for the leading roles, especially when the more celebrated visiting stars were in town. She remarked, a bit cattishly, how disconcerted E. L. Davenport became when he discovered that Morris was to fill the secondary role of Emilia, while he had to play Othello opposite the Desdemona of a matron whose "middle-aged prosperity expressed itself in a startling number of inches about the waist of her short little body." Morris was also undoubtedly aware that the Ellslers' daughter, little Effie, was being groomed in the wings as a future leading lady.

Despite her lingering respect for Ellsler, Morris finally accepted an offer to become a leading lady at Wood's Museum in Cincinnati. She made her farewells to "the city that I loved"—its schools and churches, Fourth of July picnics on Lake Erie, even the "great green silence" of the Erie Street Cemetery in the midst of the booming growth around it. Although Ellsler had been laid up with a sore throat, he showed up to see her off and presented her with the first watch she ever owned.

After only a year in Cincinnati, she was invited to join the famous Fifth Avenue Theatre company of Augustin Daly. She quickly gained a reputation as America's leading "emotional actress" in such vehicles as *Man and Wife, Alixe, Camille,* and *L'Article 47.* For the latter she had visited insane asylums in her effort to present a realistic portrayal of madness. Such intensity eventually took its toll, and her later years were marked by poor health, including temporary blindness and financial reverses. By the time of her death at age seventy-nine, she was known as "the woman of sorrow." Hundreds came to view her at the Little Church

Around the Corner, where it was remarked that "the beauty of her youth had seemed to come back to her at her death."

There were other notable alumni of Ellsler's "Old Drury," as many fondly called the Academy of Music in reference to London's venerable Drury Lane Theatre. The roll includes Laura Don, Harold Forsberg, R. E. Graham, Eliza Hudson, Roland Reed, and William Young. Mrs. G. H. Gilbert, who became a favorite in Daly's Fifth Avenue company as a comedienne, gave Ellsler credit for valuable training. John McCullough, who inherited the mantle of Edwin Forrest in the tragic roles, learned much of his business there. So did Joseph Haworth, a Clevelander who often supported McCullough and stepped into stardom following the latter's mental breakdown.

One of Ellsler's leading men found more than dramatic instruction in Cleveland. A handsome Irishman of twenty-four years or so, James O'Neill appeared in everything from *Hamlet* and *Mary Stuart* to *Minnie's Luck* and *Mickey Free.* According to one Cleveland reporter, he was "the patron saint of the matinee girls." Offstage, he began stopping in at a book and stationery shop on Superior Avenue run by fellow countryman Thomas Quinlan. Invited to Quinlan's home, he took note of a teenage daughter named Ella.

O'Neill soon "graduated" to the McVicker company in Chicago, while Ella went off to college. Quinlan died, and Ella went with her mother to New York to study music. There they crossed paths again with James O'Neill, who now became romantically inclined toward the pale delicate beauty of the sheltered girl. It took him nearly a year to win over the mother. O'Neill and Ella Quinlan were married in New York, perhaps to avoid the gossip and censure of the bride's Cleveland friends over her marriage to an actor. James would become quite famous for his portrayal of the title role in *The Count of Monte Cristo.* If he is remembered today, however, it is because he and his bride from Cleveland had a son named Eugene O'Neill.

Another of Ellsler's protégés, a pop-eyed, red-headed comedian named James Lewis, did not wait for family approval as did O'Neill but eloped with a Cleveland girl named Frankie Hurlburt. According to Clara Morris, it was the closest any of Ellsler's company ever came to a real scandal.

Ellsler was known as "Uncle John," or even as "Father John" by some, but not solely for his specialization in "old men" roles. He maintained a paternalistic attitude toward his company, continuing their

Another actor who honed his craft at the Academy of Music was leading man James O'Neill. He met his future wife, Ella, in Cleveland, a union that produced playwright Eugene O'Neill. James O'Neill revisited Cleveland frequently in his signature role of *The Count of Monte Cristo*. *Cleveland Public Library*

salaries during an illness or a layoff for lack of a suitable role. Though "never famous for the size of the salaries he paid," in Morris's words, Ellsler underwent agonies of conscience whenever it became necessary to dismiss a bad actor. "One fault he possessed," said one of his neighbors, "and even that was really a virtue; he was too generous."

Christmas at the Academy seems like something scripted by Dickens. There was usually a special holiday production such as *Aladdin,* which Ellsler would later refer to as "a Christmas mascot." At the special matinee on Christmas Day, toys were given to all the children in the audience. Following the evening performance, the stage was set for a turkey dinner for members of the company and theater employees. Tables and chairs were then moved aside for dancing and the distribution of gifts to the Academy of Music family.

The Ellsler family resided in a house on the corner of Wood and Lake Streets—Lake is now Lakeside Avenue, and Wood is now part of the Mall, which would have placed the Ellsler residence close to Zion Evangelical Lutheran Church, site of one of the first Christmas trees displayed in America. There were four children in the family, two girls and two boys: Effie, Annie, Will, and John. All became involved in theatrical activities, with Effie already beginning to blossom as a soubrette and potential leading lady. Her nontheatrical education was entrusted to the nuns of the Ursuline Academy on Euclid Avenue.

Ellsler seemed to make a special effort to avoid a bohemian lifestyle and to win acceptance as a "solid" citizen. He became active in several orders of the Masons. Having spent his younger years on the theatrical road, he was pleased to regard Cleveland as "HOME" (his emphasis) and to number some of the city's pioneering spirits among his friends. "He had all the agreeable qualities of the typical actor, with none of the vices," summarized John Ryder, who lived across the street.

For the most part since his return, Ellsler had little serious competition in the theatrical field. The Melodeon had become Brainard's Hall; as a branch of the music-publishing house of the same name, it was devoted primarily to concert activity. The Atheneum, Ellsler's bitter rival during his first Cleveland venture, burned down in 1865. Case Hall was erected two years later on Superior at Public Square, but it was used largely for lectures.

There was still the old Cleveland Theater on Center Street, which had been renamed Frankfort Street. After its short career as a circus, it became the Varieties Theater under the proprietorship of one Adolphe Montpellier. It appears to have been a beer hall that offered a variety of entertainment—"the can-can and other indecencies that flourished in those days," according to local historian Maurice Weidenthal. "It was a place where men could go back of the stage and form the acquaintance of the actresses," wrote Weidenthal, adding that "many a boy took his first lesson in vice in that pesthouse called a theater." One of the "vilest" of the acts they saw there was a sketch called *The Female Bathers* with Denham Thompson. Eventually, Thompson must have

Like many nineteenth-century stock companies, John Ellsler's was a family affair. His eldest daughter, Effie, made her stage debut at the age of eight as Little Eva in *Uncle Tom's Cabin*. Ellsler's younger daughter and two sons also found employment, either in the front or the back of the house, at the Academy of Music. *Western Reserve Historical Society*

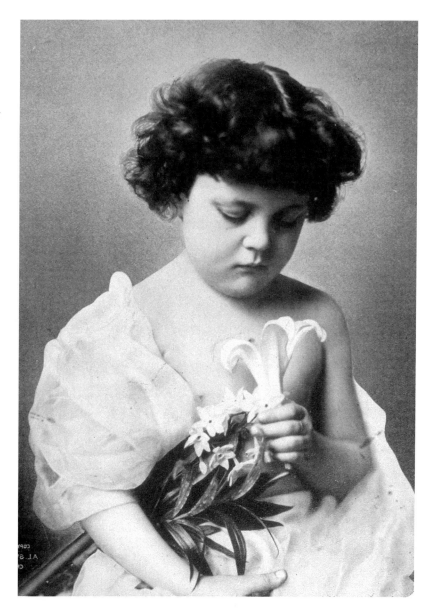

cleaned up his act, developing a wholesome character from his sketch named Joshua Whitcomb and putting him into a play entitled *The Old Homestead,* which provided him with a lifetime occupation.

It was Weidenthal who claimed that Clara Morris had made her stage debut in the Varieties before moving over to Ellsler's Academy of Music. Given the reputation of the Varieties, it is understandable why Morris would not have wanted to acknowledge the fact—if true—in her own accounts of her career. The Varieties was temporarily closed down by the city in 1865. Calling it "a hotbed of vulgarity, immorality and vice," the *Leader* noted that "the wonder is, that the place has not been broken up before this." It didn't remain broken up, for after a year or so it was reopened as the National Theater. Once again it was closed, but in 1867 it re-emerged in all its gaudy glory as the Theatre Comique. Though the names had changed, the product appeared to be the same.

Not even Ellsler's "Old Drury," the Academy of Music, was above an occasional fling in risqué territory. Easily the most notable was a local production of the celebrated musical spectacle *The Black Crook*. Often cited as the progenitor of the American musical, it was a pastiche born of the marriage of a Gothic play with a stranded French ballet troupe. It had almost anything one could want: magic, melodrama, song, dance, elaborate scenery, spectacular effects—none of which seemed to make as strong an impression as the presence of a large corps de ballet clad in pink tights. Opened at Niblo's Garden in 1866, it was well on its way to a record New York run of 475 performances.

It had already played in Cincinnati and St. Louis and was still running in New York when Cleveland got its chance to see *The Black Crook*. Ellsler had secured the rights and much of the scenery from a producer in Buffalo and advertised it as "The most costly and magnificent Dramatic Spectacle ever produced in Cleveland." Seven "Premier Danseurs," a ballet of thirty ladies, special new music, calcium lights, an incantation scene, and a final transformation scene—"the Glittering Palace of Diamonds!"—were among the promised wonders.

A large crowd filled the Academy of Music for the opening on June 17, 1867. The *Cleveland Leader*'s review stretched out a sentence to 207 words in trying to convey "the enchanting beauties of this wonderful spectacle, unsurpassed by anything in its line ever before conceived by man." The only flaws were a couple of long waits during scene changes and a ballet girl rendered hors de combat by a fall through a trapdoor on the stage.

Word of this attraction spread throughout the hinterland. A hundred people came from Norwalk to see it, followed the next evening by two hundred from Sandusky, who arrived with their own band on the steamer *Evening Star* at $2 a head. Newsman Charles E. Kennedy later recalled the "envy of the loafers in Jim Crane's store" in his native West Farmington, Ohio, when one of their cronies returned from the big city with tales of "dancing girls actually clad in black tights!" Black tights in place of pink must have constituted Ellsler's concession to any lingering New England prudery on the Western Reserve. Regardless, "photograms" of *The Black Crook* dancing girls were announced for sale at James Ryder's photography studio on Superior Avenue.

Dancing girls were obviously no liability at the box office. Just in case they weren't enough, however, Ellsler interpolated fresh novelties such as the "Demon Dance" into later performances. Many were said to be going back "night after night." By the time it closed four weeks later, *The Black Crook* had set a new Cleveland record of twenty-nine consecutive performances. It was seen by an estimated twenty thousand Clevelanders, and the total box office take amounted to $14,285.

The Black Crook may have danced to the edge of permissiveness with its chorus in black tights, but two years later the Academy apparently crossed the line with the can-can of Jacques Offenbach. Impresario Jacob Grau brought a company to the Academy of Music for a three-night stand of the effervescent French operettas that had swept Europe and the eastern seaboard. The *Cleveland Leader* was not amused. While it found *Geneviève de Brabant* to contain "much pretty and exceedingly agreeable music," that was not enough to redeem the "vulgarity, touching the bounds of nastiness" of the plot, which rendered it "utterly unfit to be presented in public." What seemed especially to distress the *Leader* was the fact that the French farce attracted not the coarser classes, but "mainly the people of education, wealth, and social influence."

As the city's preeminent theatrical showplace, the Academy welcomed all the leading acts in the decade following the Civil War. Ellsler's old partner, Joseph Jefferson, came in 1871 with his perennial favorite *Rip Van Winkle.* It was not much of a play, decided the *Leader,* but the genius of Jefferson elevated it to "the most perfect example of stage art which the theater presents." Yet, there were Clevelanders who considered John Ellsler's interpretation of the part to be unmatched even by that of Jefferson.

In fact, *Rip Van Winkle* proved to be the most popular play of the Ellsler era, with fifty-five performances in Cleveland. Its closest competitors were *Uncle Tom's Cabin* and *Hamlet.* Repertoire was often dictated by the desires and abilities of the visiting star. If Edwin Booth wanted to do *The Merchant of Venice,* members of the Academy company would fill the other roles and Ellsler would rummage backstage for the necessary backdrops and props. Some stars were beginning to travel with their own companies, but Ellsler could in that case move his own company over to the Pittsburgh Opera House, which he began to manage in 1871.

The brightest stars of the American stage all took their turns on the Academy's boards: Booth, Jefferson, Frank Chanfrau, Rose Eytinge, Alice Oates, John T. Raymond, George Fawcett Rowe, Joseph Proctor, Frank Mayo, James Murdock, John McCullough, Adelaide Ristori, Lucille Western, William Florence, Mrs. D. P. Bowers, Dion Boucicault, Jean Lander, Lydia Thompson, Maggie Mitchell, Adelaide Neilson, and E. L. Davenport. Charles and Ellen Kean appeared together in *Macbeth,* and E. A. Sothern played his Lord Dundreary in *Our American Cousin.* Clara Morris returned to her alma mater in triumph with *L'Article 47* and *Alixe.* The Czech star Fannie Janauschek came despite her imperfect command of English in *Chesney Wold,* an adaptation of Dickens's *Bleak House.* She delighted the "boys in the gallery," according to Charles Asa Post, by turning the line "We will have none but lovers here" into "We will have none but loafers here."

But hints began dropping in the early 1870s that the Academy of Music was having trouble attracting some of the bigger names. It was said that many came in spite of inadequate houses solely out of loyalty to "Uncle John," who had sustained many of them in less prosperous days. All over America, growing cities were announcing their sophistication by the raising of imposing town halls or, in the larger ones, full-fledged opera houses. The *Cleveland Leader* pointed to such civic monuments in rival towns such as Akron, Mansfield, Detroit, and Columbus, concluding, "In common with the majority of our community we hold that an opera building is the first and greatest public necessity of Cleveland."

Though he had redecorated the Academy at least twice since his return, Ellsler himself threw in his lot with the opera house promoters. In a letter to the *Cleveland Herald,* he wished his critics could see "what energy and inducements it requires, to bring the better class of stars to play here; and what energy, tact and labor, is needful, to induce the citizens to come to such a place as Cleveland now calls a theater." After barely twenty years of operation, it was apparent that Cleveland had outgrown the Academy of Music.

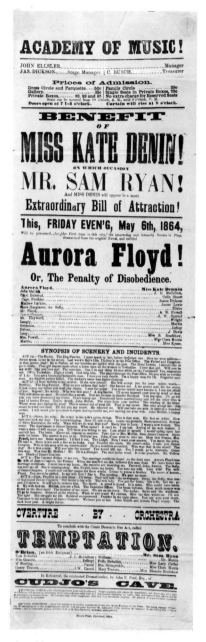

The oldest extant program in Cleveland's theatrical history is this broadside from the Academy of Music for May 6, 1864. Visiting star Kate Denin is featured with such members of John Ellsler's stock company as John McCollom, James Lewis, Ellsler himself, and a very young Clara Morris at the threshold of her career. The original measures seven by twenty-one inches. *Cleveland Public Library*

CLEVELAND'S SWEETHEART

She was known as "Cleveland's sweetheart." That appellation came much later, of course, after she had achieved national exposure. Her parents called her Effie Ellsler; she was the daughter of Cleveland's first family of the stage, John and Euphemia (Effie) Ellsler.

She made her theatrical debut at the tender age of eight, playing Little Eva to her father's Tom in *Uncle Tom's Cabin*. Another early triumph was as Mary in *Ten Nights in a Barroom*.

This was during the Civil War, when John Wilkes Booth performed at her father's theater and spent some offstage hours playing "like a big boy" with Effie and her siblings. Onstage, she played the little Duke of York to his Richard III and developed a crush on the dashing actor. She would show up at the theater every day in her best gowns, according to one of her father's actresses, and looked at him with "fervid eyes that might well have served for Juliet." "How's my little girl?" Booth inquired in a letter to her father.

She matured into leading roles. At eighteen she left Ursuline Academy to play the part of Virginia opposite the Virginius of Edwin Forrest in that actor's farewell tour. When her father opened his Euclid Avenue Opera House in 1875, she appeared with her parents in the opening production of *Saratoga*.

Bartley Campbell, one of the leading playwrights of the period, then wrote *Heroine in Rags* for her. "The acting of Miss Effie Ellsler in the part of *Jeanette Brashear* is . . . an embodiment of all the pure, loving, gentle qualities that nature could implant in the bosom of a young girl," said the *Cleveland Leader*. "It is as sweet and full of poetry as the wild flowers and simple ballads she offers to the villagers."

New York beckoned next, and in 1880 she created the title role in Steele MacKaye's *Hazel Kirke,* the opening attraction at his Madison Square Theatre. It was a hybrid of the old melodrama with the newer realism. Hazel was disowned by her father for marrying against his wishes, but the dialogue leaned toward the natural rather than the emotional.

The *New York Times* found the Clevelander's acting to be "the most interesting part of the performance; it was natural acting, equally notable for truthfulness and method." *Hazel Kirke* went on to establish a New York run of 486 performances, a record that held for a quarter-century. Effie Ellsler went on to marry popular actor Frank Weston, who also appeared with her in the long-running hit.

Effie Ellsler went from ingénue in her father's Academy of Music stock company to stardom on the New York stage. She is pictured here as Hazel Kirke in Steele MacKaye's 1880 play of the same name. In an acting career spanning seven decades, she earned the nickname "Cleveland's Sweetheart." *Western Reserve Historical Society*

Not long afterward she embarked upon a western tour under the management of former Clevelander Abe Erlanger. They played what Erlanger called the "Silver Circuit," the mining towns of Colorado, performing a piece entitled *Woman vs. Woman*. Opening a new opera house in Montrose, Colorado, Erlanger charged "Patti prices" of $5 a head and filled the house with an audience "composed principally of Indians and cow boys."

Though she never quite equaled her success in *Hazel Kirke*, Ellsler managed to sustain a prosperous career in such plays as *Storm Beaters,*

Camille, A Daughter of the Nile, and *Barbara Frietchie.* She and Weston made their home in New Jersey, where her parents spent their last days. "Cleveland's sweetheart" made her last appearance in her hometown in *Old Lady 31* at the Colonial Theatre in 1919, when she also planted a tree in the Shakespeare Garden in Rockefeller Park.

There was one more triumph, however, and it came in a play by another former Clevelander, Avery Hopwood. Cowritten with Mary Roberts Rinehart, *The Bat* was a mystery in which Effie played the elderly spinster Cornelia Van Gorder, who eventually cracks the case in the manner of television's Angela Lansbury during the 1990s.

Opening on August 23, 1920, *The Bat* ran for more than two years to become one of the decade's greatest successes. During a matinee performance in 1922, Effie was informed that her husband, Frank Weston, had died. There was no understudy, so she went on and played the evening performance, just as "Uncle John" Ellsler might have wanted her to do.

Effie then joined her sister and one of her brothers in moving to the West Coast. There was a place for her in Hollywood specializing as old ladies in such movies as *Black Fury* and *Daddy Long Legs.* She died at age eighty-seven in 1942.

That was not quite the final scene, however. A curtain call of sorts occurred a year later when some of her trunks were opened in a storage building in Lakewood. One of her grandnieces carefully unpacked old costumes of velvet, satin, and brocade along with press notices, programs, and dozens of fans and wigs. There were also letters from such stage legends as Joseph Jefferson, Edwin Booth, and the ill-starred John Wilkes Booth.

Best of all, the trunks yielded the personal stage memoirs of John Ellsler, lovingly edited and preserved by his daughter. It was Effie Ellsler's last and most precious gift to her native Cleveland.

Three

THE GILDED STAGE

IT WAS A REACTION that would be replicated more than a century later by the first Opening Day crowd at Jacobs Field. According to the *Cleveland Leader* of September 7, 1875, sixteen hundred Clevelanders the previous evening had looked about, blinking in wonderment. They could not believe "that this was all really happening in Cleveland." Dressed in formal attire, this crowd had gathered not for the opening of a ballpark but for the dedication of a "New Temple of Art"—the opening of the Euclid Avenue Opera House.

Entering through an arched doorway on Euclid Avenue, the throng had progressed down a long hallway a hundred feet in length, treading expectantly on a floor containing four thousand pieces of marble and tile. This brought them to the true lobby of the theater, which was actually built to front on the side street of Sheriff (now East 4th) Street. The first thing to catch their eyes was a magnificent box office, profusely ornamented with woodcarvings of flowers, ferns, leaves, and wreaths, all topped with gold foil. It was the work of John Herkomer, a German-born woodcarver who had similarly graced the mantelpieces and staircases of the "Millionaires' Row" of stately mansions being built along Euclid Avenue. Stairways leading from the lobby to the upper levels were likewise finished in carved oak and walnut with twelve-foot newel posts at the bottom of each flight supporting bronze figures bearing gas lighting brackets. Those fixtures alone carried a price tag of $320 apiece, the *Leader* informed its readers.

Passing into the auditorium, first-nighters undoubtedly gaped first at the great central chandelier suspended from the domed ceiling, containing "countless prismatic chains, drops, spiers [spires?], festoons and glass bells, arranged around its surface in a beautiful series of brackets." Weighing two tons and measuring fourteen feet in diameter and twenty-nine feet in length, it was described as the largest prismatic fixture in the United States. It was illuminated by 325 gas jets that, with the rest of the over 1,000 gas jets in the auditorium and around the stage, could be lighted electrically in a single second by turning a pointer on a marble dial. Ceiling frescoes by Clevelander Charles Piccini featured representational figures of tragedy, comedy, poetry, and music. Around the edges of the dome were portraits of Shakespeare, Byron, Rossini, and Mozart.

A total of 1,638 playgoers could be seated under that ceiling, said to be nearly twice the capacity of the "old house," the Academy of Music. They were ranked on three levels with a balcony and upper gallery opening above the orchestra. Seats were covered with red velvet, which was also draped around the family circle and boxes. This, combined with the general white-and-gold decor of the auditorium, must have anticipated the overall effect of the future Palace Theatre on Playhouse Square. Gold leaf was applied liberally on all the interior columns, capitals, panels, and figures of the Euclid Avenue Opera House, making it the epitome of what historians would dub the "Gilded Age."

Behind a $1,500 curtain of red satin, velvet ribbon, and heavy fringe, lay a stage of generous proportions. Measuring seventy-six feet in width by fifty-five feet in depth, it harbored seven entrances and twenty-one traps. Every detail had been overseen by John Ellsler, who would manage the new house. In the wings were carpeted dressing rooms, a comfortable greenroom for players to relax in offstage, as well as rooms for props, scenery, and wardrobe. It was said to be the first theater to provide a separate room for the use of the musicians; the pit itself could accommodate twenty-one. Underneath the stage was machinery for sinking scenes, lifts for players, and waterpower for fountains. In the words of actor E. A. Sothern, who appeared there later that season, it was "the most perfect theater in America or England."

For his premiere attraction, Ellsler chose the society comedy *Saratoga; or, Pistols for Seven*. Written by Bronson Howard, it had recently reopened McVicker's Theater in Chicago following that city's great fire.

As summarized by the *Cleveland Leader,* "It is a jolly, entertaining five act farce, in which five women of various ages and conditions become enamored of a very successful love making young man, and succeed in persuading their several lovers to arrange duels with the resistless cavalier." Ellsler's daughter Effie was the leading lady, supported by Joseph Whiting, Joseph Haworth, and her parents.

Though a highly regarded play, *Saratoga* was inevitably upstaged that night by the new house. Prior to the rise of the curtain, a short dedication was delivered by George Willey, local lawyer and arts patron. Cleveland may have lagged behind her sister cities in erecting its "Temple of Art," said Willey, but the "triumphant success and beauty" being celebrated that night was well worth the wait. As Ellsler and his daughter took their bows following the third act, a visiting party from the "Smoky city" of Pittsburgh expressed their esteem with a tribute of flowers and a silver salver. Opening night was a benefit for Ellsler, and the full house raised a total of $3,150.

Ellsler deserved every cent, for he had staked his all on the new theater. Though the need for a new opera house had been argued since the 1860s, material support was slow to manifest itself. One early proposal to convert an ice skating rink on Public Square to theatrical purposes was, perhaps mercifully, abandoned. Proponents finally persuaded Ellsler to take the lead in the formation of a stock company, assuring him that support would follow. The venture was incorporated in August 1873 with capitalization set at $100,000 and partners including Ellsler, financier Jeptha H. Wade, and A. W. Fairbanks, co-owner of the *Cleveland Herald.*

As described by Ellsler, however, selling stock proved to be "up hill 'ball rolling' of the worst kind." A general depression following a financial panic in 1873 did not make the job any easier. Another unforeseen problem arose when the city failed to widen Sheriff Street, as planners had understood would be done. According to Ellsler, this necessitated the rental of a storefront in the Heard Building to build an entrance from Euclid Avenue. Though this justified the use of the prestigious avenue's name for the theater, it didn't help the project's bottom line.

It also made the elaborate four-story facade of blue sandstone on Sheriff Street somewhat superfluous. Designed by architects Charles Heard and Sons, it was reportedly modeled after Edwin Booth's theater in New York. Dominated by an impressive central tower, it featured a heavily corniced roofline and a dignified two-story arched entrance. "The finest stone carving was wasted upon the wall," wrote Maurice

From the day of its long-awaited opening in 1875, the Euclid Avenue Opera House was the pride of the city. The $175,000 theater actually fronted on Sheriff (East 4th) Street (right), but an entrance cut through an adjoining commercial block gave its lobby access to the prestigious "Millionaires' Row" of Euclid Avenue. It fulfilled a longtime dream of "Uncle John" Ellsler—and soon broke his heart. *Cleveland Press Collection*

Weidenthal, "and there are few people in Cleveland who really know that the Sheriff street front is so beautiful and ornamental."

With three stories of that facade completed in July 1874, capitalization had to be increased to $150,000. In order to save his original investment, Ellsler threw in the remainder of his personal fortune accumulated from three decades on the stage. The final cost was set at $175,000, and the Euclid Avenue Opera House opened $12,000 in debt. Few in that awestruck opening-night audience could have realized how close a thing it had been.

Despite depressions and occasional setbacks, it was overall an optimistic age in Cleveland history. Rockefeller was making the city's first great fortune in oil and taking partners such as Samuel Andrews, Henry Flagler, and Stephen V. Harkness with him. While they mined the black gold of western Pennsylvania, other Clevelanders mined the red gold of the Upper Great Lakes iron ore fields. New fortunes were being made in iron and steel for the owners of the M. A. Hanna, Oglebay Norton, Pickands Mather, and Cleveland Rolling Mill Companies. These were the nouveaux riches who were putting up the manor houses of "Millionaires' Row."

Other people were entering the crucible of Cleveland in the Gilded Age, far more numerous if not so fortunate. Laborers by the thousands were needed for the city's new industries, and the demand was increasingly being supplied directly from Europe. To the Irish and Germans who had arrived before the Civil War were being added Poles and Czechs and later Jews and Italians. A city that had needed twenty-four years to accumulate its first six hundred inhabitants was adding them at an average of ten thousand a year in the last quarter of the nineteenth century. They were coming primarily to work, but eventually they would also want to be entertained.

As the playhouse for the carriage trade, the Euclid Avenue Opera House would dominate the theatrical scene throughout the period. Ellsler hoped to run it as he had the old Academy, with a resident stock company handling most of the chores in-house and an occasional boost from visiting stars. He wanted as much as possible to keep appearances by traveling companies to a minimum. When an outside company did come in, Ellsler could transfer his Euclid Avenue company to the house he still managed in Pittsburgh. He maintained a company of thirty actors, many of them holdovers from the Academy of Music. Supporting them was a staff of twenty miscellaneous functionaries, from stage manager and orchestra conductor to scenic artists and gas superintendent.

Saratoga got the new house off to an impressive start with a run of ten performances. The repertoire during the first season included two of the period's most successful melodramas, *East Lynne* and *The Two Orphans.* The classics were represented by *As You Like It, Julius Caesar, School for Scandal,* and an adaptation of *Jane Eyre.* John McCullough, E. A. Sothern, and Lotta Crabtree were among the guest stars. All told, the stock company was employed for a total of twenty-eight weeks in a thirty-seven-week season. In the year's greatest spectacle, it combined with a company from Booth's Theatre in New York to put on a "Live Shakespeare Pageant" of *Henry V* that boasted 42 speaking parts and 150 supernumeraries.

With a showcase like the new opera house, Cleveland also began to attract an occasional premiere. One of the first was Bartley Campbell's

Heroine in Rags, which was written expressly for the Ellslers' daughter Effie. Even more prestigious was the premiere on October 25, 1878, of a new play by William Dean Howells, which happened to bear the title *A New Play.* It was an adaptation in blank verse of a tragedy of the same name by the Spanish dramatist Tamayo y Baus. The plot concerned the comedian Yorick, mentioned in Shakespeare's *Hamlet,* and what ensued when he indulged the putative aspiration of all comedians to become tragedians.

Howells was a native Ohioan already distinguished as a novelist and as editor of the literary arbiter, *The Atlantic Monthly.* As interpreted by the popular Lawrence Barrett, his play filled the Opera House with, in the words of the *Cleveland Leader,* "an audience drawn from Cleveland's most intelligent and aristocratic classes, and comprising the literary and critical judgment of the city." The *Leader* judged the performance to be more impressive than the play, which it labeled as too much of "a one-part play." Nonetheless, Barrett made the most of that part, turning in as Yorick "a long-sustained passionate fury which is perhaps the best piece of acting of this kind which he has yet done." Retitled *Yorick's Love,* the play enjoyed a modest success but failed to establish the author's reputation as a dramatist. Like his contemporary Henry James, Howells was fated to enjoy far more success between the covers of a novel than on the boards of any stage.

Barrett's appearance was the occasion of such interest that special trains were run from Ashtabula and Norwalk. A popular clamor arose to see him in *The Man of Airlie,* a Barrett specialty in which he played a mad poet, thought dead, who returned unrecognized to witness the unveiling of a statue of himself. There was no time to get the statue out of storage in New York, so Ellsler's scene painter improvised by painting one in profile on canvas glued to a board, which was then sawed out in outline and stood up backed by a brace. The character doing the unveiling was played by Otis Skinner.

Skinner later described the ensuing scene. As he gave the sheet a vigorous tug, it got caught on the jagged edge of the board and stubbornly remained in place. Skinner tried again with no more luck. A fellow actor lent a hand; the "statue" bent forward but refused to release the shroud. They could hear muttered imprecations from Barrett by this time, coming from the middle of the crowd scene. Giving a final, desperate yank, they finally succeeded in freeing the sheet from the board. The audience lost whatever restraint it had left, as the suddenly liberated statue swayed inanely back and forth as if taking its bows.

Such were the occasional perils of doing stock repertory. But a far more serious threat than an uncooperative stage prop hung over Ellsler's stock company, even as they broke in their splendid new house. A fundamental change in the organization of the American theater was taking place in the 1870s. More and more visiting stars were touring by railroad in single productions with their own sets and supporting casts, an arrangement known as the combination company. It was favored by the nascent American playwright, as it gave him more control over the standards of production as well as the collection of royalties.

Audiences also began to look forward to the traveling companies, especially since the scenery designed specifically for a single play was obviously superior in effect to the all-purpose backdrops—drawing room, cottage, city street, and such—employed by the average stock company. As theaters grew larger, spectacular stage effects began to steal the show from the finely honed performances and traditional stage business cultivated by resident companies. Dion Boucicault's *Pauvrette* called for an Alpine avalanche to bury two lovers in a mountain cabin. In an upward spiral of scenic one-upmanship that sounds all too familiar, other plays began advertising fires, explosions, speeding locomotives, and shipwrecks.

In the face of such unequal competition, the number of stock companies operating in the United States decreased from fifty in 1871 to only twenty in 1878. They simply could not afford to build new scenery for every production, nor could they cast plays as realistically, drawing constantly from a far more restricted talent pool. Ellsler was one of the last of the holdouts, and it may have been a fatal mistake. As combination companies began to monopolize the season at the Euclid Avenue Opera House, Ellsler felt compelled to lease his old Academy of Music in 1878, primarily to provide a stage for his stock players.

The continued fallout from the Panic of 1873 was also working against Ellsler. Attendance at the new house fell short of expectations, and some blamed it on a location "too far uptown" from the established business district. Ellsler saw his debt increasing, and his stockholders failed to make good on their assessments. Playing the heavies, the banks moved in to foreclose. The final act of the tragedy took place early in 1879, when the Euclid Avenue Opera House went under the auctioneer's gavel.

What happened next would have made a lively scene in a melodrama. According to the most common version, Cleveland businessman Marcus A. Hanna was walking with some friends from his office in the Warehouse District to lunch at the Union Club—or on his way back, according to a variant account. Noticing an unusual commotion in the vicinity of Sheriff Street, they went to investigate and found the opera house on the block. The bidding was already up to $40,000. On an impulse, Hanna raised it a few hundred dollars. Down banged the hammer, and Mark Hanna was suddenly in show business. As was said of the British Empire, he had seemingly acquired the Euclid Avenue Opera House in a fit of absent-mindedness.

Hanna was one of the rising class of Cleveland capitalists, having interests in iron ore and street railways. His business interests led to an interest in politics, which in turn led him to purchase part ownership in the *Cleveland Herald*. His only interest in the stage was that of an avid theatergoer. Finding himself in possession of the city's finest theater, he merely reserved a box for his private use and turned the management over to a cousin, L. G. Hanna.

That left John Ellsler out, and stories apparently later arose that it was Hanna who had foreclosed on Ellsler just to get his hands on his theater. As a conspicuous member of a breed later vilified as "Robber Barons," Hanna, of course, made almost as good a target for social critics as John D. Rockefeller. Cartoonist Homer Davenport would eventually rivet Hanna's historical image by regularly dressing him in a suit patterned with dollar signs. Yet personally, Hanna was a naturally gregarious man who would even win the grudging admiration of that prince of muckrakers, Lincoln Steffens. By a curious coincidence, he even bore the same avuncular nickname as that bestowed on Ellsler, being known in Republican Party circles as "Uncle Mark."

Ellsler himself never seemed to bear any ill will toward Hanna, and his daughter Effie later specifically denied that her father had ever borrowed from Hanna. Before he left the Opera House, Ellsler was given a farewell benefit in a production of *Pocahontas* on June 13, 1879. Portraying the character of Chief Powhatan, he was called upon for a speech at the end. "I wish I could go among you all, loyal to me," he said, "shake every one of you by the hand, that I might prove to you that I have my heart in my hand." After taking his final bow in the house he had built, "Uncle John" Ellsler made his way back to the Academy of Music.

That season also marked the end of a resident stock company at the Euclid Avenue Opera House. Under the Hanna regime, the theater would be run strictly as a combination-company house. The legendary French actress Sarah Bernhardt made her Cleveland debut there during her first American tour in 1881. She appeared in one of her specialties, *Frou-Frou,* and delivered her lines, as was her custom no matter where she appeared, in presumably flawless French. "There has nothing like it been seen on our stage, and consequently it cannot be compared," wrote the *Leader* of the performance. "She abandons herself to the passion of the situation quite as completely as would Clara Morris, and the effect on her audience is electrical." Begging to differ, the *Herald* noted: "With all her wonderful ease and grace, her picturesqueness of attitude, her fascinating brilliancy, she appeals only to the intellect and senses. She rarely touches the heart."

Clara Morris herself appeared at the Opera House a few years later in another Bernhardt specialty, *Camille,* among other works. As she emoted on stage one night, she glanced across to the left-stage box and nearly froze at the apparition of a forbidding figure sitting with "his arms folded high upon his chest. . . . White as marble, immovable as stone." The ghost of Daniel Webster was her immediate reaction. Mentioning the incident backstage to another actress, she learned that the spectral figure was in fact "our Major McKinley." Morris was thereupon introduced by "big and cheery Mr. Hanna" to his guest, William McKinley, then governor of Ohio and future president of the United States.

Hanna used his box regularly to entertain fellow businessmen and visiting politicians. He enjoyed comedy and tragedy alike, but could express disapproval of a performance by rubbing his fist into his ear or, worse, stalking out to the lobby for a cigar. Often Hanna went backstage after a performance to introduce himself to actors and invite them to Glenmere, his estate on the west side. He formed an especially close bond with Lawrence Barrett, exchanging letters and on one occasion buying up a good part of the house to fill it during the actor's appearance on a slow Tuesday. Toward actresses, however, he could be uncharacteristically shy.

As a businessman, Hanna expected his opera house to be run efficiently, though as a theater aficionado he did not expect the same profit margin as from his other enterprises. According to a later lessee, he was always willing to wait for his rent until after everyone else had been paid. One of the things he inherited from Ellsler was a young man who had begun working at the opera-glass stand and worked his way up to the ticket booth. His name was Abraham Lincoln Erlanger, and Hanna soon made him treasurer and business manager. One of the lessons he learned from Hanna, Erlanger said later, was: "If you want to retain command of a situation, always let the other fellow ask the questions." Eventually, Hanna realized a small profit on his theatrical investment.

It is unlikely that Hanna had to paper the house for the Cleveland premiere of Gilbert and Sullivan's *H.M.S. Pinafore* in 1879. John T. Ford's (he of Ford's Theatre in Washington) Comic Opera Company brought the popular operetta to the Euclid Avenue Opera House for what the *Herald* anticipated as "the event of the season." In its review the following day, however, the *Herald* charged that the vessel had been sabotaged by a mediocre crew. Many Clevelanders had already seen the show in the East, observed the *Leader,* which had "raised expectations which it would have probably been difficult to entirely fulfill." *Pinafore* itself was "all that could have been expected of it," said the *Leader,* with the added bonus of being "wholly free from the adroit indelicacies that defile so universally the opera bouffe of French origin." Three months later, a local amateur production of the same work at the Opera House gathered highly favorable reviews.

Part of the problem with *Pinafore* was the absence of an international copyright agreement, which allowed American managers to produce "pirated" and often second-rate versions of foreign dramatic works without the nuisance of royalty payments. Only by producing the work here himself, before anyone had a chance to steal the material, could an English or Continental dramatist be sure of earning any profits from his work in America. So Gilbert and Sullivan arranged for the premiere of their second full-length operetta, ironically entitled *The Pirates of Penzance,* to take place in the United States.

Pirates had its premiere in New York City on the last day of 1879, and the authors immediately began training several touring companies. One of them arrived at the Euclid Avenue Opera House the following May bearing the official imprimatur of D'Oyly Carte's Opera Company. "It labors under a disadvantage to a certain extent from the public not being made familiar with the text through the customary libretto," observed the *Leader,* explaining the extraordinary measures being taken to ensure copyright protection. That did not stand in the way of a favorable Cleveland reception, and the *Leader* predicted that "the operetta is doubtless marked for success."

While the Euclid Avenue Opera House enjoyed a practical monopoly of the class acts, other theaters were at hand to fill the recreational needs of the city's growing underclass. The old Theatre Comique was still in business on Frankfort Street despite the continued disapproval of the "moral majority" of its day. Its ads were refused by the *Cleveland Herald* in 1875 on the old charge that its bar served as a front for prostitution. "We recognize the need of cheap amusements for the people," said the *Herald,* but it insisted that such places "need not be and should not be vicious and degrading." A few months later, however, a proposed ordinance "to prohibit immoral and immodest public entertainments" failed to win passage in the City Council.

Nonetheless, the Theatre Comique soon tried to reform itself. Evidently hoping to cash in on the growing demand for popular entertainment, the house lowered its admission to ten cents and began referring to itself as the "Workingmen's Theatre." Under the motto of "Refinement," it even offered one hundred dollars to anyone who could find "anything in any performance any evening that the most sensitive person, lady or gentleman, cannot witness with safety." Along with its regular variety acts, it offered short dramatic afterpieces bearing such titles as *Working Girls of Cleveland.*

Whether the Theatre Comique ever had to make good on its one-hundred-dollar challenge remains, unfortunately, unrecorded. Neither family fare nor sin could work its ultimate salvation, for by the early 1890s the house had finally been razed. None seemed to recall that C. W. Couldock and Caroline Richings, as well as the Ellslers, had once played there under Joseph Foster. "No amount of atonement by those responsible can ever wash away the sins caused by the harm that place inflicted on the youth of Cleveland," moralized theater historian Maurice Weidenthal.

By that time, two other popular houses had made their appearance. The curiously named White Elephant opened in 1884 on Sheriff Street several blocks south of the Euclid Avenue Opera House and convenient to the plebian Central Market area. Besides a bowling alley, billiard tables, and a bar, it also included a concert hall for variety acts. It eventually gave way to a provision house, which was burned out in 1937.

Just a few doors east of the Euclid Avenue entrance to the Opera House, the People's Theater opened in 1885 for programs ranging from variety to melodrama. Examples of the latter included *East Lynne* and *Poppie, the Mail Girl*. Converted from a former skating rink, after two years it was made over again into a circus. There was also a Reeves Opera House situated on Broadway near Harvard on the southern fringes of the city. Basically a hall with an attached stage, it had opened in 1876 and was occasionally given over to melodrama.

Of all the popular amusements of the era, none could beat Drew's Dime Museum for sheer sensationalism. The proprietor was Frank M. Drew, a cousin of the Drew-Barrymore stage dynasty. Located on the northeast corner of Superior and Bank (now West 6th) Streets in the old theater district, Drew's operation occupied the third floor of a building emblazoned with placards advertising "Human Freaks," "Animal Monsters," "Wild Men," and the like. As one old timer remembered, patrons climbed a stairway leading to a long, wide hallway lined on either side with platforms bearing such curiosities as a snake charmer, a strong man who could bite through iron bars, or a "legless man with feet growing out of his hips." In the rear was a small stage for the presentation of variety acts.

Dime museums became a staple of urban entertainment in the late nineteenth century. They were modeled after the phenomenally successful American Museum of P. T. Barnum, who organized a circuit to supply similar enterprises across the country with attractions. Opened in 1882, Drew's Dime Museum offered continuous performances and weekly changes of bill. A typical week's program included a pair of comedies, an acrobatic act, and a banjo soloist on the specialty stage along with such sideshows as a "Transparent Girl," a four-year-old girl weighing 150 pounds, and a tribe of Tongans. It all sounded a bit like Artemus Ward's last stand: Drew even had wax figures!

Trying to put a positive spin on the exploitative nature of such exhibitions, Cleveland's *Penny Press* called the dime museum a "Godsend" for "natural curiosities," providing them with employment during the long winter layoffs from the circus season. It proved far from a blessing, however, for a group of Australian aborigines booked into Drew's Dime Museum that very week. Sharing a bill with "the 'armless' phenomenon!" and "The Marvelous Elastic-Skin Man!" they were advertised as "Australian Boomerang Throwers. . . . Veritable bloodthirsty beasts in distorted human form, with but a glimmering of reason." Believed kidnapped from their native Queensland, they were touring under the management of a Barnum agent.

Shortly after they were checked into the Forest City House, one of the group died of a severe cold contracted in Baltimore three weeks earlier. His name was Tambo Tambo; he was twenty-one years old and weighed barely a hundred pounds. As his eight countrymen attempted to prepare the body for ritual burial, their manager intervened to put a stop to such heathenish customs. Instead, the corpse was removed in civilized fashion to an undertaker's establishment, where the curious were freely admitted to gawk. The *Cleveland Herald* deemed Tambo "a victim to the mania for curiosity exhibitions which has raged in this country and Europe for the past ten years." Even yet, Tambo Tambo's odyssey wasn't ended. According to historian William Ganson Rose, the mummified remains were exhibited in a downtown ambulance station for several years before disappearing. They turned up in a funeral home more than a century later, when two of his descendants came to Cleveland and finally took Tambo Tambo home.

Now that the theatrical season was regularized on a fall-to-spring axis, an opportunity arose for the rise of summer theaters. Before the advent of air conditioning, the earliest examples inevitably had an outdoor orientation. The most prominent establishment locally evolved from a beer garden opened during the Civil War–era by German immigrant Frederick Haltnorth. Located originally on Kinsman Avenue, Haltnorth's Gardens moved by 1872 to the corner of Willson (now East 55th) and Woodland Avenue. As this happened to be just outside the city limits of that time, the move apparently was an attempt to evade the jurisdiction of the Sunday blue laws.

Soon a covered theater was added to the premises and eventually enlarged to a capacity of several hundred. Summer concerts were given as early as 1878, and light opera companies began mounting fully staged operettas. The surroundings were bucolic, centering on a pond crossed by a rustic bridge. Gilbert and Sullivan shared the grounds with other attractions ranging from a bear cub to fireworks.

A more formal operation appeared downtown near the lakefront in 1885. Known as the Cleveland Pavilion Theater, it offered light operas such as *The Chimes of Normandy* under a tent seating two thousand spectators. On the west side, a Detroit Avenue roller rink also presented operetta as the Olympic Theater under L. G. Hanna.

In 1880 one of the city's oldest theaters rang down its final curtain. Watson's Hall, known variously as the Melodeon, Brainard's Hall, and by this time the Globe Theater, came to the end of its career with a

At the turn of the century, the Lyceum Theatre stood between the fourth Cuyahoga County Courthouse (left) and the Old Stone Church on Public Square. Opened in 1883 as the Park, the theater burned to the ground a few months later, taking the Old Stone Church with it. Both were rebuilt, and Mrs. Fiske introduced Ibsen to Cleveland at the Lyceum in 1895. *Western Reserve Historical Society*

farewell performance of *Uncle Tom's Cabin*. It was demolished to make way on Superior Avenue for the Wiltshire Block. During the ensuing decade, however, three new first-class theaters arose downtown to challenge the hegemony of the Euclid Avenue Opera House.

The first of the newcomers, the Park, was built opposite the northwest quadrant of Public Square next door to a former adversary of all theater, the Old Stone Church. It was part of an office building erected by the banking firm of Henry Wick and Son. Though not theater people themselves, the Wicks had a veteran showman on hand to manage their venture.

Augustus F. (Gus) Hartz was a native Englishman who had toured America for seventeen years as one of the greatest magicians of the era. One of his most famous illusions was to make a woman vanish from a chair into thin air. For another, he would borrow a hat and then proceed to fill the stage with various articles extracted from it. But Hartz had two daughters and was looking for a place to settle down and raise them. He quit the road in 1880 when Cleveland financier Jeptha Wade gave him a job managing his real estate holdings. After the Wicks offered to build him a theater, however, the smell of grease-paint enticed him back into show business.

In the Park, Hartz had a worthy rival to the Euclid Avenue Opera House. Its name was highlighted in stained glass over the main entrance on the square. Its lobby was encased within red marble wainscoting and anchored by a main staircase of rich oak and mahogany. Described as "Moorish" in decor, the auditorium was dominated by gold and vivid primary colors. There were 1,425 seats distributed among four boxes, orchestra, balcony, and upper gallery, the latter reached by way of a separate entrance off Public Square. Not only were seats outfitted with hat holders underneath, they also tilted back and forth to facilitate passage. The stage, eighty feet wide by forty feet deep, was equipped with twelve traps and fifty stock scene sets. Much was made of the innovative ceiling of fluted sheet iron ornamented with frescoes. Largely because of this feature, the Park was advertised as "The Only Fire Proof Theater in the Country."

The School for Scandal was the inaugural event on October 22, 1883. The cast was headed by M'lle Rhea, the stage name of Hortense Lobet. Manager Hartz was on hand to receive the "beauty and fashion of the city" and to present each lady with a specially bound souvenir program. A reception for star and cast was given after the play at the Superior Avenue residence of Mr. and Mrs. Dudley Wick. After a week of repertory, M'lle Rhea was followed by such attractions as *The Black Crook,* Augustin Daly's company, Wilson & Company's Minstrels, and George H. Adams in *Humpty Dumpty.* Beginning to feel at home again, Gus moved his large collection of magical apparatus into the Park for storage. If he had any thoughts of ever taking his show back on the road, it was a bad career move.

On the morning of January 5, 1884, a watchman thought he smelled gas underneath the stage and took an oil lamp to investigate. The explosion knocked him back twenty feet. In the lobby, an early ticket buyer was launched back into Public Square. In minutes, the fireproof theater was belching flames that eventually spread to the Old Stone Church. While nobody died, the theater was a total loss after less than three months of operation. "It would be difficult to conceive a more perfect wreck," observed the *Cleveland Leader.* "Musical instruments, and the tin, iron, and other apparatus in use about the stage had been

Former magician Augustus "Gus" Hartz returned to show business as manager of the Park Theatre in 1883. When the new house was destroyed by fire, Hartz moved over to Mark Hanna's Euclid Avenue Opera House, which he managed for thirty-five years. *Cleveland Press Collection*

melted together in an inextricable mass." Gus Hartz had lost $15,000 worth of magic props before he had had a chance to update his insurance policy. All that remained of the church next door were the walls. (The most permanent legacy of the fire is the restored interior of the Old Stone Church, which was one of the first important local commissions of architect Charles F. Schweinfurth. More than a century would pass before the main steeple was replaced.)

Luckily for Hartz, Mark Hanna came around with an offer he couldn't refuse. Telling Hartz to draw up his own contract, Hanna made him the manager of his Euclid Avenue Opera House. Perhaps cousin L. G. Hanna's days as manager had been numbered since the time "Uncle Mark" had unexpectedly wandered into his theater to find a professional wrestling match underway on stage. At any rate, Hartz moved in with a production of *Uncle Tom's Cabin,* claiming later to have drafted a black headwaiter from the Weddell House for the title role. When the Wicks rebuilt the Park two years later, they brought in John Ellsler as manager.

Between the time of the Park's destruction and resurrection, another new theater raised its curtain on the north side of St. Clair Avenue between Ontario and Seneca (now West 3rd) Streets. It was the third playhouse to bear the name Cleveland Theatre, the old Theatre Comique and the Academy of Music previously having used the name for brief periods. Local businessman and civic promoter Charles H. Bulkley financed construction, and the theater opened on October 19, 1885, under the management of Frank Drew of Drew's Dime Museum.

In the words of the *Cleveland Leader and Herald,* the Cleveland Theatre was regarded as "a popular amusement place for the masses." There were 1,790 seats, but Drew envisioned a standing-room capacity of 2,500 patrons. Decor was largely unremarkable, featuring papered rather than frescoed walls. Opening night was not a dress affair; the gallery was packed but the lower floor was not quite filled. The play was *Michael Strogoff* with a cast of 150. Among the stage Tatars was an eighteen-year-old youth from Brooklyn who had joined the company as a "super" in his pursuit of two of the actresses. He unwittingly provided the dramatic high point of the week when his father appeared with a detective to fetch him home.

Drew withdrew as manager at the end of the Cleveland's first season, and operation was assumed by H. R. Jacobs, manager of a nationwide circuit of theaters. After dressing up the ornamentation, Jacobs changed the name to H. R. Jacobs's Cleveland Theatre, later simply Jacobs's Theatre. It became the city's chief melodrama house with such attractions as *Under the Gas Light, Streets of New York,* and *The White Slave.* During the run of the latter in 1891, this theater too was entirely gutted by fire. It was another early morning blaze, so again there fortunately were no casualties. One of the members of *The White Slave* company, all the members of which lost their costumes, happened to be Frank Drew Sr., father of the theater's original manager. Although Jacobs rebuilt the theater, he soon surrendered management to another syndicate. By 1900 it had reassumed its original name of Cleveland Theatre.

Though the Park and the Cleveland had been built on the fringe of the old theater district west of Public Square, the last new theater of the period joined the Euclid Avenue Opera House in the eastward march of downtown Cleveland. Opened as the Columbia Theatre, it was built by Waldemar Otis on the north side of Euclid between Bond (now East 6th) and Erie (now East 9th) Streets. "It is a handsome little place," said the *Leader and Herald,* "and, as a cheap theater, is a credit to the city." Cheap it may have been, but no one could accuse the Columbia of being dry. A bar could be reached by a flight of marble stairs from the Euclid Avenue entrance, while a passageway tunneled underneath a block northward to the Oaks Cafe on Vincent Street.

Inside, the Columbia was plainly furnished with plush maroon folding chairs downstairs but plain wooden ones in the balcony. Seating was estimated at between twelve hundred and fifteen hundred, with seats on both levels steeply pitched for optimal sightlines. Overhead, the ceiling was papered to resemble a blue sky broken by clouds. The theater opened in September 1887 with the "Grand Fairy Spectacular," *Fantasma,* featuring a cast of fifty and "the most realistic exhibition of swordsmanship ever witnessed on any stage." Within two years it changed its name to the Star Theatre and came under the management of Frank Drew.

Cleveland greeted the "Gay Nineties," then, with four major theaters and various peripheral showplaces. The Euclid Avenue Opera House remained the city's showcase, but it faced strong competition from the rebuilt Park, which entered the decade rechristened as the Lyceum. Aiming at a more popular audience were the Jacobs's and the Star. The old Academy of Music limped into the 1880s as a variety theater until a fire finally put an end to its dramatic career in 1892. The building itself survived into the 1960s.

Only a generation had passed since observers had doubted whether Cleveland could support more than one theater. Now four venues did not seem too many for a city of 300,000. Theatergoing had become so commonplace that the Cleveland and Canton Railroad in 1888 had advertised a theater special leaving nightly except Sundays after the last curtain and running through Bedford. Women were attending in numbers, although the large hats fashionable in the period created a new problem in theater etiquette. Men reportedly broke into applause when one removed her millinery of her own volition at the Opera House, and newspapers added their approbation to encourage the practice.

Variety, or vaudeville, programs became increasingly popular among the new masses of theatergoers. Under Frank Drew, the Star Theatre became almost exclusively a vaudeville house in the 1890s. Eaton's Afro-American Vaudeville Company, said to be the first black troupe to visit Cleveland, played the Star in 1893. Drew also brought burlesque into the house with such acts as Weber and Fields and later Clark and McCullough. A portion of the balcony could be sequestered by a heavy curtain on such occasions, so that ladies could view the show safe from the ogling eyes of the male audience. When Jacobs's Theatre reopened after its fire, however, couples could enjoy the shows together on special two-seat Corinne sofas, which went for fifty cents rather than the ten to thirty cents for seats in the rest of the house.

Early in the 1890s, Cleveland experienced the greatest theatrical disaster in its history. A series of destructive fires had the entire city on edge during the last week of October 1892. Then on Saturday morning, October 29, the fire department received a still alarm from the Euclid Avenue Opera House. Before an extra call for engines could be answered, the "pride of the city" was doomed. The blaze, probably the result of faulty wiring, had been discovered in the cupola by stage-hands. In minutes the great central chandelier had plunged into the orchestra. The entire auditorium was a complete ruin, with only a portion of the balcony and gallery along with the Sheriff Street lobbies and facade left standing.

"Everywhere is seen destruction, and destruction in its most repulsive shape," summarized the *Leader*. "The scene is a pathetic one, considering the glories, now faded and departed of such a short time ago." It was the fourth major theater fire in the city's history, the third in the past eight years. Perhaps the most astounding phenomenon behind that statistic was the fact that not a single life was directly lost in any of those conflagrations. Cleveland was fortunate in that all its theater fires broke out after audiences had left. The Hanlon Brothers company, appearing at the Opera House that week in *Superba,* lost the scenery of the new show before it had been insured; the actors were out for the cost of their costumes, too. Though the Opera House was covered, Hanna announced that he was out of the theater business. "I shall not rebuild," he stated flatly.

Completely gutted by fire in 1892, the Euclid Avenue Opera House rose like a phoenix to reopen with even greater opulence the following year. One of the boxes pictured here—no doubt the largest—was reserved for owner Mark Hanna, who used it to entertain visiting business and political figures. He also liked to invite visiting actors to his estate at Glenmere on the west side. *Picture from* Cleveland Amusement Gazette, *December 16, 1893; Cleveland Public Library*

EUCLID AVE
OPERA
HOUSE

For once, fortunately, "Uncle Mark" was not as good as his word. By the start of the next theater season, the Euclid Avenue Opera House was back in business, grander than ever. Hanna increased the number of boxes to a dozen, and they were profitably filled. According to the *Cleveland Press,* they held "a score of millionaires" for the gala reopening on September 11, 1893. Besides a host of Hannas, these high-profile patrons included the William Chisholms, Col. and Mrs. James Pickands, the Frank DeHaas Robisons, and the Andrew Squires. Operatic diva Rita Elandi, whose stage name was supposedly an Italianization of her native Cleveland, attracted notice in a box with her brother, George Groll. Seats were sold by auction in a benefit for manager Hartz. Despite a recent financial panic, boxes had brought in from $50 to $250, and seats overall averaged $5 apiece. In the orchestra seats, sharp-eyed first-nighters might have picked out inventor Charles F. Brush, *Plain Dealer* owner L. E. Holden, chemical manufacturer Caesar Grasselli, and band promoter Conrad Mizer.

So brilliant an audience nearly upstaged the house and the play. Once spectators had finished eying celebrities, they might have taken note of a house highlighted by pink and salmon tints and entirely illuminated by electricity. When the asbestos curtain rose a few minutes past eight, actor Richard Mansfield made his entrance as the lead in Clyde Fitch's *Beau Brummel*. He looked younger and thinner since his last Cleveland appearance two years previously, according to the *Press*. "No one who saw it last night can doubt Mr. Mansfield's own words that Beau Brummel is a greater tragedy than 'Othello,' " raved the *Cleveland Plain Dealer*, "and that Mr. Mansfield has won a place in his profession which few can hope to achieve is equally evident."

Notwithstanding such critical acclaim, the temperamental Mansfield appeared to save his best acting that week for behind the scenes. The trouble began on Wednesday evening, following the first act of *The Scarlet Letter*. The curtain came down a few seconds late, leaving the actor in an awkward pose with outstretched arm. "All my work is done with my nerves anyhow, and it made me more nervous to stand there like a fool," Mansfield explained later. He sent for Gus Hartz, who asked his star for patience in view of the newness of the machinery. According to Hartz, Mansfield replied, "It is my stage; I want things done my way." Hartz's rejoinder was that he thought the stage belonged to Mr. Hanna, from whom he leased it.

Hartz left the actor to mull over that line, thinking perhaps that he had had the last word. A few minutes later, he was informed that Mansfield was donning his street clothes, pleading nervous prostration. While the star returned to his hotel, an understudy finished the show. Hartz claimed that he not only had to pay out numerous refunds for that performance, but also that many ticket holders demanded refunds for the remainder of the week.

Mansfield obviously expected some sort of reprisal from the manager. Before the final act of *Dr. Jekyll and Mr. Hyde* on the last night of the stand, he delayed the raising of the curtain for twenty-seven minutes demanding his share of the day's receipts before he would go on.

But former magician Gus Hartz had an even better trick up his sleeve. When Mansfield returned to his dressing room after the final curtain, he found Sheriff W. R. Ryan and a deputy on the scene to attach the property of the company against a claim from Hartz for $1,500 in damages. Not even the actor's watch was to be spared. "You shall not rob me of this watch. I'll die first," declaimed the actor. "This watch is a keepsake from my father."

It was probably the performance of a lifetime, even if delivered behind the curtain. At one point Mansfield vowed to quit the stage and devote the rest of his life to playwriting. "I have had a surfeit of Hartz, and I said today that I would never come to Cleveland again, especially to his theater," said Mansfield, adding the Forest City to a blacklist that already included Indianapolis and St. Louis. On that point, at least, he and the manager saw eye to eye. "Of course Mr. Mansfield will never again play in this house while I am the manager," verified Hartz.

In the end, Mansfield and his manager posted a bond so they could recover their sets and keep their scheduled engagement in Boston. Nevertheless, Mansfield not only returned to Cleveland but also apparently conquered his aversion to Hartz's Euclid Avenue Opera House. His performance there in *Cyrano de Bergerac* was considered the dramatic high point of the decade by many. By that time, of course, Hartz must have had the kinks ironed out of his curtain.

This was the period of prime performances by William Gillette in *Secret Service* and Helena Modjeska as Lady Macbeth. Otis Skinner came in *A Soldier of Fortune* and E. H. Sothern in *The Prisoner of Zenda*. James O'Neill returned in *The Count of Monte Cristo* as did Effie Ellsler in *Hazel Kirke*. Sir Henry Irving also visited and appeared with Ellen Terry in *The Merchant of Venice*. A new generation of stars was heralded by Maude Adams in *The Little Minister* and Ethel Barrymore in *Rosemary*.

But after seventy years of theater, the dramatic diet offered Clevelanders was not that far improved over *The Benevolent Tar* in Mowrey's Tavern. Shakespeare and the Restoration comedies were still popular, but few would have endorsed Mansfield's dictum that Fitch's *Beau Brummel* was a match for Shakespeare's *Othello*. American playwrights there were, but they were producing little more than stereotypical comedies and artificial melodramas. As one recent critic put it, nineteenth-century American plays were so bad that they're only studied at the graduate level. In Europe, theater was beginning to stir under the prodding of such writers as Henrik Ibscn, George Bernard Shaw, and Anton

MRS FISKE IN "ROSMERSHOLM"

Minnie Maddern Fiske introduced the drama of Henrik Ibsen to Cleveland with *A Doll's House* in 1895. She continued to champion the works of the Norwegian playwright in later visits. She was caricatured during a 1908 appearance in *Rosmersholm* at the Colonial Theatre. Cleveland Press, *May 5, 1908*

Chekhov, but Americans had had little opportunity to sample their work outside the covers of books.

It was in Cleveland that a young actress named Minnie Maddern was handed a package from actor Lawrence Barrett while appearing at the Euclid Avenue Opera House. Opening it, she discovered a copy of Ibsen's *A Doll's House.* It was so different, with its absence of big scenes and emotional asides, from what she normally thought of as drama, that she did not quite know what to make of it. At any rate, she soon married editor Harrison Fiske, retired from the stage, and forgot about Ibsen.

Barrett died in 1891, reportedly disappointed that he had been unable to interest any American actress in Ibsen. When Minnie Maddern decided to return to the stage as Mrs. Fiske, therefore, she took up the cause of *A Doll's House* as somewhat of a sacred trust. She gave a single benefit performance of the play in New York in 1894, only the second time it had been seen there. The following year she took it on the road in tandem with a conventional adaptation of a French work entitled *The Queen of Liars.*

After a couple of performances in Pittsburgh, Fiske brought *A Doll's House* back to the city where she had first encountered it. "For years the works of Henrik Ibsen have been discussed in literary societies and in clubs and read in the homes of the cultured," said the *Cleveland World,* "but on Friday evening at the Lyceum one of the Norwegian author's plays was presented [for] the first time in the history of the Cleveland stage." The date was October 11, 1895, and the *World's* four-inch column was the longest Cleveland review of the production.

Overall, the *World* was impressed by the ensemble acting of the cast and especially by the understated style of the diminutive, redheaded star. "She did not act the part, she lived it, and no higher praise can be bestowed upon any actress," observed the critic of Fiske's Nora. As for the play, he wrote: "There is no poetry in the characters represented in 'A Doll's House'; they are every-day folks who move about in every-day clothes and discuss every-day happenings just like people we all know and as unlike characters created for stage representation can possibly be. In 'A Doll's House' Ibsen tries to show how little husband and wife really know each other after a married existence of many years until the unexpected happens, until the hum-drum of every-day life is rudely interrupted by an event calculated to bring out man's true character." There is no evidence that Cleveland was as perplexed by the new style as was the audience in Pittsburgh, which remained seated after Nora's exit expecting her to return to her family in a nonexistent fourth act. The stage manager had to come out to assure them that the play was indeed ended.

Though years would pass before another opportunity came their way, Cleveland audiences at least had a glimpse of the new drama before the nineteenth century had expired. As the twentieth century got underway, it brought signs of the passing of the old guard. In August 1903, word arrived in the city of the death of John Ellsler.

With his departure from the Euclid Avenue Opera House in 1879, Ellsler's days as a manager had been numbered. His attempt to maintain a stock company in his old Academy of Music went nowhere. His subsequent tenure at the rebuilt Park lasted only two years, and in 1887 he made his last appearance as a Clevelander there in the familiar role of the slave Kazrac in *Aladdin*. Moving to New York, he lived with his daughter Effie and occasionally toured with her in his "old men" roles.

Upon reflection, Ellsler thought that Pittsburgh had provided him a more theater-oriented public and more generous financial support than Cleveland. Yet his body was returned to Cleveland for burial in Lake View Cemetery. By bringing the city its first permanent resident acting company, he had turned theater here from a happenstance novelty into a vital component of cultural activity. In building the Euclid Avenue Opera House, he had given Cleveland a dramatic centerpiece unexcelled for a half-century. Cleveland for its part may not have made him rich, but it gave Ellsler the only real home he had ever known.

A few days after Ellsler's passing, actor Joseph Haworth was discovered dead in his hotel room in Willoughby. Brought to Cleveland as a boy, he had joined Ellsler's company at the Academy of Music and maintained a residence in the city through his years on the road. He played Gilbert and Sullivan in Boston, leads opposite Modjeska, and stole the show from Blanche Walsh in an adaptation of Tolstoy's *The Resurrection*.

Mrs. Euphemia Ellsler survived as the last of her generation. When she died at age ninety-five in 1918, it was believed that she had been the oldest living actress in America.

FROM SHERIFF STREET TO PLAYHOUSE SQUARE

It was around 1893, when the Euclid Avenue Opera House reopened following its fire, that Otto Moser hung his tavern shingle out across from the theater on Sheriff Street. In the Gay Nineties, it was in the heart of Cleveland's theater district.

In addition to the Opera House, the Star Theatre was located around the corner on Euclid and the White Elephant variety theater in the opposite direction down Sheriff Street. They would be joined in a few more years by the Prospect, a vaudeville house around one end of the block, and the colossal Hippodrome at the other.

Moser faced lively competition in his own line too. Across the street was Julius Deutsch's drugstore, where behind the soda fountain Fred Gillen served up cocktails in genteel teacups for female matinee-goers

Otto Moser's bar was the "in" place on East 4th Street during the heyday of the Euclid Avenue Opera House. The proprietor is pictured in front of one of his display cases filled with faded pictures of yesterday's stars. *Photograph by James Meli; Cleveland Press Collection*

of the Opera House. An attraction of a different nature at Deutsch's was a resident tomcat that sported a gold tooth. Behind the drugstore, the Opera House operated its own bar with a free lunch featuring turkey and fried oyster sandwiches.

But Otto Moser's saloon soon became the "in" place on the narrow street. Stagehands from the theaters made it the headquarters for their social club. So too did a group of theater aficionados known as the

Cheese Club, who began meeting there in 1896 around a table bearing a huge wheel of cheese.

The place's reputation was really made by the stage stars themselves, who got into the habit of dropping in—often between acts—and leaving behind their autographed pictures. Moser began displaying them in glass cases opposite his fifty-two-foot bar. Even after they ran into the hundreds, Moser was said to be able to find anyone you could name: C. W. Couldock, Blanche Ring, William Farnum, or Will Rogers, who once threatened to "shoot the place full of holes" if he did not find his picture up with the rest on his next visit.

Outside, Sheriff Street continued to provide a colorful show of its own. The stentorian voice of Gus Morris could be heard nightly, calling out numbers of the carriages lined up waiting for their owners to emerge from the theater. He didn't need one for Mark Hanna, owner of the Opera House, who had his own private streetcar waiting (he also happened to own the railway company).

Krause's costume shop catered to masqueraders as well as thespians. A fortuneteller known as the Indian Queen doubtlessly built up a profitable clientele among superstitious show folk. A neighboring tavern called the Rathskeller featured dinner music by Louis Rich, who would then cross the street to lead the theater orchestra at the Opera House.

Another musical moonlighter was Claud Foster, a country boy from Brooklyn, Ohio, who played trombone in the Opera House orchestra pit by night and tinkered with machinery by day. His playing won him the friendship of famed actor Joseph Jefferson, who would take him along to a nearby restaurant for Kartoffel salad and sauerkraut. Watching fellow musician Frank Hruby shaping a reed for his clarinet gave Foster an idea. Finding some workspace in a shop on Sheriff Street, he came up with the Gabriel automobile horn. It made him a millionaire.

Otto Moser never struck it that rich, especially after a pair of shock waves hit his business shortly after World War I. One was the Eighteenth Amendment, which outlawed the manufacture and sale of alcoholic beverages. And if that wasn't enough to slow business, the Euclid Avenue Opera House was torn down in 1922. Cleveland's new theater district moved up Euclid Avenue some ten blocks away.

Somehow, Moser survived by serving near beer and corned beef sandwiches. Moser himself was part of the place's ambience in his striped shirtsleeves with galluses and bow tie. He stuck around long enough to see the repeal of Prohibition bring some relief from the Depression before retiring.

Yet the place hung on under later proprietors long after Sheriff Street became East 4th. Curious customers eating their sandwiches beneath the timeworn display cases registered various degrees of surprise when told that the run-down street once boasted the city's most opulent theater. One young man was sobered by the discovery of his own mother's image looking back at him through the smoky glass.

Finally, a new pair of owners decided they had had enough—of the street, not the business. It was 1994, a century after Moser arrived on Sheriff Street, and solid signs of revival were apparent in the newer Playhouse Square theater district. So the display cases were carefully taken down, packed, and moved to a new location between the Allen and Ohio Theatres. Some thought they chose the wrong time to leave, since Jacobs Field was about to pump new life into the area. But what did baseball fans know about Al Jolson, Fanny Brice, or Gertrude Lawrence? Like Dolly Levi, Otto Moser is back where he belongs.

WHEN VAUDEVILLE WAS KING

SIX HUNDRED CLEVELANDERS WERE gathered for the annual banquet at the old Chamber of Commerce on Public Square, now the site of Key Tower. It was as many people as the entire city had held eighty years earlier. They had dined on Blue Point oysters, sweetbreads, beef tenderloin, and Saratoga chips. Relaxing over Benedictine punch and cigars, they were listening and responding to a long series of toasts when from outside came the jarring clang of fire bells followed by a cacophony of cannons, church bells, and a shouting drunk or two. All eyes turned toward the speakers' table, where President Ryerson Ritchie rose and solemnly proposed a new toast: "The 19th century—God rest it. The 20th century—God bless it."

The date was January 1, 1901. (Our forebears were somewhat more punctilious than their descendants regarding the inauguration of new centuries.) In response to a campaign by the *Cleveland Plain Dealer,* thousands of businesses and homes across the city observed the occasion by turning on electric lights in every window. The most brilliant display could be seen in the new Rose Building, the largest in Ohio, at Erie (now East 9th) and Prospect Avenue. There was also a new theater around the corner on Huron Avenue, and developers were touting the six-way intersection as "The New Center."

The new theater was the Empire, and its New Year's attraction was a vaudeville bill headlined by operetta songster Pauline Hall. At the Euclid Avenue Opera House, Charles Dalton was appearing in the historical drama *The Sign of the Cross*. Comedy was the offering at the Lyceum, where Johnny and Emma Ray held forth in *A Hot Old Time*. Though it failed to specify which century, the Cleveland Theatre was advertising *King of the Opium Ring* as "The Melodramatic Sensation of the Century." Weber's Dainty Duchess Company was booked at the Star in a twin bill of burlesques, *Queen of Bohemia* and *Pickings from Puck*.

It could be said that Cleveland itself had finally arrived along with the new century. With a population of 382,000, it had broken into the front rank of American cities as the seventh largest. Besides the Rose Building, its skyline was dominated by several other first-generation skyscrapers including the Western Reserve Building, Cuyahoga Building, and the Society for Savings. All three were designed by the rising Chicago firm of Burnham and Root.

Daniel Burnham was also brought in early in the century to advise on the creation of Cleveland's forward-looking Group Plan of buildings to be erected on the Mall. This was one of the reforms associated with the administration of Cleveland's great progressive mayor during the century's opening decade, Tom L. Johnson. Other advances credited to Johnson included tax reform, city collection of refuse, municipal ownership of public utilities, and opening up the parks to the people. Not even street names escaped the reformers' broom; this was when the names of north-south thoroughfares were changed to the more logical, if less colorful, numbered system.

It was a productive, turbulent era. Johnson's eight-year struggle for the three-cent streetcar fare even reverberated within the walls of the theater. When George Broadhurst's play *The Man of the Hour* was postponed at the Euclid Avenue Opera House from October 21, 1907, to a month later, the *Cleveland Press* charged censorship. Broadhurst's melodrama dealt with a reform mayor who thwarts the schemes of a political boss to obtain a monopoly on his city's public transportation. Mark Hanna had died in 1904, but his heirs still owned the Opera House as well as a large chunk of the Cleveland Electric Railway Company. Democrat Johnson was up for re-election in 1907, and the Hanna interests were so determined to stop him that they imported cartoonist Homer Davenport to demonize Johnson as he had once done to Mark Hanna. As the pro-Johnson *Press* saw it, the Hannas must have also applied pressure on

Gus Hartz to hold off on Broadhurst's antifranchise polemic until after the election. If so, the plan did not work: Tom Johnson won again.

Though Johnson happened to live on "Millionaires' Row," the populist mayor probably did not get many votes from the Opera House crowd. Cleveland was big enough now to support a wide range of theaters, though. More would be opened during the first two decades of the new century, in sizes and shapes unimagined in the days of "Uncle John" Ellsler.

Already in place next to the Cleveland Homeopathic Hospital on Huron Road was the Empire Theatre. As the first local house built expressly for vaudeville, it opened on August 20, 1900, with a bill headed by contralto Jessie Bartlett Davis at a salary trumpeted as $1,000 a week. Also on the program were musical clowns Bimm-Bomm-Brrr and American Biograph moving pictures. The Empire presented a dignified front to the street, with a permanent canopy and a two-story facade topped with a classical pediment and balustrade. The auditorium inside was lined along the sides with double rows of boxes but lacked a balcony.

For some reason, perhaps because of its proximity to a hospital, the Empire in time acquired the reputation of being a jinxed house. An act known as Jimmy Blaine and the Paris Cuties left in the middle of a run, only to be involved in a train wreck on the way back east. The box office was once held up—on the most profitable night of the season. And a chorus girl named Frances Stockwell, after shooing a theater cat from her dressing room in a fit of petulance, was found lying outside in the snow the next day, murdered. From "high class fashionable vaudeville," the Empire eventually came under the management of the Columbus Amusement Company and was given over to burlesque.

Hailed as Cleveland's sixth theater, the Colonial opened its doors on March 16, 1903, on the north side of Superior Avenue between East 6th and 9th Streets. The last of its carpeting and curtains were installed barely an hour before the arrival of a standing-room crowd on opening night. Boxes had been auctioned off for as high as $35, and the entire house had been sold out days in advance. Illusionist Ida Fuller topped an all-star vaudeville program with her sensational fire dance. Mimic Henry Lee won equal billing for his impersonations of William Shakespeare, Teddy Roosevelt, and Pope Leo XIII. Singing comedienne Nora Bayes got no better than seventh billing, but several encores hinted that she would be heard from again.

One of Cleveland's most notable legitimate theaters was the Colonial, which opened in 1903. It was located on Superior Avenue between East 6th and East 9th Streets, a site now occupied by the annex to the Federal Reserve Bank of Cleveland. At the time of this picture, it featured the record-breaking stock run of the Vaughan Glaser Company. *Collection of Author*

Though it opened with vaudeville, the Colonial had been designed by George D. Mason of Detroit for loftier purposes. "Mason has planned the Colonial as an ideal comedy theater," revealed the *Cleveland World,* "having in mind the accepted theory that a comedy house must be compact and every auditor must be as near as possible to the stage." It seated 1,700 on three levels with leather-upholstered, swiveling opera chairs in the orchestra and balcony. Over the following quarter-century, the Colonial would fulfill many of the original hopes of its planners.

Before the end of the Colonial's first season, Cleveland had yet another new theater. It would have liked to call itself the Colonial too, since it was built next to the Colonial Hotel and Arcade on Prospect Avenue. Those naming rights having been preempted by the theater on Superior, the newcomer settled for the name of Prospect Theatre. Located on the north side of Prospect between East 4th and 9th Streets, it was described as "French in design," its three-story brick facade with stone trim being topped by a fourth story behind a mansard roofline.

Interior decorations at the Prospect featured a generous distribution of statuary throughout the lobby and auditorium. Much admiration was expressed over a large, comfortable lounge on the mezzanine level leading to the balcony. Seats went from fifteen cents in the gallery to one dollar in the boxes. The Baldwin-Melville Stock Company in

The Christian was the opening attraction on April 4, 1904. A cast party was given afterward at the neighboring Hofbrau Haus.

Still, Cleveland wanted a theater worthy of the nation's seventh-largest city. A music director named Max Faetkenheuer, who was in the pit for the openings of both the Empire and the Colonial, had illusions of even greater theatrical grandeur. By 1907 he had formed a company to build what was ballyhooed as the largest theater west of New York. Aptly christened the Hippodrome, it straddled a city block with its lobby connecting a main entrance at 720 Euclid Avenue and a secondary entrance on Prospect just east of the Prospect Theatre. Masking the auditorium as part of the structure was an eleven-story office tower on the Euclid facade and a seven-story building on the Prospect side.

More than four thousand Clevelanders crowded into the huge auditorium for the opening program on December 30, guided to their seats by innovative usherettes in blue uniforms. Manager Faetkenheuer proceeded to regale them with a three-part extravaganza opened by "Coaching Days," an original "pantomimic spectacle" with music by local composer John Zamecnic. Essentially a plotless succession of stage pictures, it featured mounted hunters dashing across stage, wagonloads of chorus girls, and coaches climbing hillsides—all borne presumably by real horses. This was followed by a vaudeville program featuring the usual acrobats and singers and a headline appearance by Power's Hippodrome Elephants, direct from one thousand performances at the New York Hippodrome.

After a fifteen-minute intermission called the "Hippodrome Promenade," affording the audience an opportunity to drink in the gold, ivory, and old rose splendors of the house and lobby, Faetkenheuer was ready with his grand finale. Entitled "The Cloudburst," it was summarized in the *Cleveland Leader:* "A wedding is in progress in the Swiss Alps when a sudden storm falls. This is followed by a realistic cloudburst. The mountain streams swell, overreaching their banks, the mill-dam bursts; the entire village is swept away. The cattle stampede, people cling to floating roofs, the mountain patrol, mounted on the diving horses, plunges into the raging torrent in an effort to rescue the drowning villagers. All ends in pandemonium and a fight of man and beast for life." The forces assembled for this "Hippodrama" included 150 actors and 455,000 gallons of water.

Such spectacles were well within the capacity of the Hippodrome. It offered forty-four dressing rooms on nine floors. At 130 feet in width

Seen from its second balcony is Cleveland's largest theater, the huge Hippodrome. Pictured here in its later remodeling for movies, the four-thousand-seat house opened in 1907 as a venue for grand opera, vaudeville, and water spectacles staged in its 455,000-gallon tank. Still visible is the bell-shaped proscenium, which provided it with excellent natural acoustics in a time before electronic "enhancements." The theater was razed in the 1980s and replaced with a parking lot. *Photograph by David Thum; Cleveland Press Collection*

by 104 feet in depth, its stage was second in size only to its New York namesake. Underneath was an eighty-by-forty-foot tank for the water spectacles and holding pens for the animal acts. As pictured on post-cards of the day, the theater in itself became one of the city's leading tourist attractions. As pictured in the dreams of Max Faetkenheuer, it might have been one of the world's great opera houses. Aided by a unique bell-shaped proscenium designed by architect John H. Elliot, it boasted perfect acoustics despite a distance of 148 feet from stage to the back of the house. The Metropolitan Opera Company played there in 1910 and 1911, giving Enrico Caruso and Arturo Toscanini their only operatic exposure in Cleveland.

The Hippodrome had risen in the center of what was now Cleveland's new theater district. Extending from Public Square to East 9th Street, it was bounded by Superior on the north and Huron Road to the south. Cleveland's counterpart to New York's Lambs Club, the Hermit Club, built its headquarters there in 1904. Designed by local architect Frank Bell Meade, the club's half-timbered and stuccoed "abbey" was located on East 3rd Street. Sharing a love for the performing arts, the group soon inaugurated an annual series of original musical shows at the nearby Euclid Avenue Opera House.

Generally ignored amid the hoopla over the Hippodrome and other theaters was the unheralded appearance of a theater genre that eventually would humble even the mighty Hipp. So obscure were its origins, in fact, that the *Plain Dealer*'s W. Ward Marsh, dean of movie critics, would have to appeal to the memories of his readers to determine the site of Cleveland's first movie house. He finally concluded that it must have been a makeshift establishment called the American, located just east of the Hollenden Hotel at East 6th and Superior. According to one reader, the projection booth was a tin box suspended precariously from the ceiling with strap iron. If anyone walked across it during a showing, the image on the screen moved in more ways than one. It was in business by 1903 with a screening of *The Great Train Robbery*. Owner Samuel Bullock actually paid women to lend the movies an air of respectability by their presence. For all others, admission was three cents.

But the heyday of the movies lay in the future. This was the age of vaudeville, which served as a precursor to the mass entertainment of the cinema. Evolving from primitive concert saloons like the stigmatized Theatre Comique on Frankfort Street, vaudeville or variety had struggled through the last quarter of the nineteenth century to gain respectability as wholesome family entertainment. Whereas the Theatre Comique had been the city's only variety house in 1875, ten years later all Cleveland theaters had presented variety programs at one time or another, including the hallowed Academy of Music and the exclusive Euclid Avenue Opera House.

Vaudeville, as it was called in the new century, was the ideal entertainment for the new urban masses. The dramatic skits were short and frequently physical in their humor. Even immigrants with little command of the language could appreciate the animal and acrobatic acts. For those in the transition stage to Americanization, ethnic comedy acts provided a means of shared humor, good-natured if crude, with native members of the audience. Offering something for everyone, vaudeville was the perfect amusement for a democracy. As the century progressed, it also paved the way to the mass entertainment of the future—and its own demise—by working movie shorts into the programs.

As reconstructed by Allen Churchill in *The Great White Way,* a typical vaudeville bill might get its audience settled with a "dumb act" featuring jugglers, acrobats, or animals. This would be followed by a succession of stock routines such as magic acts, ventriloquists, song-and-dance men, comedy teams, sister acts, tap dancers, and even monologues. Occasionally the bill might be varied with a one-act play or short musical revue.

All was calculated to build toward the "headline act" at the top of the bill. It might be a magician such as Houdini or a blackface act such as Lew Dockstadter. It could be a family act such as the Four Cohans, or it might be something exotic, like Julian Eltinge, the female impersonator who had a Broadway theater named after him. But "the most dazzling act on any bill," according to Churchill, was the solo female headliner. Nora Bayes became one with the song "Shine On, Harvest Moon," and Eva Tanguay became known as the "I Don't Care" Girl.

Historian Maurice Weidenthal counted seven vaudeville houses in Cleveland by 1910. Dating the "real craze for that form of amusement" from the construction of the Empire Theatre, he saw vaudeville as "run[ning] riot" ten years later. The Prospect had become a vaudeville house as a link in the Keith-Albee vaudeville circuit. Even the Hippodrome was leased to the Keith chain by 1910. Another new vaudeville theater, the Miles, opened the following year at East 9th Street and Huron. Reflecting its standard range of admission prices, it was known as a "ten-twen-thirt" (10-20-30-cent) house. A west side vaudeville theater named the Gordon Square opened in 1912 on Detroit Avenue near West 65th Street. It would weather the Depression and neglect, surviving at the close of the century as Cleveland's oldest extant theater.

A typical bill at Keith's Prospect in 1904 opened with American Biograph moving pictures. Then followed a pair of European jugglers, a song-and-dance team, a comedy act, a quartet of acrobats, and George Evans, a singer billed as "The Honey Boy." Working up toward the top of the bill, comedian R. C. Herz appeared in a comedy sketch, "Rice and Old Shoes," written by William Ganson Rose, then dramatic editor of the *Plain Dealer.* Next came the eight Vassar Girls with a ballet act. Finally, the program reached the headline act, Austrian soprano Mme. Slofoffski, "Engaged at Enormous Expense," in her first American appearance.

Nora Bayes, who appeared on the opening bill of the Colonial Theatre in 1903, became one of the most celebrated female headliners of the vaudeville era. She married Jack Norworth, who wrote her signature song, "Shine On, Harvest Moon," as well as the lyrics for "Take Me Out to the Ball Game." *Cleveland Press Collection*

A far more unconventional headliner came to the Miles Theater in the first week of December 1913. Billed as "The Biggest Attraction Ever Presented in Cleveland," it was Elbert Hubbard, the reputed Sage of East Aurora, New York. Monologists were accepted acts on the vaudeville boards, but these speakers were generally popular heroes such as explorers and athletes. Boxers John L. Sullivan and "Gentleman Jim" Corbett had done their turns as Babe Ruth would do later. Elbert Hubbard, however, was in a class by himself. Founder of an arts and crafts community near Buffalo known as the Roycrofters, he edited and published two magazines disseminating his pragmatic views on business, politics, art, and life. With his long hair and flowing artist's tie, Hubbard undoubtedly cut a more theatrical figure than the average athlete.

For his twelve-minute stint, offered both afternoons and evenings, Hubbard took home a week's fee of $1,000. Six other acts shared the bill, including jugglers, a triple-bar routine, and a "comedy-suffraget act." When his own number came up, Hubbard fired off such one-liners as "If you do not have a good time in your business you will never enjoy yourself," "An executive is a man who decides quickly and sometimes is right," and "Lawyers know only one way to get money, and that is to get yours." "Verily the Miles Theater this week has Ben Franklin redivivus," said the *Cleveland Plain Dealer.* Reviewing himself in his monthly *The Fra,* Hubbard wrote, "So the matinee went gleefully, with Archie Bell sitting in a box paralyzed with astonishment that a highbrow was able to meet *hoi polloi* without special loss of 'dig.'" Bell was the drama critic of the *Cleveland Leader;* "dig" was Hubbardese for "dignity."

"Fra Elbertus," as he styled himself, managed to squeeze in a few extracurricular activities during his weeklong gig. Juggling his own stage turns at the Miles, he was able to review the white slavery drama *The Fight,* then playing at the Euclid Avenue Opera House. "Women predominated in the audience—and they were right with the sentiment of the whole thing," Hubbard wrote for the *Cleveland Press.* "The only people disappointed were men who came expecting to see what they didn't get." Topping off his chores with a bit of pleasure, business guru Hubbard went out to Forest Hills in East Cleveland on Saturday morning for a round of golf with John D. Rockefeller.

Roughly contemporaneous with the rise of vaudeville, and for some of the same reasons, was the flourishing of ethnic theater in Cleveland. This was the era when Cleveland was the largest Hungarian city after Budapest and was said to be the largest Slovak city bar none; census takers counted 10,000 Czechs there in 1890, 40,000 Germans in 1900, and 35,000 Poles in 1920. Vaudeville had something to offer them, with its swift flow of sensations, many of them not dependent on language. Where their numbers were sufficient, however, ethnic groups with theatrical traditions could and did supplement the offerings of the native stage with theaters in their own languages.

First among the newcomers had been the Irish and Germans of the "Old Immigration," those who began arriving in numbers during the 1850s. A German troupe from Cincinnati found enough compatriots in Cleveland to stage a performance there in 1851. Soon thereafter, the German Freemen's Society began producing such works as Schiller's *Die Raeuber (The Robbers)* locally with a combination of amateur and professional talent. By 1855 they had opened their own theater on Ontario Street.

With their prior command of the language, the Irish were a special case as far as theater was concerned. Irish characters and themes, albeit exaggerated, appeared almost immediately on the mainstream stage in such works as *Paddy the Piper.* One of the most popular plays locally during the post–Civil War period was a spoof entitled *The Irish Aristocracy; or Muldoon's Picnic.* From a figure of fun on the fringes of respectability, the Irish by the twentieth century had moved to center stage. Talents such as Harrigan and Hart, George M. Cohan, and Victor Herbert didn't hurt their cause. In the era leading to World War I, the Irish had become a dominant force in the American theater.

Germans continued to maintain their own theaters. There were two of them in Cleveland during the Gilded Age, the Stadt and the German. In 1904 the German Theater Company converted a former German Lutheran church on the corner of East 9th Street and Bolivar Avenue into the Lyric Theater. After a few seasons of German drama and opera, however, it failed. By 1910 it had become a mainstream vaudeville house known as the Grand. In an interesting succession of ethnic associations, part of the site later was occupied by the New York Spaghetti House. Germans were more successful in their operation of summer theaters such as Haltnorth's Gardens and the later Euclid Avenue Garden Theater, where a repertoire of light opera could draw general, rather than exclusively German, audiences.

Another ethnic group that became active in theater at an early date were the Czechs. They began presenting their native drama in Cleveland as early as the Civil War, when only a few hundred Czech families had established residence there. By 1881 they had formed the Budivoy Dramatic Club, which in 1903 honored a noted Czech dramatist by adopting the name Tyl Dramatic Society. Beginning with the Bohemian National Hall in 1897, Czechs built several halls that served as centers of dramatic activities. Shortly after World War I, there were six active Czech drama groups, headed by the Tyl Dramatic Society with an average of one production a month. Working in their favor was a 98.5 percent literacy rate among Czech Americans, higher even than that of the native population.

Few ethnic groups were more active dramatically than the Jews. It began with the earlier arrivals from Germany, who brought in a German troupe to perform a comedy at Haltnorth's Gardens in 1887 as a fund-raiser for a new Anshe Chesed temple. With the later Jewish immigration from eastern Europe, however, came the more distinctive Yiddish theatrical tradition. Yiddish troupes from New York began visiting Cleveland in the late 1890s. Then "Czar" Harry Bernstein, the Jewish ward leader, established the Perry Theater in the Jewish neighborhood along Perry (now East 22nd) Street in 1899. It provided a stage not only for visiting groups such as Jacob Adler's famous Yiddish troupe from New York, but also for a resident local company under the direction of J. Weinstock. Among its attractions were the opera bouffa *King Solomon* and *Chayim in America,* a comedy about the problems faced by a "greenhorn" immigrant.

Bernstein's theatrical enterprise eventually failed as Jews began moving out of the neighborhood. Yiddish theater remained viable for a time with a group under the management of I. M. Cooperman playing in the old Haltnorth's Gardens, renamed the Coliseum. In 1910 they offered such comedies as *A Good Wine in a Bad Barrel* and *The All-Rightnik.* There was also an audience for visiting Yiddish stars such as Boris Thomashefsky in 1918 and Max Gabel in 1920. A decided decline had set in by that time, however, abetted by the growing popularity of the movies and the diminishing base of the Yiddish-speaking population.

Despite the dominance of vaudeville, the traditional English theater not only survived but managed to flourish during the century's first two decades. Theater historians generally venerate this as a golden age, with as many as four hundred stock and touring companies covering the country. Most of them had come under the domination of the Theatrical Syndicate, organized in the 1890s by a small group of producers including Marc Klaw and his partner, Abe Erlanger, Mark Hanna's one-time treasurer at the Euclid Avenue Opera House. Gaining control of the best houses in every city, including the Opera House in Cleveland, the syndicate was in a position to dictate terms to practically every manager and star in the business. As happened in more conventional industries such as oil and steel, this was done also in the name of eliminating cutthroat competition and imposing greater efficiency upon show business.

One thing the traditional stage gained from the competition of vaudeville was an elevation in status. In order to distinguish traditional forms from such upstarts as vaudeville, burlesque, and moving pictures, trade journals such as *Variety* (founded in 1905) adopted the designation of "legitimate" for straight plays or for musicals with unified librettos. *Plain Dealer* critic William McDermott later traced the term back to the English practice of granting a monopoly on the production of serious drama only to certain favored theaters. It was revived as a term of convenience, though it inevitably conveyed an elitist connotation that all other forms of entertainment were somehow "illegitimate."

At any rate, the "legitimate" stage continued to thrive in Cleveland at the Euclid Avenue Opera House and elsewhere. This was also the time when theater programs dropped their old broadsheet formats in favor of compact booklets. Those for most Cleveland theaters were printed by the Dan S. Wertheimer Company, located near the Cleveland Theatre on St. Clair. For a first-class house like the Euclid Avenue, they often displayed colorful art nouveau covers featuring allegorical representations of the muses.

Through the opening years of the century, the great stars of the era continued to wheel their latest vehicles into Gus Hartz's Opera House on East 4th Street. Bernhardt returned in 1901 with *Tosca,* as did Ethel Barrymore with *Captain Jinks of the Horse Marines.* Maude Adams re-created her most memorable role there in *Peter Pan.* Twenty-two trucks were needed to bring in the elaborate David Belasco production of *Du Barry* with Mrs. Leslie Carter. Even Belasco was outdone the following year by the colossal Klaw and Erlanger production of *Ben-Hur,* with a cast of 350 and its celebrated chariot race. "The twelve horses running at full speed on the treadmill track certainly offered one of the most inspiring sights that the theater has ever known and last evening's audience applauded it vigorously," reported the *Plain Dealer.*

On a somewhat less frenetic level, the Euclid Avenue Opera House in 1906 presented a pair of world premieres by Clyde Fitch, the foremost American playwright of his day. First came *The Girl Who Has Everything* with Eleanor Robson and H. B. Warner in February. Gaining access somehow to a closed dress rehearsal, the *Cleveland Press* revealed that between adjusting stage props and demonstrating the proper method of sliding down a banister, the author "moved so rapidly at times that the tails of his coat stuck out straight behind." As for the play, "'The Girl Who Has Everything' is a typical New York play, with a contested will and a well-dressed villain with an evil mind." Though Cleveland's "Smart Set" received it enthusiastically the following evening,

An artist from the *Cleveland Press* captured playwright Clyde Fitch rehearsing his latest play at the Euclid Avenue Opera House. *The Girl Who Has Everything,* with Eleanor Robson, had its world premiere there on February 1, 1906. Cleveland Press, *February 1, 1906*

the critics were less impressed. In compromising the name of his deceased wife, thought the *Plain Dealer,* the villain carried even villainy beyond the bounds of taste.

A better reception awaited Fitch's *The Truth* the following October. It featured Clara Bloodgood as a young wife whose penchant for prevarication brings her marriage to the brink of ruin. First-nighters were aided by detailed summaries of the convoluted plot printed beforehand on the drama pages. All was revealed but the ending, which as the *Plain Dealer* noted later, did not fail to satisfy the audience's demand for the reinstatement of the heroine. According to the *Cleveland Leader,* producer Charles Frohman was launching plays in Cleveland because "local playgoers are so clammily critical that if he can please them, success in other towns, including easy New York, is assured." Yet, though the *Cleveland Press* pronounced *The Truth* to be Clyde Fitch's "best," it did better on the road than in New York. It was also a personal favorite of the author, who died four years later.

While the Euclid Avenue Opera House maintained its status as the city's premiere showplace, the new Colonial Theatre soon established itself as a solid "legitimate" contender. After a year of vaudeville, the theater on Superior Avenue turned its stage over to the Vaughan Glaser stock company in 1904. A native Clevelander, Glaser was born on Willson Avenue (now East 55th Street), the son of a tanner turned shoe store proprietor. His company included Laura Nelson Hall as leading lady and scenic designer Robert Brunton.

Permanent stock companies had died with John Ellsler, but temporary companies were still formed to keep theaters lit during the summer off-season. Glaser's company was originally engaged for the spring and summer season but, as the audiences kept coming, Glaser kept going into the following fall and winter too. Opening with William Gillette's *Secret Service,* they prepared a new play every week. For their fifth week, they advertised Richard Wagner's opera *Parsifal,* before anyone else had done it in Cleveland, with an "augmented" orchestra of twenty pieces. (Seismic disturbances may have been recorded in the vicinity of Bayreuth that week.) Mostly, they did conventional stock fare such as *Charley's Aunt, The Prisoner of Zenda, At the White Horse Tavern,* and *Too Much Johnson.* Cleveland's Republicans found local relevance in the title of the latter comedy, and "Too Much Johnson" buttons showed up on well-tailored lapels in the next mayoral campaign.

More than a year after they opened, Glaser's company had established what was regarded as a local stock record of sixty-one consecutive weeks. Incredibly, they had performed fifty-seven different plays within that period, repeating only four shows for a second week. If anyone was more exhausted than the actors, it had to be scenic designer Brunton, who had been raiding the parlors of local theater patrons for his furnishings and props.

Heading several companies in varied venues, Vaughan Glaser was the city's most recognizable actor for nearly two decades. By 1907 he had starred in a thousand stock performances in Cleveland. Darkly handsome, he had the chiseled features of a Gibson man with just the right touch of gray at the temples of his thick raven hair. "When he got his hair cut in the local barber shops," said theater manager Robert McLaughlin, "girls crowded into the shop and fought for locks of his

The clean-cut features of Vaughan Glaser, Cleveland's most popular matinee idol, adorned the dressing tables of hundreds of local girls in the first two decades of the twentieth century. His stock company set a record of sixty-one consecutive weeks at the Colonial Theatre. *Cleveland Public Library*

hair as the barber clipped them off." "His picture was on the dressing tables of hundreds of girls," averred a newspaperman. Even after he married one of his leading ladies, Fay Courteney, the pair could stop traffic as they drove down Euclid Avenue with the top down in their 1912 Winton.

Out of character, Glaser was said to have been an indifferent dresser. He lived in the Hollenden Hotel, where he could be seen walking through the lobby in a soiled raincoat. If not bareheaded, he was crowned with a battered felt hat. Following World War I, he left Cleveland to pursue his career in Toronto and later in movies. He scored a final success in the stage and screen versions of *What a Life,* creating the role of Principal Bradley, nemesis of teenager Henry Aldrich.

Sometime after Glaser's record stock run, the Colonial came under the management of Robert McLaughlin. Born in Pennsylvania, McLaughlin passed through Fostoria, Ohio, and Canton on his way to Cleveland. A newspaperman by trade, he joined the *Plain Dealer* in 1905. Some five years later, a story he did on the Prospect Theatre led to a job as local press agent for B. F. Keith. He remained hooked on the theater for life.

It would be hard to imagine anyone less innately theatrical than the round-faced bespectacled McLaughlin. He hated even to speak in public, let alone think of appearing on stage himself. Yet he had an instinct for what worked on stage and what would appeal to the public taste. In the first three decades of the century, at one time or another, he would manage every important legitimate stage in Cleveland. Under his management, he recalled, the Colonial booked

the big Shubert shows with Al Jolson and all the Wintergarden players and other important musical shows. We were rivals of the Opera House which had long been Cleveland's leading theatre and on account of the importance of our productions we split up the business. Sothern and Marlowe were regular annual visitors in Shakespear's [sic] annual repertory company and always sold out the house long before the opening.

When David Warfield played the Colonial in "The Music Master" the box-office line extended from the theatre clear around the corner where the Federal [Reserve] Bank now stands and almost down to St. Clair Avenue.

During off seasons, McLaughlin became especially adept at keeping his theaters lit by forming stock companies. One year he signed up May Buckley and Jack Halliday, who proved as popular as Vaughan Glaser and Fay Courteney. When McLaughlin sponsored a tea party for the pair in the Hollenden Ballroom across the street, he told the hotel manager to prepare for four hundred guests. More than ten times that number showed up, spilling out into the corridors and the street and prompting the Hollenden to politely proscribe any more tea parties from the Colonial Theatre.

Another unrehearsed scene occurred when *The Chocolate Soldier* was playing the Colonial on the night of April 15, 1912. A box of chocolates and a souvenir silk banner were presented to every lady in attendance, but that's not what made the night so memorable. During the intermission, someone returned to the theater with an "Extra" announcing that the *Titanic* had gone down. The entire theater was emptied in a flash, leaving the actors stranded on stage with no one to sing to but themselves. "It was a great night," commented McLaughlin with heavy irony.

Barring similar disasters, book musicals remained as popular as ever even in the vaudeville era. Victor Herbert dominated the genre with his European-style operettas, and he opened one of his best at the Colonial Theatre on New Year's Day, 1917. Originally entitled *Hearts of Erin,* it was a musical tribute to his native Ireland. Herbert himself conducted the premiere of what he considered his favorite score, containing such numbers as "Thine Alone" and "The Irish Have a Great Day Tonight." It entered the annals of Broadway under the title of *Eileen.* Two weeks later, the Colonial offered a pre-Broadway tryout of an entirely different kind of musical show. *Oh, Boy!* was its name, the fourth in a series of innovative Princess Theatre shows of Guy Bolton, P. G. Wodehouse, and Jerome Kern. "Smart and tuneful" was the verdict of the *Cleveland News* on the basis of such Kern melodies as "Till the Clouds Roll By."

Operetta continued to dominate the summer theatrical scene. Haltnorth's Gardens surrendered its preeminence in this area to the Euclid Avenue Garden Theater, which opened in March 1904, on Euclid opposite East 46th Street. Set back more than two hundred feet from the street, it occupied a structure of Moorish-Spanish architecture with arches open to the outdoors on three sides and the stage on the fourth. There were spacious grounds outside, where one patron remembered sodas and root beer served between the acts. Such light operatic works as *The Mikado* and *The Chimes of Normandy* were presented there under the direction of Max Faetkenheuer.

When the Euclid Garden was torn down to clear the site for other uses, the indefatigable Faetkenheuer promoted a more permanent theater across the street at East 49th and Euclid. Living up to his soubriquet of "the Oscar Hammerstein of Cleveland," he named it the Metropolitan and envisioned it as a more manageable venue for opera than the ponderous Hippodrome. The two-thousand-seat house opened on March 31, 1913, with a production of *Aida* in English. Some thought the theater was located too far uptown for success; after a few seasons of opera and operetta, the Metropolitan sank to such attractions as movies and even boxing matches.

Against the main current of operetta, melodrama, and vaudeville, the new drama from Europe made fitful progress at best. Nearly a decade after her pioneering performance of *A Doll's House,* Mrs. Fiske returned to Cleveland in 1904 with Ibsen's *Hedda Gabler.* Closed out of the country's leading houses because of her opposition to the Theatrical Syndicate, she appeared in Cleveland at the new Colonial. In 1908 she brought Ibsen's *Rosmersholm* to the same theater. The *Cleveland Press* deemed it "an academic triumph," but could not resist spoofing what it regarded as the "grewsome" tendencies of the Norwegian dramatist. Those who actually understood it, imagined the *Press,* had to be the sort who would get a good laugh out of a visit to the morgue. Nonetheless, others followed in the footsteps of Fiske. By 1910, Cleveland had also seen performances of Ibsen's *Peer Gynt, The Master Builder,* and *The Pillars of Society.*

Whether they understood him any better than they did Ibsen, few playgoers would have found George Bernard Shaw morbid. If 1905 was the "Shaw Year" in New York, as one writer put it, Cleveland's Shaw Year arrived a few months later. *Candida* and *You Never Can Tell* came to the Colonial in March 1906, followed later in the year by *Man and Superman* and *Caesar and Cleopatra* at the Euclid Avenue Opera House. The *Cleveland Leader* found *Man and Superman* "marked with unusual brilliancy of dialogue, in which the hero especially advances his modern philosophy in so forceful a manner that it is actually made convincing." When *Misalliance* was scheduled for Cleveland a decade later, the *Press* called it "the worst play Shaw has written." Still, it added, "it is much better than three-fourths of the new plays to view in Cleveland."

While Cleveland was far from producing its own Ibsen or Shaw, it was at least beginning to send playwrights out into the world. There had been a few primitive stirrings of dramaturgy during the nineteenth century. George Jamieson, one of the first actors to reside in Cleveland, had written a few plays including *Our Old Plantation; or, Uncle Tom as He Is,* a pro-Southern answer to *Uncle Tom's Cabin,* which was given four local performances in 1854. An Austrian immigrant named Ferdinand Puehringer composed several operettas during the Gilded Age, some on local themes; *The Hero of Lake Erie* dealt with Perry's victory during the War of 1812.

Not until the new century, however, did a native Clevelander make his mark in the wider theater world. Avery Hopwood was born on the

Native Clevelander Avery Hopwood (1882–1928) was America's most successful playwright, with four hits running on Broadway, in 1920. He specialized in "bedroom farces" bearing such enticing titles as *The Gold Diggers*, *Getting Gertie's Garter*, and *The Demi-Virgin*. Hopwood is buried with his mother in Riverside Cemetery. *Cleveland Press Collection*

west side, the son of a neighborhood butcher. From West High he went on to the University of Michigan, graduating in 1905. Returning home, he managed to get sent to New York as a special correspondent for the *Cleveland Leader*.

From the start, Hopwood had set his sights on a successful writing career and saw Broadway as the place to achieve it. With the help of the experienced Channing Pollock as coauthor, his first play, *Clothes,* became a hit. After an early attempt at serious drama met with failure, Hopwood found his métier in the genre of bedroom farce. *Seven Days* earned him more than $100,000. *Fair and Warmer* ran more than a year in both New York and London and sent out nine road companies. By the 1920–21 season, his royalties amounted to nearly half a million dollars a year.

A Hopwood farce always promised more than it actually delivered. "Of course, everything is quite innocent," wrote the *Plain Dealer's* W. Ward Marsh of one of Hopwood's collaborative efforts. "That always is the basis of bedroom comedy. The situations are compromising; everyone believes that everyone else is dyed in scarlet most thoroughly and continues to believe until along about 10:45, when it is necessary to wind up the plot and speak the tag."

No one made it work like Hopwood, who in the words of one New York critic "was the only living man who could write French farce better than a Frenchman." In the fall of 1920, the boyish-looking bachelor had four hits running simultaneously on the Great White Way, a feat unmatched since Clyde Fitch. *The Gold Diggers* ran up 720 performances; *The Bat,* written with Mary Roberts Rinehart, topped that with 878, replacing the former as the second-longest running show in Broadway history. Hopwood's plays were always popular in his hometown, collectively running in Cleveland for more than twenty weeks in the 1920s.

Though Hopwood admitted without apology that he tailored his plays for the public taste, he seemed to become increasingly torn by a desire to write something of more significance. Plagued by personal problems involving his sexuality and various addictions, he drowned on the Riviera in 1928. The body was brought back by his mother to Cleveland for burial. His legacy included the establishment of a creative-writing award at the University of Michigan and an unpublished novel exposing the American theatrical system. Its autobiographical hero was a writer "who had sold his own birthright for a mess of pottage."

Eugene Walter never quite achieved Hopwood's level of success, but he did manage to produce at least one play of genuine distinction. A product of the public schools, the native Clevelander broke into writing as a reporter for the *Press* and the *Plain Dealer.* While unimpressed with his journalistic efforts, one of his editors recalled Walter's propensity for loitering around the city's theaters. "I never then sized

Gene up for any very deep thinking or strenuosity of application to work," wrote Charles E. Kennedy.

New York was scarcely more impressed when Walter first arrived. Columnist O. O. McIntyre later claimed to remember seeing him by himself in a corner at the Waldorf bar, brooding over a play he could not sell. According to Frank Ward O'Malley, Walter offered part of the rights to Frank Case of the Algonquin in return for his unpaid hotel tabs. After reading the play, Case turned him down.

Such were the legends that accrued around Walter's *The Easiest Way.* David Belasco gave it one of his typically meticulous productions, buying up the contents of a theatrical boarding house to lend authenticity to his set. Walter's uncompromising portrayal of a "kept woman" could have probably stood on its own. What made it especially exceptional was the absence of a conventional resolution, as heroine Laura Murdock neither keeps her fiancé nor repents her past errors. Her defiant curtain line, "I'm going to Rector's to make a hit, and to hell with the rest," was probably the most sensational exit since Nora's from *A Doll's House.* Many of Walter's peers, including Owen Davis and Booth Tarkington, came to regard *The Easiest Way* as the great American play.

One playwright who never left Cleveland to ply his craft was Robert McLaughlin. As a theatrical manager who sometimes filled his stages with his own works, he was Cleveland's answer to David Belasco. One of his early efforts was the one-act *Demi-Tasse,* which he produced with the popular May Buckley and Jack Halliday; another, *The Sixth Commandment,* toured in several other cities.

Early in 1915, McLaughlin saw dramatic possibilities in the headlines of the Cleveland newspapers. Under orders from City Hall, the Police Department prepared to close down the city's brothels in the segregated vice district on Hamilton Avenue. "We'll make Cleveland one of the cleanest, if not the cleanest [city], in the country," promised Chief William Rowe. Two of the threatened madams took their case to the city's ministers, one of them asking, "Will you let me come to work as a cook or housekeeper in your home?" One of the ministers lamely replied, "The problem has never come up before."

Several months later, Robert McLaughlin's *The Eternal Magdalene* had its premiere at the Colonial Theatre. Although the action is set in a fictitious Illinois town, the ads confirmed that it was "Suggested by Cleveland's Recent Vice Crusade." It takes place in the home of a businessman who has brought an evangelist to town to undertake a similar crusade. After the rest of the family leaves for the revival, a mysterious woman makes her appearance. Seeing a resemblance to a woman he had abandoned in his youth, the man takes her in.

Misfortunes commence to rain upon him with unbelievable swiftness. His son is exposed in an affair with a married woman; his daughter runs away with a philanderer; his wife dies, leaving evidence of past unfaithfulness; a mob gathers outside his house demanding that he throw out the strange woman. Having finally learned his lesson, the businessman confronts his fellow townspeople with the challenge, "Let him among you who is without sin first cast a stone at her." Revealing herself as the "Eternal Magdalene," the woman makes her departure. Then the audience receives its reward, as the family returns intact and the hero's misfortunes are revealed as all a dream. Finished with crusades, he promises to take them to the theater the next night.

Cleveland critics praised the play as an effective attack on hypocrisy. "Mr. McLaughlin has written a big play on a tremendous theme and it is given an excellent performance by the Colonial players," said Archie Bell in the *News*. A few weeks later, *The Eternal Magdalene* went on to New York as a vehicle for the return of Julia Arthur to the stage. She fared much better with the big city critics than did McLaughlin. He had been inspired by "a fine idea," said *The New York Times,* but "the trouble is that Mr. McLaughlin is one of those dramatists who talk too much." Though it enjoyed a good run, Broadway wags soon dubbed the play "The Eternal Maudlin."

McLaughlin gained further notice a few years later when he produced a film version of his play, *The House without Children*. It was shot with a New York cast in the former Euclid Avenue mansion of Mayor Tom L. Johnson. McLaughlin then booked a showing of the movie at the Euclid Avenue Opera House to run simultaneously with a live revival of the play at the Colonial: "The idea being to see the picture and then see the play or see the play and then see the picture," he explained. At least two members of the movie cast re-created their roles on stage with members of the Colonial Players stock company. Both versions played to full houses, but the experiment, or "stunt" as McLaughlin termed it, was not followed up by anyone else.

By World War I, movies had come a long way in Cleveland from the days of the jerry-rigged American on Superior Avenue. The city supported more than thirty movie houses in 1917, including half a dozen downtown. Among the latter were the Mall near Public Square and the Standard at Prospect and East 8th. East side houses included Max Faetkenheuer's Metropolitan and the Alhambra near University Circle. West siders were going to the Southern on West 25th and Clark and the Homestead in Lakewood.

America's entry into the war signaled the dawn of a new epoch, and the winds of change were evident in the theater as elsewhere. By 1920 the last of the city's original theater district had disappeared. The Lyceum had been torn down to make room on Public Square for the old Illuminating Building. On West 6th the old Academy of Music stood dark, irrevocably converted to business purposes. In 1920 the Cleveland Theatre on St. Clair, dark for several years, was turned into a warehouse for a paper company. The old melodrama house where, in the words of one historian, "murders were committed and heroic rescues 'pulled off' every night in the week and six matinees," was eventually superceded, in a neat stroke of poetic justice, by the headquarters of the Cleveland Police Department.

A farewell of a different sort took place on the stage of Keith's Hippodrome in February 1918. Making a "Farewell Tour" of America, Sarah Bernhardt, "The Spirit of France," appeared as the headliner of a vaudeville program in the short play *From Theatre to Field of Honor*. Blurring the line between "two-a-day" and "legit," the "Divine Lady of the Drama" didn't consider it beneath her dignity to share a bill with an all-girl band, a blackface comedian, and a Hearst-Pathe newsreel. It was not her first farewell, of course; "Much adieu about nothing" is how one wit summed up the series. Yet there was a feeling that this time might really be "it" for the seventy-two-year-old actress.

"One may question if a more fitting playlet could have been furnished Sarah Bernhardt for what may well prove her farewell," noted I. S. Metcalf in the *Plain Dealer*. In another of her male impersonations, she played a young French soldier, formerly an actor, wounded at the front in the still-raging World War I. Too badly hurt to rise—which covered up the amputated leg of the actress portraying him—he tells a British soldier, less seriously wounded, that the last thing he remembered was picking up a fallen flag. When the medics finally arrive, he remembers where he had put it and retrieves the tricolor with his final effort. "When She Said 'Vive La France' 7,000 Hearts Were Thrilled," proclaimed the Hipp's ad in the next day's *Cleveland News*. "Madam's voice rang out thrillingly vibrant yesterday and had she spoken in Sanskrit, it would have made little difference," wrote Archie Bell. "Her audience caught the message and they appreciated the wonderful power of this wonderful woman."

Bernhardt left—for good, this time—and the war ended. In August 1919 the Actors Equity strike closed the theaters in New York. Long-standing abuses such as lack of compensation for rehearsal periods and closing shows on the road with neither notice nor return train fare were at the root of the shutdown. For a couple of weeks, theatrical activity continued unaffected in Cleveland, though managers kept an anxious eye turned toward Broadway. Lee and J. J. Shubert of New York, who had leased the Colonial here and renamed it the Shubert-Colonial, opened the 1919–20 season with the A. S. Stern Company in *She Walked in Her Sleep*. By the following week, however, the Colonial was dark and the Euclid Avenue Opera House was showing a movie. Fortunately, the strike was settled soon afterward with the actors gaining all of their demands. Delayed only a week or two, the rest of the Cleveland season unfolded without event.

A "return to normalcy" would be the winning slogan in the presidential campaign of 1920—if a nation without alcohol could be considered normal. Vaughan Glaser thought it would be a good idea to salute the coming of Prohibition with a revival of *Ten Nights in a Bar Room* at the Prospect Theatre. As he remembered it, the show was received about as enthusiastically as the "noble experiment" it was intended to herald.

THE HEAVY AND THE HERO

In the first half of the twentieth century, they were the bad angel and the good angel of Broadway: diabolic Abe Erlanger, embodiment of the omnivorous and reviled Theatrical Syndicate, and the cherubic Arthur Hopkins, independent producer of many of the landmarks of the American theater's golden age. Coincidentally, both came from Cleveland.

First came the heavy. Abraham Lincoln Erlanger was born in Buffalo in the year his namesake was elected president. Brought to Cleveland as a boy, he worked for a coal dealer by day but moonlighted at John Ellsler's Academy of Music, where he ran the cloakroom and opera-glass concession. Soon he was serving as assistant stage manager and even filling an occasional part on stage.

In one of only two known pictures of the entire Hopkins clan, future Broadway producer Arthur Hopkins appears (upper left) with his seven older brothers (continuing clockwise) George, Jeffrey, Thomas, Ben, Martin, William, and Evan. Ben became one of the city's leading industrialists; William was Cleveland's first city manager in the 1920s; Evan became the first dean of Western Reserve University's law school. Being Welsh, they would naturally gather together in the old neighborhood at Christmas to sing. *Cleveland Press Collection*

He followed Ellsler in 1876 to the Euclid Avenue Opera House, where he found his true domain in the box office. When Mark Hanna purchased the failing theater, he ascertained that the short, smooth-faced Erlanger was its greatest asset and put him in charge of the front of the house as treasurer. A few years later, Gus Hartz became manager of the house and claimed that Erlanger asked to be retained in his position. "No, Abie," Hartz said he replied, "inside of a year you would be the manager and I the treasurer."

True or not, the story made its point. Erlanger headed east and teamed up with Marc Klaw as theatrical owners and managers. They were part of the small group that met in 1895 to plan a central clearinghouse to end the haphazard booking practices of the day. Within a decade, the resulting Theatrical Syndicate controlled, through lease or outright ownership, nearly seven hundred houses throughout America.

In the center of the web, occupying a dingy theatrical office on 42nd Street in New York City, sat the chunky, balding Erlanger. As the architect and administrator of the operation's booking system, he attracted the enmity and resentments of all who were ground in its meshes. Actors who refused to buckle under were denied bookings until the last holdouts, Sarah Bernhardt and Minnie Maddern Fiske, were reduced to acting in abandoned churches and even tents.

They called him the "little Napoleon of the theater," and Erlanger reinforced the typecasting by accumulating a collection of Napoleana. Stories of his boorishness were legion along the Great White Way. One of the favorites claimed that he once eliminated the adjective from a show entitled *Little Miss Sunshine,* because he wanted nothing "little" in his New Amsterdam Theatre. Though his stranglehold on the theater was eventually broken, Abe Erlanger managed to die with a fortune estimated at $75 million.

Enter the hero. Arthur Melancthon Hopkins was the youngest of a remarkable family of Welsh steelworkers in the Cleveland neighborhood of Newburgh. Among his seven brothers he could count a doctor, a dean of the Western Reserve law school, an industrialist, and Cleveland's first city manager.

Arthur bypassed college and went to work as a reporter for the *Cleveland Press.* When President McKinley was assassinated in 1901, something clicked in Hopkins's memory bank, and he went back to the old neighborhood in Newburgh. There he tracked down the family of the assassin, Leon Czolgosz, and returned with the first interview.

Moving from newspaper work into the theater, Hopkins became a vaudeville press agent for Keith's Prospect Theatre. He soon left for New York, where he became a booking agent for the Orpheum vaudeville circuit. He also visited Europe, where he studied the production techniques of Max Reinhardt and Berlin's Deutches Theatre.

One of Hopkins's first successful productions was *On Trial,* the first play of Elmer Rice. He also brought Eugene O'Neill uptown from Greenwich Village with productions of *Anna Christie* and *The Hairy Ape.* Hopkins frequently worked with the Barrymores, presenting John in *Hamlet* and *Richard III,* Lionel in *Macbeth,* and both brothers in *The Jest.*

"For more than thirty years," said *The New York Times,* "the words 'Arthur Hopkins Presents' meant, almost invariably, that something new, something exciting, something great was to be shown on the New York stage." He directed most of his eighty productions himself.

A few of the highlights included *What Price Glory?, Holiday,* and *The Petrified Forest.* It was the latter that transformed Humphrey Bogart from a "Tennis, anyone?" type into the timeless tough guy.

Hopkins himself remained the mildest of men, a perfect candidate for the "Starkeeper" role in *Carousel.* The only regret he expressed over *What Price Glory?* was not its profanity but the fact that it had unloosed "a flood of gratuitous profanity on the stage" by other playwrights in the false belief that *Glory*'s "success was due to its profanity."

Though quite successful, Arthur Hopkins managed to convey the impression that he sought other returns than solely those of the box office. He closed John Gielgud's performance of *Hamlet,* while still attracting full houses, over the protests of his Ophelia, Lillian Gish. "My dear," he consoled her, "don't you know that a fine *Hamlet* will always wear out its Hamlet before it does its audience?"

Five

NEW VOICES

IN THE CLEVELAND FOUNDATION'S 1918 survey entitled *Wholesome Citizens and Spare Time,* one of the case studies included in the work was a library worker identified as "H." Daughter of a Presbyterian mother and freethinking father, she had been reared in a small Ohio mining town. Her father's position as a plant supervisor placed her among the town's ruling establishment. Though attending the local public schools, she also took special lessons in music and German and went on to earn a degree from an Ohio college. She had lived for periods in San Francisco and Brooklyn and studied painting and art history in Munich. "H" also completed a four-year course at the Cleveland School of Art, developing a special interest in Asian art. Her library work in Cleveland involved visiting clubs and conducting luncheon interviews with people engaged in dramatic studies. "About twice a month," recorded the survey, "Sunday evening is given to a little playhouse fostered by a local group of artistically interested people who engage actively in dramatical and musical activities and in bringing before the community the folk culture of the various race groups that make up the city."

That last sentence sounds very much like the group that began gathering in the fall of 1915 in the parlor of Charles and Minerva Brooks on East 115th Street. It has been described as a mixture of "businessmen

Businessman and writer Charles Brooks hosted meetings in his living room that resulted in the birth of the Cleveland Play House. He twice served as president of the little theater and saw three of his own plays premiered on its stage. *Photograph by Trout-Ware Studios; Cleveland Press Collection*

and Bohemians." Their host would qualify in both categories, being an executive in his family's paper business as well as a writer of essays and plays. His wife was a prominent suffragette and student of dance. The group also included Harry Hohnhorst, editorial cartoonist for the *Cleveland Leader;* his wife, Anna; Marathena Barrie; and art students

Grace and Ida Treat. One of the women may well have been the "H" of the Cleveland Foundation study.

But the nucleus of the group was undoubtedly Raymond O'Neil, drama and music critic for the *Cleveland Leader*. The son of an electrician at the Colonial Theatre, O'Neil had watched his father experiment with lighting effects on a model stage in his home. More important, he had been to Europe the previous year to study the revolutionary theater techniques of Gordon Craig, Max Reinhardt, and especially Konstantin Stanislavski's Moscow Art Theatre. His demonstrations in the miniature laboratory of his home theater of what he had witnessed had led to the informal theatrical gab sessions in the Brooks living room.

By the end of the year, the stage-struck little circle had decided to organize a real theater of its own. Drafting a constitution, they elected Brooks as president and O'Neil as artistic director. The growing number of members divided according to individual predilections into three different production groups. One was interested in puppet productions; another would experiment with living forms behind screens in the production of silhouette pantomimes, or "shadowgraphs." The third would apply themselves to the live performance of experimental plays.

Incorporated as the Play House, the embryonic theater was part of a national dramatic renaissance—the Little Theater movement. As described by future Play House director Frederic McConnell, "It was an insurgence against the sterility of the so-called legitimate theatre, which under the compulsive attraction of commercial magnets had been drained of any appeal save that of melodrama, bed-room farce and corruption." The popular but formulaic farces of Cleveland son Avery Hopwood were not likely to get exposure on a Play House stage (nor, in fact, did they). The local rebels had their counterparts in the Chicago Little Theatre and New York's Provincetown Players. Gordon Craig was their god, with his vision of a theater where narrow realism might be replaced, under the expert guidance of an omnipotent director, with "the entire beauty of life." In accepting the post of director for the Play House group, O'Neil, in the spirit of Craig, had demanded complete autonomy.

Even rebels need angels in the theater, however, and a stove manufacturer named Francis Drury filled that role for the Cleveland Play House. Having built one of the last mansions on Euclid Avenue at East 86th Street, he acquired an extensive lot across the street as the future site of a planned formal garden. In the meantime, he offered the players the use of an abandoned house on the property.

So the first production of the Cleveland Play House took place in what was known as the Ammon House in May 1916. It was a puppet play by Maurice Maeterlinck, *The Death of Tintagiles,* performed on O'Neil's relocated model stage. That was followed shortly by the first shadowgraph, Ida Treat's adaptation of the Grimm fairytale, *Forty at a Blow.* The first fully acted play, August Strindberg's *Mother Love,* was given on the third floor of the house on May 31 with future Broadway star Claire Eames in the cast.

When Drury had the Ammon House razed, the group moved to an old barn in back. O'Neil and Ida Treat, recently married, literally moved in. Their "living room" did double duty as an auditorium, and their sleeping quarters also served as dressing rooms. A double bill of Anton Chekhov's *The Bear* and W. B. Yeats's *The Hour Glass* was produced there early in 1917. The group also continued its "nationality nights," consisting of various ethnic music and dance demonstrations.

Before long the Play House needed another home when Drury scheduled their barn for demolition. They found temporary refuge in the ballroom of the old Tom L. Johnson mansion, the same location Robert McLaughlin would use to film his play, *The House without Children.* Then Francis Drury rode to the rescue again with a gift of $6,000, which was used to purchase an abandoned Lutheran church on Cedar Avenue at East 73rd Street. With the further aid of a $9,000 loan and materials from the Ammon House, the structure's back wall was removed in favor of a new stagehouse to convert the little church, originally designed by Charles Schweinfurth, into a 160-seat theater.

Now in possession of its first permanent home, the Cleveland Play House was in a position to make an impact on the city's cultural scene. Lawyer Walter Flory was elected president in place of Charles Brooks, who had left to pursue a writing career in New York. A membership drive netted the group nearly three hundred active and supporting members within a year. In December 1917, O'Neil inaugurated the new theater with a production of *The Garden of Semiramis* enacted in pantomimic silhouette against the backdrop of a stark white cyclorama.

Cycloramas were standard fixtures in the Little Theater movement, lending themselves to the creation of atmospheric effects achieved through the interplay of creative lighting against their reflective surfaces. O'Neil gave the one at the Play House a good workout, particularly in the production of a couple of more shadowgraphs. He was said to have been fond of dimly obscure settings. There were also more marionette plays under the direction of Helen Haiman Joseph, who would attain a national reputation in that branch of theater. Fully acted productions included Strindberg's *The Stranger* and the medieval morality play *Everyman*. Included in the large cast of the latter were Ruth Feather, Margaret Hamilton, and Katherine Wick Kelly. All acting yet was technically amateur, roles being filled from the ranks of the group's active members. Others contributed skills according to their training or ability; composer Charles DeHarrack, for example, provided incidental music for several early productions. Two original one-act plays done in 1918 came from *Cleveland Plain Dealer* columnist Ted Robinson and Joseph Remenyi, a writer for Cleveland's Hungarian newspaper, *Szabadsag*.

But O'Neil was a perfectionist, and his artistic temperament soon grated on the sensibilities of some of the more sober-minded members. As *Plain Dealer* drama critic Harlowe Hoyt remembered him, O'Neil was "a modified beatnik. He wore no hat, affected an old-fashioned necktie in a soft drooping bow, and sported open sandals without socks. . . . He was, it seems to me, a dreamer without the capacity for consideration of the finances involved." A rift opened up between the bohemians and the business types. Subscribers were not getting the number of productions they had been promised, and the director became increasingly hard to pin down for explanations. At the annual meeting in 1919, President Flory gave voice to these complaints and called for greater accountability from the artistic director. He then resigned in favor of a new president and expanded board, and new members were promised at least six productions for the 1919–20 season.

It worked at least for that season, with the six productions including Hugo von Hofmannsthal's *Death and the Fool* and John M. Synge's *Deirdre of the Sorrows*. The following season, however, O'Neil chafed under the strain of a twelve-play schedule. After seven productions including Oscar Wilde's *Salome* and Maeterlinck's *Pelleas and Melisande,* he snapped. Tendering his resignation, he made plans to go to Europe.

Fortunately, Charles Brooks came back to Cleveland at this point, and he and Walter Flory returned to the Play House Board of Directors. The two headed a search committee to hire a new director. After consulting with George Pierce Baker of the famous Harvard 47 Workshop for playwrights, they approached Thomas Wood Stevens of the Carnegie Institute of Technology's School of Theatre in Pittsburgh. Stevens spoke highly of a former student named Frederic McConnell, who at the time was serving as codirector of the Pittsburgh Guild

Players. After stopping in Cleveland to view the Play House in action, McConnell agreed to take charge of the organization but wanted the assistance of two former Carnegie Tech colleagues, K. Elmo Lowe and Max Eisenstadt. With the concurrence of the board, Frederic McConnell became the second director of the Cleveland Play House.

McConnell, Lowe, and Eisenstadt: in Play House lore, they became bracketed as "the Triumvirate." A native Nebraskan, McConnell seemed to offset the broad forehead of the intellectual with the common sense of the Midwesterner. "Mr. McConnell is not representative of the long-haired, sandal-footed type of little theatre artists which, unfortunately, we are prone to think of in connection with little theatre management," said *Cleveland Topics* magazine in a none too subtle comparison with his predecessor. Indeed, McConnell had earned a law degree before transferring his loyalties to the theater. During World War I he spent five months in a German POW camp. He had prosaic sandy hair, sunken cheekbones, and wore a conventional necktie. As with John Ellsler in an earlier day, his avoidance of a bohemian image inspired confidence in the business community.

No one at the Play House ever seemed to know what the first initial of K. Elmo Lowe represented, though it was once reported that his Polish mother had named him after the national patriot Kosciuszko. Even his actress wife, Dorothy Paxton, whom he brought with him from Pittsburgh, referred to him simply as "Kay." Raised in California, he brought the classic looks of a matinee idol to the Play House, where his pictures developed a vexing tendency to disappear from lobby displays. Less visible than Lowe or McConnell was the third member of the triumvirate, Max Eisenstadt. A native of Russia, he conveyed a dark, somewhat shy aspect reminiscent of screen actor Peter Lorre. His domain was backstage, where he became head technician at the Play House and a recognized authority on stage lighting.

Although O'Neil had also drawn a salary, McConnell and his colleagues were the first trained professionals at the Play House. It was such a fundamental departure from the amateur origins of the group that McConnell later claimed he had had to sneak Eisenstadt in "ostensibly as a janitor." If taken for his word at the time, however, his campaign was not as much of a stealth operation as he implied. His goal, he told the *Plain Dealer* at the very beginning, was to make the Play House America's first real repertory theater by gradually assembling a full-time group of professional actors and technicians. "The amateur theatre is a

One of several husband-and-wife acting teams to have flourished in Cleveland was K. Elmo Lowe and Dorothy Paxton of the Cleveland Play House. Pictures of Lowe, a member with Frederic McConnell and Max Eisenstadt of the Play House "Triumvirate," tended to disappear from the theater's display cases. Paxton, who appeared in two hundred roles at the Play House, also wrote songs and a play, *It's Better fo' to Sing*. *Cleveland Press Collection*

myth," he announced at a theater conference in 1925. "You cannot take a step in the realm of the theatre without becoming professional and the great mistake is to compromise in the matter."

Yet McConnell had made an excellent beginning at the Play House with his combination of enthusiastic amateurs laced with the experience of a few well-chosen professionals. He opened his debut season of 1921–22 with a production of Wilde's *The Importance of Being Earnest.* That was followed by two works that became specialties of the house— George Bernard Shaw's *Candida* and *Beyond the Horizon,* the breakthrough play of Eugene O'Neill. The most spectacular effort of the year was a production in the spring of Christopher Marlowe's *The Tragical History of Dr. Faustus.* Scenery was designed by a recent Czech immigrant named Richard Rychtarik, who would provide sets for the epic opera scries at Severance Hall in the 1930s. Minor roles were filled by Charles Brooks as the Pope and future *Cleveland Press* society columnist Winsor French as a devil. For the title role, McConnell once again raided Carnegie Tech and came back with Russell Collins. The spare, glum-faced actor would appear in ninety Play House productions over the next decade.

Brooks has left a charming picture of the eclectic spirit of the Play House in its adolescence. "Our actors are not confined within the club," he wrote, "for anyone who can win our director's credulity and confidence may take a part, and we have tapped the city from east to west."

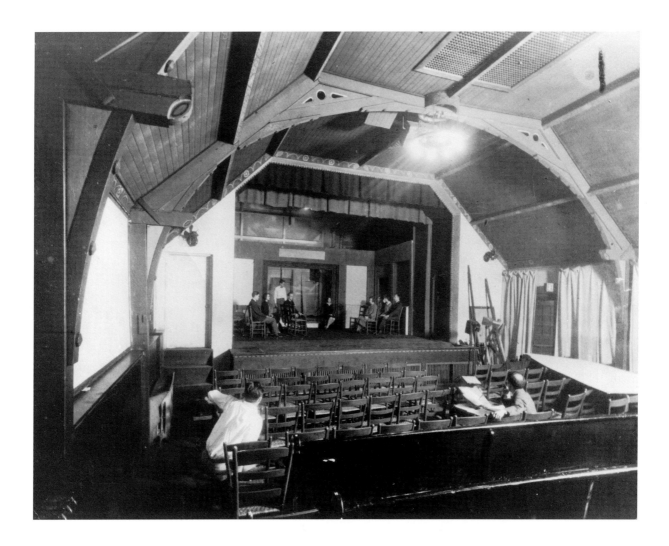

From its beginnings in an abandoned house and barn, the Cleveland Play House moved into this former Lutheran church on Cedar Avenue at East 73rd Street. Supervising a rehearsal are K. Elmo Lowe (left foreground) and Frederic McConnell, two of the three professionals hired to manage the little theater in 1921. The company occupied the Cedar Avenue theater from 1917 to 1927. *Cleveland Play House*

He had played the Pope in a robe cut from a sheet with a red ruby in his midriff that "had begun life as a red gum-drop in a candy shop across the way." One of the plays that season had been his own *Wappin' Wharf,* a bit of piratical whimsy that might be described as J. M. Barrie meets *Treasure Island.* Brooks later dramatized his novel, *Luca Sarto,* for a Play House production.

If anyone was the house playwright at East 73rd and Cedar, however, it had to be George Bernard Shaw. Fifteen of the Irish dramatist's works were presented by the Play House in the 1920s, headed by five productions of *Candida.* Given three showings each were *Arms and the Man* and *The Admirable Bashville.* Other Shavian offerings included *Man and Superman, Caesar and Cleopatra,* and *Heartbreak House—Saint Joan,* strangely, would wait until 1941. Shaw himself expressed his appreciation by granting the Play House a blanket dispensation to do any of his works without prior consent. His only constraint was to place a two-week limit on single runs, thereby encouraging the maintenance of a true repertory company.

Building a resident repertory company remained foremost among McConnell's goals too. While avoiding the clichés of the commercial theater, he hoped nonetheless to appeal to a wider audience than that of the Play House's "purple light and misty figure" period under O'Neil. From providing a means for the self-expression of its members, the primary function of the Play House would shift to providing a stage for dramatic works of literary distinction. By his third season, McConnell was preparing twelve new productions a year in addition to periodic revivals of such standards as *Candida, Doctor Faustus, Beyond the Horizon,* and Elmer Rice's *The Adding Machine.* The O'Neill and Rice works were among the few American plays to be seen at the Play House that decade. McConnell tended at first to concentrate on developing the modern European repertoire of Shaw, Ibsen, Chekhov, Synge, Luigi Pirandello, John Galsworthy, and Sean O'Casey.

It was with the Cleveland premiere of O'Casey's *Juno and the Paycock* in 1927 that the Play House gained the attention of the wider community. Cast as a young Irish girl, McConnell's wife, Katherine Wick Kelly, downed a slug of whiskey and commenced a drunken reel. A fusillade of eggs was thereupon launched toward the stage from the audience. One of them struck Ruth Feather, playing the role of Juno. Max Eisenstadt immediately lowered the curtain, and McConnell called the cops. Six young men from a group of forty-five Irishmen in attendance were identified as the eggers and hauled away. One of them told the judge in extenuation that O'Casey's play "is represented as a portrayal of Irish character. . . . But it is Irish caricature." Some of them were evidently under the impression that the play had caused a similar protest in Dublin, though the Donnybrook in that case had actually been sparked by O'Casey's *The Plough and the Stars.*

That contingent of Irish chauvinists may have been the Play House's first large theater party from the west side. But McConnell had also been drawing the daily drama critics to the theater since his second season, and they were throwing bouquets rather than eggs. Within

Russell Collins (left) and Carl Reid Benton appeared as Joxer Daly and Capt'n Boyle, respectively, in the 1927 Play House production of *Juno and the Paycock*. The Sean O'Casey play was interrupted during one performance by a barrage of eggs laid down by a group of Irish men, who took it as an insult to Irish character. *Photograph by Julia Butler Sanker; Cleveland Play House*

two seasons, attendance had increased tenfold to 40,000 a year. By the beginning of McConnell's fourth season, the Play House could burn the mortgage on the Cedar Avenue building.

The Play House had become an important component of an amazing cultural awakening in Cleveland. "An angel must have troubled the waters of the Cuyahoga in the 1900's second decade, for Cleveland began to stir with cultural activity," is how Play House historian Julia McCune Flory described it. Indeed, the year (1916) that saw those first tentative performances in the Ammon House also brought the opening of the Cleveland Museum of Art in University Circle. Two years later, the Cleveland Orchestra gave its first concert downtown in Grays

Armory. Rounding out the decade, the Cleveland Institute of Music opened its doors in 1920, housed in a former residence at East 31st Street and Euclid Avenue.

Perhaps because its lingering amateur aura invited participation, the Play House seemed to become a hub of cultural activity during those early years. Among the members of Minerva Brooks's dancing classes back in the Ammon House had been Boris Sokoloff, son of the Cleveland Orchestra's first conductor. His father, Nikolai, later recommended a play he had viewed in London, *Anne Pedersdotter,* which became the hit of the Play House's 1922–23 season. Local artists became welcome collaborators at the Cedar Avenue theater, where the interior decorations had been designed by Carl Broemel. Among the first to exhibit their work there were William Zorach and Charles Burchfield.

Personnel from the Cleveland Institute of Music also got involved with the Play House. Faculty member Roger Sessions composed incidental music for a production of *Turandot, Princess of China.* A harp accompaniment for *Francesca da Rimini* was provided by CIM director Ernest Bloch's daughter Suzanne, who later was married for a time to Play House actor Russell Collins. Another musician who began spending off-hours at the Play House was Douglas Moore, curator of music at the Cleveland Museum of Art. Moore's contribution was histrionic rather than musical, as he began filling roles on stage. He soon worked his way up to Henry Higgins in *Pygmalion* and the title role in *Rollo's Wild Oats.*

Moore also chose the intimate Play House as the venue for a cross-cultural "experiment" he cooked up in 1923 with his poet friend, Stephen Vincent Benét. They called it "Poly-Poetry," or poetry developed along the lines of a musical fugue. It began with a straight-faced lecture on the new form by Benét, after which Moore "conducted" simultaneous recitations by various groupings of readers. One poem, for example, was recited by three voices, each entering one line later than the previous reader. "Of course," said one who witnessed it, "when the evening was over no one would admit he had been the least taken in."

Much of the extracurricular activity at the Play House centered in the greenroom, which had been added to the converted church along with dressing and rehearsal rooms. It became a favorite haunt of Charles Brooks, who instituted the custom of serving afternoon tea there. Someone was always dropping in to sit before the fireplace with the balding former businessman with the gentle eyes. Among the regulars were painter William Sommer and poet Hart Crane. Occasionally something special occurred, as when designer Norman Bel Geddes took a break from his downtown production of *The Miracle* to come and deliver an informal talk on the topic of "Art in the Theater Today."

The Cleveland Play House was unique among hundreds of similar enterprises primarily in its evolution into institutional status. From only an estimated fifty in 1917, the Little Theater movement had burgeoned to around three thousand groups a decade later. Locally, the Cleveland Association of Amateur Dramatic Clubs numbered eighty-seven member organizations in 1923. Most were ephemeral, but the Shaker Players was one of the few to accompany the Play House into the 1930s. The group numbered Barclay Leathem and Shaker Heights High School dramatics instructor Elbert B. Sargent among its volunteer directors.

Barclay Leathem was instrumental in an even more significant local dramatic development of the 1920s. Joining the English department of Western Reserve University in 1921, he proceeded to work tirelessly for the creation of a full-fledged drama department at Cleveland's leading liberal arts institution. All there was at the beginning was a course or two on dramatic literature and an extracurricular Adelbert Dramatic Club. By mid-decade Leathem had gotten a course on play production into the curriculum, and in 1926 a 137-seat theater was installed in Eldred Hall. The dramatic club, renamed the Sock and Buskin Club, began tackling more ambitious works such as Edmond Rostand's *The Romancers* and Hatcher Hughes's *Hell-Bent for Heaven*. By 1931 Leathem had overseen the creation of the Department of Drama and Theater at WRU.

In some ways, the public secondary schools were as dramatically progressive as Cleveland's colleges. These were the glory years of the Cleveland Public Schools, and English supervisor Dr. Clarence Stratton pushed drama in the senior and junior highs. Outstanding was the program at Glenville High School, headed by Cleveland Play House actress Katherine Wick Kelly. Among the four hundred plays done annually in the school system were works by Shakespeare, Shaw, Yeats, Wilde, and George Kaufman and Marc Connelly.

Aside from the rise of the Cleveland Play House, however, the most noteworthy theatrical development of the period came from what might have appeared an unlikely source. In the beginning, it had nothing whatever to do with the theater. It was in 1915, the year that the Play House began to take form in the home of Charles Brooks, that a pair of newlyweds named Russell and Rowena Jelliffe arrived in Cleveland to launch a neighborhood settlement house.

They came from Oberlin by way of Chicago. Russell had entered the nearby Ohio college from his native Mansfield, where he was a boyhood friend of novelist Louis Bromfield. Rowena came to Oberlin from Albion, Illinois, where she had grown up in the shadow of Robert Owens's utopian settlement at New Harmony. They met each other on the first day of their freshman year.

For the next seven decades they were inseparable. Both concentrated their studies in political science and sociology. Rowena was somewhat interested in drama and thoroughly committed as president to the local women's suffrage league. They would ride into Cleveland on the interurban railroad to attend council meetings, take in the shows at the theaters, or just walk around. "It was our laboratory," said Rowena, who recalled being there in 1912 for the dedication of the Tom L. Johnson statue on Public Square. After Oberlin the couple put in a year of graduate study at the University of Chicago, where they could also visit the famed Hull House settlement of Jane Addams. In a few crowded weeks in the spring of 1915, they received their masters' in sociology, got married, and set out for a waiting job in Cleveland.

Their original sponsor was the Second Presbyterian Church, then located on Prospect Avenue at East 30th Street. It happened to be in the midst of a neighborhood undergoing cataclysmic social changes, a district of poolrooms, saloons, and gambling dens known as the "Roaring Third." One intersection in particular earned the even less inviting nickname of "dead man's corner." In an eleemosynary effort to uplift its neighbors, the Second Presbyterian had been led to the Jelliffes through contacts at Oberlin.

Purchasing a pair of frame houses occupying a narrow double lot on East 38th Street, the young couple moved into the smaller cottage in the rear and converted the front dwelling into a neighborhood settlement, or meeting place. Since it was located next to Grant Playground, it became known as the "Playground House," or simply the "Playhouse," at first and was later incorporated as the Playhouse Settlement of the Neighborhood Association. Further changes were coming to the area during the years of World War I, as earlier ethnic groups moved out in favor of blacks arriving as part of the "Great Migration" from the South.

Among the activities organized by the Jelliffes to bring the children off the streets, inevitably, was dramatics. As early as 1917, a children's production they had put together at a neighborhood school gained favorable comment in a black weekly, the *Cleveland Advocate*. It was

Rowena and Russell Jelliffe saw their neighborhood settlement house evolve into Karamu, the nation's foremost African American theater. Most of the early artistic direction was handled by Rowena, who was described by one of Karamu's actresses as a "cast-iron Dresden doll." She lived to be one hundred years old. *Cleveland Press Collection*

Cinderella, and it happened to feature a black Cinderella and a white (and also female) Prince Charming.

Interest soon spread to the adults, and a half-dozen young blacks began meeting in the Jelliffes' living room late in 1920 to discuss plays and theater. They called themselves the Dumas Dramatic Club, after the partly black French novelist, and were joined by like-minded whites. It was more than a little like the first gatherings of the Cleveland Play House in the Brooks living room—some of which had, in fact, been attended by the Jelliffes. In the fall of 1921, the Dumas Club put on its first one-act play, George Middleton's *The Little Stone House,* at Central High School. Rowena Jelliffe, looking for worthwhile programs for their settlement, saw real possibilities here. The group worked on several other one-acts throughout the fall and winter.

It was at this point that a defining moment occurred for blacks interested in theater: Charles Gilpin came to the Shubert-Colonial Theatre downtown to re-create his trail-blazing title role in Eugene O'Neill's *The Emperor Jones.* It was more than the first success on Broadway by

CHARLES
GILPIN
AS
"THE
EMPEROR
JONES"
—LITTLE
THEATER

Charles Gilpin's appearance in Eugene O'Neill's *The Emperor Jones* at the Colonial Theatre in 1922 inspired a largely black little theater group in Cleveland to rename themselves the Gilpin Players. Gilpin was depicted above by a *Plain Dealer* artist in a 1928 appearance at the Little Theatre, where he was supported by some members of the group named after him. The Gilpin Players eventually became known as the Karamu Theatre. Cleveland Plain Dealer, *July 10, 1928. Reprinted with permission from* The Plain Dealer ©*2000. All rights reserved.*

a black actor in a serious role; O'Neill later said that Gilpin was the only actor who had "carried out every notion of a character I had in mind." Some of the Dumas group went backstage to meet him and invite him to one of their rehearsals.

Gilpin showed up at the club's borrowed stage, a Bohemian hall on Quincy Avenue. After watching them rehearse, he agreed to say a few words. Though some blacks were critical of the debauched character he portrayed in Brutus Jones, Gilpin expressed his debt to O'Neill for giving him the chance to be something more than "a song-and-dance man." Instead of condescending to praise their own efforts, as the group later recalled, he issued a challenge:

> Look here, you're just fooling. Why don't you take yourselves seriously and do something about it? You can make this a real Negro theatre, maybe the best in the world. You could do it. If there aren't any plays get somebody to write them for you. . . .
>
> Learn to see the drama in your own lives, ape no one, and some day the world will come to see you.

Then, with all the instincts of the great actor he was, he walked up to the stage, extracted fifty dollars from his pocket, and placed it on the apron as if leaving an offering on an altar. "This is to say that I believe in your future," were his parting words.

It is doubtful whether fifty dollars ever carried a dramatic troupe further than the Dumas group went on Gilpin's inspired gesture. The very next night they voted to rename themselves the Gilpin Players. It took a bit longer, however, before they were ready to assume Gilpin's mandate to build an African American theater. Rowena Jelliffe had been waiting for the group to tackle plays on black life but declined to press the issue until they came to it of their own volition.

For about three years, the members rejected the bait, continuing with such little theater staples as Susan Glaspel and George Cook's *Suppressed Desires.* There was reason enough for their circumspection, as most black opinion makers of the day were vehemently opposed to any dramatizations that might deal too realistically with the problems of the black experience. The dean of Cleveland's black editors, Harry C. Smith of the *Gazette,* had blistered *The Emperor Jones* as well as O'Neill's later play on a racial theme, *All God's Chillun Got Wings.*

Finally, early in 1925, the Gilpin Players were ready to present their first play on black themes. It was the one-act *Granny Maumee* by Ridgeley Torrence, with a Cleveland elementary school teacher named Hazel Mountain Walker in the title role. Some of their apprehensions initially appeared to be justified. "I was almost laughed out of court," recalled Walker, who also happened to have a law degree. "It was a mixed audience, but it seemed that the Negroes came to make it difficult for me." Harry Smith objected to the performance as a perpetuation of the old "granny" stereotype.

Regardless, Walker and her fellow players persevered. The following month they did *Compromise,* a black-content play by Willis Richardson. A couple of months later they presented two more—O'Neill's *The Dreamy Kid* and Paul Green's *The No 'Count Boy.* Repeating the latter in a special performance at the Cleveland Museum of Art, they gained the attention of Archie Bell of the *Cleveland News.* "This group, unless all signs fail, is destined to win a national reputation," he wrote.

With increasingly active groups in drama as well as art, music, and dance, the Playhouse Settlement was evolving from a settlement house into an arts center. After five seasons, the Gilpin Players had thirty members and forty-three plays to their credit. One of their recent efforts, Charles Brooks's *Wappin' Wharf,* was their first full-length production. Rowena Jelliffe, who assumed the preponderance of the directing responsibilities, spent two summers studying theater and dance in New York. "We determined to build a program centered in the arts," she would recall, "for we had seen the creative capacity which our people were revealing."

The stature of the Gilpin Players took a dramatic leap in 1927 with the opening of their own theater. They built it themselves in the shell of a former saloon, a victim of Prohibition, on Central Avenue and East 38th Street. Russell Jelliffe collected materials from the neighborhood, including used pews purchased on credit from a church for $10 apiece. Volunteers came in the evenings after their regular jobs to help fashion a small sixteen-foot stage and an auditorium seating 120. Elmer Cheeks, an electrical engineer, built a light board with the advice of Max Eisenstadt from the Play House. Olive Hale brought in African designs to utilize in the interior decorations.

They took great pains to find the right name for their new theater; Hazel Walker headed a search committee. They found what they were looking for in a Swahili dictionary from the John Griswold White Folklore Collection at the Cleveland Public Library. They would call it "Karamu," a word meaning "place of enjoyment." In time the entire center would become known, and famous, as Karamu.

Still known as the Gilpin Players, the company opened its Karamu Theatre on February 24, 1927, with a trio of one-acts including Ridgeley Torrence's *Simon the Cyrenean.* This was another play with a black theme, a genre composing an increasingly more prominent segment of the Gilpins' repertoire. They had done nine such works by then, most to the intermittent distress of the more conservative elements in the black community. There had been white members in the Gilpin Players all along; except for those plays with specific racial content, casting was normally handled without regard to race.

Somewhat more than a year after moving into their new theater, the Gilpin Players found themselves on the theatrical map. It came with their performance of Paul Green's *In Abraham's Bosom,* a Pulitzer Prize–winning study of a North Carolina mulatto's tragic failure in his attempts to assert his manhood and elevate his race. This was the play's first production outside New York, and cast members prepared for it by talking to Jules Bledsoe and Rose McClendon from the original cast. Fitzhugh Woodford essayed the title role for the Gilpins. They opened it for a week's run at Karamu and then were invited to move the production downtown for two more weeks at the Little Theatre on East 9th Street.

Besides exposing them to a wider audience, the downtown engagement brought the Gilpin Players for the first time to the general notice of the daily drama critics. "In a sense, it was their first public appearance," wrote Don Muir Strouse of the *Cleveland News,* who found in Fitzhugh Woodford "as finished and polished an actor as one would hope to see." George Davis of the *Cleveland Press* confessed that, having read the play, he had just dropped in to catch a couple of scenes to see how it acted. "We found the acting so interesting that we stayed to the end," he stated. Yes, these were actors who had day jobs, he observed, but so were the villagers in Germany who put on the famed Passion Play at Oberammergau. "Here are players who have little of the amateur flavor about themselves," W. Ward Marsh said of the Gilpins in the *Plain Dealer.* "And here, it seems to me, is a finer example of teamwork in the drama; every player contributes his share to the production rather than to self-gratification." That was the sort of praise generally reserved for ensembles like the Moscow Art Theatre.

Not long after the opening of Eldred Theater at Western Reserve and the launching of Karamu by the Gilpin Players, Cleveland's foremost little theater also moved into a new home. Under the ambitious program of professionalism undertaken by Frederic McConnell, the Cleveland Play House was hardly little anymore. Even after the addition of a small balcony, the company had outgrown the capacity of its former church on Cedar Avenue. By the beginning of their twelfth season in 1926, they had presented seventy-three full-length plays, forty

In 1926 the Cleveland Play House moved into its new Tudor-style quarters on East 86th Street. The original $225,000 complex boasted two theaters. Pictured here is the entrance, with the larger Drury Theatre in the background. *Photograph by Hastings-Willinger and Assoc.; Cleveland Play House*

of them new to Cleveland. For the 1926–27 season, McConnell planned an ambitious schedule of nineteen different plays, including twelve new productions.

Ground for a new building had already been broken the previous June. McConnell had visited Europe in 1924 for ideas, finding one possible model in a dual theater and opera house in Stuttgart, Germany. Once again, Francis Drury was instrumental in turning dreams into reality. Preparing to abandon his Euclid Avenue mansion for a duplicate he was building in Gates Mills, he offered the Play House part of his former garden on East 86th Street for a new theater. Walter Flory engineered the formation of a Play House Foundation to handle the institution's business and real estate activities apart from its primary artistic functions. Charles Brooks, serving once more as Play House president, headed a drive to raise the necessary $225,000.

Before the end of the 1926–27 season, the Play House was performing in its new theater complex. It was designed by the Cleveland firm of Small and Rowley in the Tudor style of their Moreland Courts apartments at Shaker Square. The site contained two stages: a larger 500-seat main theater named in honor of Francis Drury and a more intimate 160-seat space. Upstairs was a greenroom designed by the noted local decorator Louis Rorimer. William McDermott in the *Plain Dealer* approvingly noted the absence of "the gilded manner" of the downtown commercial houses. "It looks like what it was intended to be," he said of the new Play House, "an excellent and comfortable working plant for people seriously interested in the theater as an art." After holding a mock funeral for the old building on Cedar Avenue, McConnell and company dedicated the new home on East 86th with a performance of Sem Benelli's *The Jest* on April 9, 1927.

With the opening of its new theaters, the Cleveland Play House had clearly entered a new era in its history. McConnell prepared a festive 1927–28 season of twenty-seven plays, twelve of them revivals. They ran the gamut from *King Lear* to Kaufman and Connelly's *Beggar on Horseback*. By 1929 McConnell's company of a dozen professionals, fleshed out with dedicated amateurs, was referred to by Kenneth Macgowan in *Theatre Arts* magazine as "the leading little theatre of America." With attendance reaching an annual level of 100,000, the Play House in fact was no longer a "little theater." In Europe it would have been called an art theater; in America it may have become the first of what would later be referred to as regional theaters. In 1929 McConnell tentatively crossed another threshold when he engaged the Yiddish star Jacob Ben-Ami for a guest appearance in *He Who Gets Slapped*. Ben-Ami was an Equity member, and his appearance at the nonunion Play House evoked protests from both commercial manager Robert McLaughlin and the stagehands' union. Ultimately, Ben-Ami was sanctioned for a limited run of three weeks, but the incident was a straw in the wind.

"We had outgrown the little old makeshift building, the period of gumdrop jewels and volunteer productions," summarized Julia Flory in her account of the early years. It must have been a bittersweet moment for Charles Brooks, who had worn those gumdrop gems on the old stage. He had faithfully raised the money for the new stages and had the undoubted gratification of having the smaller one named after himself. He continued to pen his fanciful essays and playlets. *Wappin' Wharf* had been done by more than a hundred little theaters since its premiere in the old house, and he had the satisfaction of seeing another, *The Tragedy of Josephine Maria,* enacted at the new Play House.

And yet, the theater that had been born in his old living room on East 115th Street had decidedly grown up and moved out on its own. Divorced from his wife Minerva, Brooks had remarried and moved into a new home not far away on Magnolia Drive. In the back, inspired by a private theater they had seen in Sicily, Brooks installed his own Lamp Post Theater in an old barn. It was "a happy blend of an American stable and an English hall," with a fourteen-foot stage and room for a hundred spectators. At the time of his death in 1934 at the age of only fifty-six, he had been putting on his own plays there for the entertainment of their friends. Charles Brooks had returned, full circle, to the Little Theater movement.

GODFATHER OF THE ARTS

When Fr. John Powers, pastor of St. Ann's Church and a pretty fair Irish tenor, needed a backup band in 1918 for a planned benefit concert, he knew where to turn. He went over to the *Cleveland Leader* to see Archie Bell.

As usual, Bell had an answer. He sent Powers to see local musical impresario Adella Prentiss Hughes, who had recently lured a young conductor named Nikolai Sokoloff to town with the promise of his own orchestra. And that, to make a long story short, is how the Cleveland Orchestra was born.

For the first third of the twentieth century, Archie Bell was Cleveland's cultural arbiter. He was equally at home whether reviewing music or drama. He worked for nearly all the Cleveland dailies of his time: the *World, Plain Dealer, Leader,* and longest of all, the *Cleveland News.*

His reputation was not confined to Cleveland's city limits. "Everybody seems to have read your article," operetta star DeWolf Hopper once wrote Bell from Buffalo. "[M]ore than once in Detroit," he wrote a couple of years later, "it had been said, if Archie Bell likes us, we are 'it.'"

The greatest names of the stage curried his favor. "I am sorry I missed such a favorable opportunity the other day in Bob McLaughlin's office when I didn't know you were you," wrote actor Otis Skinner, who tried to propitiate the critic by revealing that he had had a similar experience conversing with a stranger whom he later learned was H. G. Wells.

Legendary *Cleveland Press* editor Louis B. Seltzer, who began as a copy boy for the *Leader,* recalled how the entire office had once been thrown into turmoil by an impending call from Sarah Bernhardt. The only one unperturbed happened to be the object of the French actress's visit, Archie Bell. "He sat in his little office smoking a pipe and reading a book."

Cleveland's cultural czar early in the twentieth century was the formidable Archie Bell, drama critic of the *Cleveland News*. His frowns were feared and smiles solicited by the greatest names in the theater. *Cleveland Press Collection*

A large, heavyset man with a Buddha-like presence, Bell evidently was not always a merciful god. A French actress named Alice Delysia once wrote "Cher Monsieur Bell" a note of abject apology: "I am really very hurt about the letter you send me but it was absolutely impossible for me to keep my appointment[.] I WAS REALLY ILL[.] I am very sorry you take it personally and I can tell you that it is not in my habit to be rude with anybody."

Even waspish Alexander Woollcott, panjandrum of the Algonquin Round Table, was wary of Bell's sting when, after missing an appointment through a misunderstanding, he was unable to get a reply to his messages. "What the hell are you in Cleveland, anyway?" he asked in mock frustration. "The Pope, or something?"

In cultural matters, that was not too far-fetched an analogy. It was Bell who reputedly talked Morris Gest into bringing Max Reinhardt's *The Miracle* to Public Hall, which in turn paved the way for the annual visits by the Metropolitan Opera Company over a period of six decades. When the Wagnerian Opera Company brought Wagner's Ring Cycle to Cleveland in 1923, Bell placed his imprimatur on the reappearance of German opera following the hysteria of World War I with a reverential article for the program book.

Bell at various times took leave of the dramatic desk to do press agentry. He was an early publicity director for the Hippodrome Theatre and also managed tours for actress Olga Nethersole and German contralto Ernestine Schumann-Heink. He formed a particularly warm relationship with the latter, who habitually addressed him as "Son o' mine, Archie Bell."

On the day she learned that her own son had lost his life serving in the German Navy during World War I, Schumann-Heink found time to write to Bell. "Oh Archie, my heart breaks," she poured out her grief. "Why, why—God—I better stop—."

Stricken with a heart ailment, Bell retired from the *News* in 1933. He had traveled extensively, writing several books on his experiences, but spent his last ten years as a virtual recluse. Occasionally, the great names from the past, such as Schumann-Heink and Otis Skinner's daughter Cornelia, would stop to visit at his home on East 85th Street.

Otherwise, he had his books and his letters—and his memories.

ENTER PLAYHOUSE SQUARE

UPPER EUCLID AVENUE MUST have been littered with little snippets of ceremonial ribbons in the spring of 1921. Within the space of two months, four new theaters had opened their box offices near the intersection of Euclid Avenue and East 14th Street.

And what theaters! First came the lordly State with its 320-foot lobby, billed as the longest in the world serving a single theater. It enabled the State, with its auditorium set far back on East 17th Street toward Chester Avenue, to reach out to Euclid for its front entrance, much as the old Euclid Avenue Opera House had once done from Sheriff Street.

The builders made good use of the main lobby's expansive walls, filling them with mahogany pillars, a huge marble fireplace, and four colorful murals by James Daugherty depicting the essences of the four principal continents. That for America was dedicated to "The Spirit of Cinema," and it would play a supporting role half a century later in preserving the State for posterity.

Though described as "Italian Renaissance," the auditorium was actually a blend of Roman, Greek, and baroque elements united under a coffered ceiling and highlighted by backlit oval insets of art glass. With 3,400 seats, the State rivaled the Hippodrome in capacity and was intended for mixed programs of vaudeville and movies. It opened on

Lobby of the Ohio

February 5, 1921, with the Ina Claire movie *A Polly with a Past,* a Buster Keaton featurette, and live music from Hyman Spitalny and his orchestra.

Barely a week had passed before the State was joined by a new next-door neighbor. Like its big brother, the Ohio Theatre was one of the three hundred theaters designed nationally by Thomas Lamb. It too communicated with Euclid Avenue through a long series of lobbies, culminating in a grand foyer enhanced with scenes from the life of Venus. Inside, the auditorium was decorated in soft green and ivory highlighted by a golden sunburst above the proscenium. A pair of pastoral murals flanked the balcony, which was lighted by a crystal chandelier imported from a palace near Milan, Italy.

Like its sister Loew's theater, the State, the Ohio Theatre was connected to Euclid Avenue via a series of antechambers culminating in the awesome grand lobby pictured above. While those of the State, Allen, and Palace Theatres have been faithfully restored, the lobbies of the Ohio have been altered beyond recognition from their original appearance. *Cleveland Press Collection*

Less than half as large as the State, the 1,400-seat Ohio was a comparatively intimate house designed for live drama and musicals. The stage measured forty feet wide by eighty feet deep behind a proscenium opening of thirty-eight by twenty-eight feet. David Warfield in *The Return of Peter Grimm* was the opening attraction on February 14.

Both the State and the Ohio were conceived as part of a real estate development meant to transform Euclid Avenue from East 9th to East 17th Streets into a thoroughfare of shops and restaurants catering to the carriage trade. The last of the Romanesque and Gothic mansions of "Millionaires' Row" had given way to such high-end retailers as Cowell & Hubbard Jewelers, Sterling & Welch, and the Halle Brothers Department Store. Theaters were part of the equation, and realtor Joseph Laronge had formed Loew's Ohio Theatres with New Yorker Marcus Loew to build and operate the State and the Ohio. They were hailed by the *Cleveland Plain Dealer* as harbingers of a new era in Cleveland theater, putting the city in a league with Detroit, Pittsburgh, Boston, and Philadelphia, if not quite in a class with Chicago and New York.

Others were already getting into the act. Close on the heels of the Ohio, the Hanna Theatre opened its doors on March 28, 1921. Built by Daniel R. Hanna in tribute to his theater-loving father, Mark Hanna, erstwhile owner of the Euclid Avenue Opera House, the Hanna was a Broadway-style legitimate theater. Like its New York counterparts, it was located not on the main strip of Euclid Avenue but around the corner on the side street of East 14th. Likewise, it devoted little space or expense for an ostentatious lobby, impelling its audiences, weather permitting, to spill out during intermissions onto the sidewalk outside.

Little was stinted on the Hanna's interior decor, however. The 1,400-seat auditorium was finished in what was described as a combination of Italian Renaissance and Pompeian style, with light travertine walls highlighted by green and gold furnishings. An impressive ceiling pattern of gilded plaster medallions displayed classical images of cupids, maidens, griffons, and Pegasuses. Above the proscenium were Hellenic landscapes surmounted by names indicative of the theater's high purpose: Aeschylus, Euripides, Shakespeare, Calderon, Molière, Goldoni, Goethe, and Hugo.

Architect Charles A. Platt gave the Hanna a sizable stage of forty-two feet wide by forty feet in depth. It was equipped with a fireproof asbestos curtain, an ultramodern lighting switchboard, and an illuminated signboard to control the handling of scenery. "There's none better in the country," said Crosby Gaige, a co-lessee of the theater. "It's large enough so its managers can afford to present in it the best plays offered; but it is 'intimate' enough to present the quietest comedy or drama to the best advantage. It's a gem." William Faversham broke in the new house as Miles Hendon in an adaptation of Mark Twain's *The Prince and the Pauper.*

Four nights later, the Allen Theatre rounded out the quartet of openings that spring on what the newspapers soon dubbed Playhouse Square. It was built by two brothers from Toronto, Jules and Jay Allen, exclusively for the showing of motion pictures. Hence there was no stage to speak of, and the three-thousand-seat auditorium had the shoebox shape of a concert hall. With the house lights on, the ceiling suggested a cloudy blue sky; when the lights dimmed, twinkling stars appeared. In place of boxes, six side windows were softly lit from behind to suggest twilight outside.

A crowd of thousands lined up on Euclid Avenue on April 1 for the opening bill of Vera Gordon in *The Greatest Love,* backed by a thirty-five-piece orchestra led by Hyman's brother, Phil Spitalny. Those who were not turned away were admitted into a lobby every bit as impressive, if not as long, as those of the Allen's two neighbors on Euclid. Architect C. Howard Crane, who also designed Detroit's Fox Theater, planned it in the form of a great thirty-three-foot-high rotunda encircled by sixteen Corinthian columns of black walnut and richly accented in blues and gold. An interior rotunda opened from the mezzanine level over the rear of the orchestra section.

After four acts such as the Allen, Hanna, Ohio, and State, what could Playhouse Square possibly do for an encore? Vaudeville impresario Edward F. Albee answered that in spectacular fashion eighteen months later with the opening of the B. F. Keith Palace Theatre. It was named in honor of Albee's late partner, founder of the dominant Keith vaudeville circuit. Designed by the Chicago architectural firm of C. W. and George Rapp, the 3,680-seat theater was constructed as part of the twenty-one-story Keith Building on the northwest corner of Euclid and East 17th Street.

Both the auditorium and lobby were finished with white Carrara marble from Italy personally selected by Albee. Its starkness was offset by wall panels and hangings of rich brocade in a mulberry shade known as "Albee Red." The main lobby, or "Great Hall," was finished in a manner fully justifying the theater's name. The sixty-seven- by forty-foot floral carpet from Czechoslovakia was said to be the largest ever woven by hand. Twin marble staircases on either side led to a mezzanine bordered by bronze grillwork reputedly taken from a building in Nuremberg. The entire space was lit by five massive Czech crystal chandeliers modeled after Versailles originals.

On display throughout both levels of the lobby was antique Louis XIV furniture, including a satinwood and bronze commode once owned by Geraldine Farrar. There was a veritable art gallery of some thirty paintings including a Corot, a Sully, and a Josef Israels. "Here pause again and realize what you are seeing," wrote theater critic Archie Bell. "An Israels in an American vaudeville theater!" Dominating the scene, on the mezzanine level opposite the outer lobby entrance, was the great Sevres urn of cobalt blue that would come to symbolize the entire theater.

All was described in occasionally fulsome detail by Bell in a small booklet entitled *A Little Journey to B. F. Keith Palace, Cleveland*. Modeled after the "Little Journey" series of Elbert Hubbard, the privately printed tract offered a populist rationale for the ostentatious excesses of not only the Palace, but of all the vaudeville, movie, and dramatic showplaces of the era. "It was erected, decorated and furnished with the same good taste and elegance that a monarch would expend upon his residential palace," wrote Bell. "And guests are not *commanded* to Keith's Cleveland Palace; all are invited, even urged to partake of the hospitality offered. There is no precedent as in foreign palaces. All are equal when once inside and beyond the bronze gates. First come, first admitted. It's all decidedly a Yankee idea! . . . A palace for the masses! Who ever heard of such a thing before E. F. Albee had his wonderful dream that came true?"

Even the "Men's Smoking and Retiring Room" provided grist for this democratic parable, with its Old English decor and custom-covered selection of current magazines spread out on a large table. Others might choose to think of this as just another men's room, but to Bell it was "A beautiful clubroom for the visitor or for the man who has no club."

Nor were the Palace's splendors confined to the front of the house. Performers backstage had the use of twenty-three main dressing rooms, their own Louis XIV drawing room, a kitchenette, nursery, barbershop, and even an indoor putting green. Mimic Elsie Janis was the first headliner to enjoy these perks when she opened the theater on November 6, 1922. She would be followed through the years by Fanny Brice, Harry Houdini, Sophie Tucker, Sally Rand, Bob Hope, Gene and Glenn, and Sammy Kaye.

Unfortunately for one Palace tradition, Nathan Birnbaum and Grace C. Allen were *not* married in that theater. It was too bad, because a carved gold table in the lobby originally used by the French aristocracy for the signing of marriage contracts might have served as a splendid prop. Actually, the two vaudevillians *did* arrive in Cleveland on January 7, 1926, sitting in the lobby of the Statler Hotel for two hours while waiting for lower rates to take effect. Once checked in, however, they simply went to City Hall to be married like any other couple. They didn't even play the Palace that week, though they returned two months later to appear as George Burns and Gracie Allen.

As the Palace became the city's premiere vaudeville house, so the Ohio and the Hanna brought the best of the commercial "legitimate" drama to Playhouse Square. Each was the main Cleveland outlet of one of the two national theatrical syndicates: the Ohio flew the colors of the once-dominant Klaw-Erlanger chain, while the Hanna was leased by the upstart Shubert organization. If either had an edge in Cleveland, it would have been Erlanger, who secured the services of the veteran playwright-manager Robert McLaughlin to direct operations at the Ohio. McLaughlin had been active in the planning of the Ohio as a Klaw-Erlanger showcase from the beginning. "Cleveland is big enough to support attractions for a two-week period," he announced, "and I am already arranging with that end in view."

These were indeed heady days in Cleveland, which at 800,000 inhabitants, was touting itself as the nation's "Fifth City." Playhouse Square marked only the beginning of the "can-do" spirit of the city's leadership. During the remainder of the decade, Cleveland would add such monuments of civic pride as the huge Public Auditorium and the truly colossal Terminal Tower complex of the Van Sweringen brothers.

But the theatrical "road" in the 1920s was contracting, not expanding. Around the turn of the century, hundreds of shows had toured the country every year out of such theatrical centers as New York and Chicago. Following World War I, it was as if someone had turned off the spigot. Increasing competition from movies and later radio were most often cited as the cause of this decline, compounded by rising railroad rates and other production costs. Producers increasingly began to look for shows that might score a long run in New York, sending out on tour only those that had established solid "Broadway hit" credentials.

McLaughlin managed to make the best of a deteriorating situation. In the weeks following the Ohio's opening, he offered Helen Hayes in *Bab*

Dean of Cleveland's theatrical managers, Robert McLaughlin is seen strolling on Playhouse Square in the 1920s. Having previously run the Prospect and Colonial Theatres, McLaughlin took charge of the new Ohio Theatre in its early legitimate phase. He began wearing spats following the London premiere of one of his own plays. *Cleveland Press Collection*

and Fred and Adele Astaire in *Apple Blossoms.* High points of the following two seasons included Lynn Fontanne in *Dulcy,* one of the new New York–style comedies, and the Theatre Guild's production of *He Who Gets Slapped.* The desired two-week road runs were few and far between, however. Among these few were *Rain* with Jeanne Eagels and George Kelly's *The Show-Off.* Musical revues such as the *Ziegfeld Follies* and the *Earl Carroll Vanities* were occasionally good for a two-week stand also.

Nonetheless, McLaughlin kept the Ohio lit by resorting to what he knew best—summer stock. To kick off the first season at the Ohio, he asked Alfred Lunt to come and repeat his recent Broadway success in *Clarence.* Lunt wired his terms from his summer home in Genesee Depot, Wisconsin. McLaughlin wired back his acceptance but named a weekly figure one hundred dollars less than Lunt had indicated. It turned out that Lunt's figure had struck the Genesee Depot telegrapher as a mite steep, so he "just cut it down to size." Consequently, Cleveland got to see the rising star for two weeks at a bargain rate.

For the most part, McLaughlin cast his summer seasons with such veteran stock players as Jack Norworth and Francine Larrimore as well as occasional guest stars such as Lunt and Ruth Gordon. The repertoire was classic stock fare, leaning heavily on the melodramas and farces of David Belasco, George M. Cohan, and Avery Hopwood. In 1924 McLaughlin got a five-week run out of Hopwood's *The Demi-Virgin.* Thanks in large part to summer stock, the Ohio was dark only three weeks in its first three years.

With no McLaughlin in the manager's office, the Hanna marquee burned less steadily than that of the Ohio. Artistic high points included the Theatre Guild's production of *Liliom* with Joseph Schildkraut and Eva Le Gallienne in 1922. John Barrymore closed his tour of *Hamlet* there in 1924, netting the theater $4,500 and throwing a champagne party for the cast at the Hollenden Hotel. He was followed by the Moscow Art Theatre, which cleared a less princely $855. William McDermott, the *Plain Dealer's* new drama critic, found even this sum remarkable in view of the fact that the week's repertory was performed entirely in Russian.

Operettas, churned out wholesale by the Shubert organization, were what really made the Hanna's box office hum. This was the era of *The Student Prince,* which opened a five-week stand there late in 1925. McDermott thought it "quite the heartiest and most robust combination of sentiment and good, rousing, Pilsener music that the local theater has known in my time here." Cleveland agreed, as it called *Student Prince* companies back numerous times over the following two decades.

Not even *The Student Prince,* however, approached the phenomenal success of *Blossom Time.* A maudlin and largely mythical rendition of the life of composer Franz Schubert, it contained the saving grace of real Schubert melodies as arranged by Sigmund Romberg, composer of *The Student Prince. Blossom Time* hit the Hanna in 1923, making *Cleveland News* critic Archie Bell "glad that in a day like this, a jazz-ridden period, real music still has an appeal." That appeal kept the show coming back to

A medieval jester was emblazoned on the earliest covers of Hanna Theatre programs. Originally managed by New York's Shubert syndicate, the Hanna shared touring Broadway shows of the period with the nearby Ohio Theatre. *Collection of Author*

The HANNA THEATRE

COPYRIGHTED

Lee and J.J. Shubert and Crosby Gaige
Lessees & Managers

the Hanna, racking up eleven return engagements (including three "Farewell" appearances) in the 1920s alone. Still, it kept coming. "'Blossom Time' returns to the Hanna this week," William McDermott would announce in 1949. "I do not know how many times I have written that sentence or its equivalent." The answer was twenty, and still counting. By the time it was done, *Blossom Time* had achieved an accumulated run of half a year at the Hanna spread over nearly three decades.

There were no *Blossom Time*s in summer, unfortunately, and the Hanna was totally dark three out of its first five summers. It tried a summer-stock season of its own in 1923, and two years later Robert McLaughlin produced simultaneous summer-stock seasons in both the Hanna and his own Ohio. The melodrama *White Cargo* scored at the Hanna, running there nine weeks before moving over in the fall for four more weeks at the Metropolitan. Occasionally, both the Ohio and Hanna dodged dark periods by booking movies such as *Ben Hur* at the former and *The Big Parade* at the latter. Each had its share of occasional artistic successes and popular musical comedies. *No, No, Nanette* at the Ohio was answered by *Yes, Yes, Yvette* at the Hanna.

While the Hanna and the Ohio duked it out on Playhouse Square, Cleveland's older houses settled into a general twilight relieved by only occasional flashes of former brilliance. The fate of the Euclid Avenue Opera House, it was generally understood, was sealed with the advance of the theater district up the street. It lingered for another year, subsisting largely on a diet of vaudeville, revivals, and movies. Following a week's run of George M. Cohan's *The O'Brien Girl,* a "Final Goodbye Performance" was advertised for April 2, 1922. Included on the gala program were the entire second act of *The Bohemian Girl* and shorter selections by soprano Adelaide Norwood and a woodwind ensemble from the recently formed Cleveland Orchestra. The featured attraction, offered in tribute to former manager Gus Hartz, consisted of several of the best-known scenes from the play with which he had begun his tenure at the Opera House—*Uncle Tom's Cabin.* The next morning wreckers moved in to dismantle the house that had broken "Uncle John" Ellsler's heart, clearing the site for a commercial block.

As the Euclid Avenue Opera House gave up its ghosts, the Colonial put up a spirited holding action on Superior Avenue. At times, it operated as part of the Shubert organization as the Shubert-Colonial; at others, it was under the management of the ubiquitous Robert McLaughlin. Early in the 1920s it was dark for more than a year, then it enjoyed a long last hurrah when it housed the Cleveland company of the theatrical sensation of the decade.

Abie's Irish Rose was anything but a sensation when it made its New York debut in 1922. A corny comedy by Anne Nichols about an Irish-Jewish mixed marriage, it received tepid reviews from the critics and aroused little initial interest at the box office. The author resorted to New York mobster Arnold Rothstein as an unlikely angel to keep it going while the show found an audience. To the consternation of the city's more advanced thinkers, it soon did just that. *Abie's Irish Rose* went on to a record-shattering run of 2,327 performances, which made critic Robert Benchley's weekly chore of writing the thumbnail theater summaries for (the old) *Life* magazine an excruciating one. "People laugh at this every night," he wrote in defiance, "which explains why democracy can never be a success." As his resistance wore down, he promised, "In another two or three years we'll have this play driven out of town." Finally, in total surrender, he simply referred the reader to "Hebrews 13:8." Those who consulted the Good Book got the message: "Jesus Christ the same yesterday, and to day, and for ever."

Cleveland, then, had a good idea of what to expect when *Abie's Irish Rose* opened at the Colonial on September 10, 1923. Fresh from ten weeks in Atlantic City, the Cleveland company was one of four then playing in the country. According to Robert McLaughlin, "When the actors came here they inquired regarding good places to live so that they could put their children in schools."

Forewarned by the play's history, Cleveland critics gave *Abie's Irish Rose* a thumbs up. "Never has a stage play so openly and cruelly exposed the pretensions of the boys who write dramatic criticisms for the newspapers and the magazines," stated William McDermott in the *Plain Dealer*. "Miss Nichols set out to write hilarious farce comedy. She has succeeded beyond all expectations," observed Archie Bell in the *News*. "And she has done it by a technique that all of her critics would like to imitate or achieve." Sure, the humor in the play was more than a little dated, admitted McDermott, but what of it? "One rarely sees in the playhouse an audience that seemed more thoroughly entertained."

By this time, the producers knew their audiences well, taking out ads in both Catholic and Jewish weeklies. The *Catholic Universe* did not normally review plays but gave *Abie* at least tacit approval by accepting its ad. The two Jewish papers each gave the production some ink. "It deals with the marriage of an Irish girl and a Jewish boy, first made man and wife by a Methodist minister, then again in rapid succession by a rabbi and a Catholic priest—all this to appease their storming fathers," explained the *Jewish Review and Observer*. "Under its coating of fun, the play has a good deal of power. It would not do a bit of harm if about 95 per cent of the Clevelanders went to see the play during its stay here."

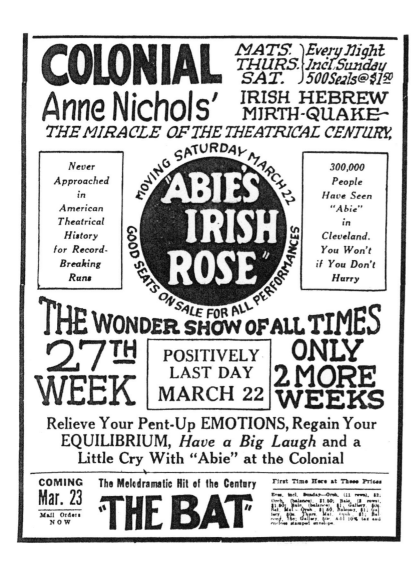

A touring company brought the phenomenally popular *Abie's Irish Rose* to the Colonial Theatre in September 1923. Before they left twenty-eight weeks later, they had established a record run for a straight play in Cleveland that still stands. There were no seals in the cast, trained or otherwise; the ad meant to say "500 Seats @ $1.50." Cleveland Plain Dealer, *March 9, 1924*

It soon appeared as if the *Review and Observer*'s wish might be fulfilled. McDermott had predicted a two-month run, but after six weeks seats were still selling two weeks in advance. It continued running through the fall and winter right up to the first appearance of spring, closing after twenty-eight weeks on March 22, 1924, which should have taken the cast's kids pretty nearly through the school year. Calculated at nine performances a week (including two matinees), *Abie's Irish Rose* achieved a Cleveland run of 252 consecutive performances, still a local record for a straight play. The Cleveland run was just short of those in Boston (thirty-two weeks) and Pittsburgh (twenty-nine weeks), and well ahead of Toronto (seventeen weeks), St. Louis (thirteen weeks), Columbus (thirteen weeks), Cincinnati (twelve weeks), and Buffalo (eleven weeks).

Nor was that all. Three years later, *Abie's Irish Rose* turned up again at the Colonial for a "Gala Return Engagement." It managed to run up another ten weeks, giving it a total Cleveland record of thirty-eight weeks for the decade—nine months in all.

Not even *Abie's Irish Rose* could save the Colonial Theatre, however. It was demolished in 1932, although its ghostly silhouette would be visible for another six decades on the side of the neighboring Superior Building. Other older houses had come to similar ends. The Empire, the Huron Road vaudeville house where John L. Sullivan had once delivered his monologue, was knocked out to make way for the art-deco building of the Ohio Bell Telephone Company; the last denizen of the reputedly jinxed playhouse was a black theater cat. On lower Prospect Avenue, the Prospect Theatre was replaced by retail shops. As if to confirm the passing of the old theater district, even the Hermit Club abandoned its original quarters on East 3rd Street in favor of a new "abbey" built on Dodge Court in Playhouse Square.

Some theaters managed to sidestep the wrecking ball only by surrendering to the silver blandishments of the cinema. The Star Theatre on lower Euclid reinvented itself as a movie house named the Cameo in 1926. It was almost completely razed and rebuilt in the 1930s as the Embassy. Across the street, the huge Hippodrome succumbed in 1931, ripping out the old boxes, the organ, and even the water tank in order to advertise itself as one of the nation's largest theaters devoted exclusively to motion pictures. It already had been mixing movies with vaudeville for several years. Squeezed between the movies and the upstart radio, vaudeville was believed by many to be on its last legs. Even the proud B. F. Keith Palace on Playhouse Square began interpolating movies into its vaudeville bills in 1926.

Movies were coming of age in the 1920s, especially after the introduction of sound. *The Jazz Singer,* generally regarded as the first "talkie," came to Cleveland early in 1928 at the Stillman, a Euclid Avenue movie palace built in 1916 on the fringe of the future Playhouse Square. The demand for the medium occasioned a building boom during the decade that spread far beyond the first-run houses downtown and often emulated them in decoration. On the east side the Doan ushered moviegoers into a lobby rotunda modeled after an Aztec temple, while the Granada brought a hint of Moorish Spain to the west side.

In one instance, however, a theater bucked the trend of the decade by converting from the showing of movies to live performances. It happened at the Little Theatre on East 9th Street and Chester Avenue, a former burlesque house previously known as the Priscilla and the Band Box. In the fall of 1927, it had become Cleveland's first art-film theater, the Little Theatre of the Movies, opening with a screening of Eisenstein's *Potemkin*. That must have been an idea ahead of its time, and by the end of that year the Little Theatre had metamorphosed yet again into a "legitimate" house.

Producer S. W. Manheim planned to use the Little Theatre to develop live productions that would then travel to Detroit, Chicago, and other road towns. Evidently a believer in audacity, he decided to launch his venture with a Shakespearean repertory. A company of actors was assembled under the auspices of the Shakespearean Association of America. Fritz Leiber, a veteran stock player from the Robert Mantell company, headed the troupe.

Leiber, who was said to have played a hundred Shakespearean roles during his long career, had sound ideas on putting the Bard over in the Jazz Age. He prided himself and his company on avoiding the traditional stilted declamatory style in favor of a more flowing, naturalistic reading. Another tradition eliminated was the arbitrary five-act division imposed on the plays by later interpreters. They would be given at the Little Theatre with a minimum of breaks ranging from a few seconds to no more than three minutes.

They opened on December 11, 1927, with a week of *Hamlet* followed by a week of *The Merchant of Venice*. "For the people to whom 'Hamlet' has always been an exercise in swooning sanctity, Fritz Leiber's is a 'Hamlet' good for them to see," praised Elrick Davis in the *Cleveland Press*. Attendance was nonetheless poor those first two weeks until Manheim dropped his admission charge to a maximum of one dollar. Shakespeare was good for another seven weeks after that, often to capacity houses. The initial two offerings were succeeded by week-long runs of *Macbeth, Julius Caesar,* and *Romeo and Juliet. The Taming of the Shrew* ran for a week and a half, the second week filled out with *Othello*. For his final two weeks, Leiber revived *Hamlet* for half a week in traditional costume and half a week in modern dress and then closed out the series with a week of repertory. There had been seven plays in nine weeks—the most intense exposure to Shakespeare in the city's history.

Some of the most challenging productions in the history of Cleveland's commercial theaters were mounted in the Little Theatre, which occupied the former Priscilla vaudeville house at East 9th Street and Chester Avenue. After nine weeks of Shakespeare, there were local premieres of works by Eugene O'Neill and Maxwell Anderson. *Cleveland Public Library*

As Leiber led his troupe to Chicago and other points west, Manheim brought another company into the Little Theatre. To top the Bard marathon, they gave the first local production of Edouard Bourdet's drama of lesbianism, *The Captive.* It played to record audiences for six weeks, possibly in spite of the fact that it avoided sensationalism in its treatment of the subject. "Those who came to laugh stayed to cough," reported William McDermott. "So acutely bronchial an audience I do not remember having previously observed in the theater." There were no problems of censorship in Cleveland, but the production was later kept out of Detroit by a court injunction.

The remainder of the season at the Little Theatre was filled out by shorter runs. Bertha Kalich, the legendary Yiddish actress, appeared in weeklong runs of *The Kreutzer Sonata* and Sudermann's *Magda*. Transplanted from their home base at Karamu, the Gilpin Players were good for a two-week stand of Paul Green's *In Abraham's Bosom*. Some of them then joined their namesake, Charles Gilpin, in a revival of Eugene O'Neill's *The Emperor Jones*.

O'Neill was a cornerstone of the Little Theatre's second season, which opened in the fall of 1928 with a list of subscribers signed during a short summer hiatus. On September 9 they saw the Cleveland premiere of O'Neill's controversial treatment of interracial marriage, *All God's Chillun Got Wings*. When the play opened in New York in 1924, it had caused such an uproar that the producing Provincetown Players claimed they spent more on clipping press items than on constructing scenery. O'Neill had already published the play in *The American Mercury,* so everyone knew in advance about the scene where a white woman kissed a black man's hand. A nervous city administration had let the show go on but not before withholding a license allowing children to appear in the first scene, ostensibly to shield them from threatened violence. The scene was read to the audience by the director.

Four years later, *All God's Chillun* could be given in Cleveland with children onstage and without turmoil. Karamu, after all, had accustomed local theatergoers to racial as well as interracial plays and casts. Actors from Karamu, in fact, were recruited by the Little Theatre for the black members of the cast, headed by Fitzhugh Woodford as Jim, the role created by Paul Robeson. To Ward Marsh in the *Plain Dealer,* a rather flat first act was redeemed in the second and final act. "The crumbling of the white girl's mind, the dogged ambition of the colored man, the fears his sister and mother entertain, the superstitions and racial hatreds blaze forth mightily in carefully studied lines and movements and make this a decidedly interesting production." George Davis of the *Press* applied a much simpler standard to conclude that the play packed "a real kick." When the deranged heroine onstage attempted to stab her husband, Davis described how "a young woman who sat two seats away from this reviewer in the first row, screamed and seemed about to climb over the back of her seat."

All God's Chillun played two weeks at the Little. Other O'Neill works seen there that fall were *Anna Christie,* which had previously been seen at the Hanna, and the first local production of *The Fountain,* O'Neill's treatment of Ponce de Leon's quest for immortality. Fritz Leiber returned to star in the latter. Another Cleveland premiere was Maxwell Anderson's first take on the Sacco and Vanzetti affair, *Gods of the Lightning,* written with Harold Hickerson. Perhaps the East 9th house at that point had reached the limit of Cleveland's inclination for experimentation, for it went dark a week before Christmas. It reopened Christmas Day as the Empress Theater, coming full circle as a burlesque house once again. In the interval, however, the Little Theatre had provided as challenging a year as the commercial theater had ever produced in Cleveland.

As the 1920s wound down, then, Playhouse Square was rapidly becoming the last refuge of commercial theater in Cleveland. Thanks to the managerial ability of Robert McLaughlin, it was doing just fine at the Ohio Theatre. McLaughlin would later recall running the Ohio for a U.S. record of ten years without a dark week. He may have exaggerated, but not by much. From March 26, 1923, to December 16, 1928, he ran it for 299 weeks, or nearly six years, without a break. During its first nine-and-a-half years, the Ohio's marquee was dark for a total of only eight weeks.

Like a veteran vaudeville juggler, McLaughlin managed to keep the Ohio bobbing aloft without dropping any of his numerous related interests. Early in the 1920s he operated the Ohio School of Stage Arts for a couple of years. In 1922 his *Decameron Nights* became the first American play ever produced at London's Theatre Royal, Drury Lane, earning him an invitation to meet King George V in the royal box. Upon his return, he began to offset his round, prosaic face by adopting the walking stick and even the spats of a Continental *boulevardier.* He collected fine paintings, rare books, and antique furniture. His luxurious office at the Ohio was crowded with curiosities including masks, ivories, and an owl with blinking electronic eyes.

McLaughlin kept the Ohio fully booked thanks in large part to his perennial summer stock seasons, which in poor road years might begin as early as April. During the 1927–28 season, he also managed a winter-stock company in the Alhambra Theater near University Circle. His summer seasons at the Ohio attracted such guest stars as William Boyd, Spencer Tracy, and Melvyn Douglas. He filled out one season with the premiere of one of his last plays, the allegorical *The Pearl of Great Price,* which ran for four weeks.

The diminished road managed to provide its share of highlights at the Ohio. One of the brightest was the world premiere of one of

The famous Barrymore profile is featured in this ad for the world premiere of Somerset Maugham's *The Constant Wife* at the Ohio Theatre in 1926. In the words of *Plain Dealer* critic William McDermott, Ethel Barrymore turned in "certainly the finest performance . . . given by an actress who did not know her lines." Cleveland Plain Dealer, *October 31, 1926*

W. Somerset Maugham's most successful plays, *The Constant Wife*. It opened on November 1, 1926, with Ethel Barrymore in the lead. Unfortunately, it opened before the star had managed to master her lines. Scraps of written dialogue were left for Barrymore at strategic locations all over the set. When all else failed, the heroine could beat a graceful retreat to a stage fireplace, where critic William McDermott spotted "a gentleman, who sat, like Santa Claus," feeding her lines in plain sight straight from the script. The cramped Santa in fact was the director, George Cukor, which might explain why he would soon desert Broadway for the more controlled environment of Hollywood. "As he got [the lines] out of his mouth," reported McDermott, "Miss Barrymore caught them up with her own huskily velvet voice and turned them very frequently into opalescent and living jewels, glowing with vibrancy, and of a melancholy and melting tenderness. It was a feat of a sort, certainly the finest performance that most of us in the theater had ever seen given by an actress who did not know her lines."

Maugham was nowhere to be found when the capacity house clamored for the author. Tight-lipped, he later confronted his star backstage. "Darling, I've ruined your play," she headed him off, "but don't worry, it'll run for two years." It very nearly did. Years later, when McDermott visited Maugham in his villa on the Riviera, the author pointed out several pieces of fine furniture that, he stated, were purchased with the royalties from *The Constant Wife*. "Ethel Barrymore bought that for me," is how he put it to the critic.

Even more memorable than Barrymore was the pre-Broadway appearance of *Show Boat,* which put in at the Ohio en route from its premiere in Washington to immortality in New York. The Florenz Ziegfeld production, with music by Jerome Kern and lyrics by Oscar Hammerstein II, played the week of November 28, 1927. William McDermott, who had expressed the wish in advance that Ziegfeld and company would concentrate on the earlier Mississippi River scenes from the Edna Ferber novel, was not disappointed in that respect. His only complaint in his *Plain Dealer* review was that, at more than three hours' running time, "there is too much of it and too much of it is good." Near the end of a long list of kudos, he included "a remarkable Negro singer whose name I lost." His name happened to be Jules Bledsoe, and he had just introduced Clevelanders to "Ol' Man River." George Davis in the *Cleveland Press* remembered not only the singer, but quoted the entire chorus of the song. "There aren't many musical shows that this reviewer cares to see twice," wrote Davis. "One of these is 'The [*sic*] Show Boat.'" He would have ample opportunity to do so in the years to come.

Show Boat had given Cleveland an advance peek at the musical of the future. With *The New Moon,* the Hanna Theatre brought Cleveland the world premiere of one of the last of the traditional operettas. (An earlier version had bombed so decidedly in Philadelphia the previous year that little more than the title survived for the Cleveland reincarnation.) Composer Sigmund Romberg personally conducted a number at the Hanna premiere on August 27, 1928. Due to the numerous encores given such numbers as "Stout-Hearted Men" and "Lover, Come Back to Me," *The New Moon* ended even later than *Show Boat*. Another

Several weeks before its Broadway debut in 1927, the legendary musical *Show Boat* docked in Cleveland for a week of tryouts. Although the name of Jules Bledsoe was misspelled in this *Plain Dealer* ad, and the paper's critic couldn't recall his name, no one was likely to forget his rendition of "Ol' Man River." Cleveland Plain Dealer, *November 27, 1927*

popular success at the Hanna that year was the George Abbott and Philip Dunning melodrama *Broadway,* which ran for four weeks. While George Davis thought the acting not quite up to that in the New York cast, he reported in the *Press,* "Few plays get as much or as spontaneous applause as this play got from the Hanna audience Monday."

If the quantity of road attractions was declining in the 1920s, some were taking note of a decided improvement in quality. As early as 1923, William McDermott had written of the burgeoning of a new theater in America as exemplified by the productions of such organizations as New York's Theatre Guild and Provincetown Players. Other signs mentioned by the *Plain Dealer* critic included "the growing splendor of the revue, the interest of the colleges in the theater, and ready hospitality to alien drama and so on." His main cavil was the failure of a new generation of American playwrights to emerge. "But with, what is to me, the somewhat doubtful exception of Eugene O'Neill," wrote McDermott, "there is very little contemporary playwriting that gives any great promise of permanence or that shows any revolutionary breaking off from the past in America." Even as McDermott's ink dried, however, O'Neill continued to mature and was soon joined by other promising talents. *Anna Christie* and *The Hairy Ape* came to the Hanna, while the Ohio exposed Clevelanders to George Kaufman and Marc Connelly's *Merton of the Movies* and Sidney Howard's *They Knew What They Wanted*.

O'Neill's *Desire under the Elms* must have convinced any doubters that a new theatrical era had opened when it arrived at the Ohio in a "Positively UNEXPURGATED Version" for a three-week stand in April 1926. Both McDermott and Archie Bell expressed fears that the majority of the capacity opening-night crowd had been attracted by the play's sensational subject matter of forbidden love and infanticide. "Above all, don't think that this is a risque bedroom farce," Bell warned *News* readers. "If you see it (and you should see it) you will find tragedy stalking about as you have rarely have had the opportunity to see it, if ever, in a play of American authorship." While McDermott quarreled with the audience for its self-conscious restlessness and with the cast for its inclination to "prettify" the play, he was convinced of the work's innate stature: "With all of what many will take as gaucherie, as mere sensationalism and offensive crudity, there is in this American play some of that pure and noble and sad beauty one finds under the stars on a soft night or in the haze of the dawn over a green field."

Several weeks earlier the Hanna had hosted another milestone of the American theater in Maxwell Anderson and Laurence Stallings's *What Price Glory?* Billed as "The Great War Comedy," it came with Louis Wolheim and William Boyd in their original roles of Captain Flagg and Sergeant Quirt. "It's sordid stuff. War stuff," noted Archie Bell. "They say what they want to say and as they are accustomed to saying it. If you don't like it, you can lump it. But you cannot say that it isn't something that belongs." McDermott praised the authors for the "shrewd theatricality" with which they had interwoven the feud of the two protagonists with the larger conflict of World War I.

And so the infiltration of the new national drama continued on Playhouse Square: George Kelly's *Craig's Wife* and Sidney Howard's *The Silver Cord* at the Ohio; Maxwell Anderson's *Saturday's Children* and Robert E. Sherwood's *The Road to Rome* at the Hanna.

A landmark was reached in November 1929, when the Theatre Guild brought O'Neill's *Strange Interlude* to the Ohio. Much had been written about this Pulitzer Prize winner, with its monumental nine-act structure and dramatic asides in which the characters voiced their inner thoughts. Curtain time was set for 5:30 P.M. with a dinner break from 7:40 to 9:00 o'clock and the final curtain sometime around 11:00 P.M. "Some business executives in the audience hadn't quit work so early in months for anything less important than golf," quipped the *Cleveland Press*. Many in the full house on opening night had done their homework by reading the printed text in advance. Similar foresight was recommended in making dinner reservations for Playhouse Square restaurants. Playgoers could choose from among the swanky Monaco's in the Hanna Building or three of the more modest Clark restaurants in the vicinity.

"The astonishing thing is that sometimes the realization approaches the intent," wrote William McDermott of the play itself, which he had previously viewed in New York. "You sit through this play and at moments you are stung with the impression that in the lives of these neurotics there is a sort of strange vitality to which the stage is not accustomed." There were other moments, however, when McDermott thought O'Neill laid himself open to charges of "pretentiousness and windiness." George Davis reduced *Strange Interlude* to much simpler terms in the *Press*. "It recognizes that tangled love affairs aren't conducive to peace of mind," he observed of Nina and the three men in her life. Also, "People don't say all they think"; so much for nine acts of O'Neill.

McDermott had recently speculated in the *Plain Dealer* that perhaps the American theater had outdistanced the capacity of its audience. Responding to reader complaints of boorish audience behavior, he observed: "A few years ago all plays produced in America were conventionally sentimental, or farcical or melodramatic. Except for revivals of classics they presented no subtleties, nothing that would tax the ordinary intelligence." Serious playgoers were consoled with the thought that "Such imbecile laughers as ruined several scenes for many in the local performances of 'Desire Under the Elms'" were, merely by their attendance, at least helping subsidize the drama for those mature enough to appreciate it. His advice to the latter was to stop being so polite and just "say shush!"

New York's Shubert brothers had no complaints with Cleveland audiences. In fact, producers Lee and J. J. Shubert told the *Plain Dealer*'s Ward Marsh in the summer of 1929 that they were thinking of using

Cleveland more regularly as a tryout town for their Broadway productions. Among the city's assets, they listed its population of one million, its location midway between Chicago and New York, its toleration of Sunday night shows, and the modern equipment and amicable union relations of the Hanna Theatre. Perhaps outweighing all of the foregoing was simply the fact that the Shuberts considered Cleveland to be a good "show town."

It certainly seemed like a good show town in the fall of 1929. Besides *Strange Interlude,* the Ohio had booked the Theatre Guild production of *Porgy* and Rodgers and Hart's *A Connecticut Yankee.* Around the corner at the Hanna, Katharine Cornell was appearing in *The Age of Innocence,* which was followed by the umpteenth return of *Blossom Time.*

In New York such future road attractions as *June Moon, Whoopee* with Eddie Cantor, and Elmer Rice's *Street Scene* were running on Broadway. A few dozen blocks southward, however, some rather heavy real-life drama was being acted out in the financial district downtown.

In the parlance of the show business weekly *Variety,* Wall Street was laying an egg.

THE MIRACLE ON EAST 6TH STREET

Public Auditorium was barely two years old in December 1924 when carpenters and painters moved in to transform it into a huge medieval cathedral.

Their motive was theatrical, not theological. As a Christmas present for the city of Cleveland, a group of sponsors had secured a local run for the spectacular Max Reinhardt pageant *The Miracle.*

All year it had been the talk of New York, where the metamorphosis of the Century Theatre into a Gothic nave would become one of the legends of the American stage. An announcement in the official souvenir program for that production had promised, " 'The Miracle' will be presented only in New York and will not be played in any other city in the United States."

Whoever wrote that did not take into account the civic enterprise of the nation's "Fifth City" in the 1920s. Cleveland's movers and shakers had not only built the mammoth auditorium at East 6th and Lakeside, but they had already filled it with a visit from the Metropolitan Opera

Company and the 1924 Republican National Convention. That spirit, with the help of a $315,000 guarantee, ensured that *The Miracle* would be on its way to a three-week stay in Cleveland upon the conclusion of its 298-performance run in New York.

Reinhardt had first presented *The Miracle* in London in 1911. Productions followed in other European capitals until World War I turned out the lights. Following the Armistice, producers F. Ray Comstock and Morris Gest secured the New York production rights from Reinhardt. For scenery and costumes, they hired a revolutionary young designer from New Philadelphia, Ohio, named Norman Bel Geddes.

Part of the Cleveland deal stipulated that Bel Geddes be on hand personally to supervise installation of the thirty carloads of scenery in Public Auditorium. He was no stranger to the city, having studied at the Cleveland School of Art in 1911. (Back then the city's nude models had been "too relaxed" to suit him; but on this return visit, he would find the rhythms of the Spitalny dance band to be just right.) Seated at a drawing board in the middle of the cavernous auditorium, Bel Geddes directed the installation of two dozen sixty-foot columns to form the chancel of the "cathedral." The first three sections of the balcony were masked to accommodate "stained windows" of painted canvas lit from behind. That still left more than six thousand seats, twice the capacity of New York's Century Theatre. All the action would take place in front of the regular stage on a platform extended seventy-two feet into the hall.

Members of the cast began arriving, headed by Lady Diana Manners of England, who had the role of the Virgin Mary. Playing the nun Megildis was an American socialite discovered by Reinhardt on a transatlantic passage from Europe. She was Rosamond Pinchot, a niece of former Pennsylvania governor Gifford Pinchot. Both were quickly taken up by the local press, which duly reported that "Lady Di" had a weakness for ham and eggs, and Pinchot had successfully challenged the Hotel Cleveland's ban against smoking in the dining room.

There would be a cast of hundreds, with Cleveland supernumeraries hired to augment the core members brought from New York. The ticket scale ranged from one to four dollars. Critic William McDermott advised a concerned *Plain Dealer* reader not to fret over the proper attire for such a spectacle: "The auditorium is pretty dark, anyway." True, the audience was ushered into a semidark hall with a perfectly motionless Lady Di already standing in front of a pillar as a statue of the Virgin.

Former socialite Rosamond Pinchot appeared as the errant nun Megildis in the 1924 production of Max Reinhardt's *The Miracle* at Cleveland's Public Auditorium. She is pictured with one of a supporting cast of hundreds. The spectacle came to Cleveland immediately following its legendary New York run. *Cleveland Press Collection*

The entire pageant was performed in pantomime to a musical score by Engelbert Humperdinck, composer of *Hänsel und Gretel*. Based on a medieval legend, it disclosed what happened when Megildis broke her vows and left the convent. After straying for seven years, she returned only to discover that she had never been missed. The statue of the Virgin, however, had just made a miraculous reappearance in the chapel after an inexplicable absence of seven years.

It got rave reviews from the local critics, whose chief concern seemed to be reassuring their readers that the Cleveland version, if anything, surpassed that seen in New York. After slow business on Christmas Eve and Christmas, sellout houses were the norm for the final two weeks. A total attendance of 137,000 patrons resulted in an unexpected profit of $20,000 for the backers.

Eventually, *The Miracle* traveled to other major cities, but Clevelanders could congratulate themselves on having seen it first after New York. In that respect, its effect on civic pride was far more important than its contribution to the city's dramatic experience. As the *Cleveland Press* put it, "'The Miracle' has centered attention upon Cleveland as the one city in which nothing great is impossible."

There was a curious and somewhat macabre postscript involving costar Rosamond Pinchot. Pursuing her acting career, she became a friend of native Clevelander Kay Halle of the department-store Halle family, who also numbered notables ranging from Winston Churchill to George Gershwin among her intimates.

Pinchot married a prominent lawyer, while Halle continued shuttling from Cleveland to New York to Washington. At Cleveland's Great Lakes Exposition, Halle added a palm reader named Madame Zouiza to her coterie.

As *Cleveland Press* society writer Winsor French told it, Kay Halle was awakened by a phone call one night in 1938. It was Madame Zouiza, warning her to watch out for her friend Rosamond Pinchot. Before she could act upon that advice, Halle got another call.

This one was from Pinchot's father. He informed Halle that his daughter, depressed over a failing marriage, had been discovered dead in her automobile. There was a rubber hose leading from the exhaust of the running motor through a crack in the window of the closed car.

Seven

THE FABULOUS INVALID SURVIVES

SOON AFTER THE HOLIDAY season of 1929–30, *Plain Dealer* critic William F. McDermott took note of an unprecedented situation: "For the first time in Cleveland theatrical history, so far as my knowledge of it goes, there will be no attractions in the legitimate playhouses next week." It was nearly three months after the stock market crash, but the full impact of the Depression still lay in the future. As McDermott saw it, the theater's troubles that season stemmed from "simply a lack of attractions on the road and the cause of that lack, primarily, is poor business."

He could not have foreseen it then, but business would not get better for a very long time. Not even Robert McLaughlin could keep the Ohio Theatre open that summer, as he closed his summer-stock season in June after only six weeks. As for the regular season, the dearth of road shows noted in the 1920s intensified in the following decade. "Dozens of shows that garner a mild success in New York and which would in ordinary years most certainly be sent on the road are dispatched instead to the storehouse," observed McDermott in 1932. A year later he pointed out that of the ten plays chosen for Burns Mantle's *Best Plays of 1932–33,* only one had come to Cleveland on tour.

Of Cleveland's two remaining commercial playhouses, the Ohio proved more vulnerable than the Hanna to hard times. The theater that

Robert McLaughlin had kept lit for 299 consecutive weeks in the 1920s had more dark weeks than lit by 1931. Part of the problem was that McLaughlin was gone by then. A. L. Erlanger, the theater's lessee, had died in March 1930, and his heirs let the veteran Cleveland manager go.

There were still some memorable moments in the house that had seen *Show Boat* before Broadway. *The Front Page,* Ben Hecht and Charles MacArthur's manic romp through the Chicago newspaper wars, enjoyed a four-week run in 1930. Alfred Lunt and Lynn Fontanne stopped there twice the following year, first with Maxwell Anderson's *Elizabeth the Queen* and then with Robert E. Sherwood's *Reunion in Vienna.* Judith Anderson appeared in a second nine-act opus by Eugene O'Neill. While *Strange Interlude* had played two weeks in 1929, *Mourning Becomes Electra* was good for only a week in 1932.

Robert McLaughlin even returned to the Ohio for a last hurrah of summer stock in 1932. He brought in Alice Brady, who managed to milk *Mourning Becomes Electra* for a two-week stand at summer prices. Jane Cowl, appearing in *Camille,* publicly praised McLaughlin as "one of the few men in this country who has shown the courage to step out and forge ahead, while others are closing their shows and their shops." The manager revealed that his task was facilitated by the willingness of a star such as Cowl to appear for $1,000 a week instead of the $2,500 she had commanded only two years earlier.

But by 1933 McLaughlin had taken a job as manager of events at Cleveland Public Hall, and the Ohio was booking more movies than plays. It was dark for thirty consecutive weeks in 1933 except for a single one-night stand. "In the matter of the touring stage we have sunk to the level of a country village," William McDermott remarked in 1934. "It is depressing to walk along Euclid Avenue at a busy hour these autumn days and to know that you will not, by any chance, see the familiar face of an actor, or shake the hand of a player. It is as if a plague had struck the city, warning away old friends and famous visitors who gave us pleasure." A few weeks later, after three performances of *The Green Pastures* with Richard B. Harrison as The Lord, the Ohio dimmed its marquee for the last time. Prohibition was also gone, however, and a year later the remodeled theater was opened as a short-lived nightclub called the Mayfair Casino.

Robert McLaughlin had no better luck than the theater he had kept going for so long. Leaving Public Hall, he went to Hollywood to try his hand at screenwriting but found no takers. Utilizing his vast network of theatrical acquaintances, he managed to eke out a living as a casting consultant. By the end of the 1930s, he had returned to Cleveland with bad kidneys and a weak heart. He estimated that he had given employment to two thousand Equity actors but spent his last months in the home of a friend.

For better or worse, legitimate commercial theater in Cleveland was now synonymous with the Hanna Theatre on East 14th Street. Some of the better moments early in the Depression included a two-week stand by the Marx Brothers in *Animal Crackers* and Elmer Rice's slice-of-life melodrama, *Street Scene.* In 1932, however, the Hanna was dark nearly three-quarters of the year. By then the rival Shubert and Erlanger syndicates had been merged into New York's United Booking Office. The retrenching Shubert organization surrendered its lease on the Hanna Theatre, which was operated thereafter under managers appointed by Carl Hanna.

Despite hard times, at least some of the premieres promised at the end of the 1920s by the Shuberts managed to show up at the Hanna in the following decade. First came the American premiere of Rudolf Besier's *The Barretts of Wimpole Street* on January 29, 1931. "That combination of a premiere and Miss [Katharine] Cornell brought out the largest audience of the season," observed William McDermott in the *Plain Dealer,* "an audience that overflowed the theater's standing room and gave more than mute evidence of the vitality of the taste for the spoken drama, at least when spoken by Miss Cornell." The play went on to a long New York run, after which the actress took the show on an extensive tour that brought live theater to some remote backwaters that had gone without for years.

Later that year, on October 19 the Hanna offered the world premiere of *Brief Moment,* a play by S. N. Behrman. Although Francine Larrimore received top billing, the chief interest in the event centered upon the stage debut of Alexander Woollcott, the renowned critic and raconteur. His role reputedly was not only written for him but also had been based on his astringent personality. "Seldom, in recent years, have so many dressed up for a first night," noted George Davis in the *Cleveland Press.* "At least four wore opera hats. That's somethin', in Cleveland."

According to actress Margalo Gillmore, who came to give moral support, Woollcott made a pathetic debut, feeling his way timorously around the stage and failing to connect with his fellow players. When he asked for her opinion, she had a simple enough piece of advice: "Put on your glasses." In the eyes of the Cleveland critics, however, Woollcott had come through with flying colors. Archie Bell gave him credit in the *News* for daring to do "exactly what all actors have been daring all dramatic critics to do for years" and showing "that he knows much more about acting than most of the actors who never wrote dramatic criticism."

One of Woollcott's most untouchable acting icons also happened to be in town during the week of his debut. Woollcott made a call to Mrs. Fiske, who was appearing at the Ohio in *Against the Wind*. "You've been responsible for this!" he accused her in reference to his incursion into her side of the footlights. Whether he realized it or not, Minnie Maddern Fiske was on her final tour. She had only joined her cast in Cleveland in mid-week, leaving a sickbed to try to pick up the play after disappointing reviews. After Cleveland, she played a couple more weeks in Chicago and then gave it up. A few months later, the actress who had brought Ibsen to Cleveland was dead.

Openings were rarely more dazzling than the one offered by the Hanna on January 2, 1933: Alfred Lunt, Lynn Fontanne, and Noel Coward in the world premiere of Coward's *Design for Living*. It was on the Hanna marquee that week that the Lunts, following their departure from the Theatre Guild, were being given star billing for the first time in their career as America's foremost acting team. The entire week's run was sold out before the opening, with ticket orders ranging from Toledo to Buffalo. Extra chairs were placed in the aisles to accommodate a first-night crowd described by one reporter as a hodgepodge of "Society folk, bootleggers, cloak and suit merchants, wrestlers, doctors, lawyers, poor men and others." Conspicuous among the society folk was Kay Halle in a black velvet gown with shoulder straps consisting of tiny ermine tails.

"We're all very good I think," wrote Coward to a friend after taking eight curtain calls with the Lunts. William McDermott deemed the play "not as nearly perfect as the audience," but admitted nonetheless that the three stars in its best moments produced "electricity in the air." The play represented the fulfillment of a promise made by Coward to the Lunts, years before any of them were famous, to someday write a vehicle for the three of them. It took the form of a sophisticated comedy about a *ménage à trois*. While McDermott thought it "would have shocked Queen Victoria and may even disturb some of her descendants," Clevelanders took in *Design for Living* with hardly the bat of an eyelash.

Nearly four years would pass, however, before another premiere would hit the Hanna. While he could scarcely match *Design for Living* for sheer brilliance, Maxwell Anderson in *High Tor* brought a much more substantive work to the Hanna—arguably the most distinguished American play ever to make its debut in Cleveland. It also brought back to his hometown actor Burgess Meredith in the lead role of Van Dorn, playing opposite English actress Peggy Ashcroft in her American debut. Raised in Lakewood, Meredith had acted in some school plays before moving to New York while still a boy. The next time Cleveland saw

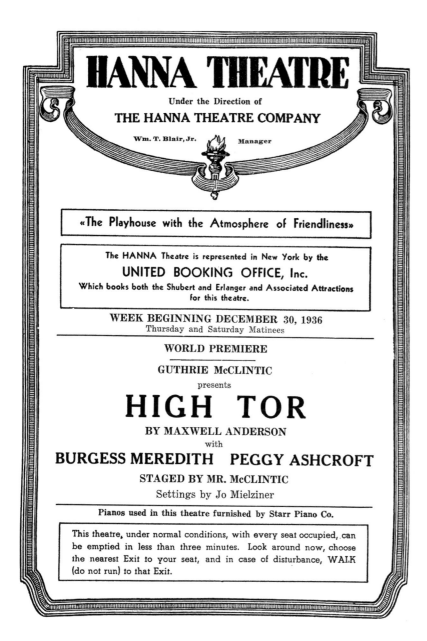

One of the most distinguished plays ever to premiere in Cleveland was Maxwell Anderson's *High Tor* at the Hanna at the end of 1936. Heading the cast were Cleveland native Burgess Meredith and British actress Peggy Ashcroft in her American debut. The play received the Critics' Circle prize for 1937. *Hanna Theatre program for December 30, 1936, Collection of Author*

him on stage was in the lead role of Anderson's second play about the Sacco and Vanzetti case, *Winterset,* which played the Hanna a few months before *High Tor.*

Opening on December 30, 1936, *High Tor* was a poetic fantasy dealing with such values as materialism and environmentalism. *Cleveland Press* critic Charles Schneider summarized its general effect upon a large audience: "It's tremendous, but what is it all about?" In its mixture of poetry and prose, realism and fancy, seriousness and slapstick, William McDermott found "a lift and freshness . . . which our thin and repetitious theater ought to welcome." All the critics admired the Jo Mielziner set, which evoked the Hudson Valley mountain of the title. The play went on to a modest New York run and the Critics' Circle prize for 1937.

But *High Tor* played the Hanna only half a week, as had the theater's previous three offerings. Producers by this time had begun splitting single-week runs between Columbus and Cleveland. In the 1935–36 season, the Hanna had offered a total of only eleven weeks of live drama. As far as the commercial road was concerned, Cleveland was becoming a three-night stand.

With the rise of the Cleveland Play House and Karamu, however, Cleveland was not as dependent on commercial theater as earlier in the century. In 1930, when remarking on the unprecedented darkness of the "legitimate playhouses," William McDermott had noted, "One of the interesting developments in the local situation is the growing popularity of the Play House." From 1928 to 1931, Frederic McConnell was averaging twenty-two productions a season in his two new stages on East 86th Street. "I suppose the most ardent missionaries of the little theaters," McDermott remarked a little later, "never visualized a day when such cities as Cleveland would be almost exclusively dependent for theatrical entertainment on a survivor of the movement to which they gave their hearts."

Even noncommercial theater was subject to the economic adversities of the Depression, however. Dwindling audiences produced a $20,000 deficit at the Play House by 1931. Ticket prices were raised from $1 to $1.50, and the number of productions was slowly whittled to a low of thirteen in the 1933–34 season. Salaries, inevitably, were also cut, leading to defections from McConnell's core of professional actors. Russell Collins left for New York, where he found a home with the Group Theatre. K. Elmo Lowe took a year's leave of absence to tour with Jane Cowl in *Camille,* where in the views of some, he stole the show from the star. McConnell mitigated the effects of the belt tightening by establishing a summer Play House repertory season at the Chautauqua Institute in New York, a series that endured from 1930 to 1980. And not even the Depression could prevent the Play House from retiring the mortgage on its new plant by the 1935–36 season.

Inspired perhaps by President Herbert Hoover's preferred strategy of willing away the Depression, McConnell hoped to keep it off the

Play House stage with a season of escapist works in 1931–32. It included Dion Boucicault's nineteenth-century melodrama *The Streets of New York,* as well as Charles Brooks's one-act *The Tragedy of Josephine Maria.* Free tickets were provided for the unemployed. But somehow, a Soviet play entitled *Red Rust* managed to sneak into the schedule. It did not, however, escape the vigilance of one *Plain Dealer* reader, who wrote in protest.

"In these times, when this country, not to mention the rest of the world, is struggling against Bolshevism, I can't help but feel that the Cleveland Play House . . . would do well to eschew the Soviet drama," wrote one C. M. Streator. Admitting that he had not "darkened its doors" in years, he described the Play House of earlier days as "a nest

Red Rust, a Soviet play depicting Russian youth after the revolution, was given at the Cleveland Play House in the depths of the Depression. Though he didn't come to see it, one reader of the *Plain Dealer* nevertheless wrote to protest what he perceived as the left-leaning slant of the Play House company. *Photograph by Trout-Ware Studios; Cleveland Play House*

of 'parlor socialists.' . . . I very well remember hearing a prominent Clevelander then very much in evidence on the acting staff, make the statement that a Soviet form of government was the only one worth having." There were plenty of other works to choose from without promoting "Red" propaganda, suggested Streator. "For instance there is 'Uncle Tom's Cabin'—something we can ALL enjoy."

Though McConnell actually took him up on that idea three seasons later, he also began to include at least one play of social consciousness in each season during the Depression. The year after *Red Rust,* it was *Merry-go-Round,* a play by Albert Maltz and George Sklar about a man locked up in jail as a material witness to a gangland slaying, who later is discovered mysteriously hanged in his cell. Though set in New York, it was reportedly based upon an actual incident that happened in Cleveland. The following year saw the Play House take on Maxwell Anderson's *Both Your Houses,* a Pulitzer Prize–winning diatribe against politics-as-usual.

In 1935–36 McConnell offered *Between Two Worlds,* Elmer Rice's exploration into the possibilities of romance between an American heiress and a Soviet commissar. Russell Collins returned to the Play House stage the following season to re-create the title role of *Johnny Johnson,* an antiwar musical by Paul Green and Kurt Weill he had originally done with the Group Theatre. Only seven of Weill's songs were used by the Play House in this early venture into musical theater. The result was called "a superb blending of propaganda and entertainment" by Charles Schneider in the *Cleveland Press.* Arthur Spaeth in the *News* judged it "a pleasant change from the conventional fare—something the Play House should offer more often."

It could be said that the Play House belatedly discovered American drama in the 1930s. Shaw was relatively ignored, as native dramatists such as Paul Green, John Van Druten, Sidney Howard, Robert E. Sherwood, Lillian Hellman, and Thornton Wilder broke into the Play House repertoire. Although O'Neill failed to make an appearance during the decade, Elmer Rice was represented by no fewer than five different works.

There were some significant world premieres, including Rice's *Not for Children* in 1936. W. Ward Marsh found some of it "vastly amusing" but a lot of it "sheer twaddle" in the *Plain Dealer.* A play entitled *A Very Great Man* had been given its premiere at the Play House in 1932. John Houseman was its coauthor, but his reputation ultimately would be made as a producer, director, and finally, actor. In 1943 the Play House premiered another collaboration, *You Touched Me,* by Donald Windham and a fledgling playwright named Tennessee Williams. "It is so good you keep wishing it might be better," said William McDermott in the *Plain Dealer.* Williams would fulfill that wish in more mature works.

Despite the general hard times, the Play House managed to broaden its community profile during the 1930s. The Children's Theater was formed in 1933 under the guidance of Play House actress Esther Mullin. Known later as the Curtain Pullers, it would give such youngsters as Paul Newman, Joel (Katz) Grey, and Joan Diener their first whiffs of greasepaint. Theatrical training at a more advanced level was provided by the Play House in connection with Western Reserve University's School of the Theater. Members of the Play House staff taught college courses for credit while graduate students earned credits toward masters' degrees through training at the Play House. Another outreach activity of the Play House involved the formation of a traveling troupe to lend dramatic support for Cleveland's annual Community Fund campaigns.

Community support for such activities probably helped the Play House withstand a sustained challenge by organized labor in the 1930s, at a time when public sympathy generally leaned in the opposite direction. The Theatrical Stage Employees Union rather than Actors Equity made the most concerted effort to organize the Play House during the decade. Just prior to the opening of the 1937–38 season, a bomb went off in the Play House ballet room. Sporadic picketing and stench bombings also marked the following two seasons. Such tactics, as well as the Play House's nonprofit status, served mainly to solidify newspaper and public support behind the theater. Perhaps C. M. Streator, the protestor against *Red Rust,* wasn't far from the truth when he wrote, "I believe I have the distinction of being the only person in Cleveland who doesn't think [the Play House] is one of the noblest works of God."

Such veneration was becoming increasingly common outside of Cleveland by the end of the decade. Completing a first-hand examination of the state of the American theater beyond Broadway in 1941, author Norris Houghton mentioned the Cleveland Play House along with the Pasadena Playhouse as the country's two outstanding products of the Little Theater movement. Going even further, he believed that the Clevelanders had the right "to command comparison with the Theatre Guild and the Group Theatre in New York, with the Abbey Theatre in Dublin, with perhaps even the Moscow Art Theatre." Houghton did raise a few cavils, including the production by the

Leaders of an American theatrical renaissance beyond Broadway in the 1930s included (clockwise from upper left) Barclay Leathem of Western Reserve University, E. C. Mabie of the State University of Iowa, Frederic McConnell of the Cleveland Play House, and Gilmore Brown of the Pasadena Playhouse. "The Cleveland Play House," wrote author Norris Houghton, "is generally considered the outstanding product, along with the Pasadena Playhouse, of the 'Little Theatre Movement.'" *Cleveland Press Collection*

Play House of relatively few new works, the failure to create a distinctive theatrical style, and the inability to form an artistic partnership with any first-rate dramatists. Nevertheless, Houghton concluded that if any great American theater could be created outside of New York, "Cleveland has had the opportunity to do it."

Houghton found more than the Play House to praise in Cleveland. "The Gilpin Players are the outstanding Negro community theatre in America," he stated in the same survey. Cleveland had known it since 1930, when the Gilpins became the hit of the *Plain Dealer*'s Theater of the Nations festival downtown and received a lengthy front-page review by Roelif Loveland. Later that year, critic William McDermott made his way to the troupe's home theater at Karamu for the first time, despite the stubborn determination of his cab driver to deliver him to a nearby movie theater instead. He noted a largely white audience there of the type that frequented the Play House. Onstage, he saw "a sense of spontaneity, a natural joyousness that is like nothing in the Caucasian theater." A couple of years later he found a Karamu production of *Scarlet Sister Mary* to be "enlightening," especially in comparison with a "fraudulent" Broadway version done by Ethel Barrymore and a white cast in blackface.

When Karamu next captured the attention of the wider community, however, it was for more than purely dramatic reasons. With their production in 1935 of *Stevedore,* a proletarian play by Paul Peters and George Sklar, the Gilpin Players found themselves in the middle of a censorship controversy. Once again, the opposition was spearheaded by Harry Smith's *Cleveland Gazette,* which described the play's language as *"vile*—insulting, derisive, abusive and ROTTEN*."* Smith registered a complaint even before the opening on February 27, which increased the first-night audience by several monitors from the police and law departments. They met the following day with Russell and Rowena Jelliffe in the prosecutor's office. The consensus was that the language was necessary to the play's spirit, and the show could go on.

But Smith was still determined to close it down. With the backing of a committee of local ministers, he prepared to resort directly to the courts. Karamu picked up the support of William McDermott, who observed in a *Plain Dealer* column that the profanity in *Stevedore* seemed to him excessive, but not out of character. If *Stevedore* were to be condemned on those grounds, then such plays as *What Price Glory?, The Front Page,* and *Tobacco Road,* not to mention most of Shakespeare, would have to be similarly condemned. (As the *Plain Dealer* quaintly described it elsewhere, "By actual count, the [*Stevedore*] script contains thirteen references to the deities, two references to the parentage of one of the characters, and two references to the occupation of one of the females.")

In the end, the Jelliffes toughed it out. Russell, a lank, courtly-looking man, kept a car idling outside the theater in case he had to rush downtown to obtain a last-minute counterinjunction. Generally impeccably dressed in pictures, Jelliffe would show up at strike parties after each run in jeans, hammer in hand, to help tear down the sets. Small, frail-looking Rowena, once described by Hazel Mountain Walker as a "cast-iron Dresden doll," would work right alongside him in slacks. She agreed to submit to what was termed a "technical arrest" at one point to test *Stevedore*'s legality. At no point in the play's run of fifteen performances, however, would the Jelliffes agree to the excision of a single word from the script.

With considerably less notice than that caused by the censorship tempest, Karamu embarked the following year on a collaboration that would make theatrical history. Earlier, they had premiered a play by Countee Cullen and Arna Bontemps that eventually would provide the basis of the cult musical, *St. Louis Woman*. Now, a former protégé of the Playhouse Settlement returned to inaugurate an even more memorable partnership. Langston Hughes had already achieved success on Broadway with a play entitled *Mulatto*. From 1936 to 1938, a time known at Karamu as the "Langston Hughes period," he would open five new plays there.

First came *Little Ham* on March 24, 1936, a play about the "numbers" game set in Harlem. It was a large, sprawling work with a cast of forty-three. "As a play, 'Little Ham' doesn't quite follow through," wrote William McDermott. "But as a folk-picture of Harlem life it is rich in character and humor." It was rich in other respects as well, if there is any truth to the story that cast members won considerable sums by actually playing the numbers mentioned in the play.

Weeks later, Karamu premiered *When the Jack Hollers,* a collaboration by Hughes and Arna Bontemps about Negro sharecroppers. It was the least successful of the series. *Troubled Island,* a historical panorama about Haiti during the reign of the self-proclaimed emperor Jean Jacques Dessalines, opened later that year with a cast of sixty-five, not counting dancers. It subsequently became the libretto for an opera by William Grant Still.

Karamu premiered *Joy to My Soul* to favorable reviews on April 1, 1937. A comedy about a romance begun through the mail, it was set in Cleveland in a hotel patterned after the Majestic at East 55th Street and Central Avenue. Featured as two of Hughes's Runyanesque characters were Minnie Gentry and newcomer Nolan Bell. Hughes evidently allowed Karamu considerable latitude in realizing his dramatic vision. When the third act of *Front Porch,* the last play in the series, failed to

Karamu's Gilpin Players were the hit of the first Theater of the Nations season with their production of Nan Bagby Stephens's *Roseanne* in 1930. Sponsored by the *Cleveland Plain Dealer*, the annual dramatic festival showcased the talents of the city's ethnic communities in Public Hall's Little Theater. Besides Karamu, participants also included such groups as the United Polish Players and the Cleveland Italian Dramatic Club. Cleveland Plain Dealer, *February 3, 1930. Reprinted with permission from* The Plain Dealer ©*2000. All rights reserved.*

arrive in time for its scheduled opening in November 1938, Rowena Jelliffe supplied one herself. The playwright was said to have approved.

"I probably would have started a Karamu somewhere if there wasn't one to do my own plays," Hughes later explained in an interview with Karamu historian Reuben Silver. "I wanted to see them. I wanted to see how they looked done live, and I wanted to experience learning from them. As you know, a play on paper is one thing, and a play in the theatre is quite something else. . . . You have no way really of judging until you see a thing come alive through action and direction." Karamu gave him that experience, and Hughes gave Karamu the most fruitful theatrical collaboration in Cleveland's history. "If there aren't any plays get somebody to write them for you," Charles Gilpin had told the players who adopted his name a dozen years earlier. One of the few things Norris Houghton had found lacking in the Cleveland Play House of the 1930s was flourishing a few dozen blocks away at Karamu.

At the end of the decade, however, more than the Langston Hughes period came to an end at Karamu. Late on a Sunday evening in October 1939, Rowena Jelliffe received a telephone call with a heart-stopping message: "Your theater's on fire." She and Russell arrived to see their work in ashes, save only a salvageable pair of the theater's church pews. Arson was suspected but never proven. The Jelliffes and their company didn't waste much effort in pursuing that suspicion; it was time to regroup.

Besides the Gilpin Players, the Theater of the Nations had showcased dramatic and musical groups from many of Cleveland's ethnic communities in the early 1930s. As the sponsor of the series, the *Plain Dealer* had placed at their disposal the Little Theater, a handsome, intimate space seating about five hundred tucked into a corner of the city's huge Public Hall complex. The festival opened in 1930 with a Syrian production of Schiller's *The Robbers,* given in Arabic by members of the Syrian-American Club. Technical assistance was provided by K. Elmo Lowe and Max Eisenstadt of the Cleveland Play House.

In a sense, Theater of the Nations was the "farewell tour" of ethnic theater in Cleveland. As a result of the restrictive immigration policies of the 1920s, the large pool of first-generation immigrants in Cleveland was faced with a slow but steady attrition. With them would die not only their languages but many of their arts and customs as well. During the three seasons of Theater of the Nations, however, they were still vital enough to put on quite an impressive show. Usherettes in native costumes and musical interludes between the acts added to the color and spectacle.

Following the Syrians, Cleveland's Greek Dramatic Players presented *Maria Doxipatri,* a patriotic drama set at the close of the Byzantine period in Greek history. Patriotism was also the theme of *Galuinas the Mighty,* a historical drama offered by the Lithuanian Cultural Gardens League. Described as a mixture of comedy and tragedy, *Malacarne* was the entry of the Cleveland Italian Dramatic Club. *Frock and Russet*

Coats, a dramatization of the generation gap, was presented by the United Polish Players.

Many of the participants lowered the language barrier somewhat by choosing musical works. A musical comedy called *The Village Wedding* was done by the Rusin Dramatic Club. *The Village Beauty* was the title of a musical comedy presented by the General Stefanik Circle of the Slovak League of America. Lumir Hlahol, the Czech singing society, did their national opera, Smetana's *The Bartered Bride,* one year but prepared Offenbach's French operetta, *Orpheus in the Underworld,* for another.

For some groups there was no language barrier. The Gilpin Players followed up their original sensation in *Roseanne* with O'Neill's *The Emperor Jones* and DuBose and Dorothy Heyward's *Porgy. On the Banks of Loch Lomond,* a musical based on the poems of Robert Burns, was sponsored by the city's United Scottish Societies. Invited to prepare an "American" entry for the festival, the Cleveland Heights Civic Theater responded with *Cherokee Night* by Lynn Riggs.

Community theaters such as the Cleveland Heights group continued to thrive in the 1930s. One of the most notable was started in 1930 when the Lakewood Chamber of Commerce decided that their populous western suburb was in need of some live theater. They asked a British-born accountant named Richard Kay to remedy the problem, and Kay responded by organizing the Guild of the Masque. Its first production, Robert E. Sherwood's *The Queen's Husband,* took place in the Lakewood High School auditorium in November 1931. Two years later the group was incorporated as the Lakewood Little Theatre, and in 1938 it acquired a permanent home in the old Lucier movie theater at Detroit and Wayne Avenues. They opened their 466-seat theater there with *Ladies of the Jury.*

At Western Reserve University, Barclay Leathem was nursing his young drama department into one of the country's leading educational theater centers with an emphasis on the training of stage directors. Its 125 students often acted in productions of the Cleveland Play House and obtained directing experience with local amateur companies. The department operated a 2,500-play library for outside groups and annually sponsored an Ohio High School Drama Festival. Student productions at Eldred Theater, directed by Leathem and Edwin Duerr, ranged from Thornton Wilder's farcical *The Merchant of Yonkers* (later reworked as *The Matchmaker* and, still later, *Hello, Dolly!*) to Strindberg's

Born at the beginning of the Depression, the Lakewood Little Theatre managed to gain a solid foothold in its west side suburb during the course of the 1930s. Pictured here is a scene from the second act of their 1939–40 production of Thornton Wilder's *The Merchant of Yonkers. Photograph by R. C. Hakanson; Beck Center for the Arts*

avant-garde *Spook Sonata*. Settings often featured designs by Viktor Schreckengost of the Cleveland School of Art.

One type of theater peculiar to the turbulent 1930s was proletarian, or workers', theater. The outstanding example in Cleveland was led by a returning native who had spent six years with Eva Le Gallienne's Civic Repertory Theatre in New York. Howard da Silva organized the Peoples Theatre in Cleveland during the summer of 1935 with a production of Clifford Odets's *au courant* strike drama, *Waiting for Lefty*. "Ours is a society of want in the midst of plenty, of deep going social conflicts, of men and women struggling to overcome demoralization and crisis," stated a manifesto in the mimeographed program. Da Silva served as both director and actor in what was described as "a cooperative project of playwrights, actors, theatrical technicians and audience."

After a couple of more programs of short, prolabor plays performed on a peripatetic basis, the Peoples Theatre took over a former nightclub at 4300 Carnegie Avenue and converted it into a 150-seat theater. "The People's [*sic*] Theater is not aligned with any political party," announced William McDermott in the *Plain Dealer*. "That is the euphemistic way of saying that it is not Communistic, and its organizers wish you to be clear about that." On its Advisory Board, da Silva listed Le Gallienne, Odets, *New York Times* critic Brooks Atkinson, leftist playwright John Howard Lawson, and K. Elmo Lowe of the Play House. He inaugurated the new space on December 23 with an antiwar comedy by Rudolph Wittenberg, *The Ostriches*. The opening-night curtain was delayed forty minutes while carpenters hammered backstage and fresh paint dried on the walls. When it rose, Glenn Pullen of the *Plain Dealer* reported seeing "the most bewildering as well as provacative [*sic*] play this reviewer has ever sat through."

In the first months of 1936, the Peoples Theatre presented at least two sets of one-act plays. Included in the bills were Lady Gregory's *Rising of the Moon*, Odets's *I Can't Sleep*, and Paul Green's *Hymn to the Rising Sun*. Da Silva, who was also acting at the Cleveland Play House that season, appeared in the Odets monologue. Soon he returned to New York to join the Federal Theatre there. What remained of the Peoples Theatre endured at least till November, when they did *Class of '29*, a social indictment previously done by the Federal Theatre in New York.

By that time, the Federal Theatre Project was also operating in Cleveland. There were four arts programs under the New Deal's Works Progress Administration whose goals were to put unemployed artists back to work on projects for which they had been trained: writing, painting, music making, and acting. Two Federal Theatre units were originally organized in Cleveland: a main Repertory Unit at the Carter Theater (formerly the Miles vaudeville house) on East 9th Street, and an African American unit known as the Community Laboratory Theatre based at Karamu.

It was the Karamu unit that opened first with the production of an original work, *The Big Top*, on January 25, 1936. Coexisting at Karamu with the Gilpin Players, the Community Lab members evidently shared some of the personnel and resources of the more established group. Although Federal Theatre was segregated nationally, Cleveland's Community Lab unit emulated the integrationist policies of its Karamu sponsor. Most of its productions were directed by William Johnson, a leading actor from the Gilpin Players. Subsequent Community Lab efforts included the sharecropper drama *United We Eat*, John Brownell's *Brain Sweat*, Paul Green's *End of the Road*, and Rudolph Fisher's *The Conjur' Woman Dies*.

Things did not go quite so smoothly for the main Repertory Unit. For one thing, the entire Federal Theatre concept failed to win the support of William McDermott, who thought the funds might be more efficiently spent by simply giving it to proven institutions such as the Cleveland Play House to hire more actors. Only *unemployed* actors were eligible for Federal Theatre rolls, however. In charge of hiring personnel in Cleveland was K. Elmo Lowe of the Play House, working under Frederic McConnell, who had been appointed a regional director of the Federal Theatre Project by its national director, Hallie Flanagan.

Lowe assembled a company for the Repertory Unit comprised, for the most part, of elderly players whose credits included appearances with such stars of the past as Marie Dressler and the Castles. One claimed to have been Cleveland's first booking agent; another was a veteran of the Ohio Theatre's first stock company. By March 16 the unit had managed to put together its first production, a local version of an original Federal Theatre genre known as the "Living Newspaper." It included dramatizations of national and local news events such as an investigation into the Cuyahoga County Relief Administration, which was enacted so realistically that a couple of latecomers beat a hasty retreat in the belief that they had stumbled by mistake into a political meeting.

Though this initial effort was favorably received, Lowe and McConnell evidently submitted their resignations soon afterward. Lowe in particular had expressed his frustration in trying to reconcile the social aims of the federal program with his own theatrical standards. Through the summer of 1936, in the face of such local competition as the Republican National Convention and the Great Lakes Exposition, the Cleveland Repertory Unit carried on at the Carter. Their offerings included Emmet Lavery's *The First Legion,* Bayard Veiller's *The Trial of Mary Dugan,* and Karel Capek's expressionistic *R.U.R. Mary Dugan* featured an entr'acte piece of business in which an actor dressed as a workman came out on the exposed courtroom set and proceeded to eat his lunch in pantomime. Most of the audience remained in their seats to watch as he suddenly stopped munching on his sandwich to extract a large nail from his mouth.

The climax of the Repertory Unit's brief history came with its participation in the legendary national premiere of *It Can't Happen Here.* Federal Theatre units in eighteen cities were involved in the experiment of presenting a simultaneous live opening of the dramatization of Sinclair Lewis's recent novel, which imagined a fascist take-

over of the United States. Theodore Viehman directed the local version, which shifted the locale from Vermont to central Ohio and injected allusions to Akron and Cleveland.

A full house and music by the Federal Music Project Marching Band were on hand for the local premiere on October 27, 1936. For once even William McDermott was impressed. "Sometimes it moves slowly, but it moves," he wrote in the *Plain Dealer*. "On the whole it is a satisfactory projection of a propaganda play that is worth doing." It played for three weeks at the Carter and might have run longer if not for some internal bookkeeping problems.

Soon the Cleveland theater project was faced with more than bookkeeping problems, as a cutback in funding on the national level threatened the continuance of both local units. In the end, a single new children's theater was formed largely from members of the discontinued Repertory Unit. Known as the Cleveland Federal Theatre for Youth,

Home-grown fascists arrive to confiscate the radio of a small-town newspaper editor in the Federal Theatre production of Sinclair Lewis and John Moffitt's *It Can't Happen Here*. Phil Miller (seated,) starred as Doremus Jessup in the Cleveland version, which opened simultaneously with Federal Theatre productions in seventeen other cities on October 27, 1936. *Federal Theatre Project Photograph Collection, Special Collections and Archives, George Mason University Libraries*

Enacted by adults for audiences primarily of children, the Cleveland Federal Theatre for Youth brought such plays as *The Emperor's New Clothes* and *Pinocchio* to area schools and playgrounds. Members are shown setting the stage for an outdoor performance in one of Cleveland's parks. *Cleveland Press Collection*

it was organized under the direction of Elbert Sargent, who had lost his position as a Shaker Heights drama instructor because of the Depression. Impressed by Sargent's commitment to the idea of children's theater, Hallie Flanagan hoped he might be the instrument to salvage what was left of the national project in Cleveland.

Sargent proved to be an inspired leader who soon turned the Cleveland Federal Theatre for Youth into one of the best units in the program. Like all children's units of the Federal Theatre, it was a theater enacted by adults for young audiences. They opened with Charlotte Chorpenning's *The Emperor's New Clothes* at Thomas Jefferson Junior High in May 1937. Eventually, they gave it a total of 195 performances in schools and settlement houses during the winter and at parks and playgrounds in the summer. Sets were often double-faced to facilitate ease in transportation and scene changes. Other popular pieces added to the repertoire were Isabel Anderson's *Sir Frog Goes A-Travelin'* and Sargent's own adaptation of Dickens's *A Christmas Carol*. When the Federal Theatre was terminated by Congress in June 1939, the Cleveland unit was

playing *Pinocchio*. The local project had proven so popular that a few of its members managed to keep it alive on community resources for a couple of more years as the Cleveland Theatre for Youth.

One of the last of the Federal Theatre for Youth productions, A. A. Milne's *The Ivory Door,* had helped open a new outdoor theater in 1938 at Cain Park in Cleveland Heights. It was an appropriate combination, since most of the masonry work in the handsome three-thousand-seat amphitheater had been provided by WPA bricklayers. What made Cain Park unique as a theater was its operation by the city itself rather than a commercial lessee. Under the direction of Dr. Dina Rees Evans, a drama instructor at Heights High, Cain Park presented summer seasons of plays and operettas. For a production of *High Tor,* its eighty-foot stage could accommodate a prop that even the play's world premiere at the Hanna had lacked: a *real* steam shovel. Other highlights of the early years were the George Kaufman and Moss Hart pageant *The American Way* and the Maxwell Anderson and Kurt Weill musical *Knickerbocker Holiday.*

It was a somewhat pedestrian theatrical weekend on December 7, 1941, when Clevelanders received news of the Japanese attack on Pearl

A wooded ravine in Cleveland Heights was the setting for the outdoor amphitheater of Cain Park. Ambitious sets like that for this early production were easily accommodated by its eighty-foot stage. *Photograph by Berni Rich; Cleveland Press Collection*

Harbor. The Hanna was dark that Sunday, which fell between the closing of *Claudia* the previous evening and the Monday opening of dancers Velez and Yolanda. At the Palace, Jan Savitt and his Top-Hatters headed the stage show, while Humphrey Bogart in *The Maltese Falcon* filled the screen. *Ladies in Retirement* and *Out of the Frying Pan* were beginning their last week on the two stages of the Cleveland Play House. On lower Euclid Avenue near Public Square, a new movie house called the Telenews specialized in newsreels of a world at war. Over the next few years, business would be good.

One of the first casualties on the home front in World War II happened in Playhouse Square. Herman Pirchner had opened his Alpine Village nightclub on Euclid Avenue across from the Palace Theatre, where the featured attraction on Pearl Harbor weekend was a streamlined version of Gilbert and Sullivan's *The Mikado.* By Tuesday, Pirchner had yanked the show in favor of something a little less provocative to patriotic sensibilities. Another, more serious casualty occurred at the homeless Karamu, where plans for a 1941–42 season were cancelled.

The entire company at the Cleveland Play House took a rehearsal break on December 8 to listen to President Franklin Roosevelt's war message to Congress over the radio. Wartime inflation would adversely affect the Play House budget, cutting into attendance and bringing the first deficits since the Depression years. The draft would deplete the male portion of the staff, as K. Elmo Lowe and others were called to active duty with the armed services. Those left behind also managed to do their bits for the war effort, from special midnight performances for war workers on the night shift to appearances at army bases and veterans' hospitals.

As in the Depression, Frederic McConnell made an effort to lighten up the repertoire with such fare as *Arsenic and Old Lace* (which broke all previous attendance records), *Junior Miss,* and *My Sister Eileen.* War issues did manage to put in an appearance through such works as Robert E. Sherwood's *There Shall Be No Night* and Leslie Storm's *The Heart of the City.* Probably the most memorable war-related production was that of *The Eve of St. Mark.* In a nationwide experiment, Maxwell Anderson released his play about a group of young American soldiers for simultaneous production by community theaters as well as a Broadway company. The Cleveland Play House performance of October 7, 1942, was the first in the nation along with the New York opening of the same date. William McDermott found it to be "genuinely moving" in its depiction of the readiness of citizen-soldiers to die for "what they vaguely understand but what they feel to be higher and nobler than themselves." Play House veteran Tom Ireland, already slated to enter the service, got to play an army sergeant before he left.

On Playhouse Square, World War II seemed to spark something of a revival. A Stage Door Canteen was opened near the Allen Theatre for servicemen stationed or on leave in Cleveland. Another welcome addition was the reopening after several dark years of the Ohio Theatre, even if only as a movie house. It relit its marquee in September 1943 with a showing of *For Whom the Bell Tolls.*

Even the Hanna seemed to share in the wartime revival. It had actually begun to rebound in the last years of the 1930s with such touring productions as *You Can't Take It with You, Tobacco Road, Our Town,* and *Abe Lincoln in Illinois.* Shortly before Pearl Harbor, Carl Hanna hired a young manager from Chicago named Milton Krantz. Kept out of the service by an attack of phlebitis, Krantz remained at the Hanna for the duration and more—forty-two years in all.

Krantz's first objective was to eliminate three-night stands at the Hanna. "If we continue to split this week with Columbus," he told Carl Hanna, "we're not a first-class city. We've got to take a chance and gamble." One of his first gambles, *Hold on to Your Hats* with Al Jolson, proved less than a good one. "You son of a bitch, three nights is all this town's good for," the singer told the manager in his dressing room. "That's not the trouble, Al," Krantz recalled replying. "You left legitimate theater fourteen years ago. Nobody remembers who you are anymore." Krantz's next show was *Life with Father,* which enjoyed the first two-week run at the Hanna in five years. Within another year, three-night stands at the Hanna were history.

For Irving Berlin's all-soldier revue *This Is the Army* in 1942, Krantz even rented Cleveland's Music Hall to double his seating capacity. Former Clevelander Russell Collins came to the Hanna in 1943 with the anti-Nazi drama *Tomorrow the World.* Dressing rooms must have been at a premium at the Hanna for Katharine Cornell's production of Chekhov's *The Three Sisters* that same year. In her supporting cast were Judith Anderson, Edmund Gwenn, Ruth Gordon, Dennis King, and Alexander Knox. The following year saw Paul Robeson in *Othello.*

And then there was *Oklahoma!*—the smash musical hit by Richard Rodgers and Oscar Hammerstein II. Early in its tour, the National Company stopped in November 1943 for a week at the Hanna on its way to Chicago. Not even the theater-savvy Krantz was prepared for the response to his ad in the Sunday *Plain Dealer*. "I came to the theater at 9:30 and saw ten sacks of mail in the lobby," he recalled. With only 12,000 seats to sell, he had requests for 120,000. To eliminate any suspicions of favoritism, he called in reporters from all the papers to witness his ticket-handling procedure. The postage required to return checks for unfilled orders took a considerable bite out of his profits.

None of the lucky 12,000 who attended asked for their money back. To W. Ward Marsh in the *Plain Dealer, Oklahoma!* was entitled to take a place "with the top musical play of the past generation, 'Show Boat.'" His eyes were especially taken with the choreography of Agnes de Mille for "such effective ways of furthering the story with the dance; it is exquisitely imaginative and a sensuous feast." Omar Ranney declined to get so technical in his rave review for the *Cleveland Press.* "The fact is, 'Oklahoma!' makes you feel good," he stated simply. "Naturally, then, people are going to stampede to see it be wartimes or peacetimes. Whoever didn't want to feel on top of the world?" Not quite so impressed was the new drama critic for the *Cleveland News,* Peter Bellamy. While he thought it "a fine and memorable musical comedy," he did not think *Oklahoma!* belonged in the same class as *Show Boat* and *Lady in the Dark.* He even found the ballet "draggy and monotonous."

Bellamy would have plenty of opportunities to get used to it, though, for *Oklahoma!* was the musical wave of the future. The hundred thousand Clevelanders turned away from the Hanna that week would get several more cracks at seeing the production on return trips. It would be followed by many more shows cut from the same cloth. To paraphrase its opening number, *Oklahoma!* held forth the promise of a beautiful day for the American musical.

The Cleveland Roots of the New Globe

A working replica of William Shakespeare's Globe Theatre has been in operation since 1996 on the south bank of the River Thames in London, England. With a little stretch of the imagination, one might say that the foundations were laid sixty years earlier on the southern shore of Lake Erie in Cleveland, Ohio.

It was the summer of 1936, the year of Cleveland's Great Lakes Exposition. Along the lakefront from the old Municipal Stadium to what is now Burke Lakefront Airport, the city had put together 135 acres of exhibits and entertainment for the delectation of nearly four million visitors.

One of the first attractions to greet the visitor, as he entered the midway area of the exposition from East 9th Street, was the Old Globe Theatre. Billed as "a reproduction of Shakespeare's own playhouse, built in 1600," it had been painstakingly reconstructed for the daily presentation of "the Bard's famous plays."

Since other midway attractions were bidding for the art lover's dollar, from Graham's Midgets to the Little French Nudist Colony, the

Streamlined versions of Shakespeare were performed in the Old Globe Theatre at Cleveland's Great Lakes Exposition in 1936. Here the cast of *The Comedy of Errors* winds up a convoluted plot after a whirlwind thirty-six-minute presentation. Members of the company included future stars David Wayne, Sam Wanamaker, and Arthur Kennedy. Wanamaker later led an ultimately successful campaign to resurrect a similar Shakespearean theater on its original site in London. *Cleveland Press Collection* director of the Old Globe wisely elected to edit the Immortal Bard's works down to "tabloid" versions of less than an hour apiece. Thomas Wood Stevens had first developed this concept during the second season of Chicago's Century of Progress in 1934.

Among the company of thirty players assembled for the Cleveland version was Sam Wanamaker, who had seen the Chicago Old Globe from the audience and came away with a sense of wonder at its "avoidance of the hushed quality you had to have when you went to the theater." Wayne McKeekan was a Michigan native but had been living in Cleveland three years, working for the Sherwin Williams paint firm by day and studying drama by night at Western Reserve University. John Kennedy had come from Massachusetts by way of Pittsburgh's Carnegie Tech.

They probably never worked harder than during that expo summer. The plays may have been cut to under an hour each, but they put on at least six performances a day and up to eight on holidays. There was a repertoire of six miniplays: *Julius Caesar, The Taming of the Shrew, The Comedy of Errors, As You Like It, A Midsummer Night's Dream,* and *King Henry VIII.* Most of the players appeared in as many as five of the offerings for $15 a week.

As described by critic W. Ward Marsh of the *Cleveland Plain Dealer,* the pared-down plays "retain the meat of the original if at times omitting the dessert of well turned phrases and longer dissertations which may not be dramatically constructive." He clocked *As You Like It* at forty-two minutes and *The Comedy of Errors* at a mind-blurring thirty-six minutes. At times, expo-goers seemed unable to spare even so fleeting a time for the Bard. Kennedy remembered one audience of a barely plural two, though he said attendance later picked up to full houses of more than six hundred.

One unplanned touch, which may have provided a fair approximation of the atmosphere of Shakespeare's London, came from the proximity of a submarine exhibit berthed a few yards away from the Globe. According to Kennedy, the sub blocked off a sewage outlet to the lake, exposing the Globe, when the wind was right, to a stench totally unconnected with the quality of the performance.

Though the Great Lakes Exposition returned for a second season in 1937, the Shakespearean troupe at the Old Globe was disbanded in favor of a marionette theater. Some of the actors made their way to New York. Finding another John Kennedy already listed with Actors

Equity, the Globe's Kennedy dropped his first name and used his middle name instead. As Arthur Kennedy, he was the original Biff in Arthur Miller's *Death of a Salesman.*

Wayne McKeekan made his theatrical fortune under the marquee-friendly name of David Wayne. Among the roles he created on Broadway were Og the leprechaun in *Finian's Rainbow* and Ensign Pulver in *Mr. Roberts.* His movie credits included *The Tender Trap.*

Of all the Old Globe thespians, Sam Wanamaker was the most permanently smitten by his Shakespearean experience. Early in his career he relocated to England as a director as well as actor. Naturally, he soon made his way to the Southwark District of London, where he was crestfallen to find nothing more than a bronze plaque on a brewery wall to mark the location of Shakespeare's "wooden O."

Wanamaker soon had visions of placing far more than a plaque on the Bankside site. By 1970 he headed a Globe Playhouse Trust with the intent of rebuilding Shakespeare's theater for the production of his plays and those of his contemporaries. In explaining his obsession, he always harked back to that summer of 1936 at the Old Globe in Cleveland.

By the time of Wanamaker's death in 1993, the new Globe was halfway built. It opened for a short preview season in 1996 and was in full operation by June 1997. In this latest and most reverential reincarnation of his own theater, it is unlikely that Shakespeare will ever be trimmed down to tabloid size.

$\mathcal{E}$ight
NEW DIRECTIONS

AT 7:00 P.M. ON the warm evening of August 14, 1945, Clevelanders learned over the radio that Japan had surrendered unconditionally, thus bringing World War II to a close. Although V-J ("Victory over Japan") Day would not officially be proclaimed until later, Cleveland wasn't in a mood to wait upon formalities. Within an hour there were enough people downtown to stop traffic on Euclid Avenue. From Public Square to Playhouse Square, it was soon shoulder-to-shoulder people. Fred MacMurray was playing in *Captain Eddie* (Rickenbacker) on the screen at the Allen, but there was a better show out on the street. Though bars had been closed down early in the evening, artificial stimulants seemingly were not needed. Automobile horns and fire-crackers produced a steady deafening din. An elderly man started firing a shotgun into the air at East 9th Street and St. Clair Avenue. Police managed to grab the gun, but the celebrant slipped away into the crowd. "And any number of pretty young things," observed Roelif Loveland in the *Plain Dealer,* "had had their dignity more or less affronted by fresh young men who had never heard of Emily Post." Not even a sudden summer rainstorm could dampen spirits, as the merrymaking continued to 4:30 A.M.

Downtown was still the focal point of Cleveland's entertainment scene in 1945, even if the old theatrical districts had largely succumbed to change. "The Colonial is now a parking lot, the Metropolitan no longer shelters drama, the old Opera House is a merchandising emporium and the Ohio is a film theater," William McDermott observed sadly in 1949. "These were all once first-class legitimate playhouses." Only the Hanna survived in that capacity on East 14th Street. Yet Euclid Avenue could still boast six first-run movie houses, from the Hippodrome and Stillman to the glittering row of marquees on Playhouse Square—the Allen, Ohio, State, and Palace. The latter still interspersed live stage shows with its films, celebrating its silver anniversary in 1947 with an appearance by Danny Kaye.

Night life of a different nature thrived a block north of Euclid Avenue on a narrow street running from East 6th to East 9th known as Short Vincent. Around the corner on East 9th was the city's last surviving burlesque house, the Roxy, home to baggy-pants comedians, candy pitchmen, and ecdysiasts such as Tempest Storm and Blaze Starr. (It might be considered an educational institution of sorts, since not only did it give many young males their first exposure to live theater, but in addition the income from the property was bequeathed to Oberlin College and Case Western Reserve University.)

From backstage at the Roxy, an alley led to the south side of Vincent, lined with bars and strip joints such as Freddie's Cafe and the French Quarter. Across the street, referred to by locals as the "Gaza strip," were somewhat classier establishments including the Theatrical Grill and Kornman's Back Room, host to some of the era's jazz legends. The apogee of Short Vincent was reached in the postwar decade, when a group of bons vivants known as the Jolly Set made it their stamping ground under the suzerainty of Winsor French, society columnist of the Cleveland Press.

Few would have imagined in 1945 that forces were in place that would nearly wipe out most of the nation's downtowns within a quarter-century. Cleveland emerged from the war with an aging housing stock that had not been upgraded since the onset of the Depression in the early 1930s. With the help of the GI Bill, however, many young families would opt for new homes in the suburbs over fixing up inner-city neighborhoods. A postwar freeway program would further facilitate the outward migration.

Another portent of change might be glimpsed in a ghostly blue light emanating from the doorways of neighborhood bars in the Cleveland Indian summer of 1948. Television had made its long-awaited debut in

Cleveland. Within two years there were three local stations, and receivers had spread from bars into thousands of middle-class homes. The new medium was viewed as more of a threat to movies than to live theater. Television would supercede movies as the mass entertainment of the future, just as movies had previously wrested that distinction from live theater. Many critics, in fact, believed that "legitimate" theater had gained as much as it lost due to the competition of movies, being left with a smaller but more discriminating audience. Eventually the market for vaudeville and melodrama had been completely absorbed by the newer media, but the audience that remained was ready for the drama of O'Neill and his successors.

Under Milton Krantz, the Hanna Theatre was well equipped to serve that presumably enlightened minority in Cleveland. For the opening of the 1947–48 season, Krantz and theater owner Carl Hanna unveiled a $150,000 renovation topped with a new modern marquee on East 14th Street. Much of the money went into improved lighting and ventilation systems. There was also an expanded orchestra pit to accommodate the big new musicals beginning to make the rounds.

Postwar seasons at the Hanna were keeping the marquee lit for about half the year. Krantz kept the seats filled by linking up with the Theatre Guild subscription series. His subscription lists often led the country, accounting for more than nine thousand seats out of a weekly capacity of twelve thousand. On the strength of this showing, Cleveland was earning a reputation as one of the best theater towns in the nation. Krantz emphasized personalized service, memorizing where subscribers sat and greeting them by name in his tuxedo on opening nights.

He was a born showman. Early in his tenure, when an actress wanted to autograph the gray-duck backing of his stage curtain, Krantz viewed it not as an act of defacement but as a potential theatrical tradition. Soon all of the visiting stars were adding their names: Henry Fonda, Helen Hayes, Tallulah Bankhead, Lunt and Fontanne, Hume Cronyn and Jessica Tandy. . . . Entire casts began to sign and affix their show posters and logos. Although the Smithsonian Institution once expressed its interest, the curtain eventually wound up at Cleveland State University.

Another bit of Krantz showmanship involved quite a showman in his own right, recent Cleveland Indians owner Bill Veeck. According to one account, it was Winsor French who came up with the notion that Veeck would make a good Sheridan Whiteside in Kaufman and Hart's *The Man Who Came to Dinner*. Krantz fielded the ball flawlessly,

Carl Hanna (left) and Milton Krantz inspect their Hanna Theatre after an extensive renovation. A son of the theater's builder, Carl Hanna managed the extensive Hanna real estate interests. He hired Krantz to direct the theater in 1942, launching a forty-two-year tenure that made Krantz the dean of American theatrical managers. *Cleveland Press Collection*

assembling a supporting cast and getting the script doctored with local baseball references. Critics were impressed by Veeck's mastery of his lines but agreed that he was too nice to be Sheridan Whiteside, another character based on the acerbic persona of Alexander Woollcott. (Veeck's main qualification for the role was that, having lost a leg due to a war wound, he was a natural in the wheelchair required by the plot.) As

Continuing a tradition initiated in the
1940s, the cast of *Godspell* in 1973 added
its signed poster to the backing of the
"Hanna Curtain." Once coveted by the
Smithsonian Institution, the priceless
relic of stage history is now in the
possession of the theater program at
Cleveland State University. *Photograph by
Bernie Noble; Cleveland Press Collection*

Omar Ranney saw it in the *Cleveland Press,* Veeck took a good swing
but "knocked only a slow roller to the infield." What little praise there
was went to John Price Jr. and pianist Roger Stearns as characters
based on Harpo Marx and Noel Coward, respectively. As for Veeck,
Ranney concluded, "I think he should rush, with all possible haste,
whatever baseball deal he has cooking."

On a more elevated plane, the Hanna also introduced Cleveland to
most of the great postwar American classics. Tennessee Williams was
represented by *The Glass Menagerie* and *A Streetcar Named Desire.* Of

the former William McDermott wrote in the *Plain Dealer*, "It is a rare play, a strange play and a distinguished play." When *Streetcar* arrived two years later, however, Omar Ranney of the *Press* thought that the playwright's "preoccupation . . . with man's baser impulses is beginning to wear." McDermott agreed to a certain extent, observing that "some of the shocks introduced into the play are superfluous and without validity in respect to the play as a work of theatrical craftsmanship, though I suspect they have not been unhelpful at the box office." Nonetheless, on the basis of the two works together, McDermott was ready to extol Williams as "the best new playwright America has produced since Eugene O'Neill."

Williams's principal rival, Arthur Miller, received his first Cleveland exposure at the Hanna in 1948 with *All My Sons*. Omar Ranney thought that the story of a war profiteer, with its reference to the penitentiary in Columbus, might well have been set in Cleveland. *Death of a Salesman* followed two years later. "It has the qualities of great tragedy," observed William McDermott. "It arouses pity and it moves the heart." A third young playwright, William Inge, tried out his *Picnic* at the Hanna on its way to Broadway. "Paul Newman is good as the rich but honest young man," noted W. Ward Marsh in the *Plain Dealer* of the Cleveland native.

At the other end of Euclid Avenue, the Cleveland Play House was riding the crest of its reputation as the nation's foremost resident theater. Its first postwar season saw the achievement of two new records: a total of 144,000 playgoers for the year and a run of fifty-one performances for Paul Osborn's *Morning's at Seven*.

In a sense, the Play House became a victim of its own success, as Omar Ranney in a thoughtful piece for the *Cleveland Press* accused it of being "too commercial." While admitting that attendance was a valid criterion for theatrical success, Ranney wondered whether the Play House had its eye fixed so steadily on the box office that it was in danger of forgetting its original nonprofit objectives. In particular, he believed it was falling short of its obligation to develop new talent and try out new plays. "One of the dangers in a resident theater such as this is that its acting company is apt to become a click [*sic*], and I think that is exactly the situation which Director Frederic McConnell now faces," commented Ranney.

Whether or not he regarded cliquishness as a real problem, McConnell was ready to address what he considered to be his company's greatest

A rehearsal for a 1960 production of Sophocles's *Electra* demonstrates the immediacy of the apron stage in the Euclid–77th Street Theatre of the Cleveland Play House. Revolutionary for its time, the theater was opened in a converted church building in 1949. The production above was staged by Frederic McConnell with a setting by Paul Rodgers. *Cleveland Play House*

shortcoming by launching a third stage. He had been dreaming of a new theater since 1937, hoping to situate it in a new building across East 86th Street from the Drury-Brooks complex. When economic realities precluded that plan, McConnell borrowed a page from Play House history by building his new theater in an abandoned church. In this instance, it was a former Christian Science structure on Euclid Avenue at East 77th Street, a domed edifice resembling a miniature Hagia Sophia sans minarets.

But most eyes were focused on the interior of the building, where McConnell had virtually eliminated any proscenium arch and installed a modified thrust stage. "I never saw a theater in which the sight lines were clearer," wrote William McDermott. "The stage is semicircular, and the audience is bestowed around three sides of the stage. It is altogether different from the ordinary picture-frame theater. It brings audiences into closer contact with the players and will form a wonderful background for certain types of plays, such as those of Shakespeare."

Shakespeare is precisely what McConnell chose to break in his new stage, with a performance on October 15, 1949, of *Romeo and Juliet.* Reviewing it for *The New York Times,* Brooks Atkinson observed ironically, "New York is not rich or progressive enough to afford an established drama organization like the Cleveland Play House and a new theater designed on such progressive principles as the one just opened here on Euclid Avenue." It has been called the first open-stage theater in America, anticipating Tyrone Guthrie's apron stage at Stratford by nearly a decade. McConnell and company put it to good use, presenting at least one Shakespearean work there annually for the next eighteen years.

The modern drama was hardly neglected on Play House stages, either. World War II was little more than a year past when the Play House offered the world premiere of a drama about the U.S. Bomber Command in Europe. Entitled simply *Command,* it was written by Air Force veteran William Wister Haines and opened in the Drury on November 27, 1946. Dramatic conflict was provided in the choice faced by the main character, an Air Force general, between sending bombers beyond fighter protection to bomb German factories or letting the factories survive to produce weapons that will later kill even more Americans. As described by William McDermott, dramatic tension was present in "those agonizingly anxious moments when the planes are returning from their missions and all eyes on the field are turned to the sky counting the incoming bombers to see how many that started did not come back and how many of their friends have died that day." The play went on to Broadway and later achieved wider exposure as the film *Command Decision* with Clark Gable.

A dozen years after *Command,* the Play House gave German playwright Bertolt Brecht's *Mother Courage* its American premiere. Benno Frank, a personal acquaintance of Brecht, was borrowed from Karamu to direct the production in the highly regarded translation by Eric Bentley. "Frank boldly breaks half the conventional theatrical rules in staging the sometimes ponderous, episodic drama with startling vividness," wrote Glenn Pullen in the *Plain Dealer.*

By 1955 the Play House in many respects had achieved parity with the commercial Hanna Theatre as Cleveland's principal showcase for drama. Omar Ranney that year noted that of eighty-two professional and semiprofessional productions seen in Cleveland the previous season, the Play House had mounted nineteen to only sixteen touring shows at the Hanna. As fewer and fewer touring companies were coming out of New York, it fell to the Play House by default to introduce significant new plays to Cleveland. Thornton Wilder's *The Skin of Our Teeth* received its local premiere there in 1945. The Play House also gave Cleveland its first look at Arthur Miller's *The Crucible* (1954) and *A View From the Bridge* (1957). When Tyrone Guthrie was seeking a location in which to establish a classical repertory theater, the Play House declined his overtures. Had it accepted, Cleveland might have gained a stunning classical theater at the expense of losing what was becoming its chief forum for new American drama.

One proposal the Play House did accept in 1957 was a Ford Foundation grant of $130,000 to assemble a touring company in classical repertory. Under the terms of the award, the first ever made by that foundation to a theater, a company of fifteen actors chosen through national competition would come to Cleveland for training at the Play House. After two years, they took four classical plays on a thirty-eight-week tour of Midwestern states, bringing live theater back to smaller cities in the television age. As one of the conditions set by Ford, the Play House ended its long holdout against unionization and became an Actors Equity house in 1958. Even after the expiration of the grant, the Play House continued to support the touring company for several years through its own resources.

It was at the end of the 1957–58 season that Frederic McConnell stepped down after nearly four decades as director of the Play House. He had taken an amateur little theater and built it into America's most acclaimed resident professional company. From a former church accommodating no more than two hundred, the Cleveland Play House had grown into a complex of three theaters seating more than one thousand people. After a few more years in Cleveland as consultant and guest director, McConnell left to spend the remainder of his retirement in California. He left the Play House in the hands of his longtime associate K. Elmo Lowe.

Lowe was the last of "the Triumvirate," Max Eisenstadt having died several years earlier. His hair may have silvered but his hairline had not retreated a millimeter. Lines had merely added character to his good looks. He had appeared in some three hundred productions at the Play

House, many of them with his wife, Dorothy Paxton. As a director, he had helped develop the talents of such players as Margaret Hamilton, Jack Weston, Ray Walston, Thomas Gomez, and Alan Alda.

Only nine years younger than his predecessor, Lowe was not about to deviate radically from the course laid out by McConnell. O'Neill's *A Touch of the Poet* entered the repertoire in 1961 and Brecht's *Galileo* in 1964. As part of the fiftieth anniversary season, Play House alumni Russell Collins and Margaret Hamilton returned in a revival of Molière's *Tartuffe*. Though Lowe personally hated the increasing incursion of profanity in the theater, the Play House presented Edward Albee's *Who's Afraid of Virginia Woolf?* in that same season with a precautionary audience advisory on language.

Probably the most noteworthy production of Lowe's directorate came near the end, when the Play House premiered Donald Freed's *The United States vs. Julius and Ethel Rosenberg* in March 1969. With a text drawn entirely from historical sources, the docudrama vividly retold the story of the trial and execution of the two accused spies with the aid of film, slides, and even audience participation. Critics hailed it as a tour de force despite its pro-Rosenberg bias. Reviewing it for *The New York Times,* Julius Novick observed: "It is significant enough that a non-political theater, in a midwestern city, has been willing to produce a play that sides openly with two people convicted of spying for the Soviet Union. What is amazing is that the production has created no controversy whatsoever: no indignant letters to the theater or press, no threats, no pickets. In fact, both Cleveland newspapers ran editorials congratulating the Play House on its initiative."

While K. Elmo Lowe retired at the end of that season, William Greene, his successor, got the following season off to an auspicious start with another significant world premiere. Though burdened with an even longer title than the Rosenberg play, Paul Zindel's *The Effect of Gamma Rays on Man-in-the-Moon Marigolds* was an intimate domestic drama mounted in the small Brooks Theatre. Evie McElroy was singled out for praise as the slatternly mother. Compared not unfavorably with *The Glass Menagerie, Marigolds* moved on to a long off-Broadway run and the Pulitzer Prize for drama in 1971.

Cleveland's other nationally known theater made its long-awaited return after World War II, when Karamu formally opened a new theater complex at the end of 1949. Ten trying years had passed since the conflagration at the old theater on Central Avenue. The homeless Gilpin Players

Perhaps the most notable premiere in the history of the Cleveland Play House was Paul Zindel's *The Effect of Gamma Rays on Man-in-the-Moon Marigolds*. Members of the original 1969 cast included Jana Gibson (top) as Tillie, Miriam Lapari (right) as Ruth, and Evie McElroy as the mother, Beatrice. The play's subsequent off-Broadway production won the Pulitzer Prize for drama in 1971. *Rebman Photographers; Cleveland Play House*

had put on productions at the Play House and Eldred Theater before the wartime draft called a halt to their dramatic endeavors. As the Jelliffes applied themselves to a fund-raising drive, an appearance by the Karamu Dancers at the 1940 World's Fair and an exhibition by Karamu artists in New York City helped keep the group's name in the public eye. A plug by Eleanor Roosevelt in her "My Day" column didn't hurt, either.

Eventually, more than half a million dollars was raised. At one point, racing against a deadline in order to secure a matching Rockefeller grant, the Jelliffes appealed in desperation to Katharine Cornell. Having needed three hundred dollars to meet their goal, they came away with five hundred dollars. The Jelliffes built the complex piecemeal, putting up a nursery building first. Always in the vanguard of theatrical innovation, they installed a temporary arena stage on the second floor where they produced Karamu's first Shakespearean endeavor, *The Taming of the Shrew.*

Karamu was now adopted as the name of the entire operation being completed on Quincy Avenue at East 89th Street. A proscenium theater seating 223 was dedicated December 6, 1949, with Hazel Mountain Walker appearing in Lenore Coffee and William Cowen's *Family Portrait.* The American premiere of Carl Orff's opera *The Wise Maiden* (*Die Kluge*) broke in a new 140-seat arena theater the following evening. Two nights later, a social worker named Zelma George appeared on the arena stage as Madame Flora in Gian Carlo Menotti's powerful Broadway opera *The Medium.*

"According to the record, Cleveland is one of the most progressive theatre cities in America," wrote Brooks Atkinson of *The New York Times,* who had returned to Cleveland to see the new Karamu several weeks after coming to review the new thrust stage of the Cleveland Play House. "This week Broadway is graciously sending Cleveland a production of 'Blossom Time,'" he continued. "No wonder Cleveland has to build its own theatres." Zelma George bore out his point several months later, when Menotti chose her to head an off-Broadway revival of *The Medium,* and she took the Big Apple by storm. Besides a performance described as "in the grand manner," she also provided New York with an early example of something that was second nature at Karamu: nontraditional casting.

Interracial theater was one of the things that attracted a young couple named Reuben and Dorothy Silver to Karamu in the mid-1950s. "I know we hadn't seen it before we came here," says Reuben of nontraditional casting. "I'd say a case could be made: Karamu was the first to do it as a sustained policy. The policy was casting according to talent, except in cases where race was an issue." Rowena Jelliffe had relinquished her play-directing duties with the construction of the new building. Several directors served short terms before Reuben Silver was hired as staff director for drama. With Dorothy also qualified to guest direct, many must have seen in the Silvers a serendipitous reminder of Karamu founders Russell and Rowena Jelliffe.

Minnie Gentry and Al Fann appeared as Lena and Walter Lee Younger in the 1961 production of *Raisin in the Sun* at Karamu. They were in the vanguard of a distinguished roster of Karamu-trained actors that also included Clayton Corbin, Nolan Bell, Gilbert Moses, and Robert Guillaume. *Reuben Silver and Dorothy Silver; Cleveland Press Collection*

Highlights of the postwar drama program at Karamu included the world premiere of William Branch's *A Wreath for Udomo* and the first production outside New York of Guenter Rutenborn's *The Sign of Jonah*. Perhaps the most memorable moment came with the first community theater performance of Lorraine Hansberry's *A Raisin in the Sun* in February 1961. Silver directed a cast headed by Minnie Gentry and Al Fann in this breakthrough drama of black middle-class life. "Every so often the Karamu Players find a Broadway gem reflecting all of their own idealistic sentiments and vitality," wrote Glenn Pullen in opening his laudatory review in the *Plain Dealer.* Stan Anderson in the *Press* considered Fann's performance as Walter Lee Younger the season's

best. Audiences agreed as *A Raisin in the Sun* ran for forty-three performances and drew an unusually high proportion of blacks to Karamu.

With more good plays being written for them, Karamu was gaining
a reputation as a training ground for African American actors. Clayton
Corbin heard about it as a young military veteran in California and
hopped freight trains to get to Cleveland. Nolan Bell started in Karamu's
Children's Theater and became the first black to join the company of
the Cleveland Play House. Bill Cobbs, Gilbert Moses, Dick Latessa,
Robert Guillaume, and Tom Brennan were also among those who took
their dramatic instruction at Karamu. "We developed and trained actors
I like to think of as the backbone of the business—not stars, but people
you can't do without," says Silver. "There was a period when the only
trained black actors were the ones from Karamu." When a New York
director was assembling a *Porgy and Bess* company to tour Europe and
South America in the 1950s, reported Arthur Spaeth of the *Cleveland
News,* he cast his line at Karamu and filled four important roles.

Karamu and the Play House were the bellwethers of a lively postwar theatrical scene. "The theatre here does not live in a vacuum; it is
rampant," wrote Frederic McConnell in *Theatre Arts* in 1950. Ohio had
more community theaters in the 1950s than anywhere in the world,
recalls Dorothy Silver. According to Arthur Spaeth in 1960, some forty
little theaters, beyond the first tier of the Play House and its peers,
were offering Clevelanders a total of about 120 plays a season.

One of the most ambitious was the Lakewood Little Theatre on
the west side. During the war it had purchased its rented quarters in
the old Lucier movie house, and in 1946 it hired its first paid managing
director, Gordon Klein. It also began acquiring adjacent storefronts
and properties for ancillary activities and parking space. Karl Mackey,
who became director in 1954, gave the group long-term stability.
Though the board rejected his proposal to reorganize the LLT as a
resident professional theater, he continued to direct it as a community
theater for thirty-two years.

An east side counterpart to the Lakewood group was the drama
program of the Jewish Community Center in Cleveland Heights. It
was largely the creation of Russian immigrant Mark Feder, who had
studied at Pittsburgh's Carnegie-Mellon University. He began the
center's program by jobbing in Yiddish stars such as Joseph Buloff and
Lola Kaminska to appear with local supporting casts in a storefront on

With the purchase of its own building, Lakewood Little Theatre solidified its stature as one of Cleveland's leading community theaters. Located in a former movie house on Detroit Avenue, it is seen here as it was in the 1950s. *Photograph by Chuck Humbert; Beck Center for the Arts*

Lee Road. When the community center opened a centralized headquarters on Mayfield Road in 1960, it included the 150-seat Eugene S. and Blanche R. Halle Theatre. It was the first Jewish center to specifically build a theater for its drama program.

There were two theaters of note in the far eastern suburbs. The Chagrin Valley Little Theatre, founded in 1930, opened a new 270-seat theater in Chagrin Falls in 1949. The red brick building on River Street was built at a cost of $45,000. In 1958 the theater gave former Cleveland actor Howard da Silva some relief from the Hollywood blacklist by hiring him to direct a summer season of six plays. In Lake County, the Rabbit Run Theater flourished from the 1940s into the 1960s. A classic summer straw-hat theater, it brought in professionals such as

Dustin Hoffman, Sandy Dennis, Margaret Hamilton, and Jim Backus to act in its converted dairy barn. Hume Cronyn and Jessica Tandy appeared there in a pre-Broadway tryout of *The Fourposter*. In its heyday, the Rabbit Run was enlarged from 190 to 350 seats.

On the western fringes of Cuyahoga County, two summer theaters both began distinguished careers in 1957. On the campus of Baldwin-Wallace College, a drama professor named William Allman began the Berea Summer Theatre. For the first few years he highlighted the work of a single playwright each season, beginning with John Patrick of *The Teahouse of the August Moon* and including William Inge and the northern Ohio team of Jerome Lawrence and Robert E. Lee. Patrick came out personally for that inaugural season and eventually gave Allman several new scripts to premiere in Berea. Casting from both the Baldwin-Wallace student body and the southwest community, Berea Summer Theatre was an incubator for such talent as John-Michael Tebelak, Joseph Garry, and David Frazier. In Bay Village, Holt Brown began the Huntington Playhouse in a 140-year-old barn in Huntington Park. Brown directed the straw-hat theater until 1968, when it passed into the hands of a triumvirate headed by Bud Binns.

A theater destined to become a major player on the Cleveland scene opened in the summer of 1962. It came about when a new auditorium in search of a tenant came across a company in need of a home. The house was the Lakewood Civic Auditorium on Franklin Boulevard in the western suburb. The company was Arthur Lithgow's former Antioch Shakespeare Festival, which flourished at Ohio's Antioch College in the mid-1950s. Over a period of six summer seasons, it had presented all thirty-six of the Bard's plays in an outdoor setting on the Yellow Springs campus. Since then the company had performed in various Ohio venues until beckoned to Lakewood by Dorothy Teare, president of the Lakewood Board of Education.

Rechristened the Great Lakes Shakespeare Festival, they opened on July 11, 1962, with *As You Like It*. Under the direction of Lithgow, the thirty-member professional troupe presented summer seasons of six Shakespearean works in repertory. Typical of the high level of acting was the appearance of Earl Hyman in *Othello*. Attendance was only eighteen thousand for the first season, however, leading to a chronic deficit that was ameliorated by a grant from the Cleveland Foundation to subsidize student matinees. Before Lithgow left in 1965, he had diversified the Shakespearean diet with the work of Richard Sheridan.

Under Lithgow's successor, Lawrence Carra, the company's repertoire continued to expand beyond the Shakespearean canon. Carra was formerly a drama professor at Carnegie-Mellon, where one of his students was John-Michael Tebelak, a young man from Berea, Ohio. Tebelak had been developing for his master's thesis a musical based on the life of Jesus Christ called *Godspell*. Set to a rock score by Stephen Schwartz, it had been workshopped at Cafe La Mama in New York. Its subsequent professional premiere on August 11, 1971, with Tebelak conducting at the Great Lakes Shakespeare Festival, was the highlight of the Carra years. Playing to 29,000 people in eighteen performances, it gave the festival the most profitable season of its first decade.

Carra was succeeded as director in 1976 by the charismatic Irishman, Vincent Dowling. He quickly established his style with a revival of the 1912 comedy *Peg O' My Heart,* which became the hit of the season. More American plays, from O'Neill to Wilder, followed. Under Dowling, the festival captured six out of eight awards from the Cleveland Critics Circle in 1978. Stars came, such as Celeste Holm in *Candida,* and young talent such as Tom Hanks emerged. The company's profile was raised in 1979 with a postseason tour of ten Ohio cities, from Ashtabula to Dayton.

An existing theater whose profile continued to rise was Western Reserve University's Eldred Hall. There, Barclay Leathem was joined by one of his former students, Nadine Miles, who put on an acclaimed series of avant-garde productions. Among them were Jean-Paul Sartre's *The Flies* and the American premiere in 1948–49 of Jean Anouilh's *The Carnival of Thieves,* for which she provided her own translation. Her pupils included Don Bianchi of Dobama, Bill Boehm of the Singing Angels, Gordon Davidson of the Mark Taper Forum, and Ross Hunter of Hollywood. A frequent contributor as set designer for these productions was faculty colleague Henry Kurth. Together, they collaborated with the WRU music department on the local premiere of Virgil Thomson's opera *The Mother of Us All,* which won warm approbation from the composer himself.

Other area colleges joined Western Reserve in the development of dramatic programs. At Baldwin-Wallace in Berea, Prof. Dana Burns and his wife began staging productions on the second floor of Marting Hall. After World War II, they renovated a former Navy barracks on campus for a theater-in-the-round. A theater program also emerged on the far eastern side of town at John Carroll University.

A pioneer in postwar alternative theater in Cleveland was Ed Henry's Experimental Theatre Cleveland company. Most of their challenging productions brought new scripts to the attention of local audiences. They performed in a Baptist church located just off Playhouse Square. *Ed Henry*

Outside academia, there were other notable attempts to provide Cleveland with alternative theater. A little theater and Cleveland Play House veteran named Ed Henry gathered a like-minded group in 1959 to found

Experimental Theatre Cleveland. With the backing of book dealer Peter Keisogloff among others, they found a space in the chapel of Euclid Avenue Baptist Church on the edge of Playhouse Square. The natural wood paneling of the chancel made an excellent backdrop for a production of Ayn Rand's courtroom drama, *The Night of January 16th*. Described by Stan Anderson of the *Press* as a "joining of literate writers with intelligent actors," they were primarily interested in new scripts by Clevelanders and others. From an audience of only three for their initial production, they built a following that eventually filled their hundred-seat house. After five years, however, they failed to outlast the loss of their church in 1964.

Another group formed at that time managed to survive the loss of two homes to achieve longevity in a bowling alley. Don and Marilyn Bianchi, Barry Silverman, and Mark Silverberg contributed the first syllables of their given names to found the Dobama Theatre. Silverman and Silverberg dropped out after the opening production at the Chagrin Valley Little Theatre in 1960. The Bianchis then moved to Quad Hall, a rundown former hotel on Euclid Avenue, where they gave the American premiere of the *Chicken Soup with Barley* trilogy by British playwright Arnold Wesker. Before long they had to leave Quad Hall to make room for a rock-and-roll nightclub called Leo's Casino.

It took the Bianchis four years to turn an old basement bowling alley on Coventry Road in Cleveland Heights into the future home of Dobama. They finally opened in May 1968 with the Cleveland premiere of Lorraine Hansberry's *The Sign in Sidney Brustein's Window*. More than 95 percent of Dobama's productions since then were Cleveland premieres, including many world premieres by Cleveland authors such as Don Robertson and Tom Cullinan. Surrounded by its audience on three sides of a plain acting space, Dobama continued to fulfill its mission of "Responsible productions of superior play scripts that otherwise might not be produced in Cleveland."

Dobama was clearly for the adventurous, but for the average theatergoer in the postwar period this was the golden age of the American musical. Most of the big ones first passed through Cleveland in stunning succession across the stage of the Hanna Theatre. Following *Oklahoma!*'s first visit in 1943 were *Carmen Jones* (1945), *Bloomer Girl* (1946), *Carousel* (1947), a revival of *Show Boat* (1948), *Finian's Rainbow*, and *Brigadoon* (both 1949). In the single season of 1951–52, Hanna patrons were regaled with an embarrassment of musical riches: *Oklahoma!* (seventh visit); *Kiss Me, Kate; Guys and Dolls* (two weeks); *South Pacific* (two weeks); and *Call Me Madam.*

It was the second visit for *South Pacific,* which had launched its national company in Cleveland in April 1950, a year after its Broadway debut. Though Milton Krantz took the precaution of renting the three-thousand-seat Music Hall for the blockbuster show, he still had to return three-quarters of his one million dollars' worth of ticket orders. He claimed to have gained severe headaches and lost twenty pounds in all the turmoil. One consolation was that he had only had to place a single newspaper ad. Richard Rodgers and Oscar Hammerstein II themselves were on hand to break in their touring company. A party was thrown for them afterward in the Hotel Allerton, at which Mayor Thomas A. Burke presented the pair with the keys to the city for "bringing 'South Pacific' to Cleveland first."

Though the composer and lyricist were reported to have "suffered agonizingly" over mechanical lapses during the performance, no one else was heard to complain. William McDermott called it "first-rate by any standard" and the "most suitable performance" since *Show Boat.* Arthur Spaeth's only complaint was that *South Pacific* had to leave after only two weeks. "But that's the fabulous 'South Pacific,'" he wrote in the *News,* "the only show in theatrical history that moved away from a guaranteed $1,000,000 boxoffice." Spaeth thought Dickinson Eastham better than Ezio Pinza of the original cast as Emile de Becque; McDermott wrote that her performance as Nellie Forbush "made Janet Blair a star who will always be welcomed in this area." In the role of Luther Billis, many Clevelanders would have recognized Ray Walston, who had appeared at the Play House during the war.

Milton Krantz had a good rapport with Rodgers, the more business-minded half of the songwriting team. When Rodgers and Hammerstein needed an updated facility for the premiere of their *Me and Juliet* in 1953, they chose to open it in the Hanna. Most musicals opened in New Haven, where theatrical help was only an hour's train ride from New York. *Me and Juliet* was a backstage musical, however, in which a couple of scenes actually took place in the orchestra pit—something lacking in New Haven's Shubert Theater. So *Me and Juliet*'s eighty-five tons of scenery were unloaded into Krantz's newly refurbished Hanna. The back-stage had to be reinforced to bear the weight of the $350,000 show.

Breaking the customary routine of Rodgers and Hammerstein musicals, *Me and Juliet* premiered in Cleveland rather than New Haven. Members of the cast appearing at the Hanna Theatre were sketched by *Cleveland Press* artist Jim Herron. One familiar face was that of Ray Walston, a former member of the Cleveland Play House company. Cleveland Press, *April 21, 1953*

Opening night on April 20 found Hammerstein in the eighth row of the orchestra and Rodgers at his customary station in the last row.

As the house lights went out prior to the rise of the curtain (the overture would come after the first scene), the opening-night audience burst into applause. Rodgers later described that moment as one of his biggest thrills in show business. "That applause to me was electrifying," he told the *Press*'s Omar Ranney. "It meant here was an audience that was full of anticipation. They love theater. And they were simply applauding the IDEA that they were going to see a brand new show."

What followed, unfortunately, failed to fulfill that anticipation. William McDermott's *Plain Dealer* review was respectful, praising the musical's professional polish and expressing confidence that the rather weak plot would be fixed before it reached Broadway. Rodgers and Hammerstein were not quite so confident after listening to Clevelanders raving about the Jo Mielziner sets and little else during the intermission. The audience had it right, since *Me and Juliet* has gone down since as one of the team's few misses. Nonetheless, Cleveland had at least seen a Rodgers and Hammerstein world premiere.

While Clevelanders were getting to know the new musicals at the Hanna, a group calling itself the Cleveland 500 attempted to revive operetta in Public Hall. The prime mover was local stagehand and scene builder Larry Higgins, backed by talent such as Singing Angels founder Bill Boehm and radio announcer Wayne Mack. For three seasons beginning in 1947, they staged such chestnuts as *The Merry Widow, Rose Marie,* and *The Desert Song.* Although they attracted seventy thousand people and made $7,000 their first year, they ended their third and final season $50,000 in the red. As William McDermott observed, the stilted mannerisms of *The Vagabond King* were no competition for the more realistic style of such newer musicals as *South Pacific.*

Operetta seemed to fare better in the wooded setting of Cain Park. As executive director, "Doc" Dina Rees Evans advertised and delivered "Ten shows in ten weeks" every summer. Repertoire was a medley of Shakespeare *(Julius Caesar),* operetta *(The Chimes of Normandy),* straight plays *(Ah, Wilderness!),* pure corn *(Camille in Roaring Camp),* and occasionally one of the newer musicals *(Lady in the Dark).* When famed Italian actress Marta Abba married Clevelander Severance Millikin, Evans built a production of Victorien Sardou's *Divorçons* around her, including sets by Viktor Schreckengost. Playwright Lynn Riggs came in 1944 to advise and view Cain Park's production of his *Green Grow the Lilacs,* destined to be better remembered as the source of the musical *Oklahoma!*

For many, especially those behind the footlights, Cain Park was as much a way of life as a theater. Rain was always a greater threat than unfavorable reviews. If it didn't scare the audience away, it was liable to drown the orchestra, whose pit happened to be unluckily situated right above an underground stream covered in the construction of the outdoor amphitheater. But theater hopefuls flocked to Cleveland Heights summer after summer to serve their apprenticeships under Doc Evans. Among them were Hal Holbrook (his stage debut), Dom DeLuise (he dropped his kilt in *Brigadoon*), Franklin Cover, Jack Lee, Lynn Sheldon, and Pernell Roberts. "Many have told me that whenever a group of theatre folk are gathered together one is sure to find a couple of Cain Parkers," recalled Evans.

One of "Doc Evans's boys" even started his own musical theater. U.S. Navy veteran John L. Price Jr. spotted a trend in the early 1950s of staging summer theater in the round under tents and decided to give it a try in Cleveland. He consulted local statistician Howard Whipple Green to determine the geographical center of the area's culturally inclined population. Green's bull's eye happened to fall within the suburb of Warrensville Heights, and Price opened his Musicarnival there on the grounds of Thistledown Race Track with a production of *Oklahoma!* in the summer of 1954.

Price's venture was strictly for profit, one of the last commercial legitimate theaters begun in Cleveland. One of his investors was former Clevelander Bob Hope (perhaps, speculated William McDermott, because of its proximity to a race track). Seating 1,800 originally, Musicarnival went through several tents and eventually was enlarged to a capacity of 2,561. Arena-style staging was a novelty for both directors and audiences, as the former had to keep their casts circulating and the latter had to watch for actors making their entrances and exits up and down the aisles. Set designers such as Paul Rodgers of the Play House were especially challenged to suggest scenes with little more than a few props and some decorative touches on the tent's three poles.

Musicarnival presented an average of eight to ten shows a summer. The backbone of the repertoire consisted of the integrated musical plays that followed the revolution of *Oklahoma!* For Clevelanders who may have missed the road companies at the Hanna, Musicarnival was generally their next chance to catch such classics of the genre as *Carousel; Kiss Me, Kate; Wonderful Town; Fanny; Paint Your Wagon;* and *Fiorello!* Occasionally, Price revived operettas such as *The Red Mill* and *The Student Prince* or tried to sneak in an out-and-out opera, letting the popular shows pay for his operatic flings. One temporarily local asset he tapped was the wife of *Plain Dealer* executive Peter Greenough, a soprano named Beverly Sills, giving Clevelanders a chance to see her in *Tosca* and *The Ballad of Baby Doe.*

For the first eleven seasons, Price maintained a resident stock company consisting of local talent such as Providence Hollander and imported players such as Joshua Hecht of the New York City Opera Company. If available and right for the role, he used guest stars. When he brought in Juanita Hall in 1955 to re-create her role of Bloody

Though John Price principally used a resident company during the early years of Musicarnival, he would occasionally bring in a visiting star if right for the role. Juanita Hall certainly qualified as *South Pacific*'s Bloody Mary, a role she had created on Broadway. At a backstage function on the Musicarnival grounds, the magnetic singer offers a treat to producer Price. *Cleveland Public Library*

Mary in *South Pacific,* he had to hold the show over for a fourth week. A young actor named Don Driver was promoted to director, a position he held during the "glory years" of Musicarnival. "He was the best director ever to hit the tents," recalls Price.

It was Driver who worked with Richard Rodgers, after the death of Hammerstein, to adapt the television version of Rodgers and Hammerstein's *Cinderella* for its stage premiere at Musicarnival on June 5, 1961. In expanding the work to fill a theatrical evening, Driver even wrote a lyric for an original Rodgers melody. This was the production in which a sixteen-year-old dancer from Maple Heights padded his age by a couple of years to get a job as an extra. He was Ernie Horvath, who would become a cofounder of Cleveland San Jose Ballet.

Toward the end of the 1960s, the ebullient, perennially crew-cut Price was forced to adopt the star system to keep his tent filled. Dropping the stock company, he brought in packaged productions generally headlined by popular singing or television stars. "It was never as much fun after that," he says.

An especially ambitious program of musicals during this period was being served to Clevelanders at Karamu. Sharing a common interest in the World Federalist movement, the Jelliffes established the sort of personal relationship with Oscar Hammerstein that Milton Krantz had with Richard Rodgers. Six Rodgers and Hammerstein works were seen on Karamu's stages in the 1950s, including the rarely revived *Allegro, Pipedream,* and *Me and Juliet.* Karamu also gave Cleveland its first look at Maxwell Anderson and Kurt Weill's *Lost in the Stars* and Leonard Bernstein's *Candide.* The Karamu production of Harold Arlen and E. Y. Harburg's *Jamaica* was said by one of the authors to have come closer to their concept than the Broadway version.

All musical productions at Karamu were under the general supervision of Benno Frank, who had received his training in prewar Germany. Musical plays were generally directed by J. Harold Brown, while operas were staged by Helmuth Wolfes. Karamu was especially known for its adventurous opera program, which included the American premiere of Leoš Janáček's *Kat'a Kabanova* and only the second American performance of Haydn's *The Man in the Moon.*

In the 1960s, theater began to reflect some of the forces that were confronting the America of the complacent 1950s. This was the decade of Vietnam and the civil rights revolution. The Lunts had appeared at the Hanna in Friedrich Dürrenmatt's *The Visit,* a dark study of greed and revenge quite unlike their usual vehicles. "Dear Mr. and Mrs. Lunt: I saw your play," wrote one Clevelander. "It was well acted, as is always the case with you. But it made me quite ill and I am going straight to bed."

Though *Who's Afraid of Virginia Woolf?* could appear at the Cleveland Play House with no more ado than a language advisory, one influential Clevelander may have had a hand in denying Edward Albee a Pulitzer Prize for his bitter dissection of a marriage in shambles. *Cleveland Press* editor Louis B. Seltzer happened to be on the Pulitzer Prize Advisory Board at the time. When the Drama Jury recommended the Albee play for the 1963 award, they were overruled by the Advisory Board after an attack by Seltzer on obscenity and poor taste on the stage.

A highly visible test of Cleveland's theatrical tolerance came with the arrival of the "tribal rock musical" *Hair* at the Hanna in March 1971. Language was not the only problem with *Hair,* as the show also contained a much-publicized, if brief, nude scene at the conclusion of its first act. The Concerned Catholics of Greater Cleveland sent excerpts from the script to Mayor Carl B. Stokes, asking him to stop the show as an offense to God, Catholics, and "all persons of decency." Other Clevelanders registered their opinions at the box office, where the first three weeks of a scheduled five-week stand were sold out before opening night. A smiling Mayor Stokes showed up at the opening on March 9; so did city and county prosecutors. A lone picket outside the theater carried a sign proclaiming, "Sheman scum dishonor our American flag at Hanna's Hair while our sons die serving under it."

Both the *Plain Dealer* and the *Press* began their reviews on the front page. In the latter, Tony Mastroianni deemed *Hair,* "The most over-rated and over-amplified show in the history of musicals." Peter Bellamy in the *Plain Dealer* saw it as a "flower child's version of 'Hell Za Poppin,'" referring to a burlesque revue of thirty years earlier by Olsen and Johnson. "But it is much less a menace than the social injustices it attacks," added Bellamy. "It's much pleasanter to see these kids cavorting on stage [against the draft] than to see them as war casualties." The audience gave it a standing ovation. The prosecutors ruled it "definitely not obscene," even if "vulgar, tasteless and an artistic failure."

But this was not the last of *Hair* in Cleveland. A week later a bag containing three sticks of dynamite was found outside the theater. A bomb threat phoned in during the first act emptied the Hanna that same evening. A month later, a fire broke out in the Hotel Pick Carter on Prospect Avenue, killing seven persons. Among the dead were the wives and one-year-old daughters of two members of the *Hair* company. Although the fire was coincidental, it did succeed in closing the show for at least one evening. Nonetheless, *Hair* persevered for a total run of seven weeks before it left Cleveland.

Seen by more than eighty thousand Clevelanders, *Hair* had achieved the longest run for a live production at the Hanna since the summer-stock presentation of *White Cargo* in the 1920s. It might have run an additional week if the company had not felt the need of time off to recuperate before its next engagement. On the morning of the final performance, someone threw a bomb at the Hanna. This one actually went off, shattering some forty windows and knocking three letters from the theater's name on the marquee. It failed to keep nearly a full house of patrons away from the theater that evening.

A bomb of a different nature had gone off that same season at the Cleveland Play House. In this case the explosive agent was an over-the-top production of Aristophanes' *Lysistrata*. It was blistered as needlessly vulgar (as if it could be otherwise) by both Bellamy in the *Plain Dealer* and Mastroianni in the *Press*. When schools began to cancel student bookings, the Play House took the unprecedented step of closing the production after only four performances. Only one head rolled, but it was that of managing director Rex Partington. Partington had just recently taken the place of William Greene, who had committed suicide less than a year after succeeding K. Elmo Lowe. When Lowe himself died suddenly of a stroke in the midst of the crisis, it can only have added to the sense of rudderlessness at Cleveland's most venerated dramatic institution.

To Frederick Smith, a drama professor at the recently federated Case Western Reserve University, the main lesson of the "Lysistrata affair" was to "point up the dangerous grip our two reviewers have on Cleveland theatergoers." Since the closing of the *News* in 1960, Cleveland had been a two-newspaper town. Writing in the inaugural issue of *Cleveland Magazine,* Smith singled out Bellamy for his generally negative attitude toward the theater of the absurd as practiced by Samuel Beckett, Jean Genet, and Edward Albee. Mastroianni was criticized for providing an echo of Bellamy rather than a choice. "What is most disturbing is that the two men in Cleveland who have the most influence over Clevelanders' taste in theater, have such provincial views of theater themselves," concluded Smith.

But Virginia Woolf wasn't the only thing Cleveland theater had to fear by the end of the 1960s. In the U.S. Census returns for 1970 could be seen a portentous milestone. For the first time in Cleveland's existence as a city, it contained less than half the population of Cuyahoga County; the suburbs had outgrown the central city. This might have been regarded simply as a demographic curiosity if the central city had remained healthy and vibrant, but a more ominous trend had also begun to emerge in the same decade as Cleveland's population, once on the verge of a million, began to drop sharply. A good part of suburban growth had come at the expense of Cleveland itself.

Despite Gore Vidal's dictum "That from Levittown no art may come," it must have seemed to many that culture would follow the dispersion of population. Cleveland's most prominent new company of the post-war period, the Great Lakes Shakespeare Festival, had taken root in the suburb of Lakewood, though in the inner tier just over the city line. In 1974, however, Greater Cleveland's first new permanent theater since the 1926 Play House was located far beyond the central city limits in an area that would come to be dubbed "Edge City." This was the Front Row, a 3,200-seat arena theater built just off the outer belt of I-271 in Highland Heights. Opened on July 5 with singer Sammy Davis Jr., the Front Row featured Las Vegas–style acts such as Don Rickles, Ray Charles, Joan Rivers, and Redd Foxx. Its instant success may have played a role in the demise of Musicarnival a few miles down the interstate.

One theater preoccupied with the problem of location in the early 1970s was the Cleveland Play House, only a few blocks away from the Hough Riots of 1966, Cleveland's major outbreak of civil disorder during that tumultuous decade. As some patrons began to voice concerns for their safety, talk of a new theater complex moved toward the front burner. One early idea had been to move the Play House eastward to join the aggregation of cultural institutions already concentrated in University Circle.

As the 1960s unfolded, however, the Play House shifted its focus in the opposite direction toward downtown. A site on East 9th Street in the Erieview urban renewal project was one option. More serious consideration was given to a location adjoining Playhouse Square in the block defined by Euclid and Chester Avenues between East 17th and 18th Streets. Visions of a three-theater complex were damped by the defeat of a bond issue that would have furnished the necessary urban-renewal funds.

Even as the Play House abandoned plans for moving to Playhouse Square, the theaters already there were beginning to dim their lights. With movie attendance shrinking before the competition of television and suburban lifestyles, there was no longer a need for large, first-run movie houses downtown. The Allen, despite a half-million-dollar facelift in 1961, was the first to give up the fight in March 1968. The Ohio and the State, which had both opened in February 1921, closed together in February 1969. A few months later, during a showing of the disaster movie *Krakatoa, East of Java,* the air conditioning broke down in the Palace. No effort was made to repair it.

Workers lower the sign from the State Theatre in preparation for demolition. By the end of 1969, all four theaters on Euclid Avenue in Playhouse Square had dimmed their marquees, symbolizing the death of downtown Cleveland. *Photograph by Bill Nehez; Cleveland Press Collection*

Though the Hanna was still lit on East 14th Street, Cleveland no longer could be said to have a theater district. Yes, there were still a couple of department stores, some tired hotels, and the Browns and Indians in the lakefront Municipal Stadium. But without that row of marquees twinkling in Playhouse Square, most observers considered downtown dead.

THE NIGHT MISS KITTY PLAYED BRATENAHL

The legendary actress Katharine Cornell played many one-night stands in all sorts of venues during her long illustrious career. She was noted, in fact, for her eagerness to bring the cause of drama to off-the-beaten-track locales that had not seen a live performance in years. It is doubtful, however, that she ever gave a more unusual performance than the night she appeared in an ordinary living room in Cleveland's lakefront enclave of Bratenahl.

As dean of Cleveland's drama critics, William McDermott reviewed thousands of performances including every major local appearance by Katharine Cornell. None of them could have been as memorable for him as Miss Kitty's Bratenahl gig, either. The living room in question happened to be his.

Both actress and reviewer had commenced their careers at the beginning of America's dramatic awakening in the 1920s. Raised in Buffalo, Katharine Cornell made her Broadway debut in 1921. When she came to the Hanna Theatre in Michael Arlen's *The Green Hat,* the *Cleveland Plain Dealer* appraised her as "the richest temperament and the finest potential talent that has this generation come to cross the histrionic horizon." She returned almost annually for the next twenty-five years.

McDermott made his Cleveland debut the same year Cornell hit Broadway. Though hired specifically as a drama critic, over nearly four decades he also served the *Plain Dealer* as a general columnist and war correspondent. "He was a pale, round-faced, little man, with a sky-scraper forehead, small hands, thin fingers, and an unexercised body, who kept puffing cigars as if he were laying down a barrage," observed fellow critic John Mason Brown. "But he had a cherub's bright smile, eyes bright as searchlights, and a giant's courage."

Drama remained McDermott's first love, and his admiration for Cornell was one of the constant passions of his career. When she brought the American premiere of her signature play, *The Barretts of Wimpole Street,* to the Hanna in 1931, McDermott wrote that "it marked the introduction to America of a great star, a star of such personal and affectionate popularity as we have not had in America since Maude Adams." Twenty years later, seeing her in *Antony and Cleopatra,* he thought she had "never, in my observation, reached such classic stature, or touched a higher note."

When illness prevented McDermott from catching her latest offering at the Hanna in 1951, Miss Kitty decided to take *Captain Carvallo* to McDermott. The entire company of seven players consequently trouped into the convalescing critic's home and proceeded to set the stage for an audience of two—McDermott and his wife. Even Sir Cedric Hardwicke, soon to appear as the Egyptian Pharaoh in Cecil B. De Mille's *The Ten Commandments,* was moving tables and davenports around like a Hebrew slave.

"If they were self-conscious at acting before so small an audience on a stage that frequently brought them within touching distance of the spectators, they did not show it," later reported McDermott. They played it straight, though the critic sensed an "inner wink" that hinted at their awareness that they were "doing a quixotic and extravagant thing."

Stage props were freely commandeered from the possessions of their audience and hosts. Cornell's producer-husband, Guthrie McClintic, dug up a Rudolf Friml recording that served as off-stage music. McDermott's well-stocked library was ransacked for needed "hymn books," and Nigel Bruce, better known as Dr. Watson in the Sherlock Holmes movies, made an ordinary walking stick do service as a gun he was required to fire.

Stage annals show that *Captain Carvallo* did not rank as one of Katharine Cornell's even modest successes. In fact, it has the dubious distinction of being one of only three of her vehicles that never made it to Broadway. Pinch-hitting for McDermott in the *Plain Dealer,* W. Ward Marsh had frankly pronounced the comedy as unworthy of her talent.

Under the circumstances, however, William McDermott may be excused for giving it a glowing review.

Nine

RENAISSANCE

ALL RAY SHEPARDSON WAS looking for in the beginning was a place to hold a meeting. In 1970 he was a twenty-six-year-old assistant to the superintendent of the Cleveland Public Schools. Someone mentioned the splendors of the four recently closed movie houses on Playhouse Square, so he decided to check them out.

He gained access to the State Theatre on February 5, the forty-ninth anniversary of its opening in 1921. "He emerged as dazzled as archeologist Howard Carter when he first broke into the tomb of Tutankhamen," is how one writer described it. "Well, I'm just a farm kid from Seattle," is how he explains his reaction. "I thought they were spectacular."

He was especially impressed by the colorful James Daugherty murals in the State's lobby. A couple of weeks later, when he chanced to see one of them reproduced in a *Life* magazine spread he picked up in his barber shop, the die was cast: Deciding that somehow those four theaters had to be saved, he had found his life's calling.

But saved for what? Downtown was dead. The conventional wisdom, in fact, held that the entire central city was dead. As discovered by Shepardson, the State was already stripped for demolition. If there was to be any future at all for the old theaters of Playhouse Square, Shepardson and others interested in them had to show that people would be willing to come and use them again. In the best tradition of the old movie musicals that had once played in the houses, they decided to put on a show.

They put on many shows, in fact, beginning with a successful concert appearance by the Budapest Symphony Orchestra in the Allen Theatre late in 1971. They had organized themselves as the Playhouse Square Association in July 1970. Their baby nearly died aborning when the owners of the State and the Ohio made plans to raze the two theaters in 1972 to make room for that new symbol of urban blight—a parking lot. With the aid of a $25,000 grant from the Junior League of Cleveland and the outcries of community leaders, the wrecking ball was dodged for the time being. Then they struck a mother lode.

It was a production of the musical revue *Jacques Brel Is Alive and Living in Paris,* mounted first by the Berea Summer Theatre and repeated later at Cleveland State University. Shepardson and his associates thought it might work as a cabaret-type show in the huge lobby of the State. Thus director Joseph Garry brought his Berea–Cleveland State production to Playhouse Square on April 18, 1973. If they could run it for a few weeks, it might provide further proof that Clevelanders were still willing to venture downtown for unusual entertainment.

Once it was in, *Jacques Brel* proved a hard tenant to evict. The four-member cast of Cliff Bemis, David O. Frazier, Providence Hollander, and Theresa Piteo caught on, and seeing *Jacques Brel* became the thing to do for Clevelanders—ten or twenty times, for some. Playhouse Square had more than a show—it had a phenomenon. Playing four-night weekends, it ran to June 29, 1975, for a total of 550 performances, the longest theatrical run in the history of not only Cleveland but also the entire state of Ohio. To members of the audience, seated in the faded grandeur of the once elegant State lobby, the show's closing anthem, "If We Only Have Love," must have sounded like a prescription for the recovery of a cherished landmark—possibly even an entire city.

It wasn't all that simple, of course. Throughout the 1970s, Shepardson's group juggled theatrical events and restoration work among its theaters. There were more cabarets in the Palace's Grand Hall and the State's auditorium. A series of Vegas-style acts in the State in 1977 drew a quarter-million patrons. Most of the restoration effort at first was the work of hundreds of volunteers, not all of them anonymous. Guides today will point out the spot in the State where Mary Travers of the Peter, Paul, and Mary trio picked up a paintbrush and did her bit.

An educator turned impresario, Ray Shepardson kept the former movie palaces on Playhouse Square alive by staging such cabaret shows as *Jacques Brel Is Alive and Living in Paris*. He is pictured introducing one of them in the lobby of the State. *Photograph by Frank Reed; Cleveland Press Collection*

"I didn't have a clue as to what I was doing," says Shepardson of those early years. "I thought I needed to figure out a use for the buildings; I never dreamed they could all be used as theaters." One early blueprint saw the Palace as an opera house, the State as a dinnerclub-nightclub complex, the Ohio as a dance or recital hall, and the Allen divided into the type of multiplex movie theaters that were going up in the suburbs.

Now that Shepardson had pointed out the possibilities, the city's establishment began to get involved. When the owners of the State and Ohio began to talk demolition once again, the Cuyahoga County Commissioners stepped in to purchase the Loew's complex. They leased the theaters to the recently formed Playhouse Square Foundation, which had succeeded Shepardson's original association and at the same time obtained a lease for the Palace. Others began to take note, one of whom was Wolf Von Eckardt, a visiting urban-affairs expert at Cleveland State University. "A hope for attracting people downtown is obviously full restoration and modernization of all of Playhouse Square," he wrote for the *Washington Post*.

The powerful Cleveland Foundation became a believer and a player as well. In an unprecedented move, it dipped into its principal to purchase the Bulkley Building and Allen Theatre for the benefit of Playhouse Square. It also conducted a study that revealed several of Cleveland's newer arts organizations would soon be in need of new facilities. A new plan began to emerge envisioning Playhouse Square as a performing-arts center providing stages for the Cleveland Ballet, the Cleveland Opera, and the Great Lakes Shakespeare Festival.

It would take a lot of money to realize the ambitious vision, some $38 million before it was done. The bohemians having done their job, it was time for the businessmen to take charge. As one foundation board member put it, "Ray was a fantastic idea man, but he was a terrible businessman." Shepardson left Playhouse Square to launch equally quixotic and ultimately successful theater restoration projects in Columbus, Detroit, Seattle, and elsewhere.

Under Oliver Henkel Jr. and later Lawrence Wilker, the Playhouse Square Foundation pushed the renovation of the State, Ohio, and Palace Theatres. Having been gutted by fire in the 1960s and repainted a uniform garish red, the Ohio was most in need of a facelift. With no shows scheduled there, workers proceeded freely with their restoration. Chandeliers from the demolished Erlanger Theatre in Philadelphia were hung in the lobby; when Cleveland's Hippodrome finally succumbed to the wreckers, its chandelier was salvaged for the Ohio's auditorium. On July 9, 1982, the Ohio reopened its doors for the Great Lakes Shakespeare Festival. The lights were back on in Playhouse Square.

Great Lakes had been looking for a more suitable home than its quarters in the Lakewood Civic Auditorium. Backers originally thought in terms of a new theater to be built in Edgewater Park. That would be expensive, however, and somewhat redundant with Playhouse Square then in the process of restoring three theaters some three miles away. With the encouragement of the Cleveland Foundation and a grant from

Putting the lights back on in Playhouse Square in 1982 was the Great Lakes Shakespeare Festival. Gathered under the new marquee of the renovated Ohio Theatre is the thirty-nine-member cast of *The Life and Adventures of Nicholas Nickelby*, the smash hit of that first season in the Ohio. *Great Lakes Theatre Festival*

TRW, the Great Lakes Shakespeare Festival became the first permanent tenant of Playhouse Square Center. And, it might be observed, Robert McLaughlin's Ohio Theatre was once again a "legitimate" house.

Vincent Dowling had a dynamite inaugural season in the wings. Following Shakespeare's *As You Like It,* Great Lakes presented the first American production of Dickens's *The Life and Adventures of Nicholas Nickelby.* The eight-hour marathon adaptation had originated in England with the Royal Shakespeare Company, which then took its show to New York. Clevelanders were offered the choice of seeing the Great Lakes version in two parts on successive evenings or in matinee and evening performances on the same day. Either way, they flocked to witness a spectacle enlivened with such bits of business as a tradesman lobbing genuine English scones at the actors on stage from his perch in the Ohio's balcony.

Hoping to capitalize on its success, Great Lakes scheduled a revival of *Nick-Nick,* as they called it, for the following summer, to be ushered in by a national tour. They opened in Chicago—and closed there also, unfortunately, torpedoed by the competition of a television presentation of

Lorain native Gerald Freedman (right) brought a Broadway cachet to the recently renamed Great Lakes Theatre Festival. The artistic director utilized his extensive theatrical connections to bring in an impressive roster of stars such as Hal Holbrook (left), whose Cleveland credits ranged from King Lear to Willie Loman. *Photograph by Roger Mastroianni; Great Lakes Theatre Festival*

the Royal Shakespeare production of the play. Limping back to Cleveland, the company finished the season with a formidable debt of $700,000.

In 1985 the Great Lakes Shakespeare Festival acquired a new name and a new artistic director. Reflecting the broadened scope of its repertoire over the past few seasons, it recognized the fait accompli by introducing itself as the Great Lakes Theatre Festival. Succeeding Dowling as director was Gerald Freedman. A native of Lorain, Ohio, Freedman was best known for his work with Joseph Papp's New York Shakespeare Festival, where he had directed the premiere of *Hair.* With his wire-rimmed glasses and receding hairline, Freedman seemed almost shy and retiring in comparison with his flamboyant predecessor.

Freedman's productions were anything but understated, though. Freely drawing upon his wide contacts in the theater world, he imported an impressive roll of guest stars in productions that often went on to New York. For Joseph Kesselring's *Arsenic and Old Lace* during his second season, he assembled a cast headed by Jean Stapleton, Tony Roberts, Abe Vigoda, and William Hickey. He brought in Hal Holbrook for *King Lear, Uncle Vanya,* and *Death of a Salesman;* Olympia Dukakis for *Mother Courage;* Piper Laurie for *The Cherry Orchard;* and Cleveland native David Birney for *Antony and Cleopatra.*

Yet Freedman had more to offer than just star power. Trained in art and music as well as theater, he was interested in creating large stage pictures incorporating music and choreography. Representative of this aspect of his style were productions of Frederigo Lorca's *Blood Wedding,* S. Ansky's *The Dybbuk,* and *The Bacchae* of Euripides.

It was during the Freedman era that Great Lakes shifted in 1991 from a summer to a fall through spring season. Though he never developed a resident company, Freedman made frequent use of such Cleveland actors as John Buck Jr. and Marji Dodrill. He developed a strong production team that included scene designer John Ezell and director Victoria Bussert. As one local actor put it, "Gerry Freedman was a gift to theater here." While it remained a nagging presence, the company's debt was considerably reduced. By the time of Freedman's resignation in 1997, the Great Lakes Theatre Festival was firmly established as Cleveland's second regional theater.

The city's long-recognized regional, the Play House, had entered an eventful period in its history. Richard Oberlin in 1970 restored some stability as director in the wake of the *Lysistrata* fiasco. With a staff that would number 130 by the end of the decade, Oberlin was confronted by deficit problems of his own. One response at the Play House was fewer productions per season—from sixteen on the average to about twelve—but longer runs for each play.

For its sixtieth-anniversary season of 1975–76, the Play House mounted two notable world premieres. The one that got the most attention was *First Monday in October.* Among the things it had going for it were guest appearances by Melvyn Douglas and Jean Arthur and authorship by Jerome Lawrence and Robert E. Lee, natives respectively of Cleveland and Elyria, Ohio. Lawrence's sister, Naomi Schwartz, had appeared on the Play House stage in the 1930s.

Though raised within twenty miles of one another, the playwrights hadn't teamed up until they first met in New York. Among Lawrence and Lee's greatest successes were the stage adaptation of *Auntie Mame* and the courtroom drama based on the Scopes Trial, *Inherit the Wind.* More recently, their *The Night Thoreau Spent in Jail* would become the most widely produced play of the 1970s, especially popular on college campuses.

Due largely to the presence of Arthur and Douglas, *First Monday in October* became the first production in Play House history to sell out before opening night. Critic Bill Doll in the *Plain Dealer* thought it worth seeing for its star value but not much of a play in itself. The plot revolved around the appointment of the first woman justice to the U.S. Supreme Court, an event the play anticipated by a few years.

Premiered originally by the Cleveland
Play House in 1975, Lee Kalcheim's *The
Prague Spring* is seen here in a 1978
revival. Members of the resident
company are (left to right) Norm
Berman, Wayne Turney, Sharon Bicknell,
Joe D. Lauck and Richard Halverson.
*Photograph by Herbert Ascherman Jr.;
Cleveland Play House*

Less heralded but ultimately more memorable was the second premiere, *The Prague Spring.* Written by Lee Kalcheim to music by Joseph
Raposo, it was an intimate cabaret-style revue based on the ill-fated
experiment in "socialism with a human face" in Czechoslovakia. Oberlin
appeared as Czech premier Alexander Dubcek, and the work was named
one of the best two plays of the year by the *National Observer.*

Following the collapse of its contemplated move downtown, the Play
House decided to consolidate its operations at the Drury-Brooks complex on East 86th Street. A closed Sears department store behind the
Play House on Carnegie Avenue was purchased to provide work, storage, and parking spaces. Renowned architect Philip Johnson was engaged to design a new theater to replace the Euclid-77th stage and inte-
grate it, the existing stages, and the Sears building into a unified entity.
This was the septuagenarian's first commission in his native Cleveland.

As architecture, Johnson's design was a tour de force. Likened to a
medieval village, the complex linked its three theaters with a series of
interconnected lobbies leading from an impressive central Romanesque
rotunda. As a theater, the new six-hundred-seat Bolton received mixed
reviews. It was designed by Johnson as an imitation eighteenth-century
court theater with three levels of faux boxes wrapped around the auditorium. In place of the revolutionary (for its time) apron stage of the

Euclid–77th Street Theatre, however, the Bolton offered nothing more than a traditional proscenium arrangement. "I still find this decision appallingly shortsighted," *Plain Dealer* critic Marianne Evett would write fifteen years later, "aimed at public grandeur rather than furthering the art of theater."

Oberlin opened the new house in November 1983 with Shakespeare's *The Tempest.* As the novelty of the new facility wore off, however, the Play House began to encounter some rough critical swells. A world premiere the following season for Arthur Miller's *The Archbishop's Ceiling* was found high on metaphysical discourse but short on dramatic interest. Later that season *Plain Dealer* critic Joanna Connors trashed a musical version of Noel Coward's *Blithe Spirit,* renamed *High Spirits,* as "the sort of mediocre effort that made the exit into the night feel like an escape." The Play House took out an ad in response headed "Poppycock!" Nevertheless, Oberlin resigned the directorship at the close of that season.

There was a general critical feeling by the 1980s that the Play House had played it safe for too long. In Martin Gottfried's study of the

Opened in 1983, the new wing of the Cleveland Play House joined the original Brooks/Drury complex (seen in background on left) to a new Bolton Theatre (right) designed by Cleveland native Philip Johnson. With its central rotunda and interconnected lobbies, the complex was likened to a "medieval village," but the Bolton lacked a thrust stage. *Photograph by Thom Abel; Cleveland Play House* contemporary American stage, *A Theater Divided* (1967), some two dozen leading regionals were discussed without a mention of the Cleveland Play House. As the *Plain Dealer*'s new critic, Marianne Evett, put it, "[A]ll the ideas that fired the theater nationally in the '60s and '70s passed the Play House by."

The new artistic director, appointed after an interregnum of two years, might have then assumed that the position entailed a mandate for change. She was Josephine Abady, the first woman to hold the job. She had been director for nine years of the Berkshire Theater Festival, making her the first complete "outsider" to take the Play House reins since Frederic McConnell. And she dropped a bombshell even before her first season, disbanding the resident company and making plans to cast future shows through New York.

In Abady's defense it was pointed out that she was bringing the Play House in line with the established practice of most regional theaters. Drawing from a wider pool of talent would give the Play House greater flexibility in casting, eliminating the "tired" look many had seen in recent productions. Ending a tradition of nearly seventy years was not accomplished without protest, though. "The uniqueness of the Play House was the fact that there was this resident company of actors who could live here and make a living doing what they loved," Rocky River musician Frederick Koch wrote to the *Plain Dealer*.

Abady made appreciable progress in what she saw as her mission to "bring the Play House into national and international prominence." In her first season she mounted the American premiere of English playwright David Storey's *The March on Russia* and the world premiere of novelist Reynolds Price's *New Music* trilogy. The latter attracted favorable reviews in *The New York Times* and *Time* magazine but proved confusing for some Play House subscribers who were given tickets to only one of the work's three plays—and not necessarily the first in sequence. In the aftermath of the Cold War, Abady also inaugurated theatrical exchange programs between the Play House and Eastern European theaters.

Abady also had her share of misses including an adaptation of Budd Schulberg's *On the Waterfront,* which added little to the movie, and a world premiere of Wendy Kesselman's *The Butcher's Daughter,* described as "an incoherent mess." She had the support of *Plain Dealer* critic Marianne Evett, but she lost the support of the Play House board after a series of three box-office flops at the beginning of the 1993–94 season.

Though most had come to accept it as a forward step, her dismissal of the resident company still rankled many Play House old-timers. Saying she "had accomplished the goals she had set when she came to Cleveland," the board of trustees declined to give Abady a contract for the following season.

These years were even more turbulent for the other jewel in Cleveland's theatrical crown, Karamu. As a theater primarily devoted to training black actors and interpreting the black experience, Karamu was particularly sensitive to the civil rights issues of the period. After the retirement of the Jelliffes in 1963, the institution began to pass into the hands of black leadership. Under Wilhelmina Robeson, the box office made progress in developing black audiences. In 1976, however, a newly appointed executive director asked for Reuben Silver's resignation to clear the way for the hiring of a black director.

Artistically, Mike Malone maintained Karamu's standards at their accustomed high level with such productions as *The Wiz* and *Black Nativity.* He envisioned taking the drama program to an even higher level with the formation in 1981 of a professional acting troupe known as the Karamu Company. One faction at Karamu, however, began to worry about a drop in white participation and institutional support. "The Black Nationalist era at Karamu House caused a lot of turmoil," said board president Donna Cummings. "Many people in the community don't feel welcome at Karamu House." When Malone planned a season for 1982–83 heavily weighted with plays by black writers or about black themes, he was replaced by a director who proposed more mainstream works on the order of *Guys and Dolls* and *The Music Man.*

One of Malone's legacies was a considerable deficit occasioned by the short-lived professional experiment. An artistic revival occurred in the 1990s under executive director Margaret Ford-Taylor. Highlights included the long-deferred premiere of *Mule Bone,* a Langston Hughes–Zora Neale Hurston collaboration whose scheduled production at Karamu in 1931 had been cancelled due to disagreements between the two authors. Ford-Taylor had to stage her productions on shoestring budgets, at times even dipping into trustees' or her own pockets to meet payroll. After nine years she was dismissed by the board without any public explanation.

Cleveland's extensive community-theater scene on the whole remained as lively as ever. According to a 1980 overview in the *Cleveland Press,* the city was ahead of Boston and Denver and the equal of Chicago in the number of little theaters it supported. Among the forty-nine groups covered by writer Teddi Gibson-Bianchi were the Ohio City Players, Willoughby School of Fine Arts, Royalton Players, and the Clague Playhouse. The latter claimed to be the area's oldest community theater, having spun-off from the Bay Village Players first organized in 1928.

Many of these were still present on a similar list compiled twenty years later for *Northeast Ohio Avenues* magazine. Huntington Playhouse had recovered from a disastrous fire to present the area's first community-theater productions of *Jesus Christ Superstar* and *1776*. Out in Lake County, Rabbit Run Theater seemed to have more lives than a cat. The East Cleveland Community Theater had benefited from the support of retired Karamu cofounder Rowena Jelliffe, who died in 1992 at the age of one hundred. One of the strongest of the community troupes was Greenbrier Theatre of Parma Heights, which later renamed itself the Paul W. Cassidy Theatre in honor of that suburb's mayor.

Cleveland's most venerable community theater, the Lakewood Little Theatre, moved into new prominence in the 1970s. It found a financial angel in local businessman Kenneth C. Beck, who offered a matching challenge grant of $600,000 toward the construction of a cultural-arts center. The resultant Beck Center, built next to the original theater, opened in 1976. Besides an art gallery and various classrooms, it included a new 488-seat theater, which was inaugurated with a production of Maxwell Anderson's *Mary of Scotland*. Named in honor of long-time managing director Karl Mackey, the main stage has specialized in such large-scale works as *To Kill a Mockingbird* and *Kiss of the Spider Woman*.

A beloved summer theater staged a comeback after serving as the location for the filming of a Hollywood movie. Cain Park had fallen into disuse and disrepair by 1979, when former Cain Parker David Shaber sold a script about a summer-stock company to United Artists. Even better, he talked the studio into filming *Those Lips, Those Eyes* at Cain Park, where part of the deal was $100,000 worth of restoration work. Cain Park fared better than the movie, as it reopened the amphitheater the following summer with a production of Alan Lerner and Frederick Loewe's *Camelot,* directed by Tom Fulton.

Since then, Cain Park has generally staged two musicals each summer: a large production in the amphitheater and a more intimate work in the three-hundred-seat Alma Theater. Composer-lyricist Stephen Sondheim became a house specialty with the Cleveland premiere of his *Sweeney Todd* in the Alma in 1982. Cliff Bemis played the "Demon Barber" and Patty Johnson portrayed Mrs. Lovett. Victoria Bussert of the Great Lakes Theatre Festival became a regular at Cain Park, contributing an epic production of Sondheim's *Follies* in the amphitheater in 1988. Renamed in honor of founding director Dina Rees Evans, the Evans Amphitheater was weatherproofed by the addition of a permanent canopy in 1989.

Musicals also became a staple of the Berea Summer Theatre, especially after it moved into Baldwin-Wallace College's new Kleist Art and Drama Center in 1972. Though straight plays still balanced the diet, the repertoire was dominated by such big song-and-dance shows as *Grand Hotel, Shenandoah, 42nd Street,* and *Oliver!* Following the retirement of founder William Allman in 1996, the program underwent a period of retrenchment and reorganization. In an effort to establish a closer working relationship with its host college, it was renamed the Baldwin-Wallace Summer Theatre.

The Jewish Community Center's Halle Theatre entered a creative period when Dorothy Silver became director of performing and visual arts in 1976. During her twelve-year tenure, the Halle attained a national reputation in its field of Jewish community theater with such productions as the world premiere of *Shayna Maidel,* a play on Holocaust themes by Barbara Lebow. This work was the result of a playwriting competition reactivated by Dorothy Silver at JCC and since then renamed in her honor. She has also been seen on the Halle stage as an actress, appearing with her husband Reuben in Miller's *All My Sons* and under his direction in Alfred Uhry's *Driving Miss Daisy.*

Following his departure from Karamu in 1976, Reuben Silver became head of the theater program at Cleveland State University. Founded in 1965, CSU incorporated the campus of the old Fenn College at East 24th Street and Euclid Avenue. While many new buildings were added, the university's theater program found a home in an old mattress factory on Chester Avenue, where it installed its Factory Theatre. Besides Silver, the department included director Joe Garry, scene designer Eugene Hare, and former Play House company member Wayne Turney. They mounted six productions a year, one of which was a memorable presentation of Dürrenmatt's *The Visit* with the Silvers in the two leads under the direction of Garry. Graduates of the program have established themselves as playwrights and members of such companies as the Cleveland Play House and Chicago's Steppenwolf Theater.

Theater departments at Cleveland State and the three campuses of Cuyahoga Community College joined those already thriving at John Carroll University, Baldwin-Wallace College, and Case Western Reserve. At Baldwin-Wallace, Victoria Bussert was named head of the music theater program. Case Western's Eldred Hall was the host for a few summers of a professional troupe known as the Actors Company. Led by Ken Albers, it included several Play House veterans such as William Rhys and Dudley Swetland. In 1981 the company won the Cleveland Critics Circle award for its production of *The Wakefield Plays* of Israel Horovitz. It was the first time the cycle of seven plays had been staged in its entirety.

Alternative theater was also going strong at Dobama in Coventry Village. Cofounder Don Bianchi carried on after the death of his wife in 1977, instituting the Marilyn Bianchi Kids' Playwriting Festival in her memory. Adult theater was still very much Dobama's forte, however, with a continued emphasis on producing new scripts. Among the premieres staged there were two works by Bianchi, *The Avenue as It Used to Be* and *Imperfect Strangers.*

By 1991 Bianchi had turned over the reins as artistic and managing director to Joyce Casey. Under Casey, Dobama in 1998 gave Cleveland its first full production of Tony Kushner's Pulitzer Prize–winning *Angels in America.* The $50,000 budget for the two-part *Gay Fantasia on National Themes* was the largest in Dobama's history, and the result was judged "as good as you could find anywhere" by Marianne Evett. "It seems ironic," she observed in the *Plain Dealer,* "that small theaters with limited resources should be the ones to introduce Cleveland audiences to the most interesting and best plays being done today, but such is the case." For its 1999–2000 season, Dobama announced a six-play schedule of one world, one American, two Midwest, and two Cleveland premieres.

At least Dobama was no longer alone. In 1979 Lucia Columbi began the Ensemble Theatre less than a mile away in The Civic Building on Mayfield Road. It established its presence during its first decade with a retrospective series of eight plays by Eugene O'Neill including *Dynamo, The Great God Brown,* and *A Moon for the Misbegotten.* Established area actors such as the Silvers appeared there in *The Gin Game* and *The Trip to Bountiful.* Ensemble's most ambitious venture was the Cleveland premiere of Robert Schenkkan's historical epic, *The Kentucky Cycle,* in 1996. It encompassed nine interrelated playlets covering

One of the most ambitious undertakings of Cleveland's "off-Euclid" theaters was the Dobama Theatre production of Tony Kushner's *Angels in America.* Pictured in Part Two: *Perestroika* are Laura Perrotta as The Angel and Scott Plate as Prior Walter. *Photograph by Rique Winston; Dobama Theatre*

a span of two hundred years, from the fur trade to the War on Poverty. A cast of nineteen, headed by Neil Thackaberry and Morgan Lund, crowded the theater's small stage.

Across town, a maverick lawyer named James Levin brought experimental theater to the near west side. Beginning with several seasons of free "Shakespeare at the Zoo," Levin found a performing space for his Cleveland Public Theatre in 1984 in a former dance hall on Detroit Avenue at West 65th Street. In return for legal services, he got a motorcycle gang to fix it up for an arena-style acting area. Along with a regular production schedule of "work that addresses the issues and challenges of modern life," Levin also used the theater as a stage

Robert Schenkkan's nine-part *The Kentucky Cycle* was Ensemble Theatre's bicentennial gift to Cleveland in 1996. Members of the nineteen-member cast included (clockwise from upper left) Ron Miller, Evie McElroy as Mother Jones, Steve Larry, Paula Deusing, Jason Fisher, and Glen Colerider. *Photograph by James Fry; Ensemble Theatre*

for the annual Festival of New Plays and the Performance Art Festival, which later became an independent event.

Next door to Cleveland Public Theatre was the former Gordon Square vaudeville house, the oldest-standing theater structure in the city. Levin acquired it in 1996, Cleveland's bicentennial year, and began returning it to theatrical uses after more than six decades of neglect. Among the productions staged there during the restoration process was the Midwest premiere of Viktor Ullmann's *Der Kaiser von Atlantis,* an expressionist opera composed during World War II at the Terezin concentration camp.

One of America's unparalleled theaters—one of only two of its kind in the country—is the Cleveland Signstage Theatre. Founded in 1975 by Brian Kilpatrick and Charles St. Clair, it was originally known as the Fairmount Theatre of the Deaf. Its purpose was not only to make theater available to the hearing-impaired but also to bring deaf and hearing people together through shared experience. Through the use of simultaneous double casting, it staged plays in both American Sign Language and spoken English. Quartered lately in the Mainstage Theater on the Metro Campus of Cuyahoga Community College, Signstage tours regularly in Ohio and as far abroad as Jordan and the Czech Republic. The touring program has proved so successful, in fact, that concerns have been expressed about the company's diminished presence in its Cleveland base. Its repertoire in 1999–2000 included such relevant works as William Gibson's *The Miracle Worker* and a play on the cochlear ear-implant controversy entitled *Sweet Nothing in My Ear.*

By the late 1990s, there was enough alternative theater in Cleveland to prompt talk of a local version of off-Broadway, or more properly "off-Euclid." Its nucleus by common consent consisted of Dobama, Ensemble, Karamu, Cleveland Signstage, and Cleveland Public Theatre. To this core might be added two well-established community theaters that often do off-Euclid works. One is the Halle at the Jewish Community Center when it stages plays such as Donald Margolies' *Collected Stories.* At Beck Center in Lakewood the old stage has been turned into the Studio Theater for the presentation of more offbeat work such as Sondheim's *Assassins* and Mark St. Germain's *Camping with Henry & Tom.*

For those who knew where to find it, there was even an "off-off-Euclid" of ultraexperimental theater. Dobama once again led the way with an offshoot called the Night Kitchen, which took over after the regular shows to offer such exotic fare as *This Vicious Cabaret.* Two off-off-Euclid troupes were spun-off from Cleveland Public Theatre—Theatre Labyrinth and the feminist Red Hen Productions. Other examples included Bad Epitaph Theatre and the New World Performance Lab. Many were transitory and even elusive in nature. The Guerrilla Theatre Company, active in the early 1990s, grew out of "hit-and-run" skits performed without notice in public spaces followed by equally fast exits. One advantage of such companies is an ability to take risks in inverse proportion to their lack of material resources. While a production of *Lysistrata* once caused an internal crisis at the Cleveland Play House, David Hansen's Bad Epitaph troupe won plaudits for an even racier version of the Aristophanes comedy.

Guerrilla tactics are not necessarily conducive to artistic growth and community presence, however. Seeking to raise their local profile, the more established off-Euclid theaters banded together in 1993 as the Professional Alliance of Cleveland Theatres (PACT). Under the leadership of John Orlock, chair of the theater department at Case Western Reserve, and actor Thomas Q. Fulton, they adopted a mission "to promote, support, nurture, and develop alternative professional theater companies in northeastern Ohio." The founding members included Dobama, Ensemble, Fairmount (Signstage), Karamu, Cleveland Public, Cain Park, and the Porthouse Theater at the Blossom Music Center. Three of the original members—Fulton's Cleveland Theater Company, the Eldred Company, and the Working Theatre—were no longer active by the end of the decade.

Increased professionalism was the common goal of the PACT theaters. Due to more flexible arrangements with Actors Equity, professional actors and actresses were becoming more visible in Cleveland's off-Euclid houses. In the past, Equity members who wished to perform on community-theater stages had to do so under assumed names to maintain their professional status. The only stages that could openly employ Equity actors were the Play House and Great Lakes Theatres. Only at the Play House was there a permanent professional company of actors who were also Cleveland residents, the embodiment of a tradition going back to John Ellsler's company at the Academy of Music. To some extent, that explains the consternation caused by the breakup of the Play House company in 1988.

But strangely, the dissolution of the Play House troupe did not signal the demise of the professional actor in Cleveland. Some observers, such as the *Plain Dealer*'s Marianne Evett, believed that "in the long run, it was clearly good for Cleveland theater." Besides the greater flexibility in casting it brought to the Play House, it began to open more doors for professionals in the area's alternative and community theaters. While some of the Play House company left Cleveland for job opportunities elsewhere, others remained or returned after a while. Openly identified as members of Actors Equity, they began to appear in the programs of Dobama, Ensemble, the Halle, Beck Center, Cain Park, and other theaters. While it remains difficult to make a living in Cleveland doing just theater, as one veteran actor put it, one can "patch" together a living with radio, teaching, and similar work.

Both the Play House and the Great Lakes Theatre, of course, remained the principal employers of Equity talent in Cleveland. Stability returned to the former with the arrival in 1994 of Peter Hackett as artistic director. Attendance rebounded, as five of the eight plays in the 1998–99 season were sellouts. Former members of the resident company such as Andrew May began to reappear on its stage.

Hackett's most promising initiative was the institution of a Playwrights' Unit to incubate the work of local playwrights—an attempt to fulfill a need noted fifty years earlier by Norris Houghton. A related venture was Hackett's Next Stage Festival of New Plays. It produced an early success in Michele Lowe's *The Smell of the Kill,* which after its Play House premiere in 1998 headed for New York.

A new era was also ushered in at the Great Lakes Theatre Festival, as James Bundy took charge as artistic director in 1998 following the retirement of Gerald Freedman. Here too Cleveland actors such as Dudley Swetland were familiar faces. Under Bundy, the festival cut its deficit and sought to broaden its appeal with such productions as Martin McDonagh's *The Beauty Queen of Leenane.*

Though Great Lakes has barely half the budget and play schedule of the Play House, its presence gives Cleveland a unique status among cities of its size. "How cool it is to live in a city with not one but two major regional theaters," noted the *Plain Dealer's* incoming theater critic, Tony Brown. A good part of that advantage has come from the fact that each has hitherto had a different forte to offer: world classics from Great Lakes and contemporary American and British from the Play House.

For the majority of Clevelanders, however, the focus of theatrical activity in the 1990s has been in the large houses of the revitalized Playhouse Square. Following the reopening of the Ohio for the Great Lakes Festival, Playhouse Square Foundation unveiled the completely restored State Theatre in 1984 for the spring tour of the Metropolitan Opera Company, opening on June 11 with tenor Jon Vickers in Benjamin Britten's *Peter Grimes.* While patrons reveled in the renovated richness of the Græco-Roman auditorium, performers enjoyed the amenities of a new $7 million stagehouse added behind the curtain. Although the Met soon discontinued its tours, the State has since served as the home of Cleveland Opera and the late Cleveland San Jose Ballet.

Four years later came the grand reopening of the Palace, giving the foundation a total of three renovated stages. To help get Clevelanders into the habit of using them again, the Cleveland Foundation awarded a grant in 1983 to begin a free noontime concert series. Placed under the administration of Dr. Lucille Gruber, director of cultural arts at Cuyahoga Community College, "Showtime at High Noon" has become a fixture at Playhouse Square. Its offerings include a mixture of classical and ethnic music and dance and occasional dramatic presentations such as the Black Light Theatre of Prague. Some of its most innovative programs have been informative docudramas in words and music of such topics as the federal arts programs of the New Deal.

As for the evenings, Playhouse Square with its large theaters became a natural venue for the huge new musicals that began touring out of New York. Andrew Lloyd Webber's *Cats* set the pattern in 1987, selling 7,608 seats in a single wintry day to a long line of ticket buyers. It has returned at least ten times since then, making *Cats* the *Blossom Time* of its era. Alain Boublil and Claude-Michel Schönberg's *Les Misérables* and *Miss Saigon* have also enjoyed impressive runs. The most phenomenal of the megamusicals has been Webber's *The Phantom of the Opera,* which since 1993 has run up a total of nearly two hundred performances in three visits to the State and the Allen. In order to keep the musicals coming, Playhouse Square has even invested in several successful productions, notably *The Secret Garden* and the revival of *Guys and Dolls.*

In the eyes of many, Playhouse Square was responsible for far more than a theatrical revival. Leading civic figures such as former mayor George Voinovich have given it credit for sparking the entire Cleveland renaissance of the 1980s. "There were so many grandiose schemes when we started," Ray Shepardson has noted. "We just stuck with it. I think it was the first big project to work downtown." It was far from the last, however, as others followed its lead in combining private and public initiatives to produce such attractions as the Galleria, Tower City, and Gateway. Even the emergence of the Flats may owe something to the spirit of Playhouse Square, as both banks of the Cuyahoga blossomed with the sort of nightlife that once enlivened Short Vincent.

For its own immediate neighborhood at Euclid Avenue and East 14th Street, the Playhouse Square Foundation provided more than an example. It began by erecting a new parking garage behind the theaters on Chester Avenue. With a climate-controlled walkway leading to the theater lobbies, it helped lure suburbanites back downtown and provided extra income for the foundation as well. In its front yard, the foundation spearheaded construction of the Renaissance Office Building and the Wyndham Hotel to replace some dowdy single-story structures along Euclid and Huron Avenues. A special improvement district, the first in the city, was formed to upgrade security and maintenance in the area.

In an action charged with potential demographic symbolism, the Front Row Theater in 1993 closed its doors in Highland Heights. As the nineteen-year-old theater was razed to make way for a suburban retail strip, its bookings were transferred back downtown to Playhouse Square. People were also beginning to move back into the city, opting for such possibilities as Warehouse District lofts, Ohio City rehabs, and new homes along Chester Avenue. While urban sprawl continued along the edges, there was at least a countervailing movement back toward the center. And wherever the center holds, there is the possibility of a theater district.

Led by Playhouse Square, Cleveland's theater district was growing again. In 1996–97 its basic Broadway Series lengthened bookings from one to two weeks in order to accommodate the demand for tickets to such shows as *Damn Yankees* and *How to Succeed in Business Without Really Trying.* Robert McLaughlin's old dream of two-week runs in Cleveland has been amply fulfilled. Playhouse Square passed two more milestones that season: one million patrons a year and the ten-millionth customer since the restoration.

In a development no one would have predicted twenty years earlier, the foundation decided the district needed another large theater. With the State and Palace committed to the Broadway Series, ballet, and opera, the foundation wanted a place where it could sit exceptionally popular shows like *The Phantom of the Opera* for runs of eight weeks or even longer. A third large auditorium was at hand in the nearly forgotten Allen. That house had nearly been lost when it fell into the hands of a developer during the restoration efforts in the other three theaters. In 1990 there was talk once again of razing it for a parking lot.

Under foundation president Art Falco, however, Playhouse Square reached an agreement with the owners in 1993 for a long-term lease of the Allen. Cabaret shows such as *Forever Plaid* were put on there during a $15 million restoration that included a new stagehouse for the former movie palace. With the reopening of the Allen in 1998 for the musical *Jolson,* Playhouse Square had a capacity of nearly ten thousand seats, which made it the second-largest performing arts center in the United States behind New York's Lincoln Center.

Nor was the theater renaissance quite done, even then. Around the corner on East 14th Street was the Hanna Theatre, which had finally gone dark in the late 1980s. Ironically, the success of Playhouse Square had inadvertently helped to seal its doom. With their heavily amplified sound and spectacular stage effects, megamusicals such as *Phantom* and *Les Miz* had outgrown the comparatively intimate Hanna. Ray Shepardson returned to Cleveland in the 1990s to try to revive it as a cabaret theater, but that enterprise lasted less than two seasons. His efforts were not entirely in vain, however, as the Playhouse Square Foundation purchased the entire Hanna Building complex in 1999. Ideas advanced for the venerable legitimate house included a new home with a thrust stage for the Great Lakes Theatre Festival. In the meantime, Playhouse Square quickly moved to fill the Hanna's stage with a cabaret-style spoof of an Italian wedding that had enjoyed wide success in other cities. Cleveland proved no exception, as *Tony n' Tina's Wedding* sold out its initial run in the fall of 2000 and was held over at least through the following winter. There was talk of a one- or two-year run, possibly even another *Jacques Brel*.

Playhouse Square seemed undaunted by the challenge of filling five theaters. Now that Cleveland was once again a tourist attraction, the center was drawing up to 15 percent of its audience from outside the immediate region. Art Falco also pointed out that one of Cleveland's recent visits from *The Phantom of the Opera* drew bus groups from upstate New York and Toronto. Toronto was the original American home of *Phantom,* which at least raises the question of whether Cleveland might hope to become a similar theatrical mecca.

"The Palace belongs to the days of the great hotels which are now being replaced all over the world by motels," wrote *Cleveland Press* columnist Winsor French a generation ago during the theater's decline. "An era of such extravagance, I am afraid, is something our children will never see." But today, in the Palace and its sister theaters in Playhouse Square, they once again can see what it was like.

It took Cleveland 180 years to get from a makeshift stage in Mowrey's Hall to the nation's second-largest performing arts center. It was not always a steady progress. John Ellsler, Robert McLaughlin, and Ray Shepardson all put more into theater in Cleveland than they ever got out of it, at least in material terms.

The Factory Theatre production of *The Visit* at Cleveland State University in 1991 featured (from left) Jonathan Lopez, Dorothy Silver, Michele Walker, and Reuben Silver. Embodying a tradition dating back to John and Euphemia Ellsler, the Silvers are Cleveland's current reigning acting team. As directors and actors, they have also played pivotal roles in the histories of Karamu, Ensemble Theatre, and the Jewish Community Center's Halle Theatre. *Photograph by James Fry; Reuben Silver and Dorothy Silver*

But theatrical success is more properly measured by intangible standards. Cleveland has produced at least three theaters of national stature: Ellsler's Academy of Music, Frederic McConnell's Cleveland Play House, and the Jelliffes' and Langston Hughes's Karamu. What they achieved was judged by what happened on their stages, often despite the shortcomings of the stages themselves.

Regardless of the box office, theater people have always seemed to think of Cleveland as a good place in which to live and work. It has been home to an impressive line of husband-and-wife acting teams, beginning with John and Euphemia Ellsler and continuing through Vaughan Glaser and Fay Courteney, K. Elmo Lowe and Dorothy Paxton, and Dorothy and Reuben Silver. Though various interest groups have inveighed from time to time against perceived wickedness in theatrical activity, they have never succeeded in imposing a general community censorship on the stage.

Returning, then, to Artemus Ward's original question of 140 years ago, "[H]ow about the show bisnes in Cleeveland?" "I always thought of Cleveland as far better than most towns," says Musicarnival's John Price, who also ran a tent theater in Florida. "A higher percentage of Clevelanders go to the theater than in New York." Jackie Demaline, who has reviewed theater in Cleveland, Savannah, Albany, and Cincinnati, places Cleveland in the lower rank of the country's top dozen theatrical centers—below Chicago, Boston, and Seattle, for example, and on a par with Denver and San Diego.

In its own immediate region, Cleveland at the beginning of the millennium seemed to have a theatrical edge over Cincinnati, Detroit, Buffalo, and Pittsburgh. "To have *two* regional theaters is unheard of," says Demaline, echoing the *Plain Dealer*'s Tony Brown. Probably, the city's closest rival is Pittsburgh with its new downtown facility for Pittsburgh Public Theater. The "Smoky city" of Ellsler's day can also claim a playwright of the stature of August Wilson writing for its stage.

Turning Cleveland into another Toronto may be a false goal if it means creating a theater primarily for tourists—which is what Broadway itself seems to have become. To paraphrase the counsel of one visiting urban planner, the object should be to create and support stimulating theater for Clevelanders themselves. This includes maintaining the revival of Playhouse Square, of course, but it also means ensuring the survival and prosperity of theater at all levels. It could involve fulfilling many of the items on the parting "wish list" of outgoing *Plain Dealer* critic Marianne Evett, things such as thrust stages for the Play House and Great Lakes Theatre, a new home for Dobama, reinvigorating leadership for Karamu, a "large, strong, professional acting community," and perhaps most important of all, greater civic and corporate support for all local arts.

As long as Cleveland can continue to foster innovative and exciting theater for itself at all levels, others will want to come and catch the show.

THE KIDS FROM CLEVELAND

Ever since the days of John Ellsler and his "school of the drama" at the Academy of Music, Cleveland has been sending dramatic talent to Broadway and later Hollywood.

It was the common lot of all American "road" cities. Actors and actresses such as James O'Neill and Clara Morris would no sooner catch the public fancy when they were lured away to shine on the Great White Way, leaving Clevelanders the satisfaction of being able to say "We knew them when."

One example is the case of a young English immigrant named Leslie Townes Hope, brought here by his stonemason father at the age of four. He grew up around Doan's Corners at East 105th Street and Euclid Avenue, where he got his first look at show business while watching Frank Fay at the Keith's 105th vaudeville house.

Hope had a brief, inglorious, local boxing career under the name of Packy East before making good elsewhere as radio and movie comic Bob Hope. To his credit, he never told Cleveland jokes, though his status as a minor stockholder entitled him to poke fun at the Cleveland Indians.

As an entertainer, Hope was largely self-schooled. After John Ellsler, the Cleveland Play House became the city's foremost training ground for dramatic talent. Claire Eames came from an upper class finishing-school background to join the group in its early amateur period. She soon became a favorite on the New York and London stages, especially in the plays of her husband, Sidney Howard, before her premature death at only thirty-four.

In its prime, the Play House became a revolving door for future stars of stage and screen. Margaret Hamilton passed through on her way to Oz and immortality. Russell Collins followed as did Howard da Silva, Jack Weston, and Ray Walston. A group of young players from the postwar period including Charlotte Fairchild, Jack Lee, and Sheila Smith became known on Broadway as the "Play House Gang."

Two of the most famous Cleveland kids emerged from the Play House children's unit, the Curtain Pullers. Eleven-year-old Paul Newman starred there in *St. George and the Dragon*. Most of his subsequent acting achievements were seen by Clevelanders on the screen, though he might be glimpsed in person as a spectator at the Cleveland Grand Prix auto races.

Young Joel Katz was even more precocious, earning a part at nine on the main stage in Paul Osborn's *On Borrowed Time*. His father, Mickey Katz, was a popular bandleader whose Yiddish parodies of popular hits are still revived by Klezmer groups today.

Son Joel achieved his fame under the surname of Grey, creating the role of the sinister Master of Ceremonies ("Wilkommen, bienvenue")

As a Great Lakes Shakespeare Festival intern, Tom Hanks (left) literally started at the bottom by lugging scenery around backstage. He worked his way up during his apprenticeship to a leading role in *Two Gentlemen of Verona*. *Great Lakes Theatre Festival*

in the 1966 musical *Cabaret*. It won him a Tony and later an Oscar for the film version. Grey later re-created the role for the Kenley Players in nearby Warren, Ohio, where he also appeared in *George M!* and *Pal Joey*.

Karamu can boast of nearly as distinguished an alumni roll as the Play House. One production of *Carousel* there featured Robert Guillaume in the lead role of Billy Bigelow and Ron O'Neal in the one-line part of an assistant to the Starkeeper. Guillaume went on to a distinguished career in films and television, and O'Neal worked his way up from that one-liner to the lead in *Othello* at Stratford, Ontario.

Another launching pad for future stars was the open-air amphitheater at Cain Park. Martin Fuss appeared there in *Journey's End* in 1939. It was the beginning of a journey that would take him to Hollywood as Ross Hunter. Hal Holbrook turned up a few summers later as Richard Stanley, the son in *The Man Who Came to Dinner*. Nearly half a century later, he was King Lear at the Great Lakes Theatre Festival.

Even a comparative newcomer such as Great Lakes can claim its apprentices who advanced to the master class. It was still the Great Lakes Shakespeare Festival in 1977 when director Vincent Dowling took on a twenty-year-old intern with big ears, curly hair, and a winning smile. A year later, the kid was named best actor by the Cleveland Critics Circle for his performance in *Two Gentlemen of Verona*.

Though he left after three summers and became Hollywood's most bankable star, Tom Hanks has returned for Great Lakes benefits and remains an Indians fan. He may not be a native, but he got something in Cleveland just as important to him as a birth certificate: his Actors Equity card.

APPENDIX

CLEVELAND'S BIGGEST HITS

Uncle Tom's Cabin (Atheneum)
November 7–30, 1853 (22 performances)

Aladdin; or The Wonderful Lamp (Cleveland [Academy of Music])
November 5–December 1, 1855 (24 performances)

The Black Crook (Academy of Music)
June 17–July 15, 1867 (29 performances)

Vaughan Glaser Stock Company (Colonial)
March 14, 1904–May 13, 1905 (57 plays in sixty-one consecutive weeks)

Blossom Time (Hanna)
September 3, 1923–November 10, 1950 (twenty-six weeks in twenty-eight years)

Abie's Irish Rose (Colonial)
September 10, 1923–March 22, 1924 (252 performances)

Jacques Brel Is Alive and Living in Paris (Cabaret, State Lobby)
April 18, 1973–June 29, 1975 (550 performances)

The Phantom of the Opera (State, Allen)
April 27, 1993–June 24, 2000 (188 performances in three visits)

Forever Plaid (Cabaret, prerestored Allen)
November 1, 1994–May 21, 1996 (437 performances)

Shear Madness (Cabaret, prerestored Allen)
September 26, 1996–May 18, 1997 (269 performances)

APPENDIX

WE OPENED IN CLEVELAND

A Select List of Local World Premieres

PREMIERE	WORK	AUTHOR	HOUSE
March 28, 1877	*Heroine in Rags*	Bartley Campbell	E.A.O.H.[a]
October 25, 1878	*A New Play (Yorick's Love)*	William Dean Howells	E.A.O.H.
February 17, 1897	*The Serenade*	Victor Herbert & Harry B. Smith	E.A.O.H.
February 1, 1906	*The Girl Who Has Everything*	Clyde Fitch	E.A.O.H.
October 15, 1906	*The Truth*	Clyde Fitch	E.A.O.H.
August 30, 1915	*The Eternal Magdalene*	Robert McLaughlin	Colonial
January 1, 1917	*Hearts of Erin (Eileen)*	Victor Herbert & Henry Blossom	Colonial
November 1, 1926	*The Constant Wife*	W. Somerset Maugham	Ohio
August 27, 1928	*The New Moon*	Sigmund Romberg & Oscar Hammerstein	Hanna
January 29, 1931[b]	*The Barretts of Wimpole Street*	Rudolf Besier	Hanna
October 19, 1931	*Brief Moment*	S. N. Behrman	Hanna
January 2, 1933	*Design for Living*	Noel Coward	Hanna
November 22, 1933	*St. Louis Woman*	Countee Cullen & Arna Bontemps	Karamu

236

PREMIERE	WORK	AUTHOR	HOUSE
March 24, 1936	*Little Ham*	Langston Hughes	Karamu
April 28, 1936	*When the Jack Hollers*	Langston Hughes & Arna Bontemps	Karamu
November 18, 1936	*Troubled Island (Haiti)*	Langston Hughes	Karamu
December 1, 1936	*Not for Children*	Elmer Rice	Play House
December 30, 1936	*High Tor*	Maxwell Anderson	Hanna
April 1, 1937	*Joy to My Soul*	Langston Hughes	Karamu
November 16, 1938	*Front Porch*	Langston Hughes	Karamu
April 26, 1939	*Coal Dust*	Shirley Graham	Karamu
February 21, 1940	*I Gotta Home*	Shirley Graham	Karamu
October 13, 1943	*You Touched Me*	Tennessee Williams & Donald Windham	Play House
November 27, 1946	*Command (Command Decision)*	William Wister Haines	Play House
April 20, 1953	*Me and Juliet*	Richard Rodgers & Oscar Hammerstein	Hanna
December 10, 1958[b]	*Mother Courage*	Bertolt Brecht	Play House
March 14, 1969	*The United States vs. Julius and Ethel Rosenberg*	Donald Freed	Play House
November 21, 1969	*The Effect of Gamma Rays on Man-in-the-Moon Marigolds*	Paul Zindel	Play House
October 17, 1975	*First Monday in October*	Jerome Lawrence & Robert Lee	Play House
October 24, 1975	*The Prague Spring*	Lee Kalcheim & Joe Raposo	Play House
October 12, 1984	*The Archbishop's Ceiling*	Arthur Miller	Play House
October 10, 1989	*New Music: A Trilogy*	Reynolds Price	Play House

[a] Euclid Avenue Opera House

[b] American Premiere

Bibliographical Essay

THOUGH THERE HAS BEEN no full-length study of the history of Cleveland theater prior to the present effort, some general works on American theater and Cleveland history may be of use to the reader. Of the former, Ethan Mordden's *The American Theatre* (New York: Oxford University Press, 1981) provides a good chronological narrative of the major developments. A topical arrangement—producers, playwrights, designers, and such—is furnished along with profuse illustrations in Mary C. Henderson's *Theater in America: 250 Years of Plays, Players, and Productions* (New York: Harry N. Abrams, 1996). An indispensable reference tool is Gerald Bordman, *The Oxford Companion to the American Theatre* (New York: Oxford University Press, 1984).

For Cleveland history, two indispensable works are David Van Tassel and John Grabowski, eds., *The Encyclopedia of Cleveland History* and *The Dictionary of Cleveland Biography* (both Bloomington: Indiana University Press, 1996); the former contains an excellent interpretive essay on theater by Herbert Mansfield. Still valuable for the wealth of theatrical references in its index is the chronicle by William Ganson Rose, *Cleveland: The Making of a City* (Cleveland: World Publishing, 1950). For an account of theater in context with its sister arts, see Holly Rarick Witchey with John Vacha, *Fine Arts in Cleveland: An Illustrated History* (Bloomington: Indiana University Press, 1994). A nine-part series by Stanley Friedman in the *Cleveland Press* (July 12–September 6, 1930 [Saturdays only]) reviews the highlights of Cleveland's theatrical heritage. By far the most complete collection of Cleveland theater programs, from 1864 to the present, can be found in the literature department of the Cleveland Public Library's Main Branch.

Many valuable sources are available for various participants and periods in Cleveland's theatrical history, which may be arranged in relation to the chapters of this study.

1. Early Stages

A highly detailed account of this entire period may be found in Gary W. Gaiser, "The History of the Cleveland Theatre from the Beginning to 1854" (Ph.D. diss., University of Iowa, 1953). Also useful is part two of Elbert Jay Benton, *Cultural Story of an American City: Cleveland—During the Canal Days, 1825–1850* (Cleveland: Western Reserve Historical Society, 1944). There is also a good chapter on early theater by Maurice Weidenthal in Samuel P. Orth, *A History of Cleveland, Ohio,* vol. 1 (Cleveland: S. J. Clarke Publishing, 1910). Chief newspaper sources for this period are the *Cleveland Herald,* the *Cleveland Plain Dealer,* and the *Daily True Democrat.*

2. The Ellsler Era

A good source available for this period is William S. Dix, "The Theater in Cleveland, Ohio, 1854–1875" (Ph.D. diss., University of Chicago, 1946). Part three of Elbert Jay Benton, *Cultural Story of an American City: Cleveland—Under the Shadow of Civil War and Reconstruction, 1850–1877* (Cleveland: Western Reserve Historical Society, 1946), covers theater in a larger perspective. An invaluable source, though more than half of it covers the pre-Cleveland phase of his career, is Effie Ellsler Weston, ed., *The Stage Memories of John A. Ellsler* (Cleveland: Rowfant Club, 1950). Clara Morris provides much material on her Cleveland years in *Life on the Stage: My Personal Experiences and Recollections* (New York: McClure, Phillips, 1902). Newspapers useful for this period are the *Cleveland Leader,* the *Cleveland Herald,* the *Cleveland Plain Dealer,* and the short-lived *Daily Clevelander* (1856–57).

3. THE GILDED STAGE

The first decade of this period is thoroughly analyzed in Margaret Ulmer Ezekiel, "The History of the Theatre in Cleveland: 1875 to 1885" (Ph.D. diss., Western Reserve University, 1968). M[aurice] Weidenthal, "History of the Stage in Cleveland," *Cleveland Amusement Gazette,* vol. 2, no. 1, December 16, 1893, 2–10, while surveying the entire subject, is an especially helpful source on the theaters of the Gilded Age. For Mark Hanna's excursion into theater ownership, see Herbert Croly, *Marcus Alonzo Hanna: His Life and Work* (New York: Macmillan, 1912), 72–75; and Thomas Beer, *Hanna* (New York: Octagon Books, 1973), 303. Mrs. Fiske's introduction to Ibsen and other Cleveland connections are covered in Archie Binns, *Mrs. Fiske and the American Theatre* (New York: Crown, 1955). Chief newspaper sources for this period are the *Cleveland Leader,* the *Cleveland Plain Dealer,* the *Cleveland Press,* and the *Cleveland World.*

4. WHEN VAUDEVILLE WAS KING

For a lively account of the vaudeville era on the national level, see Allen Churchill, *The Great White Way: A Re-Creation of Broadway's Golden Era of Theatrical Entertainment* (New York: E. P. Dutton, 1962). A personal recollection of Cleveland theater during this time is Edith Moriarty, "Stage Struck: Recalling the Golden Age of Cleveland's Theater as Seen Through the Eyes of One Who Loved It," *Cleveland Plain Dealer,* January 2, 1944, All Feature section, 1-2. Recollections of an insider appear in a letter of Robert McLaughlin to W. Ward Marsh, May 23, 1934, Literature Department, Main Branch, Cleveland Public Library. There is one critical biography of Avery Hopwood: Jack F. Sharrar, *Avery Hopwood: His Life and Plays* (Jefferson, N.C.: McFarland, 1989). Newspaper sources are the *Cleveland Leader,* the *Cleveland Plain Dealer,* the *Cleveland Press,* and the *Cleveland News.*

5. NEW VOICES

Local theater buffs are fortunate to have two full-length studies of the Cleveland Play House. Julia McCune Flory, *The Cleveland Play House: How It Began* (Cleveland: Press of Western Reserve University, 1965), covers the first dozen years to the opening of the Brooks-Drury theaters in captivating style from the perspective of an insider. Another insider reviews the same ground and continues the story into the 1980s and the Philip Johnson complex: Chloe Warner Oldenburg, *Leaps of Faith: History of the Cleveland Play House, 1915–85* (Pepper Pike, Ohio: Chloe Warner Oldenburg, 1985). Charles Brooks's reminiscences of the early Play House appear in the essay "A Spear in Ceasar's Army" from his *Like Summer's Cloud* (New York: Harcourt Brace, 1925), 111–21. The Moore-Benét experiment in "Poly-Poetry" is described in William Millikin's *Born Under the Sign of Libra: An Autobiography* (Cleveland: Western Reserve Historical Society, 1977), 67–71. For Karamu, see the masterful, and unfortunately unpublished, study by Reuben Silver, "A History of the Karamu Theatre of Karamu House" (Ph.D. diss., Ohio State University, 1961). An overall account of the entire Karamu settlement may be found in John Selby, *Beyond Civil Rights* (Cleveland: World Publishing, 1966). Newspaper sources for this period are the *Cleveland Plain Dealer,* the *Cleveland Press,* and the *Cleveland News.* Most of the letters written to Archie Bell quoted in "Godfather of the Arts" are preserved in the Literature Department, Main Branch, Cleveland Public Library.

6. Enter Playhouse Square

An excellent overview of Cleveland's commercial theater in the 1920s can be found in Irving Marsan Brown, "Cleveland Theatre in the Twenties" (Ph.D. diss., Ohio State University, 1961). Brown also covers contemporary developments in the Play House, educational, and community theaters. Archie Bell, "A Little Journey to B. F. Keith Palace, Cleveland" (N.p., c. 1922), offers a carpet-to-ceiling description of the flagship house of Playhouse Square. Newspaper sources are the *Cleveland Plain Dealer,* the *Cleveland Press,* and the *Cleveland News.* A longer version of "*The Miracle* on East 6th Street" appeared in an article under that title in *Northern Ohio Live,* vol. 15, no. 5, January 1995, 8–9.

7. The Fabulous Invalid Survives

For developments in the Cleveland Play House and Karamu, consult Chloe Warner Oldenburg, *Leaps of Faith;* Reuben Silver, "A History of the Karamu Theatre of Karamu House"; and John Selby, *Beyond Civil Rights.* A fascinating appraisal of these two Cleveland theaters in a national context can be found in Norris Houghton, *Advance from Broadway: 19,000 Miles of American Theatre* (New York: Harcourt, Brace,

1941), which also contains material on the origins of Western Reserve University's theater program. The origins and early years of Cain Park are retold by its founding director, Dina Rees Evans, in *Cain Park Theatre: The Halcyon Years* (Cleveland: Halcyon Printing, 1980). Much of Cleveland's role in the Federal Theatre Project may be found in the memoir by its national director, Hallie Flanagan, *Arena* (New York: Duell, Sloan, and Pearce, 1940). A short survey of the Hanna Theatre's history appears in John Vacha, "Heyday of the Hanna," *Northern Ohio Live,* vol. 16, no. 7, March 1966, 57–59. Newspaper sources are the *Cleveland Plain Dealer,* the *Cleveland Press,* and the *Cleveland News.*

8. NEW DIRECTIONS

Further developments at the Play House, Karamu, and Cain Park are covered in Chloe Warner Oldenburg, *Leaps of Faith;* Reuben Silver, "A History of the Karamu Theatre of Karamu House"; John Selby, *Beyond Civil Rights;* and Dina Rees Evans, *Cain Park Theatre.* Additional material on the Play House appears in a booklet by Roger Danforth, *The Cleveland Play House, 1915–1990* (Cleveland: Emerson Press, n.d.). For more on the antecedents of the Great Lakes Shakespeare Festival, see Donald A. Hutslar, "Under the Stars: The Antioch Shakespeare Festival," *Timeline,* vol. 16, no. 3, May–June 1990, 2–17. Newspaper sources are the *Cleveland Plain Dealer,* the *Cleveland Press,* the *Cleveland News,* and the suburban *Sun* newspaper chain. For a representative sampling of William McDermott's theatrical criticism, see William F. McDermott, *The Best of McDermott: The Selected Writings of William F. McDermott* (Cleveland: World Publishing, 1959).

9. RENAISSANCE

Marianne Evett's valedictory as drama critic for the *Cleveland Plain Dealer,* "Watching Theater Come of Age," December 26, 1999, 1-H, provides an excellent summary of this period's highlights. The history and rebirth of Playhouse Square is chronicled in print and pictures in an updated version of the center's original 1975 "Red Book," *Playhouse Square Center: The End of a Dream . . . the Beginning of a Legacy* (Cleveland: Playhouse Square Foundation, 1984). A shorter account of the rebirth is available in John Vacha, "Let There Be Lights," *Northern Ohio Live,* vol. 17, no. 5, January 1997, 18–20. Newspaper and periodical sources for this period are the *Cleveland Plain Dealer, Cleveland Magazine,* and *Northern Ohio Live.*

Index

Fulton, Thomas Q., 224, 218
Fuss, Martin, 232

Gabel, Max, 82
Gable, Clark, 183
Gaige, Crosley, 125, 130
Galileo (Brecht), 185
Galuinas the Mighty, 162
Garden of Semiramis, The, 102
Garry, Joseph, 191, 208, 219
Genet, Jean, 202
Geneviève de Brabant, 38
Gentry, Minnie, 160, *188*
George M., 232
George, Zelma, 187
Gershwin, George, 147
Gest, Morris, 121
Gibson, Jana, *186*
Gibson, William, 223
Gibson-Bianchi, Teddi, 218
Gielgud, John, 98
Gilbert, G. H., Mrs., 33
Gilbert, William S., 52, 55, 170
Gillen, Fred, 67
Gillette, William, 64, 85
Gillmore, Margalo, 150
Gilpin, Charles, 112, *113,* 114, 162
Gilpin Players, 114–16, 161–63, 165, 185
Gin Game, The, 220
Girl Who Has Everything, The (Fitch), 83–84, 236
Gish, Lillian, 98
Glaser, Vaughan, 16, 74, 85, *86,* 95, 229
Glaspel, Susan, 114
Glass Menagerie, The (Williams), 180, 185
Gods of the Lightning (Hickerson), 138
Godspell (Tebelak and Schwartz), 192
Goethe, Johann Wolfgang von, 124
Gold Diggers, The (Hopwood), 91
Goldoni, Carlo, 124
Gomez, Thomas, 185
Good Wine in a Bad Barrel, A, 82
Gordon, Ruth, 171
Gordon, Vera, 125
Gordon Square Theater, 78, 222
Gottfried, Martin, 215
Graham, R. E., 33
Grand Hotel, 219
Granny Maumee, 114
Grasselli, Caesar, 63
Grau, Jacob, 38
Great God Brown, The (O'Neill), 220

Great Train Robbery, The, 77
Great White Way, The, 78
Green, Howard Whipple, 198
Green, Paul, 115–16, 137, 156, 165
Green Grow the Lilacs (Riggs), 197
Green Hat, The, 205
Green Pastures, The, 149
Greene, William, 185, 202
Greenough, Peter, 198
Gregory, Lady, 165
Grey, Joel (Katz), 157, 231
Groll, George, 63
Gruber, Lucille, 226
Guillaume, Robert, 188–89, 232
Guthrie, Tyrone, 184
Guy Mannerling, 24
Guys and Dolls, 195, 217, 226
Gwenn, Edmund, 171

Hackett, Peter, 225
Hair, 201, 212
Hairy Ape, The (O'Neill), 97, 142
Hale, Olive, 115
Hall, Juanita, 198–*99*
Hall, Laura Nelson, 85
Hall, Pauline, 72
Halle, Kay, 147, 151
Halliday, Jack, 87
Haltnorth, Frederick, 55
Halverson, Richard, *214*
Hamilton, Margaret, 103, 185, 191
Hamlet (Shakespeare), 7, 25, 32–33, 38, 97–98, 129, 135
Hammerstein II, Oscar, 140, 195, 197
Hanks, Tom, 192, *232, 233*
Hanna, Carl, 150, 171, 177, *179*
Hanna, Daniel R., 124
Hanna, L. G., 50, 55
Hanna, Marcus (Mark) A., 47, 50–51, 62, 69, 72, 82, 96
Hanna Theatre, 124–25, 129–31, 140–42, 144, 150–54, 170–72, 178–81, *179–80,* 183–84, 194–97, 201–2, 228
Hansberry, Lorraine, 194
Hänsel und Gretel, 146
Hansen, David, 224
Harburg, E. Y., 200
Hardwicke, Cedric, 206
Hare, Eugene, 219
Harkness, Stephen V., 46
Harrison, Richard B., 149
Hart, Moss, 143, 169

Hartz, Augustus (Gus) F., 16, 56–57, *58,* 63, 73, 96, 131
Haworth, Joseph, 33, 45
Haydn, Franz Joseph, 19, 200
Hayes, Helen, 127, 178
Hazel Kirke, 40–41, 64
He Who Gets Slapped, 118, 128
Heard, Charles, 45
Heart of the City, The (Storm), 170
Heartbreak House (Shaw), 107
Hearts of Erin (Herbert), 88, 236
Hecht, Ben, 149
Hecht, Joshua, 198
Hedda Gabler (Ibsen), 89
Hell-Bent for Heaven (Hughes), 110
Hellman, Lillian, 156
Henkel, Oliver Jr., 210
Henry, Ed, *193*
Henry V (Shakespeare), 47
Herbert, Victor, 81
Herkomer, John, 43
Hero of Lake Erie, The (Puehringer), 89
Heroine in Rags (Campbell), 40, 48, 236
Herron, Jim, 196
Herz, R. C., 78
Heyward, DuBose, 144, 163
Hickerson, Harold, 138
Hickey, William, 212
Hield, William, 11
Higgins, Larry, 197
High Spirits. See Blithe Spirit
High Tor (Anderson), 152–54, 169
Hippodrome Theatre, 75, *76,* 77, 94, 121, 134, 177, 210
Hoffman, Dustin, 191
Hofmannsthal, Hugo von, 103
Hohnhorst, Harry, 100
Holbrook, Hal, 197, *212,* 232
Hold on to Your Hats, 171
Holden, L. E., 63
Holiday, 98
Hollander, Providence, 208
Holm, Celeste, 192
Honest Thieves, The, 7
Hoover, Herbert, 154
Hope, Leslie Townes (Bob Hope), 126, 198, 231
Hopkins, Arthur Melancthon, 95, *96,* 97–99
Hopper, DeWolf, 119
Hopwood, Avery, 42, 89, *90,* 129
Horvath, Ernie, 199

Showtime in Cleveland

was designed and composed by Christine Brooks

in 11.3/15 Bembo with display type in Boulevard Script

on a Macintosh G4 using PageMaker 6.5;

printed on 70# Fortune Matte stock

by Thomson-Shore, Inc. of Dexter, Michigan;

and published by

THE KENT STATE UNIVERSITY PRESS

Kent, Ohio 44242